TO THE END OF HER DAYS

TO THE END
OF HER DAYS

Malcolm Ross

PIATKUS

First published in Great Britain in 1994 by
Judy Piatkus (Publishers) Ltd of
5 Windmill Street, London W1

The moral right of the author has been asserted

*A catalogue record for this book is available
from the British Library*

ISBN 0−7499−0220−5

Typeset by the author using Spellbinder™ DTP
Glyphix™ Palatino fonts and a
Hewlett-Packard™ Laserjet III printer

Printed and bound in Great Britain by
Bookcraft (Bath) Ltd

for

George and Mona Angove

friends indeed

Contents

Part One

Life Goes On

*E*motions at a funeral. Do they run especially high at such a time? Jessica wondered. Or are they always bubbling away inside us, masked by the dull pressures of ordinary life? Ian's death had been so long coming that its arrival had been as much of a relief as a sorrow. It had certainly been a blessing to him: His last words had been, "Thank God for ...!" She remembered how his head had sunk into the pillow, denting it more than gravity alone could have managed, as if Death itself were pressing him down with unseen hands.

Thank God for what? How would he have concluded his little prayer if he had lived a minute longer?

"... for you, my darling"? It would be nice to think so.

A cold eddy of wind stirred the newly fallen leaves, showering them into the open grave. Flecks of russet on the pine.

She found it hard to grieve now, perhaps because she had grieved so much over the past two years — watching him slowly, slowly die. How could anyone grieve for a death that had finally come to him as such a mercy?

Ashes to ashes, dust to dust ... She knew the words from other funerals. She did not want to hear them now, not as individual words that made sense. All she desired was the comforting murmur of Reverend Meecher's rich, done-it-all-before cadences; his was a drone you could lean on.

God, how she longed for someone to lean on again!

There was a sudden, startling pressure against the inside of her thigh. She looked down in surprise and saw it was only young Toby, drawing to her side, clutching her tightly, leaning his tousled head against her hip. Guy, now the man of the family — as Ian had warned him he would be — glanced up at her. "Shall I make that brat behave himself?" his eyes asked.

Sarah, two years his senior, became aware of this unspoken dialogue and took a step nearer her mother — enough to get her elbow just in front of Guy's.

Jessica managed a feeble smile and shook her head at both of them. Then she slipped her hand around Toby's shoulder and held him tight against her.

It was not enough. How could she ever do enough for her three young children at a time like this? She squatted and murmured in his ear: "It's all right to cry, darling."

Ben Calloway cleared his throat; he clearly did not approve. Always a stickler for good form. She could imagine the talk over the bar at the Mouse Hole that evening: "She bent down and kissed him — forced the poor little cooze to blub. She'll molly-coddle those boys till they're spoiled — you'll see." On the other hand, they would approve of Guy's stoical coolness; they would see it as a good augury for his future. Sarah's fate would not concern the like of them for a few years yet awhile.

Toby did not oblige Ben Calloway, nor his customers; indeed, he pulled himself away and stood alone, between her and his older siblings, head down in a brooding, almost Napoleonic stance. Often the best way to stop him from doing something was to encourage him to do it.

The moment she had dreaded most of all arrived, when the first shovelful of shale hit the coffin; but she had dreaded it so much as to rob it of its power to grieve her. Muscles she had not realized were stiff now relaxed all down her spine. Friends' eyes were surreptitiously upon her. She acquitted herself well. Brave little woman.

Why was she suddenly so sensitive to the opinions of others? Because she was now alone — without Ian's reputation to hide behind?

And what would Ian's reputation be when people knew how little money he had left them?

Her heart beat now to the rhythm of questions about things she had never had to ponder before — awkward things that would now rule her life entirely.

David Carne touched her elbow gently. Time to go.

She did not like this modern custom of leaving the graveside after the sexton had tipped a few symbolic shovels of clay on the coffin; it had come in — understandably enough, she supposed — during the Great War. But to her it still seemed a discourtesy, not least to the departed. "You go." She smiled at him and inclined her head toward the children.

"You're sure?" His gaze was full of concern. From the look of her he must be thinking the sleeping draught he'd prescribed for her hadn't worked; if he asked, she'd confess she hadn't touched it. But only if he asked.

"Sure. Listen, children, you can go to the car with Uncle David if you like. I'm going to stay on here for a while. I shan't be long."

People took it as permission to leave. Some bowed gravely; some spoke the commonplaces of an impossible solace and pressed her hand. Alone at last she gestured to the sexton that he was to continue. Two gravediggers appeared from the lee of nearby gravestones; one took out a packet of Woodbines but put it back when he realized she intended to stay.

There were certain memories she had stored against this moment — a swift review, as it were, of all that was now being interred in this Cornish hillside (appropriately named Mount Misery). There was her first meeting with Ian, back in 1908, on the Curnows' tennis court ... the wedding at St Mary's when she said "... take you, Ian Philip" instead of "Ian Patrick" ... the honeymoon at Tintagel when it rained non-stop and her friends had grinned and said, "Still, I don't suppose you noticed!" ... and the birth of Sarah, when she had nearly died ... and the time when ...

It didn't work. These moments, which she had hoarded like gold to offer him at this most symbolic moment of their parting, simply refused to come alive for her. The images were there all right, but it was as if they recalled events she had forgotten — as when she turned over the pages of an old diary and read about who did what on some long-ago occasion.

Also the motion of the gravediggers distracted her — men in their fifties who had wielded the long-handled Cornish shovel all their lives. They knew how to make it almost effortless, not simply in appearance but in fact, as well. Their elbows hardly ever left their sides; their knees were behind their wrists at every dig and thrust; their backs were never unsupported. If there was ever a ballet in which the dancers used shovels (and watching them Jessica thought there most certainly ought to be), these men could teach Nijinsky himself to perform it.

The pleasure of observing their unconscious show intruded on her grieving. As soon as the coffin was decently covered, she turned and left them. And then, as she picked her way carefully down toward the gate, it was as if the floodgates opened and all those golden memories began to return without effort — and without that eerie feeling they had happened to someone else, or in a forgotten time. They flickered past her mind's eye too fast to catch in words — but it was all there, the whole of their brief time together. Twelve years of a marriage — two of idiotic bliss, four of comfortable happiness, four of war, and two that had seemed like two hundred, of a lingering death-in-life whose sands had finally run out last Wednesday.

The cloying reek of unburned motor spirit from overchoked engines hung on the autumnal air as the mourners clattered off down the winding lane toward Penzance. The hearse led the way, for other coffins were waiting in other houses of sorrow, down there in the town. Other graves lay open here, other griefs tarried in other hearts, awaiting the same quietus. Only the children's "Uncle" David remained, dear kind man that he was — and a far better uncle to them than Ian's brother-in-law had proved to be. He stood behind them, one hand on Sarah's shoulder, the other on Guy's, with Toby in between, leaning against him. The boys could accept from him the tangible comfort they were now too manly to take from her. A pang of jealousy twisted inside her but she swiftly quelled it. They needed a man's influence now, and Uncle David, childless himself, would be only too eager to supply it.

She tried to feel ashamed that, with Ian's grave not yet filled, she could think in such calculating terms. *But if not me, then who?* she asked herself. *I am all they have now.*

"Get in the car, you children," she called out. "You'll catch your deaths out there."

She saw David's eyebrows rise at her use of that particular idiom at this particular moment. He ushered the three of them into the back and turned to wait for her as she walked the last thirty-odd paces to the gate.

"I wheeled him up here in August," she said as she came within easy speaking distance. "He picked that spot."

She remembered then that she had already explained all about that to David.

"Really?" he responded, as if it were news to him. He turned and stared over the roof of the car at the unusually tranquil waters of Mount's Bay.

He still had his back to her when she reached the gate. She leaned her forehead against it, welcoming the chill touch of the iron. She closed her eyes and murmured, "Those cliffs!"

"Permanence," he said. He had an uncanny way of knowing what she meant, even when she merely hinted at what was on her mind. "It's an illusion," he added. "Bits of them are falling into the sea all the time." After a pause he went on, "You didn't take your sleeping draught last night, did you." It was not a question.

She opened the gate and came out of the graveyard. "I fully intended to. But it seemed like treachery — with Ian down there in the drawing room."

"You sat up all night."

"Not for the first time by any means." She slipped her arm in his, as if she needed steadying over the two or three paces to the car. She was determined not to look over her shoulder; how Ian had hated lingering farewells. "We must hurry now. They'll all be waiting for their tea. The funeral tea!" She made it sound ominous. "I only hope Daisy remembered to slip out for some mustard."

The moment she was in the car, while David was going round to the driver's side, she turned to the children and, deliberately using Ian's vocabulary, said, "Well, brats! Your father would have been proud of you, the way you've acquitted yourselves today. Actually, I don't know why I say 'would have been.' I'm sure he *is* proud of you, wherèver he might be at this moment." She smiled and added, "Free of his pain at last."

They smiled back, dutifully accepting her attempt to comfort them, which, in their immature selfishness, they probably did not need. What *did* they need? she wondered. They would never dream of telling her, but God help her if she failed to give it!

"The bay's as calm as I've ever seen it," David said as he let off the brake. They started to freewheel down the slope.

The mechanism protested as he engaged gear. She remembered how Ian had always winced whenever he'd seen David get into the car — which, in his case, had been a more-than-daily sight, since their two back gardens marched side-by-side and David was a busy doctor with a large rural practice between Penzance and Land's End.

He let out the clutch and they came to a juddering halt. The youngsters were thrown against the front-seat backs; their mother, half ready for some such occurrence, had braced her feet against the valance and her elbow on the dash.

David sat frowning at the steering wheel. "It's only just been serviced," he said. "That idiot Jones at the garage!" His gloved fingertip ran a gauntlet of checks on the remote chance that the fault might be his — the clock, the oil gauge, the ignition key, the reserve-tank tap; it came to rest on the lever that released the sprag designed to prevent the car from rolling backward on a hill climb. He was about to give it an experimental tweak when he saw Jessica shaking her head.

"No?" he asked.

"No, David." She pointed at the gear handle. "You're in reverse."

He cleared his throat and pulled a face at the two boys. "It keeps moving about," he complained as he engaged it uncertainly in a new position. "Is that it?"

She nodded.

"There so much *leash* in these gearboxes." He produced the technical term with pride.

Jessica heard Guy draw breath to say "lash." She turned and shook her head at him, unseen by David.

This time the engine "caught the spark," as he put it, and they settled down for the brief ride home — insofar as anyone could settle at all when David was at the wheel.

"I should hire you as my driver," he said ruefully.

After a pause she replied, "Well, I'll have to do *something* now. There's no doubt about that. The house is just about all we have."

He glanced sharply at her.

She arched her eyebrows and nodded.

He gave his head a barely perceptible tilt in the direction of the children. "We must put on our thinking caps," he said. "After the funeral tea."

"Oh, David!" She reached out impulsively and squeezed his arm. "You've been so good to us — but you've got your own practice to run. You can't afford ..."

"I can afford a locum — which is what I've done for this one day, at least. Make the most of it."

"But what about Estelle? Surely she won't be ..."

"It's not one of her brightest days," he said offhandedly. But his casual tone was belied by the way he gripped the steering wheel and stared fixedly at the road ahead.

A sense of foreboding settled on Jessica's spirit. Precisely what perturbed her, though, she could not say. It had something to do with invalid husbands, like Ian, and invalid wives, like Estelle, and the fact that they posed different sorts of constraint upon the behaviour of their respective spouses.

Also, of course, the restraint imposed by an invalid husband — in her particular case — had now gone.

arcus Corvo took a bite of his fish-paste vol-au-vent and pulled a face. He continued to munch away, however, until every last morsel had gone. And he helped himself to another. "I'll tell you one thing," he said under his breath and through the sticky bits to Ben Calloway, "she won't be turning this place into a seaside boarding house — not if this is her idea of fancy cooking!" Calloway's response was a thin, polite smile; he had come to the same opinion himself but would never have dreamed of voicing it. Only an out-and-out twicer like Corvo would do such a thing. He glanced about him, seeking some excuse to move away from the man.

And only an out-and-out twicer like Corvo would have gone on to ask, "Are you thinking of making her an offer, old boy?"

"For heaven's sake, Corvo!" Calloway murmured. "Poor old Lanyon's hardly cold in his grave."

The vicar, Rev. Meecher, who had not heard Corvo ask his question, turned and glared at Calloway.

Corvo, his voice still subliminal to the vicar, continued unabashed, "Only it would be a shame for you and me to fight over it. I could make it worth your while to hold your hand." He saw Sarah approaching with a plate of jam tarts and raised his voice to add, "Yes — a wonderful man and a great loss to Penzance. How's my favourite little gel, then, eh?"

Mummy said that Marcus Corvo was so awful you couldn't help having a sort of sneaking liking for him. Sarah disagreed. She didn't think he was awful at all. To her he was the kindest, most genial man she knew. He always called her Miss Lanyon and never smirked when she asked questions. "Bearing up, thank you, Mister Corvo," she replied, offering him the tarts.

He took two, giving her a conspiratorial wink. "One for later, if I get peckish," he said. As she circulated onward he called after her, "If you're at a loose end tomorrow morning, before church, pop over and let me take my revenge."

She grinned back over her shoulder but could make no promise.

"Snooker," Corvo explained to Calloway, whom he caught in the act of escaping. "She'll play for England when she grows up." He bit into the tart and added, "Cor — hard as bullets! We could have done with these in the trenches."

For Ben Calloway — who, unlike Corvo, actually had been in the trenches — it was the last straw. "My God!" he exclaimed in disgust and walked away.

"Control yourself, man, for heaven's sake!" the vicar whispered vehemently as he passed.

"That … that scoundrel!" Calloway replied with quiet bitterness. But he knew full well it was useless talking to Rev. Meecher about him, for "that scoundrel" had donated most generously to the Death Watch Beetle Fund.

He came to a halt, by coincidence, at Jessica's elbow. "What now?" she asked with the slightly forced, slightly solemn cheeriness that seemed to be demanded of her now that Ian was buried. "My two closest neighbours falling out again?"

"We never fell in," he replied. Then, recalling the military use of the idiom, he went on, "And as for Corvo, *he* never fell in at all. How dare he talk about the trenches like that!"

"Like what?"

"Oh … nothing. I'm sorry, Mrs Lanyon."

"My dear man, you needn't …"

"No, I mean I'm sorry to have to tell you this, but he's just made me an offer *not* to put in a bid on this property, if, of course …"

"*Mister* Calloway!" she exclaimed.

The vicar heard her and began threading his way toward them.

"I know," he replied ruefully. "I wouldn't breathe a word about it myself. I'd wait a decent interval. But I'm only warning you that Corvo is no respecter of those usual decencies. He's more than likely to make a bid before today is out."

"Everything all right, Mrs Lanyon?" Rev. Meecher asked ominously as he drew close.

She smiled wanly at him. "Life goes on, Vicar."

"It's persistent stuff." David Carne joined the group. To Jessica he murmured, "The boys are busy making medals in the nursery."

"Playroom," she corrected him with a grateful smile — and longed for the moment when all these people would go and she could give up smiling altogether, or at least until she actually wanted to smile again. All except David, of course; he was not "people."

Across the room she saw Mrs Meecher, keeping a wary watch on her man. Their eyes met. Jessica gave her a dutiful smile and was astonished at the venom in the other's gaze — before, that is, she masked it and dutifully smiled back. It rocked Jessica to the very core. She had never in her life seen such naked distrust in another's eyes, much less directed at her. Yet the woman had been perfectly friendly when they met last week; she had even taken the children down to the beach for the afternoon. To be sure, that was when Ian had been very obviously at death's door, when such friendly gestures would have been hard to withhold. But what could possibly have happened since to change her attitude so drastically?

Suddenly the answer struck Jessica, with all the force of a physical blow: What had happened since was that Ian had died. She was now a widow, a free woman — a predator!

She saw herself through Mrs Meecher's eyes, standing there with her husband to her left, the doctor at her right, and Calloway facing her — two married men and a bachelor-neighbour. It was notorious that the vicar and his wife were on cool terms, and that David and Estelle Carne were married in little more than name only ... so she could not, in fairness, grudge the woman her sudden hostility.

A great weariness depressed her. If only Polly Meecher could realize how fortunate she was to have any sort of husband at all.

The empty conversations droned on until the fish-paste and jam tarts gave out. People drifted away, saying she was to feel free to call at any time, not to wait for an At Home or a formal invitation, and, of course, if she ever needed *anything* ... vague smiles were all that completed that particular offer, however. She thought of telling them that any donations, large or small, would be welcome — her finances had more than a touch of the death watch beetle now.

The last to go was Willy Benny Angove, the undertaker, who slipped an envelope from his pocket and pressed it into her hand after the ritual parting shake.

"My dear soul!" she exclaimed, dropping into his idiom to soften the rebuke. "You're some quick!"

He did not bat an eyelid. "Bills are best sent," he remarked solemnly, "before the cheek is dry."

"Cheek is the word, all right, Angove!" David remonstrated.

But Jessica put her hand on his arm. "He's right," she said. "Life goes on." To the man himself she said, "I'll drop by when I call to the bank on Monday." Her stomach fell at the very thought.

He nodded solemnly and left.

"Where's Sarah?" Jessica asked, surveying the chaotic remnants of the funeral tea.

"Helping Daisy with the washing-up, I think," David said.

"Oh, she is good!" Jessica sank exhausted into an armchair. Ian's armchair. "People have been so kind."

"They're making up for the last year of the war," he said. "There was a sort of sympathy-fatigue then. We lost the ability to respond to death. Now the numbness is going. I think you should stay in bed for a day or two. Sleep and sleep and sleep."

"So do I."

"Ha! When you say it like that you mean you haven't the slightest intention of actually doing it." While he spoke he poured out a stiff whisky, which he handed to her, saying, "This might help."

She sipped and savoured it in her mouth awhile, breathing in afterwards to cool its fiery bite. "I mean the world won't let me. Life won't let me. Persistent stuff, as you said. Did you see the way Polly Meecher looked at me?"

He shook his head and diluted his own measure of whisky with more than its equal in water.

"Nothing could have brought home to me quite so brutally the fact that I am now a widow. It's odd. I've faced the prospect of widow-*hood* for ... well, for the past two years, I suppose. But to actually *be* a widow is something quite different."

"I don't follow." He sat on the sofa and crossed his legs; he was wearing odd socks.

"A war widow is even worse, of course. We're likely to be a good deal younger than your right-down regular sort. A widow who wears black bombazine down to her ankles and sports a dainty moustache is socially acceptable."

"Ah!" He began to catch her drift.

"But we of the nubile variety, who could not put on a long dress for fear of laughing in a most unseemly fashion — we are something altogether different. I saw it in Polly's eyes this afternoon." After a pause she said, "I think I'll only stay in mourning until Christmas."

He stared into his glass. She knew he was trying to frame himself to say something.

"Let's be lovers!" perhaps?

He had said it in so many of her daydreams — or her last-thing-at-night dreams — during Ian's long illness, that to hear it out loud now would be the most natural, least alarming thing on earth. And what about him? The way things were between him and Estelle, he must be just as lonely, just as full of needs and longings. Perhaps he, too, had said it so often in his own daydreams that to say it aloud now would also be the most natural thing possible. But how to get *his* most-natural and her most-natural to overlap? The two yards that separated them might as well have been two mountain ranges.

"D'you think Calloway was telling the truth?" he asked.

"That Corvo's interested in buying this property? Of course. The man's never made the slightest secret of it. He'd have pestered Ian to death these last weeks, if I'd let him."

"He'd probably pay over the odds for it, too. Ditto Calloway. The Mouse Hole needs to enlarge every bit as much as the Riviera-Splendide." David still shuddered fastidiously when he said the name. "You could make a fortune by setting them at each other's throats."

She nodded unhappily. "It's the only asset I have. Isn't it funny — either man could make a fortune out of owning it, but to me it's nothing but a money-hole."

"Are you really absolutely flat-broke, Jess?"

She gave a reluctant shrug. "Not absolutely, I suppose. And there's Ian's war pension."

"Ha ha," he said drily. The words were already a joke.

"And I could apply to the Benevolent Fund."

"How long could you hold out without being forced into making any sort of rushed decision?"

She tilted her head uncertainly. "Six months — with a bit of luck. More if I took a lodger."

"Did you ever discuss selling this place with Ian?"

She shook her head. "It would have broken his heart — his old family home. He died in the very room where he was born — indeed, in the very bed! All the same, he could see how things were going to be for us."

"The pension will help a *bit*," he said, feeling his earlier response had been rather harsh.

"Oh yes!" she said bitterly. "Try and bring up three young children on it! This is 'a land fit for heroes,' all right!"

She referred to a famous speech by Lloyd-George, which was rapidly becoming infamous as pledge after pledge was broken.

"The only land fit for my darling hero is the one he's in now! It measures six foot long by two foot wide by six foot deep. And it *fits* him all right — like a glove!" Her voice broke.

Without a word he rose and recharged her glass, and his own.

"Is that wise?" she asked, gathering herself again.

He shook his head. "But who says we must *always* be wise!" He moved the sofa nearer her chair and seated himself once more. "What if *I* were interested in buying you out, too?"

She laughed.

"I'm serious," he assured her.

"I'm sorry, David. I wasn't laughing at your offer. I was just remembering one of Ian's jokes. He must have told it you. About the visiting preacher enjoying his meal and being pestered by the family dog who won't leave him alone? And at last he says, 'My my, this little fellow really has taken a liking to me, eh!' And the Awful Boy of the family, who can restrain himself no longer, bursts out: ' 'Tin't you 'e do like, Mister — you got 'is plate!' Surely you heard him tell that one?"

David chuckled. "So I'm only pestering you for your plate, eh?" he said with mock chagrin.

"No!" she chided. "All the same — what could you possibly *do* with this white elephant of a house?"

"Open a sanatorium?" he suggested.

She was about to laugh again when it struck her that he was perfectly serious. She set her glass down and sat up straight. "Genuinely?" she asked.

He nodded.

She gulped and stared down at the carpet, running her eyes along the rich arabesques of its pattern, seeing it as if for the first time; meanwhile a voice in her head told her, "You will never forget this moment." It was like when she realized that Ian was no longer breathing. A ponderous moment. A moment to ponder. "A sanitarium," she mused.

"If you prefer," he replied.

She was baffled.

"Sanatorium … sanitarium — they're the same."

"Oh." She took a sip and set her glass down again. "I can't think at the moment, David. My mind was all bloated with resistance to any idea of selling — to either the Mouse Hole or the Riviera-Splendide, I mean — that I just never thought of …" She was going to say "you" but changed it to "any other possibility."

"I'm sorry I spoke, then." He reached forward and patted her arm. "I just didn't want you to enter into any irrevocable arrangement without knowing of my interest. Forget I said anything."

She fought a strong desire to give him the place at once — in return for a position as housekeeper at his new establishment. To be rid of the responsibility! To have a secure place and an assured income — bliss!

"Are you really going to resist the pair of them?" he asked.

She chortled. "Yes. You may rest easy, my dear. You won't need to top their bids."

"Heavens, I wasn't thinking along those lines, *my dear!*" It was the first time they had used even that mild familiarity, so he gave it a certain arch emphasis. "I was just intrigued by your declaration — how positive you were. What had you in mind for the place, then?"

She tilted her head awkwardly and offered: "A seaside boarding house, perhaps?"

He pursed his lips in a soundless whistle, making a parade of trying not to smile.

"I could hire a cook easily enough," she protested. "In fact, I'd have to if it were a business."

"Ah — hire a *cook!*" he said, as if that put an entirely different complexion on her plans.

"Oh, you are all so beastly about my cooking!" she exclaimed, half laughing, half genuinely annoyed. "I don't think it's as bad as all that." She closed her eyes and the tears came welling up; she was powerless to stop them.

"Oh, Jess, my dear!" he said, full of contrition now. "I'm so sorry. I didn't know — we've joked about it often enough in the past."

She shook her head; the tears fell into her angora jumper. "It's not you. I suddenly remembered the last walk I ever took along the sands with Ian, back in May. We came across the corpses of two seagulls and he looked at me solemnly and said ..." She choked on the memory but struggled on: " 'Have you been ...' " The rest struggled out, barely distinguishable from her sobbing: " 'feeding ... the birds ... again!' "

He took her by the arm and helped her out into the hall. Sarah came from the kitchen, her large blue eyes filled with anxiety. Daisy was just behind her. "You can both help," he told them.

While daughter and maid undressed her and got her into bed, he went to the bathroom to mix a glass of veronal. He brought it back to her, intending to stand over her while she drank it.

She put it aside and said, "Sit down, David." She moved her knees beneath the bedclothes to make room for him. She was quite calm again now.

He obeyed, a little nervously. "Are you sure you're feeling all right?" he asked.

She nodded. "If I don't tell you this today, I never will."

He loosened his front collar stud.

"It's the proper day to bury *everything,*" she went on. She flashed him a nervous little smile. "I'm thinking aloud, really. D'you mind? It may not make much sense."

"Go on." He forced himself to relax, though everything about this situation made him nervous. It was not just the promise of awkward revelations from Jess. There was also the knowledge that, if she were any other woman, he would now be doing his best to seduce her. Never mind the sombre occasion, the grief, he had been a doctor long enough to know their aphrodisiac value. He would loathe himself for it after — he always did — but the compulsion was too great to resist. Not with Jess, though. He had loved her from the moment they met, more than ten years ago, when Ian first brought her to Rosemergy as a bride — the same year in which he had yoked himself for life to Estelle. The purity of his love for Jess was the only thing that redeemed him from the squalor of his other little affaires.

"I don't know why you're so good to me," she said. "I have to tell someone this or I'll go mad. Perhaps I'm mad already? Madness isn't always a matter of screaming and tearing out your hair, is it."

He dipped his head in agreement.

"I'm afraid I've completely wasted my life, David," she went on. "I knew *nothing* when I married Ian ..." She relapsed into silence again.

"You were happy, though," he prompted.

"Oh, blissfully! For two years — maybe four. I don't know. But I didn't understand about love, you see. I thought *that* was love."

Again he had to prompt her out of a silence: "What makes you think it wasn't?"

"The way it all just ... fizzled out. It just all vanished. I haven't dared think about it these last two years but every now and then ... please don't be shocked now ... it's very painful to speak of it."

"Then don't. Drink your sleeping draught. This'll keep until ..."

"No, it won't!" She was suddenly insistent, even agitated.

"All right. I'm sorry I interrupted. You were saying — every now and then over the past two years ...?"

"Yes. I'd look at Ian sleeping and I'd say to myself, 'What are you doing here, Jess?' The clock was going tick-tock, tick-tock, and I'd think, *that's my life being measured out. What am I doing with it?* You *are* shocked, aren't you."

"Of course not, my dear."

"Why not? I am. When I realized I didn't love him, it wasn't a case of not loving him any more. The truth was, I never had loved him. For ten years I've simply been covering over a mistake that I wasn't aware of making at the time. But that's the nice bit. The nasty bit is that I've also realized that Ian, in his own way, was a bit of a brute."

"Oh, Jess! Really!"

"No! Hear me out. We'll bury the lot today — as I said. I don't mean he was a beast or an animal. He was never less than a gentleman ... chivalrous, courteous, and all that. But he didn't really give a damn about *me*. I'm not blaming him. It's how he was brought up. It's how *I* was brought up, too. I was brought up not to exist — or to exist as little as was absolutely necessary. There was no real *me* for him to give a damn about." She smiled feebly. "Poor David! I warned you it wouldn't make much sense."

"It makes a great deal of sense, Jess. Go on."

"What else is there to say? I was a nobody when he married me. These last two years, when I've had to *do* everything and *be* everything, I've begun to suspect there may be a *somebody* buried in here somewhere." She tapped her breastbone.

"That's wonderful," he offered.

"It's frightening!" she replied at once. "I want to run away from it. I want to find another Ian, who'll simply tell me what to ... No! Not another marriage — not without love, anyway. But I have this terrible urge to find *someone* who'll take all the responsibility off my shoulders — the responsibility for deciding things. I long to stand on my own two feet at last. I long to take my own decisions and control my own life, et cetera, et cetera ... and yet it scares me *stiff* the moment I think seriously about it! I want to yield to someone who'll take all my decisions for me."

"So that you can sulk in the corner and blame him — or her?" he suggested jovially.

"Yes!"

"Is there anyone likely to take over where Ian left off?" he asked. "His parents?"

She shook her head. "His father's quite ill, too — that's why they weren't able to be at the funeral. I don't think they've even broken the news to him."

David already knew it, of course, for she had told him — several times — over the past few days, but he said nothing.

"Even if he weren't," she went on, "I doubt he'd have much to do with me. He never really approved of the marriage. He never thought me good enough for the apple of his eye." She lowered her gaze and shook her head. "God, how I tried to please him! That's where Ian got it from, of course — that uncanny knack of making me feel unworthy. I could never live up to those secret standards in his mind. And the unfairness of it is that *he* lost us all our capital — the old man. If he wasn't so ill, I'd go and stand outside his window and shout, 'Where's our Mexican Railway stock *now*, Mister Lanyon?' He's left the children some money in his will, of course, but it's all in trust. I shan't see a penny. And Ian's sister couldn't wait to raise the drawbridge. We'd be welcome to stay for a *brief* visit at Christmas. She didn't even plead ill health for the funeral. She just said it was rather too far. Three hours by train!" She smiled wanly. "All the world loves a war widow with three young children to feed, clothe, and educate!"

He took her hand and squeezed it briefly between his. "Drink up, Jess, and get some sleep now. Something good is sure to come out of all this — you'll see."

All the things he longed to tell her! And he dared not hint at even one of them.

She did as she was told and then settled back upon her pillow. "You know the really wonderful thing about you, David? Any other man would be bristling with advice and plans — or telling me to get a grip on myself and brace up and face my responsibilities. But you ..."

"Yes?"

"You're just *there!*"

How beautiful she looked upon her pillow — eyes closed, trusting ... vulnerable. He could do anything he wanted with her — except for the *only* thing he wanted, which was for Estelle to be gone from his life and for Jessica to be ... well, she had said it herself: to be *there*.

*T*he Riviera-Splendide was a seasonal hôtel; it opened just before Easter and closed at the end of September. So for roughly half the year Marcus Corvo worked like a galley slave, raking in enough money to maintain himself and his wife Betty in fair comfort in London for the entire year — and keep their sons, Tarquin and Augustus, at a good day school in Hampstead. Betty and the two boys joined him in Penzance during the school holidays; for the rest of the summer he was on his own — or would have been if Petronella Trelawney had not been there to console him in his loneliness, and her own.

Throughout the summer term, and for two further weeks each September, Petronella was the queen of the Riviera-Splendide. She supervised the chambermaids in the mornings and the waitresses (the same females in different aprons) during the afternoons. She herself presided over the bar each night until it was time for her and Marcus to retire to his bed. When Betty and the boys arrived for the school holidays, she reverted without a murmur of complaint to the rôles of head chambermaid in the morning, head waitress in the afternoon, and barmaid at night, after which she retired, solo once again, to her own virtuous bed.

Everyone knew what was going on. An hôtel is the last place on earth where arrangements of that kind could be concealed. It was impossible that Betty Corvo could remain in ignorance of what transfers of nightclothes took place the very morning she arrived and the very night she left; yet never once did she give sign of it, not by the slightest nudge or wink, not by the most indirect hint imaginable. And nor did Marcus, either; he never showed Petronella the slightest favouritism, never touched her intimately when he thought no one was looking, never snatched a kiss in the odd corner.

He hardly needed to show favouritism, mind. Betty did it for him; she and Petronella were almost inseparable by day — forever consulting each other on this or that detail, laughing, inspecting the laundry, giggling, checking stocks, chuckling. If one of the maids inadvertently asked Petronella for time off when Mrs Corvo was in residence, she'd be sent on with her request — yet Mrs Corvo's first question was always, "What does Miss Trelawney say?"

Though Betty Corvo was in her forties and Petronella a mere twenty-three, they were not dissimilar to look at, in silhouette, at least. To see them against the daylight, you could easily have taken them for twins. But once the light picked them out, the differences overtopped the similarities; and, of course, when they opened their mouths they became as east is to west. Betty Corvo was from the School of Hard Knocks somewhere in South London; sometimes she said it was Peckham, at others she mentioned Camberwell. She had beautiful jade eyes, marooned in a face that looked as if its sculptor had given up the struggle half way. Her cheeks were flat, her nose rudimentary, her lips were sensuous in the middle but stern and forbidding at their corners; a firm chin rescued this unhappy ensemble from total collapse; and luckily a frame of short, frizzy blonde hair did nothing to mock all the rest.

Petronella, too, had frizzy hair, but there the likeness ended; for hers was a jet-black, glossy, velvety shock. Her eyes were violet-blue and seemed open in permanent surprise; when you examined them more closely, however, you saw they were almost entirely vacant, not so much observing the world as waiting passively for the world to fill them with some new wonder, however petty it might be. Her nose was her best feature, finely modelled and slightly retroussé. Her lips, though not generous, were shapely and firm, being well matched by her resolute jaw.

Yet even these differences were as nothing when set against their manner of speaking. Betty Corvo was quick, voluble, confident — not always accurate but she'd blunder on in a high, almost girlish register and get there in quick time. She said things like *nom de prah* for Noilly-Prat and *atroxious* for atrocious.

Petronella, with her low-pitched, slightly hoarse delivery, was the proverbial rural clodhopper. Ian had once described her as being "like a frightened heifer on her first appearance in the market." Sometimes she'd talk in a mad gallop, all slurred consonants and broad, slapdash vowels; at other times she'd just stand there, mouth all agape, larding her speech with so many ahs and ers that you'd want to cut a withy from the nearest hedge and tickle her on a bit. The general Cornish habit of putting sentences back-to-front did not help, either. Thus "Have you seen the boss?" becomes: "Seen the boss, have 'ee?" or, more rurally: "Seyn boss, avva?" — but, in Petronella's guttural utterance: "Simbaws 'evvy?" Even after six years at the hôtel — for she had worked there for four years before the Corvos bought it at the end of the war — she still made not the slightest concession to the linguistic needs of their largely "foreign" (that is, English) clientèle.

A week after the funeral — and a week before the Riviera-Splendide closed for the year — Sarah took up Mr Corvo's invitation to a game of snooker before church. She hopped over the low dividing wall and entered the hôtel, as usual, through the scullery. There she found Old Joe, washing up the breakfast crockery. As soon as he saw her he went into his unvarying ritual. "Morning, maid," he called out hoarsely. "How's your father going on then?"

In her shock, Sarah thought of trying to explain, but soon saw how hopeless it would be. She gave up before she even opened her mouth. "Going on, Joe," she replied. "Going on nicely, thank you."

"Proper job," he said and moved on to Part Two. He glanced conspiratorially over his shoulder, then hers, then generally all around. His little, wizened face puckered up in mild fear and he croaked urgently, "Seyn boss, avva?"

"I think I can hear him in the bar, Joe," she replied.

He cackled triumphantly and pulled out a small bottle that had once contained laxative tablets. Now it held a single, not-very-generous tot of whisky, which the boss poured into it each morning when Joe arrived. Joe's great gamble with life was based on his ability to forget that the boss had supplied the demon liquor in the first place

— and on the additional fiction that he would be sacked on the spot if caught swigging it. Several times every hour he would go through his furtive "Seen the boss?" routine before unscrewing the cap of the bottle and upending its contents into his mouth. Then, after savouring it for a few seconds, he would drop his head to his chest and let it all run back. Only Mr Salford, the chef, had a stomach strong enough to watch the final swig of the day, when the turbid tot was swallowed at long last.

By this early point on that particular Sunday morning the amber-coloured fluid was still fairly clear; even so, when he disgorged it back into the bottle, Sarah averted her gaze in a disgust of which she was still young enough to feel ashamed. After all, poor Old Joe couldn't help it. He breathed out fire and cackled again as he screwed the cap back on the bottle. The toiling masses had gained one more petty triumph over the capitalist classes. "Here, maid," he asked, "where was Moses when the light went out?"

"I don't know, Joe," she lied. "I never heard that one before."

He glanced carefully all about him before he pinched her arm in his ancient, wrinkly hand and said, "In the dark!" He threw his head back and guffawed clouds of whisky fumes at the dim light-bulb hanging from the scullery ceiling.

Sarah laughed and told him for the umpteenth time that it was a good 'un. As she went on into the kitchen he returned to his dishes and the next part of the unvarying ritual, singing, "'Oh I shan't furgit the deaay that I wuz boorn. It wuz on a vurry c-a-a-a-wld 'n frosty moorn …'"

"Good morning, Chef," was her next greeting.

Mummy said it was a wonder how Mr Salford stayed alive. The only food that ever went down his throat was the samplings of his own cooking during the day; he never sat down to a plate of anything. At nine each evening he put up his bowler hat, his spats, his gloves, and twiddled his cane as he strolled the length of the esplanade and back — and a little way beyond — past the front wall of Rosemergy and into the saloon bar of the Mouse Hole. Though he twiddled his cane with an independent air, you would never have heard the girls declare, "He must be a millionaire!" He looked every inch the sort of man he was — a man who drank himself into oblivion every night of his life. As for the days of his life, they were another story; then he drank nothing but black tea, which he kept simmering, leaves and all, in a jug at the back of the stove; the same jug, endlessly topped up, served from breakfast until dinner.

"Morning, Miss Lanyon." He cleared a frog from his throat and went to the back door to spit it far out into the yard. This was the man who made the most divine Viennese pastries; people came from all over West Penwith to taste them.

A sheet of dough stood on a thin marble slab on a side table; one third of it was covered with thin shavings of lard. When he returned she watched in silence as he folded the two-thirds over the one-third, above which he placed yet more shavings of lard before folding the last remaining third back over it. The result was a squashed-flat S-shape with two thin layers of lard sandwiched in between. He then rolled it out until it was as big as it had been before and repeated the process before carrying everything — slab, pastry, and rolling pin — back to the fridge.

"Open t'door for uz, bonny lass," he said.

"How many folds d'you do?" she asked.

"Twice every fifteen minutes till it looks right," he told her. "See?" He held it briefly close to her eyes, long enough for her to discern that the pastry was already made up of a couple of dozen layers.

"You must have started before dawn," she said.

He laughed. "Nay, bonny lass. Each fold threbles the number — one, three, nine, twenty-seven ... Think on't." He banged the slab brusquely into the fridge.

"Why d'you need so many layers?"

"When they bake, they lift apart." He kicked the door shut again. "Mill-foil, they call it." He made a beeline for his jug of black tea. "You'll find t'boss in t'bar."

When she reached the passage and looked back she saw him standing in the cold room, reaching down a side of lamb in his huge, shaking, alcoholic's hands.

"Good morning, Mister Corvo." She found the boss up to his elbows in sugar soap, stripping a wallpaper mural in the bar — a once-bright Tyrolean scene that had darkened to somewhere north of the arctic circle.

"You've come to my rescue, Miss Lanyon." He straightened himself with a groan; the neatly shaven line of his moustache reinforced his smile. "Set 'em up. I'll join you when I've dried my hands."

"Good morning, Miss Trelawney." Sarah skipped to the billiards room in time to the chant: "Yellow-green-brown, blue-pink-black," repeated over and over until the balls were set up in that order.

"'Es," Petronella drawled, following her departing figure with darkly suspicious gaze.

Marcus laughed. "You jealous?" he asked incredulously.

The woman sniffed. "Last year she weren't but a giglet. Now she'm a maid."

He rolled his eyes upward, consulting his mental picture of Sarah. "Could be right," he said in his cheerful cockney chirp. "It happens to the best of you, alas, thank God." He chuckled and rested a hand lightly on one of her buttocks.

He rolled down his sleeves as he followed in Sarah's wake; a gentleman never played snooker with his sleeves rolled up. "Time for one frame before church parade," he told her as he entered. He ran a critical eye over her arrangement of the balls.

She held her breath for his compliment.

"Couldn't have done better meself, gel," he said with another moustache-buttressed smile.

She beamed at him; when he called her "gel," he was admitting her to an inner circle.

He put the white on the line for her and cued the yellow for himself. It bounced off the far cushion and returned to within an inch of the line.

"Luck!" she sneered; her white came to rest within a creditable four inches.

"You break, gel," he decided. "You're getting too good to need any chivalry from me."

As he watched her lean over the table to cue off he realized Petronella was right. Sarah Lanyon was just beginning to show those interesting changes that mark the transition from childhood to adolescence. It was hardly anything as yet. Her chest was still as flat as a boy's but her hips were enlarging and her elbows growing more gawky in that appealing way they have. He didn't think her face was any different from the way it had appeared at the beginning of the season but those subtle changes elsewhere gave her big blue eyes and her full red lips a new significance.

Poor little bugger, he said to himself. *That's the end of the lightsome days for you.* He thought of his own boys, who, though much of an age with Sarah, were still a couple of years on the happy side of the great change. How long, he wondered, before he'd have to watch them all with the beady, jaundiced eye of the good parent?

Mind you (he brightened as he realized it), if his plans for the land next door bore fruit, Sarah Lanyon would never be part of that problem. Other girls, yes, but not little Sarah.

"Make something of that if you can, mistah!" she chortled.

He came out of his reverie to discover she had left him a useless lie on the fringe of a slightly broken triangle of reds. "Let's try and live dangerously," he exclaimed, giving them a good belt. "Also we haven't much time."

The reds scattered all over the table. One, by chance, dropped into a centre pocket but, unfortunately, the pink rolled to the top corner pocket, teetered on the brink, and then fell in.

She stared up at him and he realized she was wondering whether the fact that the red had gone in first might not legalize the potting of the pink. He grinned at her. "You don't know, do you!" he said.

She shook her head.

He swallowed hard. One day those eyes would be devastating. They were pretty unsettling now. "I could tell you it's okay and you'd have to believe me, right?"

She nodded.

He laid a finger to the side of his nose. "But you'd find me out before long, and then you'd never trust me again. Right, gel?"

She grinned and nodded.

He pretended to think out the situation aloud. Stroking his chin, he mused, "Is it worth losing all Miss Lanyon's future trust, just to save the loss of six penalty points now?" He screwed up his face and stared at her.

She shook her head slowly.

"I don't think so, either. Sell your honour by all means, but never too cheap — that's my motto. So it's minus-six to me and your go."

She lined up on an easy red.

"Now you trust me, don'tcha," he said to distract her.

She sank it with ease and came back nicely for the blue. "'Course I do, Mister Corvo."

Satisfied, he watched in what she would interpret as respectful silence while she pocketed several of the reds he had lined up so easily for her — and the colours she nominated after each. "I hope your mother's beginning to get over your loss, Miss Lanyon," he said. "It's a terrible time, as I know only too well."

"We weren't unprepared for Daddy's death," she said.

He could hear how she tried to make the sentiment sound as if it were her own. She missed a red, leaving it easy for him. He looked around the table and realized he could just about take the lot; but he decided not to — he'd merely take enough to let her feel good when she beat him at last. "I suppose your father told little Guy that he's the man of the family now," he mused aloud as the red dropped. "Black."

"Yes," she replied.

"Everyone's eyes'll be on him, now. And your mother, of course. They won't realize that *you're* the one to carry the load, really. It's all up to *you* now, gel."

"Me?" Her tone was poised half-way between alarm and pride.

"Yes." He paused in his break so as to stand upright and take a good look at her. "You're the only one that's old enough. Besides, boys live in a world of their own. If the sun turned green they wouldn't see it. It'll be another fifteen years before they've got as much sense knocked into their heads as what you've already got inside yours."

She laughed delightedly at this news, but his face turned sad as he resumed play. "What people don't realize ..." he said as he sank his third red (and, he decided, the last of this break) and nominated blue.

"Why not black?" she asked.

"Because the white will come back nicely off the blue, in line for this red, and *then* I'll take the black. Watch and learn!"

He missed the blue but lined her nicely up on the red.

Her cry of triumph was brief, however, for she remembered the sentence he had started but not finished. "What don't people realize?" she asked as she sank the red. "Black."

"See — just like I said! What people don't realize, my love, is the responsibility that's on *your* shoulders because *you've* got sense in your head where Guy and Toby keep nothing but sawdust."

She squirmed with delight that at least one other person in the world confirmed her own secret opinion of her brothers.

"Still," he went on breezily as she attacked the remaining reds with zest, "*you'll* cope all right, gel. You'll come through flying." Almost as an afterthought he added, "And if you don't ..."

She looked up at him, eyes filled with apprehension. "What then?"

He laughed dismissively. "Don't even think about it." And then, as if thinking better of his reply, he said more seriously, "If you do get in a mess, pet — ever — anytime — no matter what — and you think I could help, well — don't be too proud, eh?" He laughed uproariously. "I shan't charge you much 'cos I've tooken a liking to your face."

Later, when Sarah had gone skipping home to put on her coat for church — and only just remembering in time that skipping was hardly the done thing while they were all still in black — Petronella drifted into the billiards room. She found Marcus playing a sort of bowls and grinning at his own reflection in the mirror.

"You should ought to be 'shamed of yourself," she said.

"I am," he laughed. "But I can't 'elp it, gel. It's my nature, see!"

As he struggled into his Sunday best for church he said, "Listen, Pet, can them cows and geese live without you this autumn?"

"How?"

It still jarred with him that the Cornish said "how?" for "why?" He plumped up his breast-pocket handkerchief. "'Cos I need to stay on down here. I've *got* to get that lot next door out by next season. I don't care how, I've just got to do it. And I can't do it from London. So what I'm thinking is, I'm thinking I'll stay on — redecorate the *whole* place. Not just the bar — everything — top to bottom. What do you say? Stay and help?"

"Whoss missiz gwin say?"

He laughed. "Never mind her! I'm the one with the money around here, not her. She wants to put two boys through a posh school, so never mind her."

Petronella giggled. "All right," she said.

*J*essica and the children walked back from church along the seafront; she took care to let Marcus Corvo and Petronella get well ahead before she took her leave of the vicar, hoping that the call of the sugar-soap and the lure of the fading wallpaper in the bar would overcome any tendency on his part to linger and waylay her for a friendly chat about selling Rosemergy.

"How did you get on with Mister Corvo this morning?" she asked Sarah as they passed by the salt-water bathing pool. Its locked gates proclaimed the sabbath as silently as the church bells had shrilled it an hour or so earlier.

"I know how to make millfoil," she replied.

"Millfoil is a herbaceous plant, dear. *Achillea ... fili ...* something or other." She was forgetting so many things these days. David said it was only the effect of her sleeping draughts; she hadn't told him she just tipped them down the drain.

"You fold fat into pastry to make millions of layers."

"*Millefeuille!*"

"It couldn't be *millions*," Guy put in.

"Impossible." Toby added his penn'orth of support.

"Millfoil," Sarah insisted. "Mister Corvo says that people in the hôtel trade should never pronounce French properly, even if they know how — because it looks as if they're sneering at the guests, half of whom can't pronounce it properly themselves, anyway."

"Very wise," her mother agreed. "What other pearls does he cast? What did you talk about today?"

"I beat him," Sarah replied evasively. "He showed me how to, though. He says he could coach me to play snooker for England when I grow up."

The response that occurred to Jessica was a sarcastic: "Your father would love that!" but she resisted making it. The dead could be twisted into supporting any notion you liked — a point that had occurred to her during the reading from St Paul that morning; if Jesus had lived just ten years longer, old Paul would have got away with a lot less than he did.

"Did he say how long he'd be staying on in Penzance this time? How long is this redecorating of the bar likely to take?"

"He didn't say." Sarah stared out across the bay toward Mousehole. A stiff breeze had got up since dawn and the sea, which had been oily sleek then, was now bright with little white horses. She longed to tell her mother everything that Mr Corvo had said — how wise and responsible she was despite her tender years — but she knew it was the sort of truth that lived best in the warm, dark places of the mind, a thing to be savoured in secret. It would wilt and fade in the glare of alternative opinions.

"Who was that lady in mourning in the pew opposite us?" Guy asked suddenly.

"Yes, wasn't she pretty!" his mother said.

"I thought she had a very sad face," Sarah put in.

"Yes, that too." Jessica was amused to see that Guy's ears had gone bright pink. It had never occurred to her that an eight-year-old boy could be made bashful by feminine prettiness. "Why do you ask?" she teased him.

"Because she's following us now," he replied.

Jessica, conscious of setting an example, did not immediately turn round and stare; instead she halted and leaned against the esplanade railings. "What a day to go yachting!" she exclaimed, sweeping her hand vaguely along the horizon, following it with her eye — until Guy's assertion was confirmed. "All those disappointed yachtsmen who lolled around the harbour back in August — we should send them telegrams to come back now." The pretty young woman, about a hundred paces behind them, had stopped, too, and was also gazing out to sea.

"I have a premonition," Jessica murmured as they resumed their homeward stroll.

"What?" Sarah took her hand.

"I don't know. Just a vague feeling that she has some business with us. Or thinks she has. Perhaps it's only because she's in black, too." She stepped out more briskly. "At least Mister Corvo didn't stop when we did. I feared he was going to waylay us."

"Is fear the same as premo ... tion — what you said?" Guy asked.

"More or less," she replied gaily. "Which just goes to show they don't always come true."

*T*oward the end of luncheon that Sunday, Toby began to misbehave. Jessica thought back quickly over the day before she decided whether or not to make an issue of it. He had got up without fuss, washed without the usual stream of protests, dutifully carried his breakfast dishes to the scullery, and had sat quietly through a sermon that even the adults found tedious. She decided she was not going to insist on perfection for the whole waking day. "You can go and get your crayons and finish the card for Granny Lanyon's birthday," she told him.

When he drew breath to complain she added, "And if you've finished by three, I'll take you all down to the beach. There aren't many paddling days left before winter comes."

Weakness?

Ian would have called it that, and so would Granny Lanyon if she were here. But what did it matter? Jessica found that her moods alternated these days between a lightness that was almost shocking and a sorrow that seemed to fasten on her like an incubus; it weighed particularly heavy when, as now, she strayed into wondering whether Ian and his family would approve, as if they were a silent third party at every decision.

But the whole point of her present grief was that Ian was *not* here, and never would be, ever again. And she could not turn the children's upbringing into a kind of memorial to him; she would be forever making mental apologies to them: "I know, darling — I don't entirely agree with this or that myself, but it's the way your father would have liked it." The temptation was greatest where her own resolve was weak or where her opinion was indifferent.

"That pretty woman is still there." Toby was back at the dining-room door.

"Don't lean against things all the time. If you're tired you can go and lie down. She's still where?"

"By our front gate."

"And, anyway, why d'you say she is *still* there? When did you see her there before?"

There was a ring at the doorbell.

"She was there before we ate," Toby replied as she went past him and down the hall.

Guy beat her to it. He and Bunyan, the spaniel, seemed to be in competition to trip each other up on the slippery marble tiles. He opened the door, took one look at the pretty lady in black, and fled again, back to the dining room.

Jessica smiled and gave a vaguely apologetic wave of her hand. "Good afternoon."

The woman was even prettier close to. Her pale-green eyes had a sort of smoky, smouldering lustre, and her auburn hair fell below her shoulders in sleek, glossy waves. She tossed it nervously and said in a troubled voice, "Mrs Lanyon?"

"Yes?" Jessica stepped aside. "Do come in, Mrs ...?"

"Miss. Miss Sancreed. Lorna Sancreed." When she saw her name meant nothing she added, "I don't wish to intrude."

Jessica took a further pace back and made a sweeping-in gesture. "Of course you're not intruding. Have you eaten? I think I saw you at church, didn't I, Miss Sancreed?" The name rang the faintest bell in her mind — some scandal? A couple of years ago? Gossip, anyway ... she remembered no details.

The young woman came in, reluctantly, and then, when the door closed behind her, looked as if she wished she hadn't. "I didn't know," she said. "I came down to speak to your husband ... not knowing. I'm so sorry."

"Have you eaten?" Jessica repeated.

She shook her head.

"It's only cold lamb, I'm afraid." Jessica led the way down the hall to the dining room. "And the bubble-and-squeak is cold, too, by now — but I can reheat that easily enough."

"Oh, please don't put yourself ..."

"It's no trouble at all. Sarah will gladly do it."

"I'll light the gas! I'll light the gas!" Toby skipped to the kitchen ahead of his sister.

Guy came shyly forward, hand outstretched. "How do you do," he said. "I'm Guy Lanyon. Let me take your coat, Miss Sancreed."

"The man of the house, eh?" She shook his hand with a sad sort of sweetness. He took her hat and coat and escaped from his own embarrassment. "You're all very kind," she said to the room in general.

"It went *pwcchh!*" Toby stood in the doorway again, shaking his head around violently.

"Toby!" Jessica warned. "You're getting silly and excited. Go and get out your crayons." She set a new place for Miss Sancreed as she spoke. "Would you like a glass of ale with your meat? We permit ourselves that luxury on Sundays ..." She hesitated and then changed it to: "I permit myself that luxury, I mean. Oh dear — so many habits to unlearn!"

The woman nodded. "I know."

Something in her tone hinted that she was making a more-than-conventional response. Jessica took the plunge: "May I ask ... have you, too, suffered a bereavement *very* recently, Miss Sancreed? I see you are wearing mourning, too."

"Yes," she replied simply. She fixed Jessica with her pale, intense gaze. "Do you sometimes feel it's all a dream? That you'll wake up and find it's over?"

Jessica nodded and drew breath to speak, but the woman went on: "Of course, we *know* it isn't. We know it's all too real. But even so, we seem to be just ... swimming through the day."

"It's like being a spectator to one's own life," Jessica said.

"Yes!" Lorna Sancreed reached out a hand to squeeze Jessica's arm, but she plucked it back at the last moment and smiled down at the table as if it were a great relief to have these odd feelings confirmed.

"May I ask ...?" Jessica began hesitantly, leaving the rest of the question hanging.

"He was my fiancé," Lorna replied. "Philip Morvah." She saw that Mrs Lanyon knew the name. "Flight-Sergeant Philip Morvah," she added.

"Ah," Jessica said. "Then I begin to understand."

"Yes, I thought so."

"My husband often spoke of him. In fact" — she swallowed heavily — "as I'm sure you know, they both received their injuries in the same accident."

"That's right." There was a strange rigidity in her as she added, "And, as I'm sure you *don't* know, Philip died the very same day — the Wednesday before last."

"Oh, my dear!" Jessica sat down abruptly and took Lorna's hand between hers.

Sarah appeared with a plate piled high with sizzling bubble-and-squeak, to which she added several slices of cold lamb before bringing it to the table.

"Bless you," Miss Sancreed said, glad to have cause for smiling. "Life goes on, eh. There is life after death, but it's ours, not ..." She picked up her knife and fork. "There's nothing one can say, is there — *nothing*. Humour seems forced. Being solemn is too ghastly. And if one sticks to neutral things, it's just like ..." She hunted for words. "... floating in the middle of nowhere," she concluded.

She attacked the meat with relish and added, "What splendid lamb. Or splendid cooking."

"Cooking!" Jessica echoed scornfully.

Miss Sancreed, her mouth full, questioned her with a lift of the eyebrows.

"Sarah roasted this," Jessica explained. "She can cook. I never learned and I never will. I'd rather scrub the esplanade from end to end than scramble an egg."

Miss Sancreed swallowed her mouthful and complimented Sarah on her handiwork.

"I'm going to make millfoil this afternoon," Sarah told her. "I saw how this morning."

"*Millefeuille,*" her mother murmured.

"Flaky pastry, anyway," Miss Sancreed said. "Have you got a refrigerator? It's hopeless without."

Sarah said they had.

"Do you enjoy cooking, Miss Sancreed?" Jessica would have used the same tone in asking a sewerman if he enjoyed *his* work.

"Fortunately, yes," Miss Sancreed replied.

"Why 'fortunately'?"

"Because I have to do something with my life — and it may as well be something I enjoy."

Jessica took this to mean that she had no money. So she couldn't be the Miss Sancreed people had gossiped about — *she* had been quite rich, they said. Still, it wasn't a common name.

The woman took another forkful and ate with relish.

Jessica almost said, "My goodness, you *were* hungry!" but realized that their slender acquaintance hardly permitted such a comment; yet there was something about Miss Sancreed that seemed to bridge their unfamiliarity and invite casual intimacies of that kind. "It's shocking of me not to have heard of your fiancé's death," she said. "I suppose it was in Helston? That's where the Flight-Sergeant came from, I think? I can only plead that I had other things on my mind."

Miss Sancreed shook her head. "It was in Yeovil, as a matter of fact. At my home."

"You live in Yeovil?" It was a thin question but Jessica could think of little else to say. Also it completely ruled *this* Miss Sancreed out of the gossip about that other one. She was glad.

But was there a slight hesitation before Miss Sancreed replied? "My parents are from ... Cornwall, but lately I've lived in Yeovil. May I ask — are your parents still alive, Mrs Lanyon?"

Jessica shook her head. "My parents-in-law are, though my husband's father is quite ill. My own parents died during the war."

"I'm so sorry."

"During the war!" Jessica repeated. "I remember my grandfather commenting on that phrase just before *he* died — so it must have been nineteen-sixteen. He said that the words would have had no meaning during the entire course of his life. Sixty years of peace!" She smiled. "I'm sorry. I'm rambling. You said that Flight-Sergeant Morvah died the same day as my husband?"

Miss Sancreed nodded. A little shiver ran through her. "I couldn't believe it when I saw you in mourning."

"You recognized me?" Jessica frowned. "Do we know each other, perhaps? I'm awfully sorry. I'm sure I'd have remembered you if we'd met before."

"No. One of your neighbours pointed you out. And then I saw you all in black. In one way I couldn't believe it, and yet in another it was almost as if I'd expected it. And then when I was told it was the same *day* ... well! It's hard to believe it's just coincidence, don't you think?"

Jessica pulled a glum face. "It's even more of a coincidence than that. You realize it was also two years to the day after the accident? To the very day!"

"Yes, that, too. It's hard to believe it wasn't ... I don't know. Destiny or something. I don't know about the Squadron Leader, but Philip wasn't much more than hanging on by the tips of his fingers most of those twenty-four months."

Jessica closed her eyes and nodded. "The skin of his teeth," she agreed. "I couldn't ever claim it caught me unprepared."

"Nor me."

Their eyes met and an intuition passed between them that neither could have put into words. A death in Yeovil, twelve days ago, had driven Lorna Sancreed to this meeting — just as a death in Penzance, on the self-same day, had prepared Jessica to receive her.

Miss Sancreed's plate was almost empty. "Oh, I'm sorry," Jessica exclaimed. "I offered you a glass of beer. I'm an awful hostess. Why didn't you say?"

"No, really, a small glass of water would be perfect," Miss Sancreed assured her.

"A cup of tea, perhaps?"

"When are we going paddling?" Toby asked grumpily from the door. "I've finished Granny's card."

"Oh yes," his mother said distractedly.

"A glass of water, truly," Miss Sancreed repeated.

Sarah settled the discussion by quietly placing a tumbler of water before her.

"I did promise the children a go along the sands," Jessica said apologetically. "Perhaps you'd like to join us? And then we can come back and have that cup of tea afterwards."

"I'm going to stay here and make millfoil," Sarah announced with a sort of timid belligerence.

"I wouldn't dream of stopping you, dear," her mother replied.

*J*essica watched Bunyan barking at the waves. He behaved as if each one were a personal assault aimed deliberately at him; he rushed at it furiously, only to retreat in panic as it turned to a boiling frenzy that harried him up the beach at the speed of a galloping horse. "If that dog lives to be a hundred," she remarked, "he'll still be an idiot."

Miss Sancreed chuckled. "They're very like boys, Mrs Lanyon — don't you think? He knows all about waves, really, but it's fun to pretend otherwise. Boys are the same. They have much more imagination than girls."

Guy and Toby found a crab with only one claw. They tried to entice Bunyan into investigating the phenomenon — in the hope that the crab would nip him somewhere.

"More heartless than adventurous," Jessica commented as they left the boys to it.

"Girls are just as heartless," Miss Sancreed said. "If there were two little girls there as well, they'd stand eagerly by, grinning and egging the boys on. They wouldn't do it themselves but they'd goad the boys into doing it for them. No doubt about it — we females are a devious lot. We deserved to be thrown out of paradise."

"Ah!" Jessica was not sure she wanted to pursue this conversation; it might turn into an outdoor confessional as to what each of them had been devious about, lately. "You mentioned cooking," she said. "Did you mean that in any sort of professional way, or would you teach it ... or what?"

Miss Sancreed remained silent.

Jessica, slightly embarrassed at her own bluntness, added soothingly, "Of course, it's probably much too soon ..."

"Not at all," Miss Sancreed interrupted. "In fact, now is probably the best time of all to be thinking about it. To be *forced* to think about it. I never considered myself *apart* from Philip. D'you know what I mean? As a separate person. My future was his future. It made no sense to talk of them as two separate ... *things*." She had come to a halt during this speech and was now staring out at the western horizon, beyond Mousehole. "He was so *still*," she murmured. Then, looking directly at Jessica, she added, "Didn't you find that? It's a stillness that's impossible to describe. Rocks are still. Pebbles on the beach are still. Chairs and tables ... you know. But the stillness of death is not that sort of a stillness at all. It's far beyond, somehow."

"Yes." Jessica's voice was barely audible. "I remember that moment. I touched Ian and I suddenly realized that ... whatever mystical thing was *him*, it had fled. The body really is just a shell. That's also the moment when you realize that everything has changed ... *everything* ... you know?"

"Absolutely everything." Miss Sancreed nodded. "It's just as you say. All your thoughts about yourself ... who you are ... what you're *for* — it's all changed. All your previous thoughts are ... what's the word? Cancelled?"

"Voided!" Jessica laughed dryly. "What a wartime word! Like our holiday in Venice. That was voided. Ian and I planned to go to Venice for Christmas, nineteen-fifteen. And when I say planned, I do mean *planned*! He was the ultimate planner."

"I rather gathered that from one or two things Philip said," Miss Sancreed told her — then added hastily, "He had the greatest respect for the Chief — that's what they called him, you know. They all had. Philip said they'd rather go on a sortie planned by the Chief than by ..." She hesitated.

"Than by whom?" Jessica asked.

Miss Sancreed shook her head. "It's blasphemous. But it shows the respect they had for your husband."

Jessica reached out and touched her arm briefly. "Thank you, my dear. Anyway, as I was saying, when Ian died ..." Her voice trailed off and she turned to her companion with a broad smile. "D'you know, there's no one else I could talk to about ... all this. Of course, I have many friends who lost a husband — or son or father — in the war. Which of us hasn't! But our cases are different, aren't they. No telegram boy at the door for us. No sudden plummeting of that Sword of Damocles that hung over every family in the land for four long years. It *is* different, isn't it."

Miss Sancreed closed her eyes and nodded.

"So," Jessica went on in a determinedly cheerful voice, "when Ian died, I sat there beside him — I mean literally in the first minutes, after I realized he *was* dead ... in that stillness you talked about — and you're absolutely right, there is no other stillness like it — I just sat there beside him, relieved that all his pain was over and done with at last ... and then I was ashamed of feeling relieved, too." She broke off suddenly and turned to Miss Sancreed. "Did you sometimes long for him to die?"

The other nodded. Her manner was neither ashamed nor reluctant; in all sorts of subtle ways she encouraged Jessica to continue.

"I don't mean for his sake but for yours?" Jessica added.

Again the woman nodded encouragingly.

"To be ... well, it sounds awful to say *free*. But I felt as if my life had been taken away from me and hidden in a sort of never-never place. In the *void!*"

Miss Sancreed was still staring out across the bay. "I don't know how to start thinking about myself *without* ... you know, having to take someone else into the plan. You have the children and the house, of course." Her thoughts petered out and she stared down at her empty hands as if to say they were all she had.

"You have no idea at all?" Jessica asked. An absurd notion was taking shape in her mind, yet she shied away from it even before she could put it into words.

Miss Sancreed gave a single dry laugh. "It would have to be something shocking," she said. "I need to be shocked — you know? There was a travelling fairground in Yeovil last week, just after Philip died. I didn't go, of course, but it was camped quite close to our house. And I saw out of my bedroom window. I saw a young girl do a high dive into a tank of burning petrol — forty feet or more, and yet the tank was only six feet deep! I went out and watched her next performance, close-to, so I could see the the look on her face."

"Fear?"

"Before she climbed the ladder, yes. Fear you could almost touch. But then the triumph in her eyes when she clambered out of the water after it was all over! I envied her. I said to myself, 'You *know* you're alive, girl!' I feel I need that sort of shock each day, just to be sure I haven't died. Otherwise I feel like an automaton, simply going through the motions, you know."

Jessica nodded. "I'm afraid I do." Then, before she could have second thoughts she blurted out the idea that had been turning over in her mind. "Listen," she said, "I realize we hardly know each other, and yet in some ways — in one very obvious way — we probably know more about each other than even our own families could ever understand. Would you like to stay awhile, here with us at Rosemergy? Please say yes!"

Miss Sancreed just stared at her, jaw slack, eyes wide.

"Only if you want to," Jessica added hastily. "I'm being very selfish, I admit. Just the few things you've said since we met — what is it? Only an hour! Yet some of the things you've said are so ... oh dear, I can't express it properly. But when you talk, something in me cries out, 'Yes! That's so exactly right!' And there's no one else I know who comes near that sort of ..." She waved her hands in a rapid hither-and-thither motion between them. "Have I shocked you?" she asked hesitantly and then added with a smile, "Into feeling alive, perhaps? Your high-dive act for today!"

Miss Sancreed burst out laughing at that. Then, catching her breath, she apologized and said, "No, it's just so *generous*, Mrs Lanyon. I hope you don't believe in telepathy, though?"

Jessica smiled and frowned all at the same time, staring at her in bewilderment.

"The moment I entered your home," Miss Sancreed explained, "I felt it *was* a home. It has such an aura of ..." She sought for the word and then said simply, "home."

"I don't usually make snap decisions like that." Jessica was now rather surprised at her boldness. "In fact, I'm not too good at any kind of decision, snap or leisurely. I relied absolutely on Ian for all that."

"It sounds as if you have one hanging over you at this moment, Mrs Lanyon?"

"Oh, call me Jessica, please. Or Jess. I take it you will stay, Lorna? May I call you Lorna?"

"Please! But as for staying ... every well-bred particle of me says I can't possibly impose ..."

"Oh, but you wouldn't be imposing, I do assure you. It's really a very selfish suggestion on my part. I'm not good at reaching decisions on my own. I need to talk them over with someone. Or just talk out loud, really. Often I don't know what I'm thinking until I hear myself saying it." She smiled at her companion in a kind of joking accusation. "Somehow I don't feel *you* have that sort of difficulty!"

Lorna chuckled. "No! My difficulty is the next station down the line from yours: I often don't know what I'm thinking until I find myself *doing* it!"

"So you will stay awhile — until you find yourself doing something you really want to do?"

Lorna dipped her head gratefully. "For a day or two, anyway. You're very kind."

"One day at a time?" Jessica suggested. There was something odd about the woman's reluctance — as if she felt there were some explanation she should get out of the way before she accepted.

If so, she shrank from giving it. All she said was, "That sort of thing. I won't sing for my supper — for which you will be eternally grateful when you hear how badly I sing at any other time — but I can promise to cook it. I do quite enjoy cooking."

"And I loathe it!" Jessica caught a fleeting smile on Lorna's lips. "As you probably guessed! In the good old days we had a cook. But as things got tighter ..."

"Mummy, Mummy! That crab has lost his other claw now." The boys caught up with them. "He can't possibly live, can he? May we bury him now? He's as good as dead, isn't he?"

"In no more than three inches of sand," their mother told them. "And well below the high-tide line."

Bunyan, who had been deceived by their sprint into galloping a furlong ahead of them along the beach, turned and barked in frustration and then raced back to rejoin them.

"That was decisive enough for anyone," Lorna commented.

"The poor creature will easily get out of three inches of sand, especially with the tide coming in. But the children need to bury things now — dead animals — you know. I don't know how their minds work but they seem to need those rituals, for some reason."

Lorna shook her head in admiration. "The moment you say it I can *hear* the rightness of it, but it would never have occurred to me off my own bat."

"You will — when you have ..." She hesitated, embarrassed at what she had been about to say.

Lorna was embarrassed, too. They walked on in silence awhile, letting it fade. They came to a low, smooth rock, jutting out from the foundations of the esplanade. By unspoken agreement they sat there and rested.

"Mummy, Mummy, may we?" Jessica echoed the boys, who were now solemnly digging the crab's grave, using their hands as shovels. "Those little decisions are easy enough. It's the bigger ones, where common sense is all on one side and yet my feelings are all on the other. That's where I flounder."

"You face one now?" Lorna asked.

A faint aroma of coal and tar wafted along the beach. A freighter of some kind was steaming upwind of them; it had just left the harbour, which lay beyond the Trinity House dock at the far end of the esplanade, half a mile or so to the east.

"The biggest one possible, I suppose," Jessica told her. "Should I stay on here at Rosemergy, or sell up and move somewhere smaller and more sensible?"

"Ah! That *is* a big one, I must say. Is it your childhood home, or the Chief's, perhaps?"

"His childhood home — but only just. His parents bought it when he was on the way. Before that it belonged to a Norwegian lady, Miss Gaard. She built the turret at the corner."

"I adore it! I always wanted to live in a house with a turret."

"And sit combing your hair at the window — I know — and letting your long, fair tresses hang down for knights in shining armour to climb up! Or auburn tresses in your case."

They laughed far too much at this little pleasantry and then looked guiltily up at the esplanade above them. A red-faced gentleman with a walrus moustache glared at them disapprovingly — though it might have been his everyday expression, anyway. He probably thought that two ladies in mourning should not be sitting on the beach, laughing their heads off in the sabbath sunshine.

They moderated their laughter and turned back to face the sea. Jessica glanced across at Lorna and was surprised to observe her lips moving in some kind of silent incantation as she leaned forward, picked up a piece of driftwood, drew a face in the sand — a face with a walrus moustache — and then stabbed the stick quite viciously through the eye. "I *hate* men like that," she said when she became aware that Jessica was watching.

Jessica wondered whether she meant men with walrus moustaches or men who disapprove of female laughter or men who just happen to pause and lean on the esplanade railings at the one spot along the beach where there happen to be young women nearby — a phenomenon she had frequently noted.

"Would you get a good price for the house?" Lorna asked.

The question took Jessica aback; money was not something one talked about in polite society — or not so bluntly. In subtle ways, of course, one talked about it all the time. "Almost too good a price, I think," she replied.

Lorna turned to her in surprise.

"The fact is, all three of my neighbours are keen to acquire the place," she explained.

"Three?" Lorna was momentarily puzzled. "Oh, you mean the one at the end of your garden, too."

"Doctor Carne, yes. The house is called Trevescan. He's been very good to us. If I'm compelled to sell up and leave — which I probably will be — he's the one I'd like to sell to. But either of the others would probably outbid him."

"The pub and the hôtel," Lorna mused. But her tone was too remote, too idle. Jessica could sense that she really wanted to hear more about Doctor Carne. Had her tone in talking about David given something away? Her heart sank. She must be more careful in future — for there *was* no future in indulging those feelings.

"Yes," she put in before Lorna could steer the conversation back to David, "the pub is owned by Ben Calloway. The brewers — Rosewarne's — want to tie him into selling their beer only. He could resist them better, he thinks, if he were more of a road house. He'd build a ballroom along the front, where they could also serve banquets and put on smoking concerts and things like that. And he could use the rest of the space for parking cars. He thinks cars are going to be quite important for his sort of trade in the years ahead."

"Is he married?" Lorna asked.

In any other circumstances Jessica would have made an arch reply. Instead, she said, "There was a fiancée but she drowned rather tragically during the war, climbing down the cliffs at Hell's Mouth."

"What on earth for?" Lorna shivered at the mental image of that bleak, godforsaken spot on the north coast.

"Trying to get closer to the seals, they said. She'd swum there often. She was a Saint Ives girl — Maude Lessore. You might have read about it?"

Lorna shook her head. "So! Remember not to talk about swimming with seals and Hell's Mouth with Mister Calloway!" She closed her eyes and put an outstretched index finger to each of her temples, as if they were electrical contacts, feeding in these prohibitions.

Jessica became aware that, despite Lorna's savvy, confident manner, there was something appealingly childlike about her, too. "He served with the Gunners in the war," she added. "He has a piece of silver in his skull as a sort of memento. He was invalided out in nineteen-sixteen but immediately joined the special coastguard watch and, they say, helped save the lives of at least two crews whose ships he was the first to sight as they were sinking off Land's End. He's a well-liked man, anyway, as you can imagine. Which is more than one can say of Marcus Corvo ..."

"Ah!" Lorna interrupted. "Your hôtelier! I met him just before church — him and his wife."

Jessica cleared her throat meaningfully.

"Is she not his wife?" Lorna asked.

Jessica looked all about them. "Not the one he has all the year round, you might say."

Lorna's eyes gleamed and she smiled broadly. "Do tell!"

Jessica glanced skywards. "Where does one begin! Listen, I'll tell you the whole sordid tale after supper tonight, when little ears are safely tucked up in bed." She grinned as if she had just been very clever. "And that will make sure you stay for one night at least. Have you got any bags to collect, by the way, or did you come down on the train this morning?"

Lorna made an exaggerated show of her disappointment and then, serious again, said, "No, I came down yesterday afternoon. I stayed at a guest house in Morrab Road."

"Then let's go home, have a nice cup of tea — I can at least cook that! — and then we'll drive round and collect your things."

Sunday was high-tea day. In summer that meant bloater paste, whitebait, thunder and lightning. In winter — and that particular Sunday, though bright, was raw enough to count as winter — it began with crumpets toasted round the fire followed by a mixed grill of kidney, liver, bacon, egg, and chips, topped off with fried tomatoes and baked beans. "It's a sort-of compensation for those still young enough to find the Reverend Meecher's twenty-minute sermons rather hard going," Jessica explained to Lorna out of earshot of the children. "I'd better cook it because I know how they like it."

To Lorna's surprise the children appeared to like it as near burned as made no difference. She watched with amazement as they wolfed it down and then wiped every last drop from their plates with plain brown bread — a habit left over from the war. It confirmed her view that children are essentially barbarians.

Jessica said, "I wonder if we'll ever go back to the old rules of etiquette? Before the war we'd rather have *died* than guzzle every last morsel. But then during the war you'd look at the food on your plate and you'd think of the sailors who'd risked their lives to bring it over the ocean and you'd feel just as ashamed if you left it *uneaten!* Everything's so relative nowadays. D'you think there are *any* absolute rights and wrongs left?"

"It's very hard to know, Jess," Lorna said. "Do you keep a stockpot going? I don't see one."

Jessica bit her lip and gave a guilty smile. "I tried. It always seemed to be going wrong. I won't attempt to describe it in detail, especially as we haven't eaten yet."

Later that evening, in fact, while she was bathing the two boys, she became aware of the most heavenly fragrance drifting up the stairs and filling the entire house. It was so subtle at first that she could not have said whether it was a new perfume, or an unknown plant with a winter-evening scent, or the aroma of cooking. Guy and Toby smelled it, too; they stopped their splashing and stared at each other and then at their mother with a what's-*that?* light in their eyes.

She rose and went out to the landing — where the smell was, unmistakably, of something cooking. But what? Ambrosia! Food for the gods! It was a smell that conjured up farmhouse kitchens at harvest thanksgiving, the smell of soup tureens after a long day's hike over the moors, the smell of every grown-up dinner table that ever tantalized Jessica during a long childhood of denial — at least of that sort of richness. She closed her eyes and breathed deep draughts of it.

Sarah came skipping out into the hallway below, obviously intending to race upstairs with the good news. She was already calling out, "Mummy, Mummy, Mummy!" when she glanced up and saw her standing at the stairhead. "It's *stock!*" she said — as other children might say: "It's the circus come to town!"

"But …" Her mother was bewildered. "Where did you get the bones to make stock from?"

"I went and asked Mister Salford at the hôtel."

"Oh, you shouldn't go begging, dear."

"I didn't beg. I took my millfoil across to show him and he said it was good and I saw all the bones there ready to throw out and I asked wasn't he going to put them in his stockpot and he said it's too late in the season to bother. So he gave them to me. He said it was a prize for making the pastry so good."

"So well."

"He said good. But isn't it a scrumptious smell!"

Her mother smiled at last. "It's almost too good to believe. What's in it?"

"I don't know. Miss Sancreed went out and picked a lot of leaves in the garden."

"Oh, good for her! I didn't know we had any herbs at all." She left the two boys to towel themselves dry, or dryish, and went to draw their curtains and turn down the beds — a trivial, everyday action that always made her think of the horror her great-grandparents and people of their generation would have felt if they could only see her. A house without a dozen servants would have been a pretty poor place to them.

This evening, however, she was distracted in the midst of that small ritual. She had her hand to the curtain and was about to draw it when she noticed David Carne walking across the garden from his dispensary to the back door of Trevescan. Twilight was fairly well advanced by then; if he hadn't been moving she wouldn't have noticed him at all.

When he stepped off the lawn onto the gravelled back yard he stopped and turned toward Rosemergy. She could not see his face. Was he going to call by? He often did between his evening surgery and dinner — for a quick pick-me-up, he said. He no longer had the excuse of seeing how Ian was faring, of course. And people might talk

— especially when they all knew what a perpetual invalid Estelle was and what a wretched dance she led the poor man.

He obviously decided to brave the tongues of scandal, for he changed direction and came to the boundary fence. Jessica had not switched the light on in the boys' bedroom; she was sure he could not see her behind the darkened panes. She felt a little guilty, just standing there, staring down at him. What *was* he doing, she wondered — holding on to the top of the fence with his head raised in that peculiar attitude? Looking for her? Staring into one darkened window after another for some fleeting sign of her? Worrying about her ... thinking about her?

A great warmth filled her. Dear David! Such a *good* man, and so especially good to her during these years of trouble. And still thinking of her now. She luxuriated in his fondness for a moment or two — until it suddenly struck her that he was doing no such thing. He was *sniffing the air*, of course; that's why he held his head at that strange angle. A light southerly breeze, straight off the bay, was wafting the aroma from Rosemergy's kitchen directly to him. And that was what had made him halt in mid-stride — the reek of Lorna's stockpot! And it was holding him there now, rooted in pleasure.

A blind, raging fury filled her. It lasted only a moment for, of course, all her more civilized faculties came welling up to dowse that sudden conflagration; but its ferocity left her shaken.

David was now looking surreptitiously right and left, like a man aware he was about to act beneath his dignity; and then, placing one hand firmly on top of the nearest fence post, he vaulted lightly over, landing on the lawn with the spring of a gymnast. Jessica closed her eyes and quelled the unruly feelings his lithe, athletic grace stirred within her.

He ran tip-toe across the grass, making straight for the kitchen window; he passed out of sight beneath the boys' sill before Jessica understood his intentions. She threw open the window to greet him at the very moment he realized that the cook in the kitchen was a stranger; she also saw that the kitchen window was wide open — which explained how the aroma had carried so strongly to him.

"Go on indoors, David," she said quietly. "I'll come down and introduce you in a mo."

He glanced up in surprise. *"There* you are! I thought ..." He pointed toward the kitchen window. "It was such an irresistible smell."

"Come, come! You couldn't possibly have believed it was me!"

"Frankly, I couldn't believe it was any sort of human agency."

"Pour me a gin if you get there before me." She shut the window, still feeling slightly agitated at the force of her earlier emotion.

In an abstract way she had to admit she was rather glad of it — to feel *any* strong passion after the hopeless numbness that had pervaded her life for the past two years had to be some kind of a bonus. But even so, to feel such jealous anger against a kind, sweet soul like Lorna Sancreed, just because David was so smitten by the smell of her cooking ... well! It was a bit unhinged, surely? Resolving to watch herself more closely in future, she returned to the bathroom.

Such aggressive, knobbly, bony bodies they had — boys — even at that age. She was as proud of their muscles and their broad, fine-skinned chests as they were. "Don't skimp your teeth," she told them sternly. "And if you're quiet as churchmice, you may read for half an hour. Doctor Carne has called, so I must go down and introduce him to Miss Sancreed."

She saw David as she passed the drawing-room door; he had his back to her and was already pouring out their drinks. "I'll bring some ice," she called.

"Just the ticket," he replied, not turning round.

"Lorna, that smells absolutely heavenly," she said as she breezed into the kitchen. "What is it?"

"Stock," Sarah answered. "I told you. And leaves from the garden."

Jessica took the ice tray from the fridge. "Well, if it can be left to bubble on its own for the moment, Lorna, I'd like you to come and meet a dear friend of ours."

"Your doctor-neighbour?" Lorna wiped her hands in her apron and fumbled for the loose end of the bow. Sarah gave it a tweak.

"You've met?" Jessica asked as she broke out a small handful of ice cubes. "Did he introduce himself on the way in?"

"No, but I saw which garden he jumped out of and I remember your saying his backed on to yours."

Lorna was clearly one of those people who gained their bearings rather swiftly in any new situation, Jessica thought as she refilled the empty ice compartments at the tap.

"If you use hot water, you'll get clear ice cubes," Lorna said, then, seeing Jessica's mouth harden, added, "... though actually I prefer them with bubbles in, too."

"I must try that trick with hot water next time." Jessica inserted the tray back into the fridge. She saw Lorna patting her hair nervously and searching for a looking glass. "You look grand," she assured her, though there were, in fact, one or two wisps.

As they walked up the passage toward the drawing room she asked what herbs Lorna had managed to find. "I know we've got mint and parsley," she said, "but I've always thought of them more as garnishes than herbs."

"I found several," Lorna replied, "including *Achillea ptarmica*. I don't know its common-or-garden name. It's the one with the little white button flowers, growing near the top of the path. I noticed it on the way in."

"*Achillea ptarmica.*" Jessica tried to commit the name to memory as she led Lorna into the drawing room.

"The old apothecary's standby." David met them almost at the door; he was holding Jessica's gin and French at the ready.

"Bless you!" She took it and offered him her cheek to kiss. It was not their usual manner of greeting but he passed it off without obvious surprise. "Lorna," she went on, "meet Doctor David Carne. Miss Lorna Sancreed."

"I'm the neighbour that way, Miss Sancreed." He jerked his thumb toward the back of the house as he shook her hand.

"She saw you vault the fence," Jessica said. "We both did."

"One can't move a foot in Cornwall," he complained. "May I pour you some poison, Miss Sancreed?"

"Thank you, Doctor — the same as Jess, please."

He was obviously a little surprised at her intimate use of the Christian name.

"Miss Sancreed's fiancé was a flight-sergeant in Ian's squadron ..." Jessica began to explain.

David turned round, the vermouth bottle poised in his hand. "Philip Morvah?" he asked. "Would he have been the son of Jake Morvah — the lawyer in Helston?"

Lorna nodded gravely. "Did you know Philip, Doctor Carne?"

He shook his head. "But I remember Ian mentioning him — more than once. The backbone of the entire squadron, he called him. They were both wounded in the same accident, if I recall?"

Lorna glanced nervously at Jessica, who did the explaining for her. "The coincidence is even more ghastly, I'm afraid. Not only was he wounded in the same accident, he actually died on the very same day. Lorna came here to tell Ian — not knowing about it, of course."

"I am so very sorry, Miss Sancreed." He held out her glass as he spoke; his deep, dark voice — with just a hint of the Cornish burr in it — carried the suggestion that he was assuming some degree of personal responsibility for Philip's death.

Lorna could easily imagine that all his female patients fell for him. He had such large, sympathetic eyes, embellished with crow's feet from so much smiling and laughter. His lips were full and soft, with a downward slope from the centre; she guessed that when he was angry, or even in repose, their expression could be somewhat grim, but when he was animated and friendly, as he was now, they were most endearing.

Yet he was, after all, a doctor and he faced death and bereavement often enough not to dwell on it. "You know your late fiancé's father, of course?" he added.

Lorna shook her head. "I'm afraid Philip and his father were estranged. Mister Morvah wanted his son to go into the Royal Navy. He could have wangled him a commission there. But Philip said he'd rather be an A/C with the Chief in Six-oh-four Bomber Squadron than admiral of the fleet in any old navy."

"I quite believe you." David grinned at Jessica. "The Chief did have that effect on people, didn't he." He waited for the two women to seat themselves on the sofa before he took the arm chair opposite.

Lorna was uncomfortably aware of the way he kept glancing at her, running a quick eye up and down her figure. Normally she wouldn't have minded. She quite enjoyed it when men would eye her in the street and then be unable to look away, even when she had gone past. She would catch their reflections in shop windows, still looking at her. She didn't mind that in the least. But in these present circumstances it was most awkward. Jessica quite clearly had a rather tender spot for her doctor-neighbour.

Lorna drew her charcoal-gray cardigan more firmly across her bosom and plucked its folds to a state of unrevealing looseness. "Are you from these parts, Doctor Carne?" she asked casually.

The moment the words were out she knew it was a mistake, for it would provide him with the opening to quiz her on her family and origins; she had already seen a speculative glint in his eye − not the usual one men have, about a woman's charms and availability − this one was more particular.

"I was born not five miles from here, Miss Sancreed − in the village that bears your name, indeed." He smiled. "Or perhaps your family is named after the village. In fact, I have two patients called Sancreed − Tom and Gertie. Are you by any chance related?"

Damn! she thought − but then immediately felt resigned to it. After all, her chances of keeping her origins to herself were null in these parts. "They are my uncle and aunt," she replied.

"Ah!" In that one syllable he managed to express the fact that a lot of his other questions were now answered, too.

Jessica remembered the old scandal that had strayed briefly into her mind that afternoon, but once again its details eluded her. "Miss Sancreed will be staying for a few days," she said, warning David he had plenty of time to play the detective if he wished. She smiled at Lorna. "Many days, I hope."

His eyes, gleaming merrily, dwelled in Jessica's. "Good!" he said.

Something in the way he spoke that single word sent a little thrill of fear down Lorna's spine — fear and ... something else. "I'd better not leave the kitchen too long," she said, rising to her feet again.

He rose, too, cleared his throat meaningfully, and eased the knot on his tie.

"Would you like to stay for dinner, David?" Jessica asked heavily.

His eyes twinkled. "Now you mention it ..." he said loftily. "Nothing was further from my thoughts, of course."

"I can knock together a quick mixed grill," Jessica offered.

"Or there's still the cold lamb in the larder," Lorna put in quickly.

"Cold cuts for a Sunday dinner?" Jessica was dubious.

Lorna grinned as she rose to her feet. "By the time I serve it you won't be able to tell it from a freshly carved roast. You stay here and leave it all to me." At the door she added, "And Sarah, of course — will she join us, by the way?"

"If she wants."

The moment she had gone David murmured, "How long is she staying?"

Jessica put her hands together in an attitude of prayer.

"I'm glad for both your sakes," he said.

"And your own!" Her tone was jokingly accusatorial.

He put a hand to his stomach and nodded ruefully as he rose to his feet once more. "I'll just pop over and boil a couple of eggs for Estelle — though she probably won't eat them. The maid's off tonight."

"She won't resent your coming back here to dine?"

He paused at the door and gave a single, hollow laugh. "It's hard to tell resentment from all her other myriad moods," he replied.

*S*arah watched everything Lorna did with the minutest attention, as if she would later have to sit an examination on each little action. And what Lorna did first was to improvise a bain-marie out of two saucepans. Into it she put a dash of her as-yet-immature stock before laying out the slices of cold meat under a bed of fresh rosemary leaves. While they warmed up — absorbing the stock and generally acquiring the texture and appearance of succulent lamb cut straight from the roast — she prepared the vegetables.

Her young helper was amazed to see that she chose sprouts. "Mummy says they take *ages* to cook," she remarked. "More than half an hour."

Diplomatically, Lorna replied that, while they could, indeed, take that long if one so *wished*, they could also take only twelve minutes, if one so *chose*.

"Where did you learn to cook so beautifully, Miss Sancreed?" Sarah asked enviously.

"Nowhere, really," Lorna told her. "Come to think of it, I only ever had one lesson in cookery in all my life — when I was in the sixth form. The young ladies at *my* school were considered to be rather above such things, you know. But one Saturday afternoon, I remember, our housemistress took us sixth-form girls — all *four* of us, because we were rather an intellectual school — down into the kitchens to teach us how to make one dish. It was all a bit furtive, as if we were doing something beneath our dignity, you follow? She told us that when we were married it would happen from time to time that our husbands would fall ill. And the one thing that would speed their recovery more than anything else would be to be served a little light dish we — their devoted and adoring wives — had prepared with our own delicate hands! And guess what dish that was? What d'you think she taught us to make?"

Sarah thought of the most scrumptious dish she knew. "Fluffy kipper?" she suggested.

Lorna shrieked with laughter. "Heavens no! Nothing so delicious and sustaining, I'm afraid. She taught us to make an egg custard!"

Sarah pulled a face.

"Exactly," Lorna said. "Mind you, it would certainly speed an ailing husband's recovery — though perhaps not in quite the sense dear Miss Bowles intended." Then, after a brief silence, she added, "Actually, I don't believe cookery is something you *can* learn. It's more like painting or music, don't you think? If you're born to it, you discover that you already somehow know what to do once you have the ingredients in your hands. You're rather fond of cooking, then, are you, Sarah?"

"Yes! By the time I grow up I want to be able to cook every recipe in every book in the whole world."

"Oh, is that all!" Lorna laughed. "Now then, what are we going to do for pudding, eh? There's half a spotted dick in the pantry but I'm not sure I like the look of it. Shall we try a bit on Bunyan? Dogs are usually good guides in such cases."

Bunyan turned his nose up at even the small piece she offered him.

"As I feared," she said darkly, scraping the contents of the bowl into the slop bucket. "*Crêpes Suzettes*, perhaps? No. Too extravagant."

"Bread and milk?" Sarah suggested hesitantly. "And whatever fruit there is. There's some tinned rhubarb, I think."

"Fruit!" Lorna exclaimed. "You're a genius, Sarah. Fruit, of course. And I'll show you a very impressive, *très élégant* dessert you can throw together in less than a minute — *if*, that is, we have some bananas."

Sarah raced to the dining room to get four from the fruit bowl. Then, after further discussion with Lorna, she made a second trip to fetch half a dozen sinful chocolates from her mother's secret hoard. When she returned with them she saw that Miss Sancreed had already sliced the banana skins lengthways and opened them up, leaving the flesh exposed but still encased in its skin. She took the chocolates from Sarah and cut them in little pieces, which she studded down the length of each banana. Then she sprinkled a little brown sugar over them. Finally, still dissatisfied with their appearance, she rummaged in a cupboard and found a half-used bottle of hundreds-and-thousands, which she emptied over the concoction. "That'll frighten the natives," she remarked happily. "Now all we have to do is slip them under the grill until they start to brown. Then serve them with a dollop of whipped cream. You wouldn't get better at *Au Savarin*."

"What's it called?" Sarah wanted to know.

"Oh my!" Lorna's eyes raked the ceiling. "*Bananes au chocolat Jessica!* How about that? I'll whip the cream if you go and tell your mother that dinner is served."

"And what about Uncle David?"

Lorna, who had noticed him crossing the lawn through the circle of light from the kitchen window, said, "Abracadabra!" and made a conjuror's pass in the direction of the scullery door just at the moment she guessed — rightly — that Doctor Carne would open it and come in. To Sarah it was one more sign of the magical gifts with which their guest was endowed.

What Lorna had managed to do with a few cuts of cold lamb and a great deal of artistry amazed both Jessica and David; but it also put them in something of a social quandary. In the first place they had never sat down to dine with the person who had cooked the meal on their plates; and in the second, it was one of the most elementary rules of etiquette that one never passed any sort of remark about the quality of food one was served. And yet it seemed so churlish to say nothing at all. What on earth was one to do?

At last, toward the end of the first course, it was Sarah — unconstrained as yet by time-worn taboos — who said it: "Well, *I* think that's even tastier than a fresh-cut roast!"

The silence that followed was prickly enough to make her aware she had abused the privilege of being allowed to dine with the grownups. She laid her knife and fork side by side, adjusting them carefully several times, staring defiantly at her plate, thinking *I'm right, though!* — and wishing her ears didn't feel so hot.

"Yes, dear," her mother said awkwardly. "Since you raise the subject, I'm bound to agree. Impolite though it may be to say so ..." She smiled at Lorna. "I truly believe you are a magician, my dear."

"Hear hear, I second that!" David chimed in heartily, now that the barrier was down.

Lorna dipped her head in acknowledgement. "Thank you, kind lady and sir. And thanks to my young assistant most of all. But, like all conjuring tricks, it's terribly easy once you know how." Desperate to rescue poor Sarah, she nodded at her. "You can do the next trick, pet," she said. "Remember what I told you?"

The girl's eyes shone. "Light the grill?"

Lorna put a finger to her lips, as if to suggest she had already given away too much. "You do it all. The whipped cream is in the refrigerator."

As a delighted Sarah skipped off down the passageway, her mother said, "Are you sure?"

"Utterly," Lorna replied. "She's born to it."

"Out of the mouths of babes and sucklings," David put in. "I was racking my brains for some polite way of complimenting you, Miss Sancreed. And, of course, Sarah is right. Straight out with it! I would have bet a year's income that the lamb we've just eaten had never been a cold cut."

"A dozen times a day," Jessica murmured to herself.

They others turned inquiring eyes upon her.

"I mean that's how often I catch myself thinking, *If my grandparents could only see me now!* Or hear me now. So many of the old rules of life have ... *pffft!* And we're caught in between, aren't we." Her smile canvassed their agreement.

"Between what?" Lorna asked.

"Between old and new." She chuckled. "In my case, I'm quite literally between old and new. There's dear old Ben Calloway on one side — an old-fashioned stickler, if ever there was one. And not-so-dear-old Marcus Corvo on the other, who knows just enough of society's ways to make a profit out of it! And believe me there are an awful lot of Corvos around since the war."

"Of course!" Lorna exclaimed.

Now the other two turned their curiosity on her.

"I've been wondering what it is about that man. The moment I met him I knew he reminded me of someone, only I couldn't think who. But that's it, of course! He's the very picture of every war profiteer you ever imagined."

"You say you've met him, Miss Sancreed?" David asked.

"On the way to church this morning. He was very affable, him and his wife — or the woman I thought was his wife."

"Aha!" David's eyes twinkled. "You've heard about our little scandal, too, have you?"

Jessica put a finger to her lips. "Later," she said, tilting her head toward the kitchen.

"You imagine Sarah doesn't know?" he asked.

Jessica shrugged awkwardly. "She probably knows the facts of the situation — without grasping their significance. I didn't learn about such things until I was much older than she is."

"That was before the war," he pointed out.

They accepted that truth in glum silence. "Talking of Corvo," David went on, "I hear he's staying on till Christmas, this year. He's redecorating the place from top to bottom for next season. Did you see the advertisement in the *Tatler*, showing the Riviera-Splendide with palm trees outside? Holidays on the Cornish Riviera — that sort of thing, you know."

"But those palm trees are *ours*," Jessica objected. "He has no right to put them in *his* advertisement. Or has he? Can we stop him?"

"Perhaps he thinks they'll be his by next year?" David suggested.

Jessica pursed her lips unhappily, for she could not deny that it was at least possible.

Lorna looked from one to the other, thinking, *Can't she see that that's what he wants to talk about?* She decided to give a little push, for she wanted Doctor Carne to stop paying so much attention to her. "I think it would spoil the character of Penzance," she said, "if he acquired this site and built an annexe to his hôtel here. Big hôtels belong in resorts like Falmouth, not Penzance."

"Why d'you say that?" David leaned forward and stared at her with intense interest. "I mean, I agree with you, Miss Sancreed, but I'd like to hear your reasons."

"Oh, big hôtels go with big yachts and big, exclusive yacht clubs — like the Falmouth YC. Penzance is for middle-class families ... donkey rides on Marazion Beach, healthy walks to Land's End and back ... that sort of thing."

He smiled provocatively. "So what do you think our hostess should do with this beautiful old house?"

She narrowed her eyes and grinned at him. *"That* would surely be presumptuous of me, Doctor Carne. Until a few hours ago I was not even aware that a decision of that kind was in the offing. Whereas *you* have had days — if not weeks — to mull it over."

Jessica grinned at him, too. "Hoist on your own petard, David!" she remarked in a taunting sing-song. "You've met your match at long last, I think."

"I think so," he agreed ruefully.

She turned to Lorna. "This man, as you've already discovered, makes a point of sailing as close to the social wind as he dares — which is several points closer than most others would try. Sup with a long spoon when you sup with him!"

"Dee dah de-dah de-dah dah ..." Sarah entered at that moment bearing aloft the dish of baked bananas, still sizzling from the grill; she was singing, not quite appropriately, the opening notes of Mendelssohn's Wedding March. The aroma filled the room and provoked them all into cries of delight and compliments that would have been most unrefined if anyone but a child had produced the dish.

"I only did what Miss Sancreed told me," Sarah protested modestly — then, with an arch grin at her mother, she added, "And you'll never guess what it's called!"

When they gave up she said, *"Bananes au chocolat Jessica!"* and laughingly set it before her mother to serve.

"Oh, a dish named after *me!*" her mother chirped. "I don't see what I've done to deserve the honour." She handed Lorna the first plate. "I only wish I had."

"But you did!" Sarah giggled and pointed to the dark streaks of melted chocolate. "What d'you suppose those are?"

Jessica peered at them and frowned angrily. "I see! We shall have words about this anon, young lady." Then, rewarded by the sudden fear in the girl's eyes, she relented and, tousling her hair, added, "Go on with you. Take that to Uncle David. But you really should have asked, you know."

"It was my fault, I'm afraid," Lorna put in. She knew that Jessica was joking and yet there was also an undercurrent of genuine annoyance there — as if she were trying to reprimand her, Lorna, through her mock anger at Sarah. Because of the attention Doctor Carne had been paying her, of course. She decided she would not, after all, be staying very long at Rosemergy. A moment later it struck her that that was an extraordinary decision to reach upon such trivial provocation. Then she understood what a fragile state she was in, notwithstanding the warmth and good humour she had encountered in this household. Finally she decided not to make any decision at all.

David, who was watching the two women intently, was alert to every nuance; he certainly felt Lorna's abrupt coolness — which Jessica, busy separating the last pair of bananas, missed.

Four poised spoons dug into four *bananes au chocolat Jessica*. Four dainty morsels vanished between four pairs of lips. And four murmured variants of *mmm!* and *aaah!* filled the air.

"You are forgiven *everything*, Sarah, darling," her mother told her. "While there are bananas in this house I shall never again simply pop a chocolate in my mouth. *This* is clearly what they were created for."

When the meal was over, Sarah begged to be allowed to do the washing up all on her own. At first her mother demurred but David advised her to take such offers while they lasted. "In two years' time she'll be saying, 'Oh, do I *have* to?' and you'll remember these golden months with nostalgia."

Sarah returned jauntily to the kitchen while David followed the two women to the drawing room.

"You should have stayed alone at the table," Jessica told him, "and passed the port back and forth to yourself while we women sat here and tore your character to shreds."

"Oh, is *that* what you ladies do when you withdraw?" he asked.

"What else?"

They seated themselves while he threw a few lumps of coal onto the dying fire. "Well don't let me stop you," he said. "I'd be intrigued to hear what you might find to say about me. I have always thought my character was beyond reproach from every possible angle."

"Ho ho!" Jessica rubbed her hands avidly and winked at Lorna. "What an invitation! Good heavens, where does one *begin*?"

Lorna grinned, first at Jessica then at Doctor Carne. "I have always thought that if people *ask* for a thing, they should be given it, haven't you, Jess?"

"In a kindly way, yes, I do agree."

"And it seems to me," Lorna went on, "that the kindliest way of all, in an inquiry of this nature, is not to tell a man about his faults face-to-face, but rather to give them as if one had heard the opinions from a third party."

"And disavow them at once," Jessica put in.

"Oh, of course! For instance ..." She pretended to survey David critically. " 'Mrs Smith says your ears are too large, Doctor Carne, but I disagree. Personally, I have always *admired* men with *large* ears!' That sort of thing."

"Yes!" Jessica giggled and clapped her hands with delight. "Perfect!"

David fiddled self-consciously with his right lobe. "The size of one's ears has little connection with one's character," he complained.

"Oh but it's just a way of breaking the ice, Doctor," Lorna assured him. "We'd start with appearances — the hors d'oeuvres, you might say — progress to habits — the entrée — and finally get our teeth into the main course — your character itself."

"How civilized!" he said miserably, though his eyes sparkled. "Let's talk about something else."

Lorna turned to Jessica and spoke as if they were alone. "That doctor-friend of yours," she said, as if introducing the subject for the first time. "He's not a *stayer*, is he! A jolly good man for a sprint, perhaps, but no stamina."

Jessica laughed heartily and pointed a finger at him. "Oh, David! Little did you think when you started this ..." She left the obvious conclusion hanging.

From the kitchen came the sound of a coffee grinder — or, rather, of juvenile muscles struggling with the handle of a grinder. Lorna rose at once. "I'll just go and help her with that," she said.

Tactfully she closed the door behind her.

"And little did *you* think, either, I suspect," David said, "when you invited her to stay for ... how long is it to be?"

Jessica nodded ruefully. "I didn't really say. She's a whirlwind, isn't she. I don't know what I feel. Part of me is delighted ... ecstatic, even. But the other part is ..." She could not hit upon the word.

"Resentful?" he suggested.

"No-o-o," she replied dubiously. "Fearful, perhaps? It would be so fatally easy — in my present state of mind — to let someone walk in and take over my life. I might end up resentful but at the moment I'm simply fearful of it. I just don't want to make *any* decision." She fixed him with her gaze.

"I understand," he said. "Especially not about Rosemergy."

She nodded and gave an apologetic little smile.

He repeated his assurance: "I quite understand, Jess. For my part I could wait a year or more. I'm only afraid Calloway or Corvo will keep up the pressure until one of them makes you an offer you feel you can't resist."

"But I'd never accept anything without first discussing it with you — that's an absolute promise."

He raised his hands as if pushing the whole subject away from him. "Then I shan't say another word on the topic until you do. That's also a promise." He smiled at her and nodded.

"Bless you, my dear." There was a smile on her lips but a frown troubled her brow. "Listen," she went on, "I don't know how long Miss Sancreed will be staying, but her presence is going to make certain conversations difficult — between you and me, you understand? There are things we've never actually said to each other ..."

"And perhaps ought not to say, either," he put in swiftly.

"Why?"

He gazed into the fire awhile before responding. "Because," he said at length, "I am, after all, married to Estelle — in name, at least — and you are less than two weeks widowed ..."

"I am two *years* widowed, David — and no one knows it better than you. And the same is true of Miss Sancreed. Can't you feel it? That's why there's such an affinity between us, of course. We know things about each other — though we only met this morning — we know things that no one else could understand. Except you. You come closest to understanding because you've been through it with me."

"In the eyes of the world," he pointed out, "you're only eleven days widowed."

"Oh!" There was a challenge in her tone now. "D'you you want to start talking about the eyes of the world? And the ears of the world? And the *tongues* of the world?"

The door opened at that moment and Lorna returned bearing a tray with three demitasses and a pot of coffee. "Sarah's gone up to bath and bed," she said.

David leaned toward Jessica and murmured, "No!"

Lorna stared from one to the other. Jessica smiled at her. "He means the world is clamouring at the drawbridge but we shan't lower it just yet."

"How medieval!" Lorna responded lightly. Then, recalling an earlier conversation, she chuckled and added, "I could just sit at the window, combing out my tresses, and let them climb up!"

*A*fter the coffee Jessica went upstairs to tuck Sarah in for the night and to prepare Lorna's room. David, meanwhile, fetched his car and drove Lorna round to collect her things from the boarding house in Morrab Road.

"It really is extremely kind of you," Lorna told him as they set off.

"Not at all, Miss Sancreed," he assured her. "It's a service I'm more than happy to perform. I've been rather worried about Jess these past few days. I'm delighted you'll be staying awhile. I don't need to tell *you*, I'm sure, but when a person's death has been so long foreshadowed, there's a temptation — not always conscious — for people to say, 'Oh well, she must have been anticipating it at any time,' and so they expect her to take it in her stride without faltering."

"Nothing prepares you for a death like that," Lorna said quietly. "I know."

He slowed down to let an elderly couple cross the road; they hobbled the first half and ran the second — when he put the car back into gear. He muttered oaths about "adjusting the splines" and kangarooed forward again. The rather sombre mood between them was shattered.

"And how are you?" he asked.

"A little shaken," she confessed, "but not nearly so much as Darby and Joan back there."

He laughed and said, "No, I meant ... well, never mind."

"I'm really in no condition to analyze myself, Doctor," she pointed out. "One day at a time, as Jess said. I sometimes think one hour at a time is enough."

"Activity's the thing," he said. "I have a patient over near Zennor, a young widow whose husband was killed down Geevor mine. Her father's come to stay with her, a dour old Scottish crofter. And whenever he sees her with a faraway look in her eye he growls, 'Get some work into your hands, lassie!' Or, rather, 'Gæt som wurrk intæ yær hænds, lassie!' And he's right, too."

Lorna sighed. "He is. Sighing gets us nowhere. This is Morrab Road, by the way."

"Is it *really?*" he asked with jocular sarcasm. "I've often wondered. Actually," he confided, "we'll take the next left and go up to the top and come *down* Morrab Road so that we're facing the right way. I'm not too good at turning round in the middle of a road, you see. All that going backwards and forwards and changing gears … and *trying* not to hit things."

"Ah!" Her tone implied she could well believe it. Their eyes dwelled briefly, merrily in each other's.

"At least you don't *have* to work at anything, Miss Sancreed."

"You think not?" she asked neutrally. She was beginning to enjoy sparring with him.

"The Sancreeds aren't short of the odd guinea."

"I see very little of my parents," she replied. "We never really got on terribly well."

He wasn't deceived, of course. He knew that in rich families like hers, with lots of old money, daughters could be independently wealthy no matter how well or ill they got on with their parents. And he only needed to look at her in her black cashmere suit and hand-made shoes to know she was not on the poverty line.

"Also," he said casually, "you spoke just now of your *condition* — you remarked that you were in no condition to analyze yourself."

All at once her senses were alert. *He knew! Somehow he had guessed!* She drew a deep breath and said calmly, "I suppose people dump their secrets on you all the time, Doctor. More than on the priest or the vicar, these days?"

He dipped his head gravely. "Go on," he said.

"Will you be my doctor while I'm here?" she asked.

He smiled and, without glancing at her, said, "So I can't tell Jessica about it, eh? I wouldn't do that anyway. You have no need to bind yourself in that way."

"No, but I want you to be my doctor." She sighed again and added, "How did you guess?"

"It's my trade … one twigs this and that."

"Is it so obvious?" She put an experimental hand to her belly and rubbed it tenderly.

"Only to me. And even so, *obvious* isn't the word."

"Yet," she said heavily.

"Well," he allowed, "in the nature of things it cannot be concealed forever. When is it due, may I ask?"

Lorna sighed. "March next year I think. I'll be gone before then."

He chuckled. "I doubt it." He swung left and headed away from the esplanade, going north, more or less parallel to Morrab Road.

"Why d'you say that?" Her tone was affronted, for he seemed to accuse her of being a parasite.

He replied as mildly as ever. "To be utterly cynical about it, there is nothing in my experience as ruthless as an intelligent and capable young woman with a new-born baby."

"Now see here ..." she began angrily.

But he continued in the same benign voice, quite unstoppable: "But that won't be the reason in your case — I mean, it'll never come to that."

"Why not?" she asked, somewhat mollified.

"Because I know Jessica," he began.

"I must tell her at once," Lorna interrupted.

"If you wish to, of course — by all means. But I don't think it's necessary — not yet."

"When, then?"

He turned left at last and headed toward the top end of Morrab Road. "When she suggests you should stay at Rosemergy on a somewhat more permanent basis — that'll be time enough."

"What if she doesn't?"

"She will. If not, then you need never tell her, of course." He took his hands off the wheel to gesture his point.

Lorna reached across and grabbed it, steering them back up the camber just in time to avoid the kerb. "Have a care!" she protested.

"Have a kiss," he replied, giving her a quick peck on the ear.

She grabbed his hand and clamped it to the wheel as she sat upright again. "My God! You don't waste any time, do you!" she exclaimed breathlessly, wishing she didn't feel quite so pleased at what he'd done.

"It's my character." He sighed, pretending to be penitent.

"You'll get struck off for that."

"Don't joke! It'll happen one day, I know."

"Who said I was joking?" she asked evenly, then, favouring the ear he had kissed, she said, "But thank you, nonetheless, Doctor Carne. It was good medicine."

"I can let you have something stronger," he said, "if that ever stops working for you."

She stared at him in amazement but his eyes were fixed upon the road and not even the faintest smile twitched at his lips. "I'll forget you said that," she told him.

He laughed. "Oh no you won't!"

A fisherman had once told Ben Calloway that, on a night when his boat capsized in Mount's Bay, just off Wherry Rocks, it was the sight of the Mouse Hole and a sudden memory of the beery, smoky fug in the public bar that came to his rescue and kept him going until the Newlyn lifeboat turned up and did the job officially. Ben thought the man mad. He himself would never become accustomed to that same fug and could not help wondering about the quality of a life that could be saved by the mere memory of it. At some point during every evening the reek drove him to say, "I'll just pop out for a breather," to Molly or Peg or Sue, and then he would go for a brisk refresher on the esplanade. If it was raining, he stood in one of the new glazed shelters the council had erected and stared at the sea; on fine evenings like this one he stepped out briskly, a measured half-mile, looking neither right nor left, and then sauntered back, looking at everything.

One of the sights that met his eyes on that particular Sunday evening caused him some alarm: a pack of dogs, all hurrying toward him along the seafront, tails up, eyes aglow, tongues out — clearly bent on mischief. He glanced nervously all about, seeking a bolthole in case the intended mischief should focus on him. When he looked at the pack again, however, he saw that the "leader" was a bitch and the others were all dogs — which explained the bright eyes and drooling tongues. As they scurried past him one of the leading dogs made a leap at the bitch, who turned round and snapped at him.

Ben tried to kick the dog but missed. "You filthy ..." He did not say the word because there were too many people around.

The dog snarled at him and might have lingered to take him on if there weren't so many other rivals waiting to try their luck with the bitch as well. He watched them trotting on up the esplanade — Bunyan from next door, a collie, two mongrel terriers, a setter, a sealyham, and a little bundle of string. All of them bore their tails like flagstaffs, their balls waggling at their scuts. The cause of all the trouble, to be sure — those shiny black dangling jewels, scourging their hapless owners forward on this wild bitch chase. He thought smugly of Rex, his own alsatian, neutered since puppy days and now snoring contentedly before the snug-room fire, impervious to whatever marching orders that poor beleaguered bitch was giving out.

"Why did you try to kick him, mister?"

He spun round to see a couple of young girls of about fourteen grinning cheekily at him — fisher folk by the pail of lugworms one was hefting on her hip.

"Yes," the other girl said. "It's only natural."

They giggled at their boldness.

Ben crossed the road in disgust, to get away from them, even though it brought him to the footpath immediately outside the Riviera-Splendide — a stretch of the esplanade where he never walked if he could possibly avoid it.

A black cigarette end with a gold tip struck the pavement at his feet; there was a chuckle overhead. He glanced up to find Marcus Corvo, dressed in workman's overalls, leaning out of a window and gazing down at him with a stupid grin almost splitting his face. That vile moustache, too! "What are our youngsters coming to these days, eh, Calloway?" he said.

"Where have our dog-catchers gone!" Ben replied. "Scenes like that should not occur in Penzance — not along the esplanade." He turned round with a sneer of disgust, but the pack had vanished.

Corvo chuckled again. "They've gone in Mrs Wardle's front garden. Perhaps they share your views about the decorum of the esplanade, old boy. Care for a gin-and-it?"

Ben looked up at him and saw that the Trelawney woman, also in overalls, had joined him. Her generous bosom, straining at the bib and braces, forced him to look away. Such sights always convinced him that women could read his mind through the little black pinholes of his eyes. "No thank you, Mister Corvo," he said.

"We ought to get together for a chinwag sometime," the imperturbable Marcus responded. "About our mutual neighbour and the pot of gold she's sitting on."

Ben gave a frosty sniff. "I hardly think we have an interest in common there."

"Oh, but we do, we most definitely do! She could play you off against me, and me off against you, and both of us off against the good doctor, if he's interested. Not to mention playing him off against the pair of us. Don't tell me the same thought hasn't crossed your mind. You're a very smart gent, Mister Calloway, as I know to my cost!"

It was absurd flattery and Ben knew it. He had never schemed against Corvo ... never even had the *chance* to scheme against him. And yet he could not help feeling a little glow of pleasure at the undeserved compliment.

Corvo, seizing his moment, added, "But I think I see a way to spike her guns."

Ben fingered his tie nervously. "I'm sure Mrs Lanyon would attempt nothing dishonourable," he said.

"No doubt about that, Calloway. I'm as sure as you are. I'm not talking about sharp practice. I'm talking about good business — the game where two or more can play, but two is best. All I'm saying is I think you and I could meet her, united. And I think we should — else she'll put a wedge between us and drive us both to the wall."

It was a compelling argument, Ben had to allow. Nevertheless, he hesitated. Corvo was such an absolute ... *twicer*. It was the only word for the man.

"Still ..." Marcus toasted him jovially with his pink gin, making the ice tinkle like a silvery laugh. "If you're happy to leave all that to chance, then it's each man for himself ..."

Ben took out his watch, gazed at it but without registering the time, and put it back. "What's your idea, then?" he asked unhappily.

"Come in and I'll show you."

"Just five minutes then." Ben took out his watch again and now he did make a note of the time — twenty-forty. Military hours. Must be back behind the bar at twenty-one hundred!

"We've got him by the short and curlies, love," Marcus chortled to Petronella as he raced to meet their enemy by the front door.

"You're some lucky to find 'em on that maggot," she sneered.

"You go and mix him a good stiff gin-and-it, my gel."

Petronella mixed the cocktail in the downstairs bar and brought it up the staff stairs. The two men were on the landing above the foyer; she advanced upon them, holding the glass like a prize for a good boy. She jiggled her curves and made her bosoms wobble because she knew it made old Calloway uncomfortable.

"Now there's a sight for sore eyes!" Marcus said, ambiguously waving a hand toward the drink and Petronella.

Ben Calloway thought the woman must have ransacked the town for a pair of overalls into which she could only just be poured and squeezed like that. He hardly dared get near enough to take the drink off her; he seethed, as he always did, to think that Corvo not only had a damned attractive little wife going to waste in London but also had this Jezebel creature off the moors to keep away the chill down here.

"Careful! Almost dropped 'n," Petronella giggled. She understood his confusion very well and found it highly amusing.

"Over here, old chap!" Marcus was standing by a side window of the hôtel, overlooking the front garden of Rosemergy.

Ben hastened to join him. "So ... what's the idea, then?" he asked, staring out across the lawns and flower beds.

Petronella came and stood beside him, artlessly allowing her right breast to brush ever so lightly against the back of his left arm; he was able to save his drink only by clutching it in both hands. Marcus made an angry gesture at her. She pouted and flounced away.

"She's just a kid," Marcus muttered by way of excuse, once she was out of earshot. "The grand idea, old boy, is this. I need frontage, see? Big, classy, seafront hôtel — where the guests can spit in the briny from every window!" He stretched his fingers wide and moved his hands apart like a Kentucky Minstrel at a sentimental point in a song. "You, on the other hand, don't — not necessarily. I mean, it would be nice but it's not worth the money Madam Lanyon would squeeze out of you for it." He broke off and stared into the garden below. "Here! What's *she* doing there?" He glanced over his shoulder to make sure Petronella had not crept back. "Gawd! Cop an eyeful of *her!* She was in church this morning." He whispered a lustful whistle, which briefly clouded the pane.

Lorna glanced up toward them at that moment but all she could see was the fiery afterglow of the sunset reflected off the glazing along that side of the building. In any case, she was still trying to come to terms with her disturbing encounter in the car with David Carne.

Ben Calloway drew back nervously. "She heard you!" he accused.

Marcus chuckled. "Through plate glass? Over the roar of those waves? Pull the other one! Who is she, d'you know?"

"I believe I saw her walking along the sands this afternoon, with Mrs Lanyon," Ben replied.

"Oh!" Marcus said heavily. "That must have been when I was ... er, *resting!*" He chortled the air full of gin fumes.

What Ben meant was that he had seen, at a distance, a woman-shaped blur in mourning — a woman with light-red hair; he certainly had not seen this vision of loveliness who seemed to float like gossamer over the grass, not twelve yards below him. He was aware that Corvo was droning on at his side but not a word penetrated his reverie. The angelic face that had gazed up at him a moment ago possessed every feature he had ever counted beautiful in a woman — the pale, vulnerable-looking eyes shining so appealingly out of deep-set sockets, the high, smooth cheekbones, the soft, adorable lips, the elfin ears and chin, the swanlike neck — and all framed in a rich, chaotic tumbling of lustrous auburn hair. His heart thundered in a body that felt suddenly weak and hollow.

"So — what do you say?" Corvo asked. He stared into Calloway's uncomprehending eyes ... and then down toward the young woman in the garden again ... then back to the inn-keeper with a sly grin parting his lips. "You never listened to a word I said!" There was a kind of admiration in his tone. "You old dog!"

The image was too recent in Ben's mind to let pass. "I beg your pardon?" he demanded haughtily.

"Well, well!" Marcus clapped him on the back. "Set to! You could do a lot worse in this town — and she could be gone by tomorrow." He made as if to walk away, leaving Calloway to play the Balcony Scene in reverse.

"Wait!" Ben snapped. "Never mind this tomfoolery. What was your proposal again?"

Lorna was now bending over one of the beds, deftly tweaking out weeds and shaking off the earth.

"Well, old fellow — if you can take your eyes off the gardener and run them over the garden instead for half a tick — what I was saying is that when you see it from above like this, it's a lot bigger than what it looks from down in the road. It's the best part of two acres, you know? I reckon my frontage extension would take up no more than a third of it — up to that bush with the red flowers."

"Escallonia."

"Is that it? Okay — up to there. So from there up to the back wall of the house, say, we could split it between us for a car park, half to you, half to me. Room for fifty cars with a valet to park them. Thirty if you leave it to the mugs themselves. Then you've got all the back garden for *your* extension — plus building out over the outer half of your present parking lot, see?"

"*All* the back garden?" Ben protested. "That's not much."

"Ha-ha!" Marcus raised a cunning finger. "It's *everything*, old man! It's the key to everything." He sniffed. "What d'you think Estelle Carne is going to do when she realizes her view through Rosemergy's gardens is going to turn into a vista of your dance hall, our car parks, and the back side of my hôtel, eh! When, instead of the crash of waves and the cry of the seagull, she's got the strains of The Mouse Hole Feetwarmers and The Riviera-Splendide Orpheans wafting through the midnight air! I reckon that before our surveyors even got out their chains, she'd take any offer we care to make for Trevescan." He sniffed again and stared down at the tasty redhead, still weeding one of the beds. "Look at those fingers go!" he exclaimed in a hoarse, mock-strangulated whisper. "What wouldn't I give at this moment to be a weed down there!"

Ben stared at him in disgust.

Marcus saw his expression and burst out laughing. " 'S'all right, me old cock-sparrow," he cried, larding on the cockney. "I know your opinion of me and I don't mind a bit. There's no law says we have to like each other to do a bit of business together — and a good bit of business it is, too. So, whaddya say? Think it over, eh?" He pulled a punch on Ben's shoulder. "Stand there as long as you like. Measure it all out with your eye — if you can take it off that luscious bundle of curves. Gaww!" He raised a saintly hand before his eyes, shutting out temptation. "How can a woman bend over like that and not *know* what she's doing? They know! They *know!*"

And he wandered off, whistling "The Man Who Broke the Bank at Monte Carlo," full of satisfactions.

He left behind him a Ben Calloway too miserable to move, and too agitated to give the slightest thought to this cunning proposal — all the more cunning in that not a single figure had been mentioned.

Ben, staring down at the most beautiful young woman he had ever seen, was hoping that Corvo had been right in one particular at least — that *she* might be gone by tomorrow. For he already understood that as long as she remained at Rosemergy, he would know no peace.

*J*essica flung herself into the armchair, the one David had occupied earlier, and raised her face toward the ceiling. Eyes closed, jaw slack, she shook her head lazily enjoying the illusory feeling that her hair was shaking itself free of every little tangle. Long hair irked her. It was only because Ian had liked it ... She dropped that line of thought. The muscles of her neck and back, which now seemed to have remained tense all day, sent waves of pleasant relaxation all through her.

At that moment Lorna, also in dressing gown and slippers, nudged her arm with a cup of hot cocoa. "I found some," she said.

"Oh, bless you!" Jessica took it between both hands and breathed deeply on its aroma. "You're like a genie in a bottle, my dear. Except that one doesn't even have to rub the bottle or anything. You simply appear at magical moments with *precisely* what one's soul needs." She yawned deeply and apologized as her water-filled eyes sought her benefactress in the dimly lighted room; when her vision cleared she saw her settling on the sofa, drawing her legs up beneath her and gazing into the dying fire.

"Have you seen Bunyan anywhere?" Jessica asked.

"He was outside when I was weeding your flower bed. Why?"

"There's a bitch on heat and I wanted to keep him in."

Lorna chuckled grimly. "Which does one feel more sorry for — driven dog or harried bitch?"

Jessica thought it best to say nothing.

A piece of soft coal gave out a damp squib of an explosion and flared off its gas. The suddenly brilliant underlighting lent Lorna's prettiness a demonic cast, reminding Jessica of a beautiful but evil princess in a storybook from her childhood. She was about to make some jocular remark to that effect when it struck her that an easeful silence like this was rare and should not be lightly squandered.

She turned her own gaze upon the flaring coal, the last bright gasp of a fire that was otherwise as good as dead.

As good as dead!

She remembered Guy and Toby with the pincerless crab. As good as dead! She remembered, too, all the times she had tried *not* to think of that phrase in connection with Ian.

Were thoughts like these running through Lorna's mind at that moment? she wondered — thoughts like jackals circling the laager fire, creeping ever nearer as it sank, ready to pounce the moment it flickered to extinction.

The coal flame was bright enough to blind a little spot in her vision when she looked away from it. Where did so much gas come from? Where did dust come from in a locked room? Where had Lorna sprung from, just at the moment when there was a great big gap in life at Rosemergy, waiting for somene like her to occupy it?

The world was filled with mysterious providers.

"David Carne must surely be one of the strangest doctors ever," Lorna murmured.

Jessica gave a surprised little grunt.

"I mean," she went on, "I've met more than my share of them these last couple of years, from learned physicians to old sawbones who belong in the age of barber-surgeons. But none of them remotely like Doctor Carne."

"His informality, you mean? I'm sure he doesn't behave like that with all his patients."

"I'm sure of it, too!" Lorna replied with feeling.

Jessica raised her eyebrows in surprise — which told Lorna what she desired to know: that David had never tried to make advances to her of the brazen kind he had attempted in the car that evening. *So he's genuinely in love with her*, she thought. *I, on the other hand, am just a trollop in his eyes*. She knew she ought to feel offended, yet she could see advantages in the situation, too. For instance, there would be no danger of any *permanent* attachment with such a man. And "temporary" was an attractive word to her these days.

"Why d'you say it in that tone?" Jessica asked.

Lorna passed it off lightly. "Oh, well, all the world knows that most of medicine is faith-healing, really. There *are* no magic bullets that can pick out germs or diseased cells and leave the healthy ones to get on with it. We all know that — but we don't want to be reminded of it when we're lying in bed with a fever, or in pain, or ... just wasting away. We want our doctors to enter the sickroom, staggering under the weight of magic bullets. I like a doctor to be at least fifty, with big bushy eyebrows, a high-wing collar and morning coat. And a battered old bag. And a monocle, of course."

Jessica chuckled. "So, my dear! David won't be *your* choice of doctor while you're here!"

"Ah ..." She was nonplussed for a moment.

"I'm joking," Jessica assured her. "I doubt you'll be needing a doctor. I never met anyone who looked healthier. You're positively *blooming.* I could scratch your eyes out. I only ever looked like that when ..." She hesitated. "Well, when I was your age, I suppose — which isn't to be wondered at."

Lorna looked slightly askance at her, as if she suspected her of fishing for compliments, and quite unnecessarily, too. "There's not all that much between us, surely?" she said. "I'm twenty-two — twenty-three next February." Her raised eyebrows posed the question.

"Seven years," Jessica sighed. "I shall be thirty next August."

"Pff! That's next to nothing! Anyway, it only amounts to six and a half years' difference."

"True." Jessica's tone became philosophical. "It's not the number of years that counts but what you pack into them. I've had maids here of seventeen who know more about life than I probably ever will. I'd say I led a very sheltered existence until Ian's illness forced me to deal with the world as it really is." She looked to see whether Lorna would agree that such had been her experience, too; but the woman was gazing into the embers of the fire again, miles away. "Even then," she added in self-deprecation, "I always knew there was David Carne in the background. I wasn't exactly alone in the lion's den."

There was a further silence before Lorna said, in a rather weary, dreamy voice, "I feel I'm here under false pretences, Jess."

"Really?" Alarm and curiosity were equally mingled in the word.

"I can't believe it took me all morning to pluck up the courage to knock at your door."

"Especially now you know I don't bite!"

"No, I mean anyway. That's not like me — to be all hesitation and uncertainty. I've always been the fool that stepped in where angels feared to tread. No one ever called *me* an angel!"

"I do. You've been an angel here today."

Lorna laughed dryly. "That's what I mean by false pretences! I was expelled from school, you know — from three schools, in fact. My parents have disowned me, too. What I said about living 'at home' in Yeovil wasn't true — not exactly. I mean, it was *my* home, not my parental home. I took an apartment and cared for Philip, myself, for the last eighteen months."

"You mean ..." Jessica sat upright. "Just you and ..." She swallowed heavily. That was the scandal, of course; she remembered it a little more clearly now.

"Yes."

Jessica saw — or fancied she saw — tears beginning to form in the other's eyes. Desperate to avoid a scene, she forced herself to laugh, even though she was truly shocked. "Then you're a *fallen* angel," she cried, with a robustness that surprised even herself.

"'Fraid so!" Lorna felt compelled to pick up her hostess's dismissive tone — which then made it impossible for her to go back and complete the confession toward which she had been edging.

Well, there would be other occasions, no doubt.

Jessica continued, "I was going to tell you about my two neighbours and their ... their ..." Her hunt for the *mot juste* ended comically: "... their dark designs upon me!"

"Ah!" Lorna made a suitably exaggerated response, lifting her brows in a parody of shock. "Which two can she mean? I ask myself."

"Or, rather, their designs on Rosemergy."

"Oh." Now Lorna parodied disappointment. "In that case I know which two — Calloway and Corvo. They sound like a pair of shyster lawyers, don't they!"

Jessica frowned; the implication was clearly that David might have been included if the subject were designs upon her *person*.

"Ben Calloway," she said, brushing her irritation aside, "is, as I hinted earlier, a stickler of the old school."

"An old fogey?"

"If it's possible to be an old fogey in one's twenties. He's a year or two younger than me. Wears knitted cardigans with brown leather buttons — you must have come across the type. If you ever see him take up a poker and stir the fire, you could easily imagine he's well advanced in middle age. But he has all the old virtues, too. Straight as a die ... trust him with your life ... his word is his bond ... salt of the earth — all that sort of thing."

"But a publican!" Lorna said.

"Well, he inherited the Mouse Hole from an uncle, otherwise I don't think he'd ever have considered the trade. *Innkeeper*, he prefers to call it, by the way."

"He could have sold it," Lorna pointed out.

"He'd probably have regarded that as running away from a challenge. Besides, I'm never too sure about people with very strong principles, or views — or very strong *anything*, are you? Those men who prowl the municipal gardens, Bible in one hand, riding crop in the other, scourging out the couranting couples. They think they're consumed by the flame of righteousness but actually they're obsessed with thoughts of the very thing they seek to scourge."

"So d'you think Ben Calloway is secretly attracted by drunkenness and the sort of petty crookery that goes on in pubs and taverns?"

"I doubt it!" Jessica laughed at the very idea. "But there are degrees of fascination, as with everything else. I could easily imagine that he's intrigued by the sort of minor depravity he sees around him every day and is rather glad of an excuse not to look away."

"Mister Corvo sounds more interesting," Lorna remarked, feeling rather tired of Ben Calloway already.

"Rogues always are, aren't they."

"You're sure he is a rogue, then?"

"Well," Jessica said dismissively, "you've met the man."

"Yes, that's why I ask. I can't believe that a genuine rogue would nail his roguish colours so high on the mast. Corvo positively flaunts it. I think I should do the same if I were in the hôtel trade — just as I'd try to flaunt myself as a stickler of the old school if I were a publican."

"Come, you're just being perverse," Jessica teased, and then added, "At least, I hope you are."

"Not at all. A publican's trade is mainly among lower-class riff-raff. They still tug a reluctant forelock when they come up against the magistrate sort of character. But a hôtelier's clientèle is middle class — a horse of an altogether different colour. The middle classes are devious, hypocritical, snobbish, ruthlessly dishonest in their mean, furtive little way ..."

"Good heavens!" Jessica laughed in astonishment. "You must have had your fingers burned!"

"But apart from that, they're awwwf'ly naice people," Lorna conceded sarcastically, "and I'm really quate fond of them."

"What d'you consider yourself, then?"

"*Dé-class-ée.*" She almost made three words of it. "Have you ever been driving along in a car and you suddenly wonder what would happen if you just put the accelerator absolutely flat to the floor and kept it there?"

"On a long, straight stretch? I'll say! Penzance Green is ..."

"No! I mean in the middle of town or on a snaky mountain pass or somewhere. *Anyone* can do it on a long, straight road. Or sometimes when you're going uphill, don't you ever deliberately keep it in top gear until it stalls?"

"No." Jessica was both amused and bewildered.

"I do. The thing is, you see, the engine may be in pain but you're not. It's like being anæsthetized but remaining conscious. The engine is probably having a heart attack but you don't feel a thing."

"Why did you bring this up?"

Lorna stared at her uncertainly. "I can't remember. Oh yes! I was going to say, I often feel like that about my own life. I'm sort of anæsthetized about it. Things happen but I don't feel them. I'm tempted to push my own accelerator down and just keep it there — just to see what happens."

"You'd crash, that's what'd happen."

"Yes, but would I feel it?" She laughed. "Don't be alarmed, Jess. I only *think* about it. I'm much too sensible to *do* it. Anyway, while we're on the subject of cars and driving ... *what* about Doctor Carne!"

Jessica relaxed and laughed at last. "Yes. He leads a charmed life, of course. Anyone else would have banned himself from driving years ago — never mind waiting for the magistrate to do it. They say our local garage here doesn't bother ordering spare parts any more — they just follow David around with a bucket and shovel."

They laughed, drained the dregs of their cocoa, and looked at each other. "Time to retire, I suppose?" Jessica suggested.

"What *is* the time?" Lorna asked. "I've lost all touch with it."

By long habit Jessica looked toward the grandfather clock beside the door — and then remembered she had stopped it at half-past-two in the afternoon of the Wednesday before last. Now she rose and crossed the room to it, checking her watch as she went. "It's only five to ten," she said in surprise. She moved the hands and set the pendulum going again. "Life returns to Rosemergy!" she said. "I'll leave the chimes until tomorrow."

"Don't feel you have to stay down and entertain me, Jess," Lorna said. "Just because I'm not ready for bed, it doesn't mean ..."

"No, nor am I. I don't know why I said that. I don't feel in the least bit tired. Would you like a sip of port? I don't know what else there is." She opened the cabinet. "Sherry? Benedictine? David finished the whisky, I'm afraid, but there's some more upstairs in ..." She did not specify where.

"A drop of port would slip down the gullet a treat!" Lorna spoke the plebeian words in an ultra-refined accent.

Jessica chortled. "Yes, it is a bit of an old charlady's tipple isn't it." She poured out a small measure each and then changed it to a large one, instead.

They clinked glasses and Jessica returned to her chair; now she drew her feet beneath her, too, and tucked her dressing gown in snugly round her calves.

"I was telling you about Marcus Corvo," she said.

"Oh yes — and his two wives. That's what I really want to hear about. Don't you think men should be encouraged to have as many wives as possible — or as many as they can maintain in the lap of luxury? We could get away with a lot more if we weren't the only one our husband had to keep an eye on."

Jessica smiled indulgently. "That's one view of it, certainly. But in the Corvo ménage-à-trois I'm not sure anyone gets away with anything. He only has one of them at a time, you know."

Lorna giggled. "It's hard for a man to do anything else."

"No!" Jessica replied tetchily, for that meaning of "have" had been far from her thoughts. "I mean as soon as Betty Corvo — his legal wife — comes down from London — with their sons Augustus and Tarquin, if you please! ... As soon as Mrs Betty turns up — always well announced, of course — Petronella Trelawney — that's wife-number-two — goes back to being plain head chambermaid at the Riviera-Splendide. And barmaid in the evenings."

"Plain is not the word I'd use to describe the Mrs Corvo I met this morning — not in any circumstances."

"No, I agree there. Poor Ben Calloway thinks it's an absolute scandal, of course. Him and the Reverend Meecher. I had to talk them out of getting up a petition."

"Who *to*, for heaven's sake? The lord lieutenant? The Bishop of Truro? Who do you petition to stop a ménage-à-trois?"

"The *trois* themselves. At least, that's what Calloway proposed."

Lorna laughed in disbelief. "You mean they were actually going to present him with a piece of paper saying, 'We your neighbours think you ought to stop larking around!' Followed by all their signatures?"

Jessica nodded. "That was the general idea."

Lorna's incredulity redoubled itself. "And you *stopped* them, Jess? How could you!"

"D'you think I shouldn't have?"

"It would have looked wonderful mounted on crimson plush in a gilded frame and hung over the bar. The Riviera-Splendide would have been famous. People would have come down from London just to see it."

Jessica did not rise to this rather obvious provocation. "It's not the sort of notoriety we would have welcomed in this part of Penzance," she said.

Lorna gave up her tomfoolery and became serious again. "No," she murmured. "The Chief liked to run a pretty clean ship. I remember Philip saying that."

By "we" Jessica had meant David and herself, but she did not say so now. Instead she changed the subject. "So, as I remarked to Doctor Carne earlier this evening, that's the devil and the deep blue sea between which I am now caught. They'd each give their eye teeth to acquire Rosemergy — though I'd far rather see it pass to Doctor Carne, who wants to keep the house as it is and turn it into a nursing home or sanatorium."

"So what would be the objection? Why not simply sell out to him?"

"I've been thinking about that. If I were childless, I would. I'd not even hesitate. But I have to think of the children's best interests, too — their security, their future. I have to go for the best price."

"And those are the only three possibilities?"

"The only three in sight. What d'you think I should do?"

Within five minutes of entering Rosemergy, Lorna had decided precisely what she would do with this house if it were hers, but she held her peace for the moment. "Nothing yet," she replied. "I'm sure something better than all those will turn up before long."

*J*essica drew back her bedroom curtains at the unearthly hour of half-past six. She pulled her sumptuous padded quilt completely off the bed and turned down the sheets and blankets until they remained tucked in only at the foot. There was a pang of regret as eddies of their heat rose enticingly around her, but she slipped into her warmest dressing gown and went resolutely to the window. She threw it wide open so as to supercool her bedclothes and remove the last temptation to return to their comforting snuggery. It was the eighth of October and she was turning over a new leaf.

Recently she had been lingering longer and longer in that cocoon of oblivion between her sheets, especially since Lorna had taken over the hated chore of making the children's breakfasts and getting them off to school. But the sin of luxury had merely compounded itself, for what is one more minute when she had already enjoyed ten? And what are ten more when a whole hour has slipped by? So Friday, October 8th, was to be a new-leaf day in her life; she had intended starting at the beginning of the month but that had been a particularly cold period.

And what was the first thing she saw as she threw wide the casement on the first morning of her reformed way of life? Lorna Sancreed, with a basket of fresh-landed fish on her arm, walking up the garden path. The movement of the window attracted her attention and she waved cheerily.

"I'm trying to reform," Jessica called out, before Lorna could get in a little dig of her own. "I suppose you've been up for hours!"

"Not really. Only since five-thirty." She hefted the basket. "They landed mackerel today. How would you like yours done? Would you like it steamed? Or grilled with butter?"

"Oh, steamed please," Jessica replied at once; the very thought of any dish cooked in fat — even in butter — before noon made her queasy. "Did you actually buy them on the quayside?"

"Of course. And guess who else was there?" She gave a wide grin.

A gull swooped between them and only just decided against making a dart for one of the mackerel; it landed heavily on the path behind Lorna and screamed aggressively.

"I can't think of anyone else dedicated enough," Jessica replied. "Unless it was Mister Salford, the chef next door, perhaps? No, of course, they've shut down. Who, then?"

Lorna grinned even wider. "Doctor Carne — on his way back from delivering a baby over near Poljigga." She touched one of the fish. "That's his, in fact. I promised to cook it for him. I hope you don't mind, Jess?"

"Mind?" she echoed sharply. "Of course I don't." When the words were out she wished they had sounded less shrill. In any case, it wasn't true. She *did* mind. If David called round of an evening, that was a social matter; but if he dropped in for a spot of breakfast, well, that was … different. In any case, Lorna had no right to invite him like that.

Lorna caught her tone. "I'll wrap it in greaseproof and send it round to him, if you'd prefer," she offered.

All this while the gull had been edging nearer. Perhaps it was planning to peck Lorna from behind, hoping to make off with one of the fish in the resulting fracas.

Jessica took a grip of her anger and laughed. "Don't be absurd. I'm delighted he's coming." She was going to add a warning about the gull when a new thought diverted her. "Why greaseproof? Is he having it fried?"

Lorna nodded. "He says it's the only way to enjoy fresh mackerel."

"Oh, really? Perhaps I'll change my mind, then — since it comes so highly recommended. Fry one for me, too, there's an angel."

Without even glancing behind her Lorna kicked out at the gull with her heel. It evaded her easily but flew off in a cacophony of protesting screams. "Evil things!" she remarked as she set off for the kitchen door.

Jessica took so long over dressing and doing her hair that David had almost finished his breakfast by the time she arrived. As she descended the stairs, the laughter emanating from the kitchen was especially grating, somehow.

"Eating in the kitchen?" she asked sharply the moment she opened the door.

Lorna stared at her in surprise, implying that that was where they had been eating for the past two weeks and more, ever since she had come to stay. David scrambled to his feet, wiping his lips in his napkin as he hastened to draw out a chair for her. "Saves lighting the breakfast room fire," he said affably, though his tone also implied that she was to stop being so fussy.

It annoyed her that he should concern himself with such domestic trivia in *her* house but she masked it as best she could and — as was their new custom by now — offered him her cheek.

He brushed it with his own and made a kissing noise in the air; his breathing tickled her ear and made the nape of her neck prickle. But as he drew away again he left her in an aura of fried fish, which made her regret having changed her order. "Good morning, children," she said. "Lost your tongues?"

"Good morning, Mummy," they chorused, the boys from the table, Sarah from the stove.

"Fresh fish from the sea!" Toby added.

His brother turned on him in scorn. "Where else do fish come from? Eh?"

Toby looked around for help.

Think, boy! his mother shouted at him mentally. It had been one of Ian's principles that the children should not appeal to grown ups as a court of first resort; and if it seemed unfair on Toby that he was two years younger than Guy, well, it *was* unfair. And so was life. And he'd make a better man for overcoming the greater obstacle.

"It could come from a river," David pointed out — and wondered why Jessica's lips went ominously thin at that moment. He raised his eyebrows in a silent query.

For reply she turned to Guy and challenged him: "Are you satisfied with that reply?"

He wobbled his head awkwardly. "It's not very important."

"It was important enough to make you sneer at your brother. All I'm asking is — do you think Uncle David has given you a satisfactory answer? D'you think mackerel live in rivers?"

David cleared his throat. "Steady the buffs!" he protested. "I was trying to *smooth* the troubled waters."

Jessica laughed. "Troubled waters are what we sail on here, David. It's all in aid of sharpening the mind, so don't mistake it for a mere vulgar brawl."

His gaze flickered rapidly between her and Lorna, almost as if he wondered whether he had strayed into the wrong house.

"She told me it's her day for turning over a new leaf," Lorna said, by way of explanation.

"*Maquereau au gratin!*" Sarah set the plate before her mother with a flourish, adding: "The breadcrumbs make the butter easier to digest."

It looked and smelled so utterly mouthwatering that waves of relish and gratitude swept all Jessica's pugnacity aside. "Bless you, darling," she said, and glanced across the table to see David smiling at her — a smug, knowing sort of smile. A doctor's smile. And now it was her eyebrows that rose in query.

"You have at least one thing in common with Good Queen Bess," he told her.

"What may that be?"

"You have the stomach of a man. At least — if the old saying is true that the way to a man's heart is through his stomach. I never saw wrath more swiftly dispelled."

"Wrath!" Her scorn was humorous as she deftly filleted the fish off its bones.

"Well ..." David drained his coffee to the dregs and rose to his feet again. "If you'll forgive me, I must love you and leave you. These domestic turbulences are heady stuff at this ungodly hour. Besides, I have several painful extractions to perform today."

"Teeth?" she asked in disbelief.

He grinned and shook his head. "Guineas. It's that time of year." He turned to Lorna and took her hand between his. "You are a treasure, Miss Sancreed," he said. "If ever you should seek a new *position* ...?" He left the conclusion dangling and turned to put on his scarf, which hung beneath his cap on the back of the door.

Jessica had meanwhile filleted her fish and eaten half of it. "Actually, I want a word with you, David," she said as she rose to help him tie the scarf. "Pop my plate in the oven, there's a dear," she told Sarah.

"It'll spoil," the girl complained.

"And I can wait." David loosened the knot she had tied a token inch or two and resumed his seat, this time sitting on it back to front.

Jessica's fingers, which had enjoyed touching him, fussing over his clothing, felt deprived, but she sat down again and finished her plate as quickly as she could without setting a bad example.

"Salmon come from rivers *and* the sea," Guy said morosely.

"And eels," Toby added.

"Eels aren't fish."

"Nor are whales."

"Eels have nothing to do with whales," their sister said with the air of someone putting a stop to all argument.

"Not if they can possibly help it," David added — which allowed them all to laugh.

"Eels and whales are very snobbish," Lorna put in. "They would never *dine* together, but they might invite each other round for coffee *after* dinner, don't you know."

Jessica had noticed that Lorna never referred to social conventions unless it was to mock them — but in so good-humoured a fashion that one could not complain without seeming a fuss-budget. She watched her two boys taking in this fine distinction — knowing it was a joke and yet taking it in — and she realized they would now never forget that subtle distinction between those one invited to dinner and those one merely had round for coffee afterwards. Nor would they forget that there was, in this day and age, something comical about such distinctions. Suddenly she felt a warmth for Lorna that had been conspicuously lacking so far that morning, young as it was — a genuine warmth rather than the slightly guilty kind she had felt on seeing her up and about so early.

"What a splendid breakfast!" she said, laying knife and fork neatly together on her plate of fishbones. Her tone was so unexpectedly cheerful that the others looked at her in surprise. She stared back, her eyes twinkling. "What's the matter? Have you never seen Good Queen Bess before?"

She gave a saucy twitch to the knot in David's scarf and settled his cap at a jaunty angle. "I'll escort you off the premises," she said.

She took an old gardening coat off the back door as they went out.

"Is your every breakfast like that?" he asked as she went ahead of him down the scullery steps.

"Like what?"

"The children bickering ... and all those ... undercurrents."

"That's not bickering. That's the way children talk quite naturally."

She looked to see if he were teasing her. "Of course! I keep forgetting you're an only child. The brats go on like that *all* the time. That's normal conversation for them. If you see them laughing, heads bent toward each other like a well-matched carriage pair, don't ever say, 'Oh, how sweet!' because you can bet it's something smutty."

"I'll take your word for it." They stepped onto the lawn. "What's this bone you want to pick with me?"

"Oh, nothing like that, David." She took his arm, partly to slow him down, but also because she knew they were now in Lorna's view from the kitchen; the childishness of it made her feel ashamed but she held on, nonetheless. "It's to do with Miss Sancreed, actually. Is she a patient of yours? I wouldn't like to embarrass you."

"She has not yet consulted me. Why?"

"Oh dear! I almost wish she had — because in a way that would answer my question."

"Which is …?"

"Which is extremely awkward and difficult to ask, if not impossible."

"Are you worried about her? About anything in particular? I mean …" He stopped.

"No, don't pause until you've got over the fence. It'll look better."

He chuckled. "Dear Jess! Always worried about how things will look." But he resumed his homeward stroll.

"It's a good thing somebody does!" she exclaimed. "Anyway, I am worried about her — about one very particular thing." Her voice trailed off. After a tense silence she added, "You see, I *feel* responsible but I'm not sure where my responsibility begins or ends. She seems such a very mature and level-headed and capable young woman, but *is* she? D'you think she is?"

"My dear Jess! How on earth would *I* know? We've hardly exchanged more than the time of day."

"Because you're very good at people, David. You can diagnose character almost better than you can an illness — which is saying a lot. So stop beating about the bush. Is she or isn't she?"

"What?"

Jessica swallowed heavily and said, in a voice barely above a whisper, "Expectant. And you knew jolly well that's the bush I was beating about."

He suppressed a smile and she realized what she had said — or the other meaning. "I'm serious," she told him wearily. "Seriously worried."

He turned from David to Doctor Carne in a flash. "Has she said anything to that effect?" he asked. "Or hinted at it?"

Jessica shook her head. "You see, I wonder if she even *knows?* Lord, when I think back to how ignorant I was before I married!"

"Then what makes you think she might be?" he asked as he climbed over the dividing fence into Trevescan. "Will it 'look all right' if I stop now?"

"Ha ha! This is serious, David."

"But not, I hope, solemn."

She relented and gave him a tiny smile. "All right — not solemn."

"That's my girl! Now kindly tell me what put the idea into your head at all?"

"I almost said it the very first day — except that it would have been unthinkably intrusive, of course. But I jolly nearly did. We were talking about keeping one's complexion ..."

"Such an unlikely topic for two women! Sorry!"

"And I complimented her on hers. I came within an ace of saying that the only time *I'd* ever been blessed with a complexion as good as hers was when I was expecting. Even then, I'd have thought no more of it until that evening, I think it was — maybe the next evening, I don't know — anyway, sometime very early on she let slip ... no, not 'let slip' — it was quite deliberate — she let me know that she'd broken off all ties with her parents ..."

"Or they with her!"

"Yes, well, that's the question, isn't it! Who's broken ties with whom? Anyway, she told me she'd been looking after poor Philip in her *own* home — not her parents' home, which is what I'd naturally assumed when she mentioned it at first. It was just him and her, alone together in her apartment in Yeovil for the best part of two years. And not married, either!"

"She has a substantial private income, you know."

"What has that got to do with it?"

"Everything. No one's going to order Lorna Sancreed into the Mount Pleasant Home for Wayward Girls, are they! *She's* not going to scrub floors for a six-month penance and have her baby snatched from her by self-righteous female sadists when it's two weeks old and looks like surviving — is she!"

"David!" She touched his arm anxiously.

"Sorry!" He forced a grin. "It makes my blood boil, that's all."

"Clearly! I never knew you felt like that."

He drew a deep breath and squared his shoulders. "Perhaps I didn't until yesterday. We had a particularly distressing case at Mount Pleasant. A sixteen year old — they took her baby boy away for adoption. The usual thing. They gave her the first decent clothes her baby had ever had — pretty clothes — and told her to get him ready for a nice photograph. She believed them, of course, and by the time she realized she'd been tricked the baby was lost and gone forever — lost to her, anyway."

"And?"

"She swallowed carbolic."

Jessica felt the garden swim around her; she put her elbow on the fencepost and beat her brow with her knuckles.

"She didn't even have the good fortune to die," he went on savagely. "But I wouldn't give much for her life from now on. Oh Jess, I'm sorry. I didn't mean to mention any of this. It just ... my God, what did we fight the Great War *for!* To save civilization, they told us! Can we call *that* civilization?"

Jessica turned from him in a daze and drifted away, vaguely in the direction of the house.

"Your question," he reminded her.

She shook her head. "It hardly matters now. Another time."

"There's an easy way to find out."

His voice was soft, tempting. It suggested there was some elementary medical test that doctors had somehow managed to keep secret all these years. "What?" She turned to face him again.

"Put your present positions vis-à-vis each other on a formal basis."

"Eh?"

He sighed. "Suggest she become your companion ... chef ... children's governess ... call it whatever title you like. She'd have to come out with the truth then, wouldn't she!"

Jessica nodded glumly but gave him no indication as to whether she'd take his advice or not.

On the way back she reflected that doctors had to learn to be pretty callous about most things. One poor girl up at Mount Pleasant was enough; if David responded to everyone's woes like that, he'd probably end up taking carbolic himself.

*T*he question Jessica had asked David continued to haunt her all the following week. It would be child's play to learn whether or not Lorna was expectant; but that wasn't the problem. The really difficult question came next: *How* did it happen? Had she been an ignorant hostage of her own biology? Or had she deliberately intended to have a baby by Philip Morvah — like a keepsake of him, or a memorial to him — understanding full well how respectable people would respond, but simply not caring?

It could be ignorance. Unmarried girls from good families (especially from good families) were often amazingly ignorant of arrangements below the navel. Charley Sampson, who was killed at First Ypres, had told poor Wilhelmina Stourton it was a breathing exercise to improve her singing voice; no one had been more surprised than poor Billie when she produced a baby at the hospital garden party the following year. Yet no one had thought it odd that she had lived through all nine months in blissful ignorance of her little passenger.

It could be the same with Lorna; all her suave and sophisticated ways could be just a cloak for her fear and inexperience. Oh, how Jessica hoped that was so! To play the wise and comforting elder sister was a rôle she could happily adopt.

But what if it had all been deliberate? Not exactly a calculated plan but an angry defiance of the world?

That was too awful to contemplate.

"See if *I* care!" Lorna would cry. She'd toss that gorgeous mane of hair and you'd see that hard glint come into her eyes and you'd know there was nothing the world could do to frighten this girl. She would never be cowed into that sort of shame-faced submission which had blighted the lives of so many others — like the girl who drank carbolic and was unlucky enough not to die.

Jessica knew that look of defiance so well. She had seen it in the eyes of young men in the early months of the war — young "flanelled fools" who could not wait to join battle and "give the Hun a black eye." Such happy, carefree bravery! And such ignorance of the bestial life that lay ahead! She met them still from time to time, those few who had survived, but now the glint in their eyes was dimmed with horrors they could never speak of.

She thought of Lorna, who probably could not wait to go over the parapets, guns blazing, and she grieved already.

Yet in one way she surprised herself. Until now, she would have considered herself one of the most conventional of ladies. She thought that if everyone could just be nice to everyone else, and be considerate and a little more tolerant and patient than they were, and turn the other cheek, and not be greedy for money and power over others, then all the world's problems would vanish. She certainly disapproved of rebellious or outrageous behaviour. Yet the thought that Lorna might be quite deliberately cocking a snook at the world gave her a little tingle of excitement.

She would never have tried to put it into words — because it would have been like arguing against everything she'd ever believed in — but she knew that if she had to choose between defending her beliefs and defending Lorna, she'd stand by the girl, shoulder to shoulder, come what may. It seemed an absurd thing to be saying about someone whose very existence was unknown to her a mere month ago, but there it was.

But where did all this thinking and worrying get her at the end of the day? Nowhere!

Her mind chugged round and round the same old track, now looking inward to the dull but solid citadel of her beliefs, now outward to the exciting new vistas that Lorna's sudden irruption had opened up. And beyond them, she suspected — in the twilight self that no one enjoys exploring too minutely — lay other, subtler difficulties ... thoughts and feelings of which she was vaguely aware ...

Filled with frustration, she crossed the room to the window, where she threw the casement wide. Chill October air enveloped her, dank and salt-laden off the bay. She leaned her brow against the jamb and pressed hard enough to hurt. A feeble sun came out from behind a cloud. She closed her eyes. Her whole world shrank to within the confines of her eyelids and turned red.

Somewhere out beyond its boundaries there was a loud report and a scraping, metallic sound.

There was a bellow of: "You ... *artist!*" It was David's voice.

Her sense of relief was almost unbearable. Who but David would rescue her from these miserable reflections — always there when needed! She opened her eyes to catch him in the act of kicking the front wheel of his car, which had come to a halt against the kerb, right opposite the boundary between Rosemergy and the Mouse Hole. And on the wrong side of the road, of course.

His feelings relieved somewhat, he turned to face the house, noticed her at the window, and gave a cheery wave. A moment later he was striding up the path. "Thank heavens for old-fashioned ponies and traps!" he called out to her. "Hope you don't mind if I take this short cut to Trevescan?"

"Why did you call it an artist?" she asked.

He grinned and came to a halt, though he glanced at his watch to show it would be brief. "I heard a fisherman shouting that same oath at his donkey last week in Newlyn, when it refused to budge." Newlyn boasted a famous "colony" of artists. "It was obviously the foulest insult he could think of. I rather agreed with him."

"Where d'you have to go? Could I drive you, perhaps?" Her boldness astonished her. She added, "... if it's urgent, that is."

"It isn't," he replied, adroitly throwing the onus of decision back upon her. "But we could pretend. I have a tryst out beyond Ding Dong tin mine."

"Well, I could do with a little outing anyway," she told him, making it clear it was a matter of no great moment. "Perhaps Lorna might like to come, too — get to know our part of the country. I'll see."

She closed the window and ran to her dressing table for a quick fight with lipstick, comb, and powder puff. Her hair would never compete in glory with Lorna's. She hated it.

On her way down the stairs she passed Lorna herself. "You can hold the fort, can't you, dear?" she asked. "Doctor Carne has broken down and has an urgent call ..."

"What a bore! I'll drive him if you'd like," Lorna offered. "'Unless you actually *want* to, of course." She smiled knowingly.

Jessica hesitated — and then heard herself saying, "Oh, *would* you? You are a brick! The keys are ..."

"I know." Lorna was already leaping downstairs, three at a time. She couldn't possibly do that, surely, if she *knew*.

"Our car may need petrol," she called after her.

"I'll make *him* fill it up," Lorna promised as she struggled hastily into coat, scarf, and beret. "To the brim."

She didn't even stop to look at herself in the hall mirror.

While the silence crept back into the house, Jessica made her way slowly downstairs, wondering why on earth she had agreed to Lorna's offer. It was almost like admitting she was afraid of driving out alone with David.

Unwilling to pursue that thought, she decided that it would give David a chance to discover the truth about Lorna's condition. He had dropped by a couple of times this past week but had shown not the slightest interest in pursuing the matter. Now he'd have no excuse!

Feeling rather pleased with her own instinctive cleverness, she waited in the hall until she heard the car leave. Lorna, she noted happily, achieved two quietly well-mannered changes of gear before she even reached the front gate. Such a competent girl!

She stuck her head into the kitchen, where Betty was cleaning the silver. "I'm just popping over to the Riviera-Splendide, dear," she said. "If Mrs Carne rings, explain that Miss Sancreed has driven the doctor to an urgent call because his jalopy has broken down again. Don't say jalopy to her, of course!"

The maid smiled and continued her polishing.

"I shan't be long, anyway."

She still found it impossible to go out without gloves, even for gardening, even for a walk along the beach. These days it seemed a sufficient departure from her own upbringing that she could now put on her gloves in the hall. Her mother had once slippered her for opening the door of her bedroom while still pulling on one of her gloves — standing there where any manservant might see her in that horrifying act of shame.

Now she watched herself in the umbrella-stand looking glass, drawing on her gloves over her naked hands in a sinfully public way; and yet again the precise nature of her supposed iniquity eluded her.

She surveyed her hat critically, wondering why something so beautiful on the peg should dissatisfy her so deeply the moment the put it on her head. Suddenly the thought came to her: *I shall have my hair bobbed.*

Not I *should* ...

I shall.

Perhaps that's why she had sent Lorna off for an hour or so! No time for second thoughts. No, "What d'you think ...?" By the time she returned, the deed would be done. It had often occurred to Jessica that her mind made plans in secret, behind her own back in some absurd way — so that, as she had said to Lorna once, she only knew what she wanted when she found herself doing it.

She went back to the kitchen. "I've changed my mind. I'm popping along to Estelle's instead — not Mrs Carne — that new coiffeuse at the top of Church Street. My hair looks a fright." She touched her curls with distaste as if that were all the proof anyone needed.

The maid stared at her in disbelief. "If that's a fright, missis, I wish I could frighten like what you can!"

"Well ..." Jessica beamed at the compliment. "I just feel like a change. We'll see what she can suggest. Everyone says she's very good at all the latest styles."

As she set off up the esplanade, it struck her that, of course, it was Lorna who had said that about not knowing what she wanted until she discovered she was actually doing it. No matter. It was true of both of them.

Perhaps they were more alike — underneath the skin — than appearances would lead anyone to believe.

Back at the kitchen table Betty thought to herself: *Popping! What a word! "I'm just popping over there ... just popping out to see soandso ..." Always popping. And one day she will go pop and all, I shouldn't wonder!*

*L*orna drove with an aggressive sort of excellence that forced itself on David's attention. He could not have said how Jessica drove; as far as he was concerned she merely directed the motor from start to destination without fuss or flourish. She would have made an excellent chauffeuse. But Lorna drove as a maestro conducts an orchestra. When she double-declutched and pushed the gear lever through its gate with a deep, well-oiled *snick!* the movement of her hand was the sort that could bring in forty violins dead on cue — or else.

After observing her for a while he remarked in a disgusted tone: "You are so competent, Miss Sancreed."

"Left, I presume?" she said, not rising to his provocation. They had arrived at the top of Alexandra Road.

"If you like," he replied amiably.

"It's not a question of what I like or don't like, surely? Where does your patient live — this one who's at death's door?"

"I never said any such thing."

"But Mrs Lanyon ..."

"Mrs Lanyon asked me if it was urgent. I said it was not — which is the truth. In fact, Doctor Carmichael is covering for me today, and I intended ..."

Lorna made an exasperated gesture, not knowing whom to believe. "But she told me you had an urgent case."

He leaned back luxuriously in his seat, making the leather creak. "Then she has deceived you. You must take that up with her. My intention today was to go out and commune with nine maidens. I told her I have a tryst."

She glanced at him sidelong, warily. A horse and cart, tired of waiting for her to decide which way to turn, pulled out around them; the driver was about to shout something pithy at her when he saw the doctor at her side and held his peace.

"Nine Maidens," David explained, "is a circle of ancient stones about seven miles from here — in *that* direction." He jabbed a finger off to their left.

"Thank you," she said sarcastically, slipping the car into gear and setting off that way. Only after she'd driven a further quarter of a mile, while passing through the dell of Stable Hobba, did she suddenly thump the steering wheel with her fist and exclaim, "Heavens! Why am I bothering to chauffeur you at all — if all you're going to do is loiter among some ancient stones?"

"I did wonder about that myself." He spoke as if she had raised some abstract, philosophical question. "But I thought you probably had your own good reasons."

Her eyes flickered briefly, venomously over him and then returned to the road ahead. "I could have a lot of fun with you," she murmured softly. Her grim tone made it clear that her idea of fun and his would probably have little in common.

Her manner was sufficiently cold to deter him from making any of the obvious replies to so provocative-sounding a remark. Instead he said — as if she had not spoken — "You must, after all, have had *some* purpose in stopping Jessica from coming. She seemed quite set on it."

Lorna saw a number of fruitless exchanges ahead of them if she were foolish enough to respond to that. "Yes, I must have," was all she said. Then, weary of their banter, she turned to him and added in a direct, no-nonsense voice, "Look, may we start again — you and I?"

"No," he answered cheerfully.

After a brief silence she burst out laughing. "Actually, you're quite right. Not after what you said to me on the last occasion when we were alone in a car together. It was utterly disgraceful of you, but there's no way we can expunge it and begin again as if it had never been said."

"And even if we did start again," he pointed out, "I should only repeat my offer. I mean it quite seriously."

She inhaled deeply and said, "Tell me about your Nine Maidens."

He linked his fingers behind his head and did his best to lie at attention. "They have hearts of stone and are utterly without feeling.

You'll love them, Miss Sancreed. Opposites always do get on well, don't they."

"Like me and Jessica!"

"Oh, no. You and she are complementary. That's quite different. Complementaries get on well, too, but in a different way. They grow to *need* each other. Opposites only need each other in the sense that God needs the Devil, and the Devil needs God. Without each other they'd have no trade."

"That's a curiously old-fashioned notion, if I may say so. Surely no one believes in the Devil any more?"

"Perhaps not. Who would you put in his place?"

"Any passing doctor."

Laughing, he leaned forward and chalked an invisible mark on her side of the windscreen. "One up to you," he conceded. "Keep right at this junction, then right again. Follow the signs to Madron."

Silence returned; and now it was curiously easeful.

After a while he said, "May I go against my own selfish interests and ask you a serious question, Miss Sancreed?"

"As long as you leave me free to decide whether or not to give a serious answer, Doctor Carne."

"No one who knows you would dream of doing otherwise," he replied, but the bantering tone of his earlier remarks was absent now. "The question is this: Do you intend to make any arrangements for the birth of your baby? I'm not touting for work, mind you. In fact, I'm going to recommend Doctor Carmichael, in whom I have the utmost confidence — obviously, or I shouldn't be here now."

Something in her was sharply disappointed at this new, serious tone of his. For all her outward show of coolness she had enjoyed their flirtatious to-and-fro. She would have relished another half-hour or so, concluding with a crushing *No!* from her — or perhaps she might not have said no. That very ambiguity was part of the fun.

And yet, she realized, it was — as he had said — a serious question and one that deserved her serious consideration, even if she finally denied him a serious answer. "I do not consider it an illness," she replied defensively.

"Nor do I, I assure you. Quite the contrary. For many women it's the only time in their lives when they're entirely healthy."

"So why should I bother just yet — or are you still worried about being struck off the register? Is that why you're shovelling me off on Doctor Carmichael?"

There was just a hint of his former tone in his reply. "We can go back to that conversation at once, Miss Sancreed, if you'd prefer not to think about this one any more."

Damn him!

She sighed. "No. You're right, I suppose."

"I can't believe ... Straight over this crossing, by the way. Then left. Follow anything that says Newbridge or Ding Dong."

"So many little lanes! All these twists and turns!"

"You should try it at two in the morning in the pouring rain!"

"In your car, no thanks! You were saying — you can't believe ...?"

"Yes. I can't believe you've given your baby's birth absolutely *no* thought whatever."

"The trouble is I don't *want* to think about it. Any time I start — when I catch myself at it, so to speak — I think, why bother yet? Nothing shows. No one can even suspect. But if I start *thinking* about it, perhaps it'll show in my face. Then the secret will be out. Where's the harm in postponing it?"

He put out a hand, ready to grab the wheel if necessary. "You think Jessica doesn't know?" he asked.

Forewarned by his gesture she made less of a jerk than she might otherwise have done. Her mouth felt suddenly dry. "Has she said anything to you?"

"I wouldn't tell you, even if she *had*," he answered, allowing his emphasis to imply that she had not. "And that would be part of the rules of friendship — nothing to do with medical ethics."

A cunning light crept into Lorna's eyes. "And if she did ask you, would you tell her?"

"I would not."

"For the same reason?"

He cleared his throat grumpily. "Well, as you're not my patient, it must be, mustn't it! To get back to the point ..."

But Lorna interrupted him; other possibilities were now racing through her mind and she wanted to pin some of them down before they vanished. "Of course," she said in a speculative sort of voice, "Jessica *might* have her suspicions anyway, and she *might* pass them on to you — deliberately — hoping you *would* tell me about them. People often communicate the most important things in such roundabout ways."

"And most lives begin with a howl of rage," he pointed out.

"I don't follow?"

"I mean you're teaching me to suck eggs, young lady — and I'm not even your grannie!"

"All I'm saying is that *if* Jessica has said something about my condition, you may not be the best of friends to withhold a hint or two about it from me. A hint is all it needs. You don't have to say she did or she didn't."

"My God!" He laughed at her tenacity. "You really do want to know, don't you!"

"Why does that surprise you?"

He shrugged. "It doesn't, I suppose."

After a silence she said, "Well? Got any good hints for me today?"

He tilted his head reluctantly to one side. "Take this any way you like, but if I were you, I shouldn't delay much longer before you tell the glad tidings to Jessica."

"And how d'you think she'll take it?"

He recovered his poise and grinned at her. "How do *you* think she'll take it. You probably know her as well as I do by now."

"I doubt that!"

"I shall ignore your tone" — he lifted his chin haughtily — "and tell you this: She will probably surprise everybody — most of all, herself. Bear right again here."

Lorna had to change down into bottom to negotiate the corner, which was blind and narrow. "Jessica is a very conventional person," she said as they pulled away again. "So you imply she'll surprise herself by taking an unconventional view of my … situation."

He wondered what word she had considered and rejected first. He licked his lips nervously and said — as if something inside him were forcing the words out between his teeth, "Jessica is the dearest person to me in all the world."

Lorna was so unprepared for this thunderbolt that she had to ransack her mind for any kind of response at all. What came out was so banal she cringed the moment she heard it: "What about Mrs Carne?"

The look he gave her was so bitter, so contemptuous, she had to pull up. She left the engine running and buried her face in her right hand, leaving the left on the gearstick. "Sorry!" she whispered.

For an awful moment he thought she was going to burst into tears. "No!" he exclaimed angrily — though his tone managed to imply that his anger was not directed at her. "How on earth did *this* come about? All I wanted was a pleasant drive out into the country, a neat seduction, and a pleasant sing-song in the car on the way home — was that too much to ask, dear Lord?"

She burst into laughter — and though there were genuine tears now, she could pretend they were part of it.

"That's better." He soaped his hands and then nudged hers on the gearstick. "Come-us on, maid," he said in a Cornish accent, "or us'll never get there."

She slipped the car into first and they drove off once more.

"I'll tell you about Estelle," he said calmly.

"You don't have to."

"Oh, I'm aware of that. But I want to — though I'm sure Jessica must have told you something."

"Not a word."

He stared at her.

"Honestly," she assured him.

"Not even a hint?"

He saw her momentary hesitation and she knew she'd have to explain it. "That first night, when you came to dinner, I asked Jess if your wife wouldn't want to come, too. And she just said, 'Oh, Estelle won't miss him' ... or something vague like that. And that's the only word she's ever said on the subject. It hurts her, you know."

This final remark shook him; for a moment he could say nothing.

She drove the point home. "You're as dear to Jess as she is to you — surely you know *that*?"

"Has she told you as much?"

Lorna thought of paying him back in kind — telling him she'd never divulge such a secret, even if Jessica had told it her. "D'you suppose she needed to?" she asked sarcastically.

He stared down at his hands. "I asked for this," he said wanly.

"Whether you asked for it or not doesn't really matter," she assured him. "I was quite determined you were going to get it, the first real chance you gave me."

"What a web it's turning into!" he said. Then, in a more challenging tone, he added: "But if that's true, why has she let *you* come out alone with me now?"

She gave him a withering glance. "You understand nothing, do you! I told you — she is a very conventional person. Not just on the surface but through and through. The last person she'd ever permit to recognize the fact that she loves you is Jessica Lanyon herself! She'll tell the world that you're her dearest friend. She'll even say dearest-dearest-*dearest* friend — because, after all, the best place to hide a needle isn't in a haystack but in a sewing basket ..."

"And love *is* a needle," he put in ruefully.

"So is friendship. Well ... you see my *point*! Anyway, you were going to tell me about your wife?"

"What d'you want to know? The stone circle, by the way, is just over this next ridge. It's not actually *the* Nine Maidens. They're a mile off over the croft." He pointed westward. "But they're still pretty spectacular. Get ready to be astonished."

"Good. I was beginning to wonder. I'd like to know how you and your wife met. What she meant to you then. How things started to go wrong. It's not just idle curiosity. Philip and I never got beyond the first stage — the beautiful time. But I could feel the usual progression (if that's the right word for it) of married life *there,* you know. It was potentially there — hovering in the wings — the quarrels, the anger, the disappointments, the regrets. Like ... I can look at this noonday sunshine and yet be certain night is drawing on. But it never actually happened with us, so I can't imagine how it does."

The road, which was now an unfenced ribbon over wild moorland, crested the ridge and spread before them a scene of unparalleled grandeur. It was the last ridge before the cliffs, a mile or two farther away, with the vast reaches of the Atlantic stretching beyond them to a haze-muffled horizon that merged with the infinite sky. By contrast, the foreground colours of ling and sedge and moss seemed lush and saturated. Only the clumps of struggling furze, cut low by winter winds that howled unchecked off three thousand miles of ocean, modulated that richness with their discreet mottling of sandy beige. The scene thus divided into three elemental bands — earth, water, and air — random and unfocused. As a result, the massive stone circle, some fifty paces from the road and to their right, assumed a magnificence it could never have gained in a more humanized setting — in a field, say, like almost all the other standing stones of Cornwall.

Lorna gave a little cry of joy and, bringing the car to an abrupt halt, leaped from it and strode over the moor to the nearest of them, which was just slightly taller than she; some of the others barely came up to her waist. "What is it?" she asked, touching its weather-pocked flank with awe.

"Granite," he told her.

"No. I mean what is it *about* them that is so different from other stones? Even from cliff faces, which, after all, brave the same elements with the same vertical ... defiance. D'you know what I mean? You can understand why people thought these were once living creatures."

"You know the legend then?"

"They were supposed to be dancing on the sabbath, weren't they — village lads and maidens, a couple of fiddlers, and a motley of lookers-on? Dancing on the sabbath?" Her hand waved vaguely around the circle. "And some Cornish saint came out and turned them to stone. Typical!" She stroked the face of the granite again, trying to recapture the awe she had felt earlier; but it had gone now.

She smiled at him and said, "Thank you for bringing me here, Doctor Carne."

He smiled back. "Who brought whom, Miss Sancreed? Would you like a piece of chocolate?" He fiddled in his pockets. "Let's go for a walk, eh? To the real Nine Maidens." He gestured toward a winding sheep path, heading westward, and handed her a finger of chocolate.

"And you?" she asked.

"I'm not really hungry, honestly."

She bit off half of it and popped the rest into his mouth before he could protest. She laughed at his surprise and ran off ahead of him across the moor, heels flashing provocatively, tempting him to pursue her in every sense.

He almost did, too, but saw she would be too nimble for him.

"Too old?" she taunted, about twenty paces beyond him by now.

"It's a shattering discovery," he replied. "Yesterday I'd have risen to the challenge. Today I don't. Sometime last night — all unbeknownst to me — I passed that magic milestone where dignity takes over from fun. Ah me!" He spoke like an actor blocking out his speeches and movements rather than speaking them with sincerity.

Watching him approach her, Lorna realized she was having more fun than she had known for a long time — since her early weeks with Philip, in fact. Not that she wanted to push the parallel too closely. It had something to do with this wild place and its ancient grandeur, and with the feeling that the rest of the world was far, far away; but most of all it was to do with David Carne, who now seemed far more interesting than he had seemed on her first evening in Penzance.

She could not imagine being married to him and *not* living a richly satisfying life. Suddenly she wanted to know, more than anything, exactly what had gone wrong between him and Estelle. How could they have reached a point where she hardly cared whether he was in the house or out of it?

But not today, she thought. *It's too soon. He wouldn't tell me the truth, not all of it. He'd just gloss it. And then later, when we know each other better and he tries to tell me more, he'll remember his earlier half-truths and weave the new bits around them.*

So when he drew breath to speak — and she knew he was going to start trying to explain about Estelle — she said, "I've changed my mind. Can I talk to you about me and Philip instead?"

avid gave the car a push to the point where the slope grew steep enough for gravity to take over; as he leaped aboard, Lorna let out the clutch and "caught the spark" with only the smallest jolt.

"Is there anything you do *badly?*" he asked.

"Yes," she told him. "Pick men."

"To fall in love with?"

She shook her head. "To fall into bed with."

"Ah!" He cleared his throat. "Would this be about you and Philip?"

"Well, he's a good example." They were approaching a junction with the main road along the peninsula's north coast. "Shall I turn about here?" she asked.

"If you turn left, we can go back by way of Land's End. You've seen it before, I suppose?"

She swung the car left. "No. I've never been to the Lizard, either. I'm not a born tripper, I suppose."

"What's the opposite? A woman who puts down roots at once?"

She ignored the remark. "Is Land's End far?"

"Five or six miles." He kept his eyes on her while the twists and turns of the coastal road prevented her from looking at him. He wondered why such a young and beautiful woman had felt compelled to waste herself on a useless, dying young man. Where was the biological survival value in it? And why this deep streak of pessimism within her? Had she forced Philip to give her this baby just to "prove" how wayward and unworthy she was?

Not for the first time in his professional life he wished there were some way of springing her bonnet catches, lifting off the top of her skull, and tinkering a bit with the grey cells until she started firing smoothly again.

After a long silence she said, "You're very good at it, David."

"What?"

"Listening."

"Oh?" he asked guiltily. "Were you telling me something?"

"No!" Her exasperation implied he was too dense to take her point. "That's what I mean. You don't prompt or drum your fingers or whistle through your teeth or anything. Or perhaps you were simply miles away?"

Do not exclude a stranger from your home. You may find that you're shutting out the messenger of God, the Angel of the Lord who comes to visit you, the Angel of the Lord who comes into your life.'

Noël Colombier

"*I was a stranger and you welcomed me.*"

"No, I was thinking about you, actually."

She purred like a cat. "Tell me more!"

"I was thinking ..." He hesitated. "Before I say it, I ought to explain — so there's no misunderstanding — that I'm not developing a romantic interest in you ..."

"I hope not!" she exclaimed robustly. "Otherwise I wouldn't dream of ..." Now it was she who hesitated.

"Dream of what?"

"It doesn't matter. Say what you were going to say."

"I was wondering what prevents you from realizing what a splendid person you really are. Why this streak of misery that runs right through the core of you? Why d'you sell yourself short all the time?"

"I don't sell myself at all," she said harshly. "I *give* myself away."

He waved a hand in her direction, implying that she made the point far better than he had managed. He pressed it no further, however. "Perhaps it was you who were miles away?" he suggested.

She breathed in and forced it out in a rush. "Perhaps — though it was all connected. I was remembering once when I was a little girl and I'd eaten too much jelly and cream at a party or something and I was feeling a bit queasy. And my father didn't believe me. He thought I was being wayward and a spoilsport — not wanting to join the games. So he started tickling me to make me laugh. And I *did* laugh, of course, but I also vomited — three helpings of jelly, all over him. I was thinking — you can't have two actions much further apart than laughing and vomiting, but I managed to combine them into one!"

"And how does that connect with Philip?" he asked.

"With him it was laughter and tears," she replied. "Different opposites, but I managed to combine them in his case, too. I dressed him in his RAF uniform once. I'd taken his campaign medal ribbons off to clean them and I'd forgotten to put them back on. And I asked if he could see anything missing. Just a game, you know. And he was in a playful mood and pretended he couldn't see anything missing. And so it became a childish little frolic — me pressing him to say what was missing and him pretending it was all there. And we were both laughing because, of course, it was perfectly obvious. And then, when I said for about the fifth or sixth time, 'Come on — what's missing?' he suddenly stopped laughing and said, 'The fu...'" Her voice broke on the word and he had to guess she meant "future."

Watching her closely David saw her jaw clench tight, her lips tremble, and her knuckles whiten on the steering wheel. He reached tentatively forward to grab it, just in case.

"I'm all right," she whispered hoarsely, blinking her eyelids rapidly and not minding the tears it sent down her cheek.

He took out his handkerchief and dabbed them. "It'll take years," he said gently. "So don't be surprised. But it will go in the end."

"Speaking from experience?" she asked; the rawness of her emotions made her speak more harshly than she intended.

"I don't know whether it's worse to mourn the loss of the dead or the loss of the living. I suppose the dead can also get in the way? They, too, can lie in wait at your every homecoming, demanding to know who you laughed with today, yes? They can put a blight on every new shoot of love and tenderness just as surely as the living?" He saw she was close to tears again, this time of sympathy. He reached out and rubbed his fingertip daintily behind her ear. "It's all right, love. I'm just keeping my half of the bargain. Left here — follow the fingerposts to Saint Just."

"Saint Just!" She chuckled at a new thought. "Was Saint Just only *just* a saint, d'you think?"

They were both glad of a way out of their previous conversation. David rubbed his hands eagerly and replied, "Would you like him better if he was?"

"Who says it's a *he?* If the 'just' is merely an adverb or preposition or whatever part of speech it is, the saint could be a *she.*"

"All right. Would you like *her* better if she were — only just a saint, I mean?"

"Yes."

"Why?"

She had to think. "Because people who are *so* good — good enough to be obviously saints — are actually as dull as ditchwater, aren't they. All the interesting people I've ever known have a streak of the devil, too."

"Present company excepted."

She stared at him and burst out laughing. "Absolutely not! Your streak of the devil is as wide as the English Channel."

"That must make me very interesting."

She took one hand briefly off the wheel and rested it on his kneecap, scratching its inner edge lazily. "As if you didn't know!" She grasped the wheel again to milk the car round the corner into the village. Then, with a flirtatious giggle, she drew to a halt and wound down the window. "Excuse me," she called out to an old woman carrying a milk pail and stool from a narrow field between two houses. "Do you happen to know — was Saint Just *only just* a saint?"

The question gave the woman no trouble at all. "Why, bless my soul, missiz," she called back jovially, "this here in't no more'n a village, really."

Now it was Lorna who looked nonplussed. After staring vacantly at the woman awhile she said, "Ah, yes, I see, good — well, thank you very much."

"You'm welcome, my lover," the woman replied as Lorna rewound the window and set off again.

"That'll teach me!" she said.

After a breath-holding silence they both gave way to laughter.

*T*hey parked the car at the First And Last Inn and walked the remaining half-mile to the Land's End headland. The hôtel was already closed and shuttered; the kiosk that sold pop, ice cream, rock, and postcards was shrouded in rope and tarpaulin — a tribute to the storms that lay ahead. Today, however, the mixture of stiff breeze and hazy sunshine was enough to keep even the most casual tripper away; it was a day for visitors driven by some form of dedication — botanists, birdwatchers, coastguards, and the young at heart.

He brought the travelling rug from the car with him; she passed no comment on it. They walked in loose unison down sheep paths that parted and joined, bringing them tight together at times, forcing them yards apart at others. When they touched, they did not say "oops!" or laugh shyly; they simply touched. Lorna liked the contact; man-flesh had a special quality.

"Which is actually Land's End?" she asked when they came to rest on the tip of the headland nearest the battened-down hôtel. "Oh look! There's two seals! Three!"

"Four," he said.

"Which?" she asked when he did not respond to her first question.

He shrugged. "I don't know."

"It's not easy to tell." She shielded her eyes and stared at the long sequence of coves and points stretching away to their north; to the south it was fairly easy to see that nothing jutted more westerly than the point where they stood.

"And I don't think I ever want to find out, either," he said. "There should always be these little uncertainties in our lives."

"I'm sure the Ordnance Survey will have it all worked out," she said comfortingly. Now that she had decided to say yes she felt all warm and calm inside.

"Bully for them!"

She smiled knowingly at him. "Ho ho! Why are you in a temper all of a sudden?"

"I'm not."

"You are! I can tell."

"*I am not in a temper!*" he yelled, stamping his foot uselessly in the thick carpet of thrift beneath their feet. Then he grinned and said, "Now *that's* a temper."

"You don't want to do it, do you," she said calmly. "Now we're actually here."

He swallowed heavily and stared away across the Atlantic to the blue smudges of the Scilly Isles. "I have the feeling that it hardly matters whether I want to do it or not, Lorna."

"It doesn't."

He frowned.

"We're both in the same prison," she explained. "And it looks like an escape."

Still he did not seem to understand.

"*This* prison!" She thumped her breastbone savagely, hard enough to resonate. "*We* can see the dangers, you and I, trapped up here." She put a finger to her forehead. "We can sniff disaster a mile off. But it makes no difference." She pressed her body against his. "Does it!"

"No." He closed his eyes and shivered.

She relaxed and became calm once more. That "no" was his way of saying yes, too.

"This is too public here," he mumbled; he tried to lick his lips but his tongue was dry.

"And too windy. There seems to be a little hollow over there." She went ahead of him along the winding path, skirting the landward ends of the numerous inlets that gashed the peninsula. He saw nothing but the beautiful, lissome body ahead of him — the trim waist, the curvaceous bottom, which her progress over the tussocks and hollows did so much to accentuate, and her smooth black skirt so little to hide. His training helped his mind's eye see, in a kind of shimmering overlay, all the secret invaginations that fitted so perfectly, so snugly, between those voluptuous curves. *How odd*, he thought. *In a few moments I shall be inside there and yet I am not roused!* He shivered; he felt hollow and weak; he knew his pulse was off the clock and his blood pressure could only be guessed at; but still he was not physically roused in the only place where it mattered.

"That's enough," she said when they reached the spot. The land here fell steeply away toward the sea, dotted with large outcrops of rock and bowers of sea holly and tamarind — enough to conceal an army of lovers. "You lead now. It's my turn to look at you. Take your jacket off."

If she had not said that, it would never have struck him that she derived as much erotic pleasure from watching him move as he did her. For her benefit, then, he tried imagining he held a coin tight between his buttocks; it was enough to sharpen all his movements but not enough to make her aware of the exaggeration. To his amazement it produced the most frenzied awakening in himself he had experienced for some time — the mere thought that he could rouse her. He became aware of it the moment he found the perfect place for them to lie — and so did she.

"Hee hee! You enjoy it, too!" she said with jocular accusation, rubbing her knuckles gently over the bulge. She was trembling and breathing in little rushes.

"What?" He swallowed heavily.

"You have the most divine bottom of any man I've known."

He was so much out of control of himself he almost asked her how many that was. He spread the rug for her.

Her fingers were shivering so much she gave up the struggle with his belt and flung herself down on her back, clawing her skirt and petticoats up around her waist. He was astonished to see she was already naked beneath them, the auburn delta gleaming wet between the pink straps of her suspenders. His question must have shown in his eyes for she laughed and said, "No — I do usually wear them! I took them off behind you back there." Then her eyes went wide. "David! Is that really all you!"

He fell on her, and into her, like a wild thing, flapping like a sheet in a gale.

"Yes!" she shouted to the skies, kicking off her shoes and throwing her legs up round him to press him hard with her heels. "Now! Now! Any time you like!"

She must have realized how much he was good for, to shout that with so much confidence. In fact, it was almost two more hours, while the sun shot past the zenith, before they groaned and stirred themselves, and began gathering the scattered clothing that would restore to them the veneer of civilization.

When their nakedness was half-covered he leaned over and kissed her once again, full on her lips, which immediately became soft and receptive. "Are you already wondering about the next time?" she asked when they broke for air.

He closed his eyes but made no other response.

"There won't be one," she said.

He smiled wanly and nodded.

"It's nothing to do with you," she went on. "In fact, if it's any consolation, you're the best lover I ever had."

Now he dared ask it: "And how many was that?"

Her lips twisted in an upside-down grin. "Enough. Too many. If I'd met you at the right time, there'd only have been one." She released him and sat up to draw on her shoes. "D'you think I'm awful? I suppose you do now."

"Of course not."

"You do!"

"I don't. I promise you I don't. Do *you* think you are?"

She gave it some thought before she said — as if the notion had only just struck her — "Not any more!"

"But you did until now?"

"Yes." She still seemed a little dazed at the discovery. "It was a sort of weariness, really. Self-disgust. Of course, in the war I could always dupe myself that I was doing my bit for 'Our Boys.' But each time, after it was over, I'd think, *Is that it?* I'd push the fellow away and wonder what all the fuss was about. Why did grown-ups make it seem so exciting? It was like successfully breaking into a bank vault and finding nothing but a stale ham sandwich and a two-week-old newspaper!" She laughed — they both laughed — at the exuberance of her image.

"Well the room was hardly locked today!" he said. "The doors and windows were wide open."

"And what a feast was spread inside, eh! Oh God, David! Go and sit over there — I could start all over again!"

"I thought you said there wouldn't be a next time."

"I meant on another day."

For a joke he did as she bade. "Race you!" he proposed. "And I'll bet I'm dressed before you."

She began hastening at once. "How well you know me," she remarked. "I'll do anything to win a competition."

"You won one against me today," he admitted ruefully. "I can't deny that."

"I know — let's have an eating competition next," she suggested. "D'you think they serve steak-and-kidney pie back there at the First And Last?"

On their way back to the road she said, "That won't have hurt the baby, will it?"

He stopped and turned her to face him, shocked. "D'you honestly think I'd have so much as touched you if the answer were yes?"

His intensity did little to perturb her. "Candidly, I wouldn't mind losing it," she said.

He backed away from her. "No, Lorna! I'm not going to get involved with that sort of thing."

"I mean I think I'd rather have yours there than Philip's. I do want a baby. I didn't mean ... what you thought. Only I'd rather it was yours, now. I've come to realize I didn't actually love him — Philip — very much at all."

They started walking again.

"Now I *have* shocked you," she said.

"Would that make you happy?"

"I have, haven't I!"

"Only because I misunderstood what you were asking me to do."

"Don't you *want* children of your own? Is Estelle ever going to give you any?"

"Stop it, Lorna!" He strode out ahead of her.

"Don't you want your own flesh and blood to tread these paths after you've gone? Breathing this air? I do!" She struck him hard between the shoulder blades with her fist.

Stunned, he turned and faced her.

She burst into tears and hurled herself into his arms.

"Someone might see ..." he murmured feebly.

She did not hear him — or did not seem to hear. "Help me, David," she sobbed. "I make such huge mistakes always. I do such awful things. And I don't know *why!* Hit me! Shout at me! You were wonderful when you were angry just now. I want help!"

All he could think to do was stand there, holding her tight in his arms, wondering how it was possible to want a woman with the passion he now felt, and adore her company, and feel such enormous sympathy for her ... and yet know, too, that he did not, could not, would not ever ... love her.

When he thought of love, he thought only of Jess.

*T*he garage was rather too narrow for the car so David got out before Lorna drove it in. He, therefore, saw Jessica first, as she was turning in at the gate. "Can I help you?" he asked pleasantly as she followed them up the drive.

"David!" she exclaimed, being sure he was joking. "It's not all *that* different!" She took off her hat, patted her shingled hair nervously, and added, "Is it?"

His jaw dropped. "Jess?" he asked uncertainly.

"Well, of course it's me!" she snapped. Then, in a softer tone: "Say you're teasing — only I don't really feel quite up to a tease at the moment." She drew close enough to grip him by the arm.

Lorna came out of the garage and went through the same sequence of disbelief and horror as David had done — only silently and in a fraction of the time. She forced her face into a mask of delight and came eagerly toward her. "Jess! You brave *thing!* It's *lovely!* Who did it for you?"

Jessica pulled a *so-there!* face at David and turned to Lorna, to let her touch and stroke the small remnant of her hair. "Estelle," she said.

David's expression darkened — as Jess had hoped it would. She laughed. "Not *your* Estelle. Estelle down Church Lane. Penzance's first coiffeuse. D'you really not like it, David? Surely you've looked at the magazines in your waiting room?"

He puffed up his cheeks and expelled his breath as if winded. "Give me a chance to get used to it." He adopted a critical but kindly pose, head aslant, chin on crooked finger.

She did a slow twirl in front of him — five seconds during which she changed his ideas about femininity forever.

In fact, she had an easier task than it might otherwise have been, because of an experience he had had about a month earlier. A rather lovely young girl from a poor family in the town had been admitted to the workhouse infirmary with a severe scalp infection and the master had been compelled to crop her hair close to her skin. She, of course, had been devastated by it, despite earning two guineas from the sale of her hair. David, being the man he was — one who needed the company and affection of women and who was ever-ready to return it in kind — began at once to reassure her. He had treated her a couple of times before so he was able to say he had often noticed what lovely eyes she had but now they really came into their own ... and so on, with equal praise for her lips, the shape of her face — being careful not to lay it on so thick that it would seem like obvious flannel. The curious thing was that half-way through this simple exercise in reassurance he had realized he was speaking the plain truth! She was, indeed, every bit as lovely and as feminine as before — though in quite a different way.

"By heavens, Jess," he murmured appreciatively, "I'll say one thing for it — it's knocked years off you!"

"Well, that's a start," she said, slightly mollified.

"All these diehards one reads in the papers," he went on, "saying it makes a woman appear mannish! They just haven't *looked*, have they!" His eyes glowed and he reached out to touch her cheek, though he fought shy of it at the last moment. "If my humble opinion counts for anything at all — now that I've got over the shock of your rejuvenation — I heartily approve!" He looked to Lorna to say something encouraging, too.

Lorna knew it was all flannel, of course. David was a doctor shoring up the *amour propre* of his patient. But he did it so well and looked so sincere, she could not help a sharp pang of jealousy. "Don't look at me!" she said. "I liked it the moment I saw it."

"And tomorrow you'll go and do likewise?" he challenged.

A withering look was her only response.

"Ha!" He waved a dismissive hand at her and turned, smiling again, to Jessica. "Women are natural conservatives, Jess. Thank heavens there are a few like you, a precious few with the spirit of adventure, still! As a matter of interest, what made you do it?" Foolishly he added, "Today of all days!"

She was puzzled. "What's so special about today?"

She saw his smile fade; it occurred to her that he was avoiding looking at Lorna. "You mean I've made it special?" she suggested.

He was savvy enough not to rush to agree with her. "Well, of course you have," he said with suave jocularity. "But what I really meant was that you usually talk things over for weeks before you do them — and even then you often don't." He turned to Lorna. "Did she even mention this to you?"

Lorna, admiring his skill more and more at every turn, wondered why she could never fall in love with men like him — good, interesting, complicated men who'd keep her on her toes all the time. Infuriating men but never-a-dull-moment men. "Perhaps," she said vaguely. "I really can't recall."

David turned back to Jessica. "How much did you get for it?" he asked eagerly.

"For what?"

"Your lovely long hair, of course. I'll bet Madame Estelle gathered it carefully and put it in a box."

She stared past him, out to sea. "She did, too, come to think of it."

"She'll sell it on for two or three guineas."

Jessica's mouth hardened. "And she charged me five shillings on top of it."

"Five *shillings?*" Lorna almost shrieked.

"Mummy!" There was a shriek in a shriller register from beside the house. Guy came running toward her, his eyes filled with something close to panic. "What happened? Who did that to you?"

His sister Sarah, who had undergone her moment of shock in silence, just a few seconds before Guy, left her vantage by her bedroom window and raced downstairs, two steps per flight, filled with a "my mummy, right or wrong" sort of righteousness. "You're just so stu-u-upid, Guy," she yelled the moment she opened the front door. She flew to her mother's side shouting, "It's lovely, isn't it, Uncle David? Isn't it, Aunty Lorna?"

"That's what I've been trying to tell her," David said.

Laughing, Jessica backed away from them. "Listen — all of you! I don't really give a hoot whether you like it or not. It's my hair and my head, and *I* like it. And that's all that matters. And as for you, Guy ..." She pointed an accusing finger at him.

He stared at her, open-mouthed. It was just beginning to dawn on him that his mother had not met with some dreadful medical tragedy. She had actually *chosen* to make herself look like that. "What?" he asked faintly.

"Just beware! From now on I shall be able to hear every mumble, every mutter, every whisper you make."

"I never noticed — you've got lovely ears," Sarah told her, choosing the one good thing she felt she could honestly say about the whole awful calamity.

"Have I, dear? What a *nice* thing to say. Let me go and see." She stared meaningfully at Guy as she passed, hoping he'd take the point; but she was careful not to slip her arm around his sister, for fear of rubbing it in too hard. "Where's Toby?" she asked over her shoulder.

"Killing bats," he replied.

"What with?"

"My catapult. It's all right. He couldn't hit a barn door at two feet."

Before Jessica reached the front door they heard the sound of shattering glass from somewhere round the back. She turned and said to Guy, "Apparently he can hit *anything*, if it's made of glass!"

David stepped out toward the back garden. "I'll see what's to be done," he said.

As soon as they were indoors Jessica gave her daughter a hug. "Thank you, darling," she said. "I know you hate it but you were a brick out there."

"Why did you *do* it?" Sarah asked, reaching out a hesitant hand to touch the unbelievable shingling.

"Because I felt like it." She shook her head vigorously and luxuriated in the fact that her hair no longer repeated her movements a second or so later, dragging at her scalp all the time. "Oh, Sarah, the *freedom!* You've no idea!"

"Isn't it cold?" she asked.

"Cool. Cool. I'll get used to that."

"You do look younger."

"Go on! Go on!"

Sarah frowned. "Daddy wouldn't ..." Then she changed it to, "D'you think Daddy would have liked it?"

Jessica sighed and, taking her daughter's hand, started leading her slowly up the stairs. "Would Daddy's *father* have liked it?" she asked. "Would his grandfather? And great-grandfather?"

"But they don't count," Sarah objected.

"Why not?"

The girl saw the point, then, but did not see how to answer it.

"I know," Jessica told her. "Daddy's only been dead just over a month and the others went long before. And we remember Daddy every day — every hour of the day sometimes. So he's with us still in a way the others aren't. But it's the same thing for all of them — they're gone, and we can't go on living our lives as if they hadn't died. D'you think that's shocking?"

"No-o-o," Sarah replied slowly.

"But you still think there's a difference."

She led the girl into her bedroom while she took off her outdoor clothes and slipped into her housecoat. She tried again. "Suppose we *did* let Daddy's opinions and his likes and dislikes go on ruling our lives?" she asked.

"We would if he was still with us," Sarah pointed out.

"Yes, but that would be Daddy of October, nineteen-twenty. And next year, it would be the Daddy of nineteen-twenty-one. And then of twenty-two … and so on. Daddy wouldn't just be *with* us, you see. He'd be *growing* with us. *Changing* with us. Moving with the times, d'you see? But now — if we keep asking ourselves, 'Would Daddy approve of this … would Daddy like that?' he wouldn't be a Daddy who was moving with the times but one who's stuck forever as we remember him, and always will — but stuck back in September, nineteen-twenty." She gave a provocative little smile as she concluded: "D'you think Daddy would approve of *that*?"

Sarah saw the irony of the question and laughed. Then she drew a deep breath and stretched luxuriously, as if her mother had also settled a mighty conundrum for her.

"That's been worrying you, hasn't it," Jessica said.

The girl nodded and smiled shyly.

"We have to be *ourselves*," her mother added.

The smell of cooking — à la Lorna — crept up the stairs.

"Oh!" Sarah sprang to life again. "I must show her! I forgot!" She did not say what it was but raced out of the room and took the stairs in the same reckless fashion as before.

Jessica hurried after her, wanting to hold her back and talk a little longer. But she was too slow. As she watched her daughter's skirts fly up around her shoulders and heard the mighty thump as she hit each landing, she heard her own mother's voice saying, "Jessica! How dare you! If you cannot behave like a lady, you shall be whipped like the hoyden you are! To your bedroom, Miss, and bare your posteriors!"

It was enough to make her hold her tongue. But it was less easy to check her jealousy — that Sarah was so eager always to be with her Aunty Lorna. Hadn't she just said it, though — the girl must learn to be herself.

*J*essica stared into the fire, cradling her nightcap of cocoa between her hands. Every now and then she turned her head to one side or the other, still not able to believe how light and free it felt and how warmly the glow fell upon her skin. Lorna sat in her usual posture, inelegant but comfortable, in the sofa opposite, flipping over the pages of a *Saturday Evening Post* she had acquired from somewhere that evening. "The things they have in America!" she murmured at last. She held up a page showing a picture of what looked like a knife-polishing machine. "You turn the handle and it makes ice cream."

"Heavens, don't show the children! There isn't one that makes gold sovereigns, is there?"

Lorna chuckled.

"Did you buy that magazine?" Jessica asked.

She shook her head and dropped it on the sofa at her side. "Ben Calloway stopped me in the road and gave it to me. I suppose some tripper left it at the Mouse Hole. I don't know why he gave it to *me*. He just said, 'I thought you might like this,' and blushed, and beetled off."

Jessica giggled. "He's got a crush on you!"

Lorna pulled a face. "Don't!"

"You should be flattered. Ben's a very decent sort of fellow. He's not been known to look twice at a woman since ... well ..."

"I know. Since Maude Lessore. She was drowned at Hell's Mouth, you said?"

Jessica nodded. "At the time, people whispered it was perhaps just as well. He worshipped the ground she walked on. He could never see the slightest fault in her."

"And did she have any?"

"Who doesn't?" Jessica said reluctantly. "One shouldn't speak ill of the dead."

"But?" Lorna leaned forward with interest.

"Well ... it was rumoured that she was no better than she ought to be. People *said* she drowned deliberately, because she was with child. The sea was flat calm and she was such a strong swimmer. But people always say things like that, don't they." She stared sympathetically at Lorna — who continued to gaze into the fire.

At length she turned to Jessica and said, dryly, "No better than she ought to be — what a phrase! What does it mean, Jess?"

Jessica chuckled. "The opposite of what it appears to mean — which is quite usual in that department of life."

Lorna shook her head sadly and stared down at the carpet.

"Why?" Jessica prompted.

"*Department* of life!" Lorna echoed her words. "There's another foggy phrase! Why *department*? As if it were some unimportant little annexe … off down there, somewhere." She waved a hand vaguely behind her. "Something we can turn the key on and forget. 'Oh, that's not my *department*! … You'll have to try at our other *department* for that, I'm afraid! … I'm sorry, that *department's* closed for the winter!' Won't it be wonderful when language catches up with life at last! D'you think it ever will?" She smiled wanly at Jessica.

Was she asking for help? Jessica wondered. Or warning her that while she continued to use vague circumlocutions like that, there could be no honest discussion between them?

"Not unless we give it a push in the right direction," she suggested. "In the end, you know, it's people like us who write the grammar books and dictionaries."

Lorna nodded, her eyes still lost in the intricate pattern on the floor. She drew a deep breath and said, "You know, don't you!"

Jessica felt her stomach fall away inside her. What was she to say? The time and place became suddenly unreal — it was all there and yet somehow transformed. "It's no business of mine," she ventured. "Unless …"

She meant *unless you want to tell me*, but Lorna glossed it even more realistically: "Unless I stay on here at Rosemergy! I know."

"Well, I hope you *do* stay on," Jessica said at once — and so fervently that Lorna looked up in surprise.

"It's true!" Jessica nodded. "I honestly cannot imagine how I'd have got through these last four or five weeks without you."

"Now I feel awful!" Tears welled behind Lorna's eyelids.

She meant she felt awful about what she and David had done that day. But Jessica took her to be expressing regret at having said nothing before. "Don't!" she urged. "You've absolutely no cause. I admit, when I first suspected about the baby, I felt …"

"When was that — if I may ask?"

Jessica bit her lip guiltily. "The very first day you came, I'm afraid. Not that anything showed then — it still doesn't, come to that. It was just the way your skin glowed, and the gleam in your eye. I remember seeing myself in the mirror, looking just like that, when I was having each of mine."

"And you said nothing?"

Jessica raised both hands to heaven. "What could I have said? Anyway, as I started to explain, I did feel a little resentful at first. I thought you didn't trust me enough to tell me. I thought you were going to take advantage of, well, our hospitality, such as it is — until we were such fast friends I couldn't possibly turn you out — when it became obvious to everyone."

Lorna smiled guiltily. "Come to think of it, how d'you know that isn't exactly what I planned?"

Jessica chuckled. "Because I soon got to know you better than that, my dear. I knew you'd tell me in your own good time. Actually, I then thought you might be afraid of the opposite fate — that I might start mollycoddling you and sending you to lie in a darkened room every two hours — so that the whole town would know." She laughed at her own stupidity. "I was desperately trying to think of ways to let you know that I have never thought of ... this time in a woman's life as a sort of ..."

"Pregnancy," Lorna said firmly. "Let's call a spade a spade."

Jessica fanned her face demonstratively. "If you like, dear. I was trying to let you know I never thought pregnancy an illness. I played tennis and swam right up until the eighth month. But I thought it would sound so obvious if I said anything like that."

When they had finished laughing, Lorna said, "Was it only tennis and swimming?"

Jessica looked at her in bewilderment. "Bridge?" she offered. "Dancing was a bit awkward. What d'you mean?"

"A particular dance — what they call 'the matrimonial polka'? We're back in that *department*."

Jessica puffed up her cheeks and expelled her breath sharply — precisely the gesture David had used that afternoon. Lorna wondered if she realized how closely she modelled herself after him in little ways like that. "Tell me to mind my own business, if you want. I was just curious, that's all."

Jessica tilted her head from side to side in a trapped sort of gesture. "It hardly matters in your case, I'd have thought?" She forced a laugh. "That *was* a joke."

"Yes, wasn't it!" Lorna said bleakly. And waited.

"Well ... I suppose there's no reason *not* to tell you. I'm afraid Ian had quite different views from me on that subject. His attitude to making babies was rather similar to that of the Ministry of Aircraft Production toward the building of aircraft during the war."

After a few seconds of shock Lorna gave way to laughter — in which Jessica eventually joined, somewhat ruefully.

"What an extraordinary comparison!" Lorna exclaimed.

"But very apt," Jessica replied. "It's something I often told him to his face. Or, rather, to his *back* — while he pretended to be already asleep. God — is there anything more offensive, more insulting, than the back of a lightly snoring man when you know jolly well he's wide awake?" She grinned. "Sorry! I take it I may safely ask questions like that of you now?"

Lorna closed her eyes and stretched both fists high in the air; her yawn was of relief rather than tiredness. "Oh, it's such a weight off my conscience, Jess. Though I still can't see a connection with the Ministry of Aircraft Production ..."

"I mean Ian would sort of set me this production target — produce another heir. And you remember how the ministry went all-out when it had a production target to meet? So, it was like that. He went all-out at begetting an heir on me! Twice a night, sometimes. Then, the moment it became clear we'd succeeded, he'd stop." She snapped her fingers. "Just like that!"

"That must have been awful for you?" She made it a question.

Jessica stared into the fire and remembered her cocoa suddenly. She took a sip, found it still pleasantly warm, and said, "I nearly went mad." She swallowed a bigger mouthful and added, "However — I have to admit it was good practice for these last two years — since the accident." She gave a brave little smile, finished the mug, and tossed the dregs into the fire.

The smell of burned chocolate hung briefly on the air. Lorna thought of making a joke — asking Jess if she missed the aroma of burned food in general — but felt it might sound like an embarrassed change of subject.

"By the way, did David get to his patient in time this morning?" Jessica asked. "Unless you have any more questions for me in this ... er, department?"

Lorna made an exaggerated display of guilt. "I'm awful. I know."

"Did he?"

"In a way, yes." She smiled at Jess's incomprehension and added, "*I* was his patient, you see."

Jessica frowned. "You mean you had it all arranged? It was just bad luck I was standing at my window and offered to drive him first?"

"No, no, nothing like that. Did he actually tell you he was on his way to see a patient, Jess? Because that's what you told me."

Jessica had to think back. "No," she confessed ruefully. "Now I come to think of it, he didn't."

"But you said ..."

"I know I did. I thought it would look suspicious if I just said I'm going for a drive with him."

"Why not? You ought to do things like that."

"People would talk." Her tone dismissed the very idea but Lorna could see the gleam in her eye.

"People talk anyway. Just look at the two of us, talking about Maude Lessore just now! Besides, they'll soon have something *much* more scandalous to talk about."

"True!" Jessica sighed and returned her gaze to the fire. "Where did you go, then?"

"First to Nine Maidens, then Land's End, and we had pasties at a pub called the First And Last." After a pause she added, "He has a rotten home life, poor man." She peered at Jess to see what effect this last remark had.

"It must have been rather nippy on that coast today," she said. "Very exposed."

"The sun was quite warm if you got out of the wind. I never went to Land's End before — believe it or not. It's a bit of a disappointment, isn't it. Just headlands. And you can't really tell which one sticks out the most."

"And what did you do? Put the whole world to rights, I suppose?"

"As usual." Lorna laughed. "When we were driving from Nine Maidens I wondered whether Saint Just got his name because he was *only just* a saint." She went on to describe the incident of the old woman with the milking pail. "God knows what question she thought I'd asked her," she concluded.

"Even so," Jessica pointed out cannily, "it didn't stop her from giving you a very confident answer, did it!"

"True! It's something older women are particularly good at, actually — giving confident answers to questions they don't really understand!"

Jessica wondered if she counted as an 'older woman' yet. After a thoughtful silence, she smiled hopefully and said, "I suppose you also talked about me?"

There was another long pause before Lorna said, "There *is* a way you could drive him around the countryside, you know — and the tongues would wag in vain."

"Oh yes!" Jessica replied with surprising bitterness. "If he divorced Estelle and married me!"

Lorna stared at her and then grinned. "You old savage!"

Jessica became embarrassed. "I'm sorry. That was an awful thing to say. I don't know what … I mean I don't know why …"

Lorna, still amused, interrupted her. "Let's keep that plan in reserve," she said. "It's a jolly good one, mind. Nothing against it. But I think I have one even better."

Jessica plucked her dressing-gown lapels more tightly over her nightdress. "Go on."

"You remember telling me that David wants to buy you out and turn Rosemergy into a sanitarium?"

"Yes?" she replied warily. "But I couldn't stay on and manage it, if that's what you're thinking. David has no money of his own — or none to speak of. Estelle holds the purse-strings there and she'd never countenance that. David thinks he could talk her round, but I know Estelle better than he does."

"So why does *David* have to own the sanitarium? Or Estelle?"

Jessica frowned. "Who then?"

"Why not us! Don't you see? We could open it ourselves — and just employ him as our resident MO?"

Jessica stopped breathing and stared at her. She thought it was the most exciting — and dangerous — and idiotic — idea she'd heard in years. At length she swallowed hard and said, "But how could we possibly afford it?"

She expected Lorna to say that she had money of her own, and she prepared a few words of grateful refusal. But all Lorna said was, "How much would it take?"

"I don't know. Several hundred at least, I should think — more than I've got, anyway."

"Then I think we should find out as soon as we can, don't you?"

"And then?"

"Go and talk to a bank manager. That's what they're for."

Jessica laughed and relaxed again, for now she knew it was just a lovely pipe-dream. "They'd never take us seriously."

"They would," Lorna asserted.

"Two *women!* With no experience of any sort of business at all?"

Jessica thought her words sounded like the coup de grâce, but Lorna's confidence was undented. "They're getting quite used to that. The house I rented in Yeovil belonged to a banker, a manager for the whole of Devon and Somerset. He said that half their accounts in some branches are held by women, nowadays. He made it quite clear they'd rather deal with men — but alas, those men are just names on war memorials now. They have no choice but to deal with us." She chuckled. "I asked him if women didn't make as good a fist of running a business as the men. 'Oh, better!' he said. 'But we'd still rather deal with men.'!"

Jessica's uneasiness mounted again as the comforting pipe-dream turned back into a worrying — and oh-so-tempting — possibility. "To go into *debt!*" she murmured. "Ian would never ..." She paused. Her chin went up. The line of her lips hardened. "Well he should have thought of that before he and his father ... he should have thought of it earlier, shouldn't he!"

*T*here had actually been a debate as to whether Ian's name should be added to those already carved on the town War Memorial. Councillor Jenkins, who had spent the war snapping up businesses that could not be managed very well from the trenches, said that he yielded to none in his admiration for the squadron leader and had no *personal* objection to permitting his name to go forward; but they had to take the more responsible long-term view. There were men still suffering from mustard-gas poisoning who might linger on for years, yet. What if the funds were exhausted by the time they passed on? Who'd have to stump up then?

He repeated the question to a little huddle of people outside the church on the Sunday before Armistice Day. Marcus Corvo, standing on the outer fringes, piped up and said, "Us war profiteers, of course, old chap!"

Jenkins and his crowd stared at him coldly until he walked away, but Jessica caught up with him and thanked him.

"What are you going to be doing on Armistice Day, Mrs Lanyon?" he asked.

"Stay quietly at home, I suppose," she replied. "I'm certainly not attending any of *their* ceremonies, no matter what they decide to do about adding my husband's name."

"I was thinking of giving a little party," he told her.

She whistled softly. "That's rather going to the other extreme."

"Very quiet affair. I was hoping you'd come along. We've finished redecorating the bar, see? And a nice little party — just a few good friends — would warm it up a treat."

She shook her head dubiously. "I don't know about that, Mister Corvo." She might easily have added that she wasn't aware he had *any* good friends down here.

He started edging away from her. "Think it over. I've got some plans to show you. Calloway and I put our heads together. We think we can split the property between us, see? We each pay less but you get more." He smiled sympathetically at her and jerked his head back toward the knot of long black coats still gathered around the church door. "More than a name on a tablet of stone, anyway."

When Jessica repeated this conversation to Lorna she was full of scorn. "More for you — my foot!" she exclaimed. "I shall give that Ben Calloway a piece of my mind next time I see him. Ganging up with a rat like Corvo to diddle you out of a few hundred!"

"Don't!" Jessica said in alarm. "We're not going to negotiate with them anyway, so ..."

"Aren't we?"

To Jessica's surprise, Lorna seemed disappointed to hear it. She looked around in case any child was within earshot and murmured, "I thought we had ideas of our own?"

Lorna sighed, the sort of sigh grown-ups make when they have to explain something to a child even though they know it's way over the child's head. It made Jessica feel inadequate — as she often did with Lorna nowadays.

"Listen, Jess," Lorna said. "The first thing a bank manager is going to ask us is, what's Rosemergy worth? Of course, he'll have a good idea of its value already, but he'll want to know if we do."

"And if we don't?"

"He'll rub his hands with glee — after we've gone, of course — and tell himself it's easier than stealing sweets off babies. But if we can slap in front of him a letter from Corvo and Crony, something in black-and-white, offering us two thousand ..."

"Two *thousand!*" Jessica was incredulous.

"Well, we'll tear it up into little bits in front of them if it doesn't say at least that much — won't we?"

"Will we?" Jessica put her hands to her temples. "Oh dear — it makes my head spin."

Lorna grasped her by the wrists, gently but firmly. "Jess! I know a lot of this goes against the grain with you. At least, I'm sure you *think* it does ..."

"It does — I promise you. I lie awake at night, arguing with myself, working myself up into a frame of mind where I'm ready to come out fighting. But it never lasts. It all dies down again. It *does* go against the grain with me."

"But it's the grain of the *veneer* they put on you — your upbringing and all that. Underneath you're a tough piece of heart-of-oak with quite a different grain. Believe me, I *know!* You'll see — the minute we join battle, you'll find your true strength and amaze yourself. But if we don't join battle, you never will."

Jessica stared into her friend's hard, bright eyes and had no doubt where the real heart-of-oak between them lay. "It seems so deceitful," she objected. "To lead them on like that when we have no intention of selling to them. And two *thousand!* That's preposterous. Ian's parents didn't give more than six hundred for Rosemergy."

Lorna's eyes raked the ceiling. "And when was that?"

"Only thirty years ago. And I was reading in the *West Briton* last week that some properties round here are changing hands for *less* than they made in the eighties of the last century."

Now Lorna began to look exasperated. "A thing is worth what people are willing to pay for it," she said heavily. "Not what it says in the newspaper. Not what someone was willing to pay thirty years ago, when the the Riviera-Splendide was a field full of thistles and the Mouse Hole was a little fisherman's tavern — and the motor car was just an idea in someone's head. It's going to be at least two thousand pounds or we just laugh in their faces. Have you asked David yet what it's going to cost to turn Rosemergy into a sanitarium?"

Jessica stared guiltily at the floor. She hadn't suffered these feelings since school.

"You haven't!" Lorna said implacably.

"Don't nag, darling. I will do it."

"When?"

"When the time is right." Thinking to deflect her, she asked, "Shall I accept Corvo's invitation, then?"

Lorna laughed. "No. Let him sweat for a change. We'll just turn up on Thursday evening."

Jessica bit her lip uncertainly. "I've never failed to respond to an invitation in my life. One always lets people know whether one accepts or not."

"For social occasions, yes. But in business ..." She sighed. "Oh, never mind all that now. Listen — I accepted a social invitation yesterday that I've no intention of keeping. But you could turn up and keep it for me."

"Where?" Jessica was intrigued. "Who with?"

"The place is Lamorna. We were going to look at the artists' studios and perhaps buy a few paintings, if any took our fancy. The person is Doctor David Carne."

"Oh no!" Jessica's face fell. "I couldn't possibly do that." Her expression took on the colour of accusation. "And you *shouldn't*."

"Why not? He asked me. All I said was yes — but even then I was thinking you could go instead of me. In any case, he'd far rather go with you, I'm sure."

"Oh really?" she responded bitterly. "That's why he asked you instead, of course!"

Lorna put her head on one side and smiled pityingly at her. "How little you know about him! Don't you know he's in love with you?"

For a moment Jessica forgot to breathe. "That's a terrible thing to say!" she whispered. "A monstrous thing!" She closed her eyes and put her hands to her ears. "I shan't listen to another word."

When she opened them again she found she was alone in the room. She heard Lorna's footfall on the stairs, going up to her room. "Lorna!" she called out.

"Have it your way," the woman replied easily.

She raced after her and followed her into her room, where she found her taking her seat at the dressing table. "What are you doing?" she asked.

Lorna opened a drawer and lifted out her writing case. "I'm going to send him a note to say I've changed my mind."

"No, don't do that."

Lorna smiled at her in the looking glass. "Why not? Have you changed yours instead?"

Jessica chewed her lip in some agitation. "I don't know. What made you say he loves me? Has he told you so?"

"He hardly needs to *tell* me. In any case, it's the last thing he'd do — tell *me!*"

"Why d'you say it in that tone?"

Lorna looked past her and said, "Close the door."

"Why would it be the last thing he'd do?" Jessica repeated when she had done as Lorna asked.

The woman sized her up coolly. "Because," she said at length, "it's not the sort of thing an intelligent man like David would tell any unattached young woman whom he hopes to seduce."

For a moment she thought Jessica was going to strike her. She had never seen such a look of pure, undiluted hatred in another woman's eyes. "If you do not immediately retract that … that … monstrous slander this minute, I shall have no alternative but to ask you to leave this house!"

"Miss Sancreed," Lorna said calmly.

It threw Jessica off her stride. "What d'you mean?"

"You forgot to add, 'Miss Sancreed'."

"Oh, so cool!" Jessica's lips curled in disgust.

"One of us has to be, Jess. If you're going to spend the rest of your life refusing to see the most obvious facts, you'll end up with nothing — not even your children, perhaps."

"What d'you ... what are you saying?" Again her fingers went up and massaged her temples. "You're trying to drive me out of my mind, I know."

"Oh yes! A lot of good that would do me!"

"Well, I don't know what your purpose is, then."

"Are you asking me to tell you?"

"No!" Jessica snapped back. Then, "Yes! Oh, I don't know." She sat down on the edge of Lorna's bed and fought with herself not to break down and cry.

After a silence, punctuated only by some rather laboured breathing from both of them, Lorna said, "Perhaps you'll agree that people on the sideline, people who aren't themselves emotionally involved, can usually see the game more clearly than those who are?"

"Sometimes," Jessica admitted reluctantly.

"All right — sometimes. I think this is one of those times. I saw from the very beginning that David Carne is in love with you, Jess. God, how feeble that sounds! The man adores you. The very air you move through is magical to him ..."

Jessica felt as if her heart were trying to leap right out of her chest. She stood up and walked around, unable to think, unable to muster a single word. Only when she caught sight of herself in the looking glass did she realize she was smiling.

And then she saw Lorna smiling at her, too.

The moment their eyes met Lorna sprang up and came round behind her. She seized her by the shoulders and forced her nearer the now unobstructed glass. "Look, darling!" she insisted. "That's an honest face with an honest smile on it. If *she* can be honest — that woman in the mirror — why can't you?"

Jessica closed her eyes and two tears rolled down her cheeks. But they were not tears of misery — nor were they quite tears of joy, either. The strange thought popped into her mind that they were tears of *strength*, more than anything.

She shrugged her way out of Lorna's grasp and seated herself before the glass, where she patted her shingled hair needlessly. "Go on, then," she said. "I'll listen at least."

Lorna came and stood behind her. At first Jessica thought the young woman was going to strangle her, jokingly, of course. But then her fingers began to massage the tension out of her neck muscles and, after a moment or two of resistance, she yielded and let out a great sigh of satisfaction.

"The other thing I saw on that very first evening," Lorna went on, "was that you also love him." She felt the tension return and bore down on it quickly. "You don't need me to explain why you've never dared admit it, not even to yourself. Especially to yourself, perhaps. You'd have to be a hard-hearted trollop like me to be able to nurse a dying husband and admit to such feelings for his doctor. Besides, I don't think I *can* love. I don't know what it is. Can't you hear the envy in my voice?"

Jessica reached a hand up and stroked the fingers that were massaging her. "It's not true," she said. Her voice was quite firm again now. "But go on — say it all." She smiled. "I'll get my revenge when you've finished."

Lorna smiled wanly down at her. "There's no point my going on unless you admit that what I've said is true — about you and David, anyway."

"I'll admit it for argument's sake," was the most Jessica would concede. "I'm still waiting for you to justify your extraordinary attack on his honour."

"There you go again!" Lorna gritted her teeth in frustration. "Oh, Jess, can't you see that notions of honour like that died in the fall of nineteen-fourteen! 'Oh what a fall was there, my countrymen! There you and I and all of us fell down!' In a world where Councillor Jenkins and Marcus Corvo can claim to be 'men of honour,' we should be glad of men like David Carne."

"Men of *true* honour?"

"No! Men of true honesty. God, there's less than seven years between us — surely the world can't have changed so much? Perhaps it has, when you think of what seven years they were! When you were a young, nubile maiden there was a glut of men. They had to fight their way through a thicket of chaperons to get so much as a dance with you. But look at the world now, for young, available spinsters like me! Godfathers! Aren't we *available* — aren't we just! The chaperons are playing bridge in the next room. And the men aren't fighting to get to us any more. It's our turn now — because there's a million more of us than there are of them ..."

The expression of horror was returning to Jessica's face. "And you're saying that a decent man like David would take advantage of a situation like that?"

"No!" She stopped her massage and went over to stand by the window. "I'm not talking about behaviour like that. People don't sit down and think things out. No man will sit down and think, *Jolly good! There's a million surplus females out there — let's go out and harvest a few!* Well, perhaps one or two might, but they'd be so weird that most girls would twig it at once and have nothing to do with them. But that doesn't mean it has *no* influence at all."

"But to get back to David," Jessica insisted.

"He's a man, isn't he? I know exactly what's going through his mind when he looks at me. He's thinking, *Would she or wouldn't she?* And he's making ..."

"How can you possibly know a thing like that?"

"Because I'm thinking it, too, of course: *Shall I or shan't I?* It's as common as breathing."

"Common!" Jessica said fastidiously.

"It's what all men wonder about all women — all of the time. And the more attractive she is, the more seriously they ..."

"Lorna!" Jessica gave an incredulous laugh. "I've known dozens of gentlemen — some of them very dear and close to me. And I'm sure such thoughts have never once troubled their minds."

Lorna stared at her, equally filled with disbelief. "Have you honestly never thought of getting into bed with David?" she asked brutally.

Jessica became flustered at once. "What a question!" she protested. "You have no right ..."

"Not once? This is what I mean about being a man of honesty rather than a man of honour, Jess — it applies to women, too."

"Perhaps I have." Jessica swallowed hard and started to fiddle with the hairbrushes and powder pots in front of her. "One is bound to have such thoughts ... occasionally ..."

"Voilà! Next question: Were such thoughts pleasant?"

"They were shameful."

"But pleasant?"

"All right. What if they were? Even so, I should never *dream* of ... you know ..."

"*Doing* anything about it? Why not?"

"You know very well why not."

"Yes, but I'm not the one who's denying all this, Jess! I know why *I* think of getting into bed with David — *and* the young man in the newsagents, *and* the man who walks that English sheepdog up and down the promenade before breakfast each morning, and even Ben Calloway, for heaven's sake! And I know why *I* don't do anything about it, too."

"In David's case?" Jessica asked. "Why not? You've had plenty of opportunity." She stared at her, shocked by her own words. "Yes, you *have* had plenty of opportunity, haven't you! You've got another one this afternoon — which you're turning down!" Her eyes narrowed suspiciously. "Why?"

"I'm not turning it down, Jess." Lorna smiled sweetly. "I'm donating it in a far worthier cause!"

Besides, she thought, *I have a bone to pick with Ben Calloway.*
But she said nothing as to that.

*G*uy and Toby stared at the two massive cables, bigger than the elephant's trunk in Torquay Zoo. Despite their size they had an exposed, vulnerable look, especially to two little boys who had no experience of trying to hack through several layers of woven steel-wire sheathing. The twin cables came out of the bottom of a small, untenanted brick shed at the foot of the cliff. Side by side they ran a few yards down over the sand and then dipped beneath it and vanished under the waves. "One mighty blow with an axe," Guy said, "and you could stop everybody talking to America."

Sarah and Toby reconsidered the twin cables in the light of this information. They didn't know anybody who had ever talked to America, so they couldn't see that life would change all that much.

"You'd have to cut the other one to stop America talking back," Toby pointed out.

"How d'you know it's America and not France?" Sarah asked.

"Because France is *that* way," he explained with the weary patience brothers reserve for sisters.

"Well that doesn't prove anything. The cable could turn in that direction as soon as it got out beyond the point. It's only going this way to start with, so as to run down the middle of the cove."

"That would take a lot more cable," her brother pointed out, with slightly more weariness and slightly less patience. "Five or six yards, I shouldn't wonder." He sucked a tooth knowingly. "They don't waste that stuff." He wished he had said fathoms instead of yards. He prodded the cable gingerly with the toe of his shoe and was relieved to feel no shock from it. "It costs a fortune, cable like that."

"Pounds and pounds," Toby said in support.

Sarah could just remember the engineers working on this end of the cable. They had a big cauldron of boiling pitch. The smell had been scrumptious. She asked one of them what it was and he said it was a special soup for men who had to work out in all weathers. She had been so disappointed when she learned the truth, and ever since then she had longed to find a genuine food with that tarry tang.

"Can we touch them anywhere without getting a shock?" Toby asked his brother.

"I can," he replied, "because I know what I'm doing. You'd better not, though. I'll show you the proper way after you're seven."

Bunyan rather spoiled the effect by leaping onto the cables and straddling them, wagging his tail and waiting for the children to throw bits of kelp stem to fetch.

"They shouldn't leave it exposed like that," Sarah said.

"That's the sea's fault," Guy explained. "It came up and washed all the sand away."

"Shall we cover it up again?" Toby glanced nervously at the sea in case it took this piece of impudence amiss.

"Why?" his sister asked.

"Because Huns could come and blow it up, silly!" Toby copied his brother's impatience but failed to capture its lordly weariness.

However, neither of his elder siblings pointed out the obvious flaws in his argument. They each had a bucket and spade — and nothing very special in mind to do with it; so the project to re-bury the Transatlantic Cable and make it safe from the prowling Hun grew rapidly from a gleam in the eye to a breathless dash to where Uncle David and their mother were sitting on little camp stools in the sunny lee of a rock.

Bunyan ran excited circles around them in the sand, picking up bits of driftwood and cuttlefish shells and flinging them in the air by way of a hint.

"Mummy, Mummy! The sea has washed all the sand off the cable and it's dangerous and can we cover it up again?"

Jessica looked uncertainly at David. "What d'you think? It's not electrical, is it?"

"It can't give them a shock," he replied.

She turned back to them with a radiant smile. "What a splendid idea! I'm sure the Postmaster General will be very grateful to you all. Take your time and make a good job of it, mind — there's an hour to go until tea."

Sarah and Toby began to run but Guy caught up with them and grabbed them by the arm. "We've got to organize properly," he said before they passed out of earshot.

Bunyan went down to bark at the waves, which were slightly more predictable than humans.

"It's so odd," Jessica mused as she watched the three youngsters setting to work. "Sarah will submit to Guy's authority in a thing like this — without a murmur. But not at home. When it comes to making beds and tidying up, she's the boss."

"And Guy submits there?"

She smiled grimly. "When does that boy *ever* submit! He's his father's son. But he pretends to — the way Ian used to let me have my way sometimes."

"A diplomat!"

"Yes!" The point had never occurred so simply to Jessica before. "That's true, David. Ian would have made a good diplomat, wouldn't he." She watched Guy pacing out the sand and drawing lines in it with the edge of his spade. "The chances on which life hinges, eh! I wonder if, twenty years from now, Guy will be staring out of the window of our embassy in ... Berlin, or somewhere, and tell himself he might not be there at all but for a casual remark from his Uncle David all those years ago!"

David chuckled. "I must say, you're in a very philosophical mood today, Jess."

"No, but it's true, isn't it. Tiny little accidents early in life can produce enormous changes later on."

"Oh, that's surely true! Just go and ask the inmates of the Home for Wayward Girls!"

Jessica laughed though she was also annoyed he didn't take her point more seriously. However, he had, accidentally, given her the chance to talk about Lorna, one that was too good to miss. "Well, while we're on *that* particular subject," she said, "Lorna is beginning to show at last, don't you think? To someone who knows what's happening, I mean."

"She has talked about it openly with you, has she?"

"You're a diplomat, too! Yes, she has — two or three weeks ago, in fact. The day she drove you to Land's End."

"Ah!"

She watched his eyes traverse the horizon. Her innards experienced that familiar hollow feeling as a wave of longing for him swept through her. This time, however, it was not the usual vague sort of longing she had so often felt in the past — wishy-washy, sweet, romantic, and easily brushed aside by conscience. This was a sharp, physical craving of a kind she had not felt before — or perhaps, she was conscientious enough to admit, she had not allowed herself to feel before. She had always nipped the bud out of such feelings, leaving them to grow into those sweetly neutered sentiments that were so much easier to contain. This violent new emotion alarmed her, for it lay beyond the control of moral scruple.

It was all because of her conversation with Lorna, of course. Lorna made the unthinkable thinkable.

For the first time in her life she felt an upwelling of hatred for Estelle. *Why* should *she have him when she doesn't even want him?* she asked herself. For the first time, too, she wondered if the woman would ever really get ill enough to die. And would she, Jessica, ever stand at David's side and whisper those beautiful words: "I will"?

Her mind teetered on the brink of further impossibilities. She had a sudden vision of Adam and Eve, naked in Paradise before shame was born. "I wonder why Lorna chose to tell you on that particular day?" He licked his lower lip nervously — wondering, of course, if that was *all* Lorna had said.

Jessica shook off her daydreams. "Oh, she'd been working up to it for some time. Actually, there are lots of things she and I never need to talk about at all — not in words, anyway. Did she mention it to you that day?"

He frowned and pursed his lips.

"She's not your patient, David," she reminded him.

"There are still other kinds of confidence, though." He squared his shoulders and came to a decision. "She did, in fact." He tugged his lower lip a couple of times and added, "To be candid, Jess, I'm beginning to be quite concerned for her."

Jessica sat up in alarm. "She's not in any danger?"

"Physically? No. No worries at all on that score. She's strong, healthy, calm, optimistic ... all the right qualities. But in a way, that's the worrying thing. I don't think she has the first idea what life is going to be like with a baby to look after. I don't mean changing its nappies and feeding it, but having another *life* to care for. Has she spoken about that side of it with you?"

Jessica shook her head. "I know what you mean," she said. "Mind you, there's four or five months to go yet. Things could change. She's a highly intelligent woman."

He remained uncomforted. "I've seen it happen before. It's nothing to do with intelligence or preparation. A woman looks down at her new-born baby and she suddenly realizes it isn't a doll, it isn't a baby brother or sister, it isn't a pet — it's a *life!* It's a live person, *utterly* dependent on her ..."

"What happens then?"

"Oh, they cope, of course — most of them. Old Mother Nature sees to that. But they're never the same again." He chuckled feebly in an attempt to lighten their mood. "Mind you, in Lorna's case that may be no bad thing!"

Jessica chuckled, too. "She does have an unpredictable side to her. But oh, David — *no!* If she loses that wild ... free ... all that ... *zest!* If she loses that, we'll *all* lose something. I hope you're wrong — about Lorna, anyway. I hope she'll never lose that."

He stared at her, grinning with amazement.

She stared back pugnaciously. "Oh, I know you think I'm an old stick-in-the-mud ..."

"Not *old.*"

"Ha-ha! You think I'm a stick-in-the-mud, I know — but can you imagine what life would have been like without Lorna? For me especially — but also for you. She fascinates you, too, doesn't she! I can tell."

Bunyan deserted his predictable playmates the waves and came to try his luck with the two grown-ups.

"You all fascinate me," David responded lightly as he tried to drag a stick nearer him with his toe.

"*All* women?" she asked, putting a harsh edge to the question.

He turned sharply to her, all the humour drained from his face. "That's unlike you, Jess."

Bunyan barked a reminder. David picked up the stick and flung it with too much force into the rocks on the western side of the cove.

"And that's unlike you," she replied. "We haven't had much chance to talk lately, have we."

"And Lorna thinks we ought to?" he asked. "Or is it you? Did you put her up to arranging her outing with me to Lamorna — on the understanding she'd back out?"

Even before he had finished speaking, Jessica thought it a most extraordinary question. He must have realized it, too, for he laughed as he finished and went on to add: "Yes, you're right, it *is* a long time. Actually, Estelle has been particularly difficult lately. Since Lorna came, in fact."

"What does she think we are? A couple of harpies?"

"No. She can smell the cooking!"

"She wouldn't eat it if we sent a plate over. Anyway, she's perfectly capable of getting up and joining us. What does she want? If you keep her company she spends all the time sneering at you and criticizing. If you visit us, she moans. She'd only have herself to blame if we ..."

"Bunyan!" David shouted; he stood up and ran a few paces across the sand to pick up another bit of driftwood.

His interruption was deliberate, of course. She could see the alarm on his face.

"Here, boy!" He threw it more considerately this time.

"D'you never think about it?" she asked quietly when he sat down again. "Us? You and me?"

"Jess!" He rolled his eyes and ran his fingers through his hair. "All the time!"

Bunyan dropped the stick at his feet and growled.

David pointed to within an inch of the dog's nose. "If you nip my fingers," he warned, "I'll pull out all your teeth except one!" He snatched up the stick and threw it before the dog could pounce.

"Why except one?" Jessica asked as Bunyan skittered away.

"So he can still get toothache!" David laughed.

"Going back to what we were ..."

"Don't, Jess," he interrupted. "It's a floodgate. Don't open it!"

She ignored his warning. "When Ian was alive it was easier for us to avoid such thoughts, you and me — even though he couldn't — you know — perform."

"I know."

"We respected him too much to even ..."

"You did more than simply respect him, surely?"

She reached down and picked up another bit of stick, which she handed to him to throw.

"Jess?" he prompted.

"No," she answered bleakly. "I didn't. And I told you all that on the night of the funeral."

There was a hint of reproach that he had done nothing about it. He said, "It's hard to talk about these things, Jess. It could also be ..."

"There comes a point where it's even harder not to talk about them." Then she realized she had interupted a sentence that might be important. "It could also be what?" she asked. "What were you about to say?"

"Dangerous. It could also be dangerous to talk about them."

"Why?"

"Because talk leads to action."

"And if that's what we both want?"

"Oh, Jess!" He spoke despairingly, through clenched teeth. "I *know* it's what we both want — but it would destroy us. Estelle would *never* agree to a divorce."

"You could divorce her, then."

He gave a hopeless laugh. "On what grounds?"

"Her refusal to be your wife."

"A *doctor* — suing for refusal of conjugal rights! I'd lose my practice overnight. And what good would I be to anyone then? Least of all to you and those three children over there! We cannot live on bread and cheese and kisses!"

She stared about them; the little cove was small enough to seem like a prison. "Let's go for a walk?" she suggested.

"Where?" He waved a hand at the few dozen yards between them and the sea, and between the rocks on either side.

"Anywhere. Just up the lane a bit and back. The children won't come to any harm." She raised her voice. "Sarah? Boys? Uncle David and I are just going for a little stroll back to the car. We'll only be five minutes. All right? The blue bag is under my camp stool here."

"Blue bag?" David asked as they made for the end of the lane.

"Toby has a terror of being stung by a jellyfish again."

David chuckled. "Laundry blue won't do much against a jellyfish sting, I fear."

"Oh no! If you ever tell him that, I'll ... I'll pull all your teeth out except one!"

Their laughter made it easier to draw closer together as they gained the narrow lane; and being closer together made it easier for her to slip her arm through his. "You don't mind?" she asked.

Bunyan decided it was his duty to stay and guard the children.

David dithered so long between conceding to her or repeating his warning, that at last she said, "Doctor Carne speechless!"

"David Carne with too *much* to say," he responded.

"Close your eyes and pick the first one at random." She squeezed his arm against her breast. The heart within it turned a somersault.

Still he said nothing.

"Shall I say something, then?" she asked.

"No." He sighed.

"I will if you go on saying nothing."

"It's just that if I say anything — anything at all — I mean the least little bit of the millions of things I'd like to say to you, Jess — it will change everything between us. For ever. There'll be no going back to the way we are now."

"You're so suave with the other ladies. You flirt outrageously. Even with Lorna. You give her a squeeze and you say flirtatious things. But never with me!"

"Why d'you think that is, Jess?"

"Damn it, David! I *know* why it is. But d'you think that's enough? Just to *know* it in silence, and to go on and on just knowing it? Never a word spoken? While I watch you flirting with *them?* And d'you think I'd even open my mouth and say a word of this if I *didn't* know?"

She had won — as women always win that particular battle. He put his arm right round her and bore her hastily to the side of the lane. There he pressed her against the wall and, taking her face between his hands, kissed her with such tenderness, such reverence, she almost passed out. She had dreamed of many kisses with David, but none, even had they been real, could have moved her to such emotion as she now felt welling up inside her. Their lips did not merely touch, they fused together, making his sensations hers and hers, his. Then it seemed their entire bodies were welded together, too. Her knees buckled and locked with his. He bore her back, crushing her tighter yet against the grassy face of the stone hedge at her back.

She thought the cravings that suddenly overwhelmed her would tear her wide open. She thrust her belly forward and began a slow gyration of her hips, drowning his face in breathless kisses and gasping his name between each.

"Oh, Jess!" he pleaded, holding her tight around her shoulders but trying to ease his lower half away from her. "Please — not here!"

She was shivering too violently to speak in more than single words: "Yes ... here ... now!"

"We can't risk it. We must be patient — take your hand away from ... please!" He grasped her wrists and struggled with her to pin her hands to the wall.

"Where then?" she asked in a kind of panic. "Where? How soon? I must know. I cannot live another day like this."

"I'll think of something — I promise. I can't think at all like this."

"Good afternoon!" The jovial, manly greeting came from a little way up the lane.

They sprang apart so swiftly they might as well have turned to the stranger and shouted, "Guilty! Guilty!" at once.

But what a very strange stranger he turned out to be! Jessica pinned it down later when she said he looked exactly like the man on the Quaker Oats packet — genial smile, curly white locks, Doctor Johnson hat, and all. He also wore an Inverness cape, which may or may not be true of the original Mr Quaker. "I called as soon as I saw you," he said with an apologetic smile as he swept on by. Then, a few paces later, he turned and added, "I used to do my courting up there on the left."

David laughed politely. Jessica just went on leaning against the wall, eyes closed, face drained of all colour. "I think I'm going to be sick," she murmured.

"No you're not," David assured her. "Don't take it so seriously. D'you recognize him?"

She shook her head but still did not open her eyes.

"Nor me, either. I'm sure I've never seen him before — and he's not a man you'd forget easily. I think we're safe. I don't believe he's from round here."

"Of course he's from round here!" she said vehemently. "He said that's where he used to do his courting."

"He could be revisiting the scenes of his misspent youth. Are you still feeling sick?"

She made an effort and pulled herself together. She even managed to open her eyes and smile at him. "I know you're only trying to comfort me. Oh David, I'm so sorry! I feel *awful* now. This could ruin your career."

"If so, it'll be through carelessness."

"Mine, I know. It's my fault."

"No, I mean *my* carelessness in letting him get away from here. We must do something about that."

She looked at him aghast. "Your don't mean you'll ..." She couldn't say "kill him," but what else could he mean?

David laughed at her misunderstanding. "You little savage," he said admiringly. "But you flatter me. That is *not* what I mean. Come on!" And he led the way resolutely back to the cove.

The stranger was standing above the line of the waves, throwing sticks for Bunyan to catch.

Jessica's alarm increased with every step, for David clearly intended walking right up to the man. "What are you going to say?" she asked under her breath.

"I'm taking a risk," he agreed. "But — unless I'm an absolutely rotten judge of character — I think it's a much smaller risk than simply leaving it all to chance."

When the man saw them he dropped the stick he had been going to throw and came smiling toward them. "I'm *sorry!*" he exclaimed with self-accusing emphasis. Then he shrugged and smiled. "These things happen!"

Jessica sensed an oddly admiring look in his eyes; then she realized he thought the three children were hers and David's. He was admiring their ability to keep so much passion still alive. It was all she could do not to take to her heels and run.

One thing was certain — it had cured her forever of wanting to consummate her love for David before he was free of Estelle. The thought of provoking such terrors, day after day!

But she almost died of fright when she heard David replying, "Forgive me, too, sir. I should have introduced myself. I'm David Carne — Doctor Carne — and this is Mrs Jessica Lanyon. Those are her three children over there."

The old man grasped the true situation even before these words were out — and then Jessica saw that David had judged him perfectly, after all. He smiled genially and stretched forth both hands, saying, "Theodore Foster — Doctor Foster — though not the one who went to Gloucester, all on a summer's day. Nor, I fancy, *your* sort of doctor either, Doctor Carne. I am a professor of moral philosophy — fortunately, perhaps" — he beamed at them all over again — "retired!" He laughed and clasped Jessica's hand between his; they were astonishingly warm. "Mrs Lanyon! What lovely children you have. We had a little chat just now. They are saving the international telephone system from anarchists, I gather? Such civic consciousness is rare these days! And you, Doctor Carne." He turned to David and clasped his hand in the same way. "You would be the sort of doctor who helps bring such charming children into the world?"

David dipped his head ruefully. "Those very ones," he added meaningfully.

There was a tougher glint in the old man's eye as he said, "So it's a case of *your* life in *my* hands?"

"I'm afraid so, Doctor Foster."

"You took a risk — introducing yourselves like this."

David smiled. "I don't think I did, sir. Did I?"

"No!" he responded briskly. "The trouble with moral philosophy — as a career, I mean — is that it strips one of all absolutes. Your life is as safe in my hands, sir, as I imagine your patients" — he smiled at Jessica — "are in yours! I have taken the little cottage at the head of the lane. Porthgwarra Cottage. Just where you have parked your car. In fact, I came down to ask if you could move it."

"Oh, I'm so sorry." Jessica began making guilty movements back toward the lane. "We thought the place was deserted."

"Well, so it was until yesterday, Mrs Lanyon. But don't worry now. I had half a mind to drive over to Saint Ives, but now I'd much rather you all came and took some tea with me?"

*L*orna was so busy watching the front of the Mouse Hole that she almost missed Ben Calloway when he came round the back to start his car; in fact, if it had started first time, she would have missed him entirely. But it didn't even start the second time, nor the third ... nor the tenth — and by then Lorna herself was leaning over the fence, telling him that her oven was still hot enough, probably, to dry out the plugs.

He let go of the starting handle and wiped the sweat from his brow. "I'm sorry, Miss Sancreed, I didn't see you come up."

"You were rather preoccupied," she agreed. "I don't think she's going to fire unless you dry her out a bit."

He looked at his watch in annoyance.

She noticed a bouquet of flowers on the running board. "Are you late for an appointment?" she asked, intrigued.

He stared around him awkwardly — or, rather, all around her, as if she stood in a patch of mist that obscured her from him. "I suppose I am, in a way," he replied.

"May I help?"

"Oh, I wouldn't dream of imposing ..."

"It wouldn't be any imposition, I assure you. Weeding is *not* my favourite Sunday-afternoon occupation. I'm only doing it because no nice young fellow has seen fit to offer me any alternative."

"Oh! Ah!" He coughed and his ears flushed pink.

She laughed. "D'you think I'm awful? I'm sure you do. Would you like to push her down your drive while I sit at the controls?"

He gasped with relief — mainly at not having to respond to her earlier hint. "I say, would you? You are a brick."

It didn't work. In fact, Lorna pulled the choke out full to make sure it wouldn't work. "Let me drive you," she said, pushing the knob back before he could see what she had done. "I've got Mrs Lanyon's car, and I'm sure that'll start. Where d'you need to go?"

"Oh ..." He gazed unhappily up and down the esplanade, against whose kerb his own car had finally come to rest. "It's an ... it's ... well, it's rather awkward, really ..."

"Oh, do forgive me." She held up both hands as if to ward off a confession. "I wouldn't dream of prying. I'm sure you have your ..." A vague twiddle of her hands hinted at unspoken words.

What words might they have been? Private reasons? Private needs? Private arrangements? She smiled an understanding smile that forced him to go on: "It's the first Sunday in November, you see?"

She nodded but said nothing.

"The Sunday on which a very dear friend of mine was drowned — some years ago."

Lorna glanced at the flowers, which had meanwhile been transferred to the back seat of the car.

"Yes," he said. "I usually go and lay them close to the place where it happened."

"Hell's Mouth," Lorna said solemnly.

"You know?" He seemed surprised.

Her eyes twinkled. "You've surely noticed what gossips we women are, Mister Calloway! On my very first day in Penzance I asked Mrs Lanyon who the handsome young man next door was — and somehow she just knew I didn't mean Marcus Corvo! And then she told me the whole sad story. Oh dear — there are so many sad stories! But come on — we're wasting daylight. I'll be most happy to drive you to Hell's Mouth. What is it? Only ten miles or so? We'll do it in twenty minutes. No — I insist."

She dashed indoors, slipped on a coat, and left a note for Jessica in case she and the children returned first.

"No Mrs Lanyon?" Ben asked when he saw her lock the door and slip the key among some strands of clematis surrounding the porch.

"Doctor Carne thought she and the children were looking a bit wan, so he's taken them off to Porthgwarra. Or Land's End. Somewhere that way."

As they set off he said again, "It really is most awfully good of you, Miss Sancreed ..."

"Please! If you say it once more, I shall die of embarrassment. Besides, it's a perfect chance for us to get to know each other a little better — which we ought to do, since it looks as if we're going to be neighbours for the foreseeable future. Don't you agree?"

"Why … yes. That is … er, yes."

He was obviously wondering whether she knew anything about the possibility that Rosemergy might soon be sold. He had persuaded the unspeakable Corvo to say nothing until at least until after Armistice Day, out of respect for Mrs Lanyon's grief.

Corvo had immediately reneged, of course, but Calloway was unaware of that.

"And do I have an unfair advantage of you?" she asked. "Or do *you* know of the bereavement that brought *me* here to Rosemergy?"

"Mrs Lanyon was good enough to tell me something of it, the bare facts, at least, the Sunday after your arrival. I've often wished to find some way of letting you know how sorry I am — without seeming to intrude, don't you know."

"I know!" Lorna's tone suggested they were discussing a tragic defect of character, which they each possessed and neither could overcome. "We English are quite absurd in that respect …"

"But I am Cornish, Miss Sancreed," he interrupted.

"So am I, Mister Calloway, come to that. But, if anything, we Cornish are *worse* than the English in that respect. We imagine that to express sympathy is somehow to intrude. We end up being ashamed of our grief — which is absurd, of course."

"Oh, Miss Sancreed," he said admiringly. "How right you are! And" — he added as she swerved to avoid a knot of people who seemed to be involved in a skirmish of some kind — "how well you handle a car, if I may say so!"

"You may indeed, Mister Calloway," she told him. "My life is not so full of compliments these days that I will turn any away!"

"Ah!" He drew breath, as if he would say a great deal more, and then decided not to.

She was driving along Wharf Road, beside the Harbour, a favourite haunt of ladies of the town — even on a Sunday afternoon. As they passed one — a big, blowsy woman in her forties with her nose in a newspaper full of fish and chips — Lorna watched surreptitiously to see Calloway's reaction. He sat rigid and unblinking, staring directly ahead. He did not relax until they came to the railway station, where they joined the main road, which they would now follow to within a mile of their destination.

"Would you like to tell me about … Miss Lessore, was it?" she suggested. "Or would it still be too painful?"

"Not at all," he hastened to say. "That is, it *would* be painful, of course. But so is thinking about her — as I have been doing all day. It's an unavoidable pain. But if you can bear to listen, Miss Sancreed, I'd deem it an honour to tell you."

"Please do, Mister Calloway." She flashed him a sympathetic smile. "When I heard how tragically she died, I felt an enormous affinity with her. I myself used to swim at Hell's Mouth, you know."

"Why, Miss Sancreed!" He stared at her in amazement. "How extraordinary! Maude was an extraordinary young woman, too, you know. And beautiful."

"I'm sure. From Saint Ives, wasn't she?"

"Carbis Bay," he said, naming the posh part of the town. "We met at a garden party there. If I close my eyes, I can see her now. There was a little diverted stream running down through the gardens and she sat beside it, staring into the pool, with the sunlight dappling all around … I think I never saw such a vision of … loveliness." His voice broke but he managed to complete the sentence.

"While you are here to recall that scene, Mister Calloway," she assured him, "and others like it, Maude Lessore is not entirely dead. If she were, surely there would be no point at all in making this pilgrimage of remembrance?"

After a longish pause he said, uncomfortably, "If I am to be completely honest, Miss Sancreed, I did wonder this morning — for the first time since Maude died — whether there *was* any point in continuing … these … you know — pilgrimages. It's different with our national mourning on Armistice Sunday. That helps us all to draw together as a people. But for me to mourn Maude, all on my own, who does that draw me closer to?"

She reached across and squeezed his arm. "Today," she said, "there is no need to ask such a question."

After that there was no stopping him. About two miles beyond Penzance the road turned in a more northerly direction and took them across the Cornish peninsula at its narrowest point, from the sandy coves and bays of the English Channel to the wild and massive ramparts along the Atlantic Coast. Ben Calloway sang Maude Lessore's praises all the way.

Lorna parked the car to one side of the bumpy track that flirted with death the full length of the cliff margin to Portreath. She offered to stay in the car but he said he'd be grateful if she would accompany him. She reminded him that the place held only happy memories for her; he replied that it would comfort him to know it.

Their way led a quarter of a mile or so over the headlands, an awkward and uneven walk, mostly downhill. Several times he turned to assist her but always panicked at the last. The alarm in his eyes was the same as she had glimpsed along the harbour side in Penzance and she wondered what equivalence he could possibly see in her and that old blowsabella with her fish and chips. What could inspire that identical panic?

Some twenty paces short of the cliff edge he held out an arm and halted. "This is a treacherous place," he warned her. "Even on a calm day like this you can get sudden gusts of wind along this coast, which can take you by surprise and blow you over the edge. And it's a sheer drop, you know."

"I know!" she answered with feeling. "There's a place along the rim there where I used to sidle up to the edge and just stick my head over — or half my head — and suddenly you find yourself looking down a sheer face of rock ... a couple of hundred feet, or something."

"A good hundred and fifty, anyway," he said, as if the reduction ought to soothe her. "Anyway, I'm going on all fours from here on."

"You'll get grass on your knees. Roll your trouser legs up."

"You wouldn't be shocked?"

"At the sight of a man's knees?" She laughed — and laughed even louder when she saw how he blushed.

He joined in, guiltily, until she put a finger to her lips. "I'll go down there — the place I mentioned." She pointed toward the north-eastern edge of Hell's Mouth, which is a vast, U-shaped bite into the cliff face.

She did not turn and look at him until she had arrived at the spot, a couple of hundred paces away. He was disobeying his own warning and standing at the very edge, staring down at the waves, far below. For some reason he no longer seemed the ludicrous figure whose clumsy and embarrassed attempts at friendship had made her cringe — not that she now swung to the other extreme and began to entertain romantic feelings toward him, either. But he was beginning to interest her slightly as a person.

She forgot him for a while then as she renewed an ancient terror of heights. She dropped to her haunches and, as she had said, sidled to the very edge of the cliff. There, lying flat on the rock, she inched her eyes toward the rim, which was as near to a right angle as made no difference. She peeped over. That moment when her field of view expanded from two inches to what she still thought of as two hundred feet (which, in turn, looked like two *thousand* feet to her frightened mind) was terrifying beyond measure. She closed her eyes and withdrew

— and then did it again, and again, and again — until her heart came back to a mere gallop and she could breathe once more.

Then came a wonderful moment when her fear had so anæsthetized itself that it entirely lost the capacity to feel — or be felt. She suddenly knew herself to be immortal. She was convinced she could float out over the edge of the cliff and soar like a bird, wheeling and screaming defiance at the rocks and waves below. The place was a haunt of gulls and cormorants and her spirit joined them as they kited themselves up the sheer face, for no other purpose, it seemed, than to peel away and plummet downward once again, only to let the wind lift them with equal ease somewhere else along the cliff.

There were no seals in view today — for which Lorna felt grateful. The sight of those mournful, blubbery creatures whose friendliness had tempted Maude Lessore to her death would surely have been very melancholy to poor Ben Calloway, she thought.

There was a screaming and rushing of gulls toward a single focus at the very throat of the bay. It was a second or two before she recognized the bouquet of flowers as it tumbled and turned. It fell against the face of a wave, which immediately dashed it with some fury against the foot of the cliff. Lorna stared at the water for several minutes but was unable to discern a single surviving bloom.

"The sea took it all," she called out as she caught up with him on his way back to the car. "I'm sure that means something positive, Mister Calloway."

He turned and shook her hand, too moved to say a word.

Neither of them spoke until they were back on the main road. Then, to her surprise, he said, "However, one must be careful not to canonize the dead."

It was such a poetic turn of phrase that she knew someone had put the thought into his mind in just those words — which was not to say that he did not mean the sentiment sincerely, only that, unaided, he would have formulated it in a more commonplace way.

"She was very ..." He gave up and tried again: "She could be very ..." And then he gave up entirely.

Lorna did not press him. Instead she said, "The hardest thing I find is to remember those moments when Philip was unkind to me or said something slighting. If someone living behaves to me like that, I can either cut them or make some effort to improve things between us. But when the person is dead, all you can think is, *Could I have changed it for the better? Was it my fault?* Pointless questions, really, because there's still nothing you can *do.*"

"Maude could be like two people at times," he said.

To try to lead the conversation back to him, Lorna asked, "What did she think of your owning the Mouse Hole?"

He pulled a face. "She wasn't too keen, to be quite candid. It was her idea to develop it into something more like a road house, with a ballroom, and good, comfortable rooms to stay in."

"You'd be quite happy to go on running the place as an old-world tavern, you mean?"

He made a resigned gesture. "Likes and dislike are almost impossible to explain, aren't they. I served with a fascinating man — a barrister in civilian life — an amazing man, knew the whole of Keats by heart, could scribble you a Latin verse on the back of an envelope five minutes before a big push against the enemy. He's pushing up poppies, now. But the point I was going to make is that he was a fanatical follower of a football team called Arsenal — if you've ever heard of it — and also of professional boxing. I asked him why and all he could say was, 'It's my character!' He didn't really know why, you see. And it's a bit like my attitude to owning a tavern. I have nothing in common with my customers. Their need for beer and spirits disgusts me — and the way they cheat their wives and children to get it. And yet I find the whole business fascinating and I'd miss my customers more than anything if I had to give it up." He repeated the gesture of resignation with which he had begun. "I can't explain it." He smiled apologetically at her. "Can you, Miss Sancreed?"

She shook her head sadly. "But you're lucky to have something like that in your life," she said.

He drew a deep breath and took the plunge. "If you'd like to see it at first hand — from the other side of the counter, as it were — you'd be very welcome to join me behind the bar one evening — just for the fun of it, you know." He ground to a halt and added lamely, "I hope you don't feel insulted."

When she did not leap in to deny it, he said, "You do feel insulted."

"No!" she sighed. "I was just thinking how different you seem from the person I sort of assumed you were — are — from our few brief encounters before today. I'm so glad your own car decided to sulk, you know."

Now it was his turn to remain in thoughtful silence. "What sort of person did I seem?" he asked at length.

Rather than answer him directly she said, "I suppose I can safely confess it now: I was very worried for you when I heard that you and Marcus Corvo were making a joint offer to Mrs Lanyon for Rosemergy."

"But it wasn't — it *isn't* a partnership," he hastened to assure her. "I'd never undertake any kind of joint business with Corvo."

"It wouldn't worry me in the slightest if you did, Mister Calloway. You'd run circles around him. I can see that now."

The penny dropped. "Ah! You were worried in case he tried to cheat me!"

She cleared her throat meaningfully. "I'd hesitate to be so blunt about any man I know as slightly as I know Corvo. But even that trifling acquaintance leads me to fear that his view of the equal benefits arising out of any such arrangement might prove to be one thing before the transaction, and quite another thing after it."

He rubbed his hands happily. "Well, Miss Sancreed, if I ever feel in the need of business advice, I shall certainly come to you."

"Heavens!" she exclaimed. "I have no head for business at all."

"I wonder ..." He eyed her shrewdly. "Let's try a test. What's the most dastardly way Corvo might go about bidding for Rosemergy?"

Lorna thought it over, though the answer occurred to her at once. "I would expect him to rope you into making a combined bid for it. As he has done. This bid will be attractively low, of course, from your point of view. And then I'd expect him to make a secret bid of his own. A higher one, naturally."

"Just a few pounds but enough to tip the scales, eh!" He chuckled at the cunning of it.

"No," she said, surprising him. "Our unscrupulous friend is a knave but not a fool. I expect him to bid as much as the place was worth to him. Because you'll be so used by then to the thought that you'll be getting the place for a song ... you'd be most reluctant to go back to the fair market price. Your opponent is not really interested in keeping the price low, d'you see? He simply wants to avoid a situation in which the pair of you bid one another up among the stars."

"By jove!" Calloway exclaimed. "And you say you have no head for business, Miss Sancreed?"

She gave him a self-deprecating smile. "I played a lot of poker with Philip these last two years. Perhaps I picked up a wrinkle or two. Anyway" — she rubbed her hands eagerly — "we'll know the worst this Thursday, won't we!"

He frowned.

"Thursday," she said again. "Corvo's little cocktail party? He's going to present your joint bid to Mrs Lanyon?" She offered each reminder to him in a questioning tone, as if to jog his forgetfulness. When she saw his frown darken she said, "He didn't *tell* you?"

*W*hen Lorna heard that Jessica had "forgotten," yet again, to ask David how much capital would be needed to start the sanitarium she hid her annoyance as best she could. Jessica, however, was left in no doubt that she had failed her friend, or, rather, that she had failed their partnership. "Whereas *you*, I suppose," she said wearily, "managed to get a cast-iron promise out of Ben Calloway that he's not going to gang up with Corvo to make a low offer?"

"I wouldn't trust cast-iron guarantees from anyone," Lorna replied scornfully. "Least of all from a man whose vital business interests are at stake."

Such sentiments filled Jessica with despair and made her feel she'd never be fit for the world of commerce. "Wouldn't it be easier, dear," she would say at such moments, "just to sell up for what we can get and find somewhere quite small where I could grow a few flowers for the market, and you could bake things, and we could do teas in the season, and not be bothered with all this scheming and conniving? We'd get by, I'm sure."

Such sentiments, in their turn, filled Lorna with despair and made her wonder whether she shouldn't throw in her lot with Ben Calloway, instead; together, she was sure, they could make a road house popular enough to blast the Riviera-Splendide out of the water. True, Ben was still a bit of a bore, but not nearly as bad as she'd imagined before getting to know him a little better on that visit to Hell's Mouth. The real argument against it was that she'd always stand in Ben's shadow, whereas she and Jess, side by side, would shine equally if they made a success of *their* sanitarium.

But such cold calculations also made her feel ashamed. To keep her spirits up she had to remind herself that she was alone in the world now. Soon there'd be another mouth to feed, and many doors now open would be closed against her. If she didn't maintain a cool, level head, she could lose everything. It was an argument any woman would understand, she felt. *I understand it, anyway,* she said to herself. *And I'm a woman — so there!* Besides, she wasn't manipulating Jess into doing something against her best interests. Jess wanted two things in life, above all others — to stay near David Carne; and to give her children the best possible future. A little Cornish flower garden and teashop would never provide her with either.

At last, after Jessica funked one more attempt at getting the figure out of David, Lorna realized what was holding her back: the feeling that they would be cheating him out of something that was already "rightfully" his. Precisely what code of honour conferred that "right" on David, she, Lorna, could not see, but Jessica obviously could. Very well, Lorna thought, if one is working with people, one must accept them more or less as they are and try to work with the grain.

So when David hopped over the fence for "an after-dinner snort," as he put it, she took the chance to tackle him directly. It was the Wednesday evening before Marcus Corvo's little party at the Riviera-Splendide, so she was cutting it fine. Fortunately David himself gave her just the opening she needed.

He arrived at the moment the meal ended. The two women complimented him on his perfect sense of timing. He helped Lorna carry out the dishes while Jessica went upstairs to make sure Sarah finished reading and put out her light — and also, though she did not say so, to have a little talk with her.

Lorna slipped into her apron and held the two ribbons behind her for him to tie. He ignored the invitation and laid his hands on her hips, massaging them tenderly. "I think of you every night," he murmured.

She almost surrendered to the emotions his caress awakened. Her heart beat faster, she needed more air, her mouth went dry, her knees felt weak. "And of Jess, too, no doubt," she made herself say.

"More than ever before," he admitted, much to her surprise.

It was enough to startle her out of that urge to surrender. She tied the apron strings herself and said, "You think you'll get more miles per gallon out of brutal frankness, do you!"

"Candidly, Lorna," he replied, "I'm beyond such calculation. I'm in such a whirl, I don't know what's for the best. All I *do* know is that I'd receive nothing but contempt from you if I tried the usual sentimental flannel that rogues in my situation traditionally resort to. And I'd deserve it, too. If you came to my dispensary around midnight, I could slip out and meet you there. What about tonight?"

"Oh?" Her merry eyes dwelled in his. "Isn't it Jess's turn tonight?"

He clenched his fist; she saw the knuckles whiten. There was a potential for violence in this man that excited her. "Yes!" she sneered. "You'd never dream of proposing such an arrangement to *her*, would you! She's the Virgin, I'm the Whore!" She kissed him on the forehead and smiled forgivingly. "But I'm not going to quarrel with you, darling. I'm much too fond of you — and much too inclined to say yes to your interesting proposal."

He did not truly accept her attempts at pacification but the juices in his blood forced him to it when she spoke those last words. She exulted at the feeling of power it gave her as she watched him battle with himself. "Poor man," she added when she judged it right. "You'll never find peace and happiness with Jess until you've smashed those rose-tinted glasses. Tell me something — do you really want to have affaires with the two of us at the same time? Me knowing all about it and Jess not? Wouldn't that be like living in hell?" She put another plate in the drying rack. "You're three plates behind, man. You spend too much time thinking!"

He chuckled ruefully and took two plates at once. "I find it very hard to know what you want," he said.

"As far as *we* are concerned? You and I? You'll find that out tonight! And as far as you and Jess are concerned? I'd like you to come down out of the clouds — because until you do, she won't. You know that. She'll be as led by you as she was by Ian — as she always will be by whoever is the important man in her life."

"You speak as if you wouldn't mind at all. There's still a bit of egg on that." He slipped the plate back into the soapy water.

"Why should I mind? I have absolutely no desire to end up sitting by your fireside knitting cardigans for you and tut-tutting about your bedroom slippers while you lie snoring under the *British Medical Journal* or whatever you read for fun."

"It wouldn't be like that — and you know it." He let his knuckles run lightly down over the curve of her bottom.

She shivered. "No," she said vehemently. "But even less do I want to tie myself to a man in whom I love what I can see but don't give a damn about what I can't." She turned and kissed him briefly again, mainly to glance out of the door in case Jess was coming back downstairs. "And don't pretend you have no idea what I'm talking about because that's exactly the way you feel toward me, too. Anything between us is completely physical." She started on the cutlery. "Jess, by the way, is just longing to knit cardigans for someone and fret over his bedroom slippers."

"The more I know of you, the less I understand." By his tone he was trying to put some distance between them, she felt. "Jess is a long time with Sarah," he added.

"Sarah has noticed my tummy. I volunteered to explain it to her but Jess, for some extraordinary reason, declined. She may be up there for some time this evening — long enough for you to make a bit more effort than usual to try to understand."

He sighed. "What *do* you want, Lorna?" he asked in a slightly petulant tone.

"Oh David!" She turned to him, eyes dancing. "Would you really like to know?"

"Of course I would." His head shot back between his shoulders and he eyed her warily.

"I mean really, *really* want to know?"

"Yes?" More dubious than ever he took a pace back from her.

She said, "I want to know how much capital it would take to turn this place — Rosemergy — into a sanitarium."

Of all the things she might have said it was probably the last he'd ever have guessed. His jaw hung slack and he just stared at her.

"Seriously," she assured him. "Because that's what Jess and I are thinking of doing. Either a sanitarium with a resident medical staff or a nursing home with a doctor or two on call" — she grinned — "one of them living *very* close by!"

Although he looked for the chair before he sat down, he almost missed it. "*You* and Jess!" he said.

She laughed. "Oh! If only all the little gears and cogs in the cars you buy would run as smoothly as those in your brain are turning over at this moment, David! We'd have nothing left to laugh about. You *are* beginning to see the point, aren't you!"

He swallowed hard and nodded. "By Harry! It's the answer to everything. Estelle couldn't say a word!"

She dropped her hands and gazed down at him; for the first time that evening there was genuine warmth and even affection in her eyes. "In those few words, David," she said, "you have revealed yourself as one of the nicest men I'm ever likely to meet."

"Really?" All his distrust returned, for he suspected that a huge, backhander of a compliment was coming his way.

"Really," she assured him. "You're a bit of a fool by Marcus Corvo's standards. And you're an out-and-out cad by Ben Calloway's. But by *my* standards you reveal yourself as a man who knows what's truly important."

"To a woman!" he added, supplying the backhanded element he still felt was imminent.

She put a bundle of cold, wet cutlery into his cloth and closed his hand around it. "That goes without saying," she told him. "So tell me, how much is it going to cost?"

A new thought suddenly struck him. He relaxed and grinned lazily; his tongue lingered on his lower lip. "It's an extraordinary thing," he told her, "but I spent most of yesterday afternoon working it all out ..."

"And?" She held her breath.

"Oh, I couldn't possibly summarize it — it's far too complicated — planning for various contingencies ... making different assumptions about how much profit one may expect in each of the first five years ... all that sort of thing. It covers several sides of foolscap."

"And where are they — these sides of foolscap? I'll bet you haven't left them lying around where Estelle might see them!" She frisked his breast pocket.

"Guess!" His head gave an almost imperceptible tilt in the appropriate direction.

She threw back her head and roared with laughter. Then, lowering her voice, she murmured, "Midnight at Trevescan, you said?"

He nodded. "The dispensary."

"Midnight it is, then." She pecked him a brief kiss on the nose. "You always know the right thing to say!"

*S*arah lay in bed, staring at the confusion of patterns the street lights cast on the ceiling, trying to make out the form of a baby. The patterns always obliged in the end, even if one had to wait until summer or winter came back, for they changed throughout the year. There was the dodo she had found after *Alice in Wonderland*. There was Jabberwocky, after the other *Alice* book — she could stare at it unflinchingly now. And there was the old goat dying in the cave, from *Robinson Crusoe* — she had only lately been able to look at that. But there was no baby.

It struck her as curious she had never looked for a baby before, especially when one thought how many babies there were in all those nursery rhymes and fairy stories. Never mind. With patience she'd find one. The worst thing was to find one in a hurry and then not be able to find it again. That happened with Goosey Gander, when the breeze fluttered the curtains, and she'd cried herself to sleep at the thought that Goosey Gander had gone somewhere where she'd never find him again. She didn't know then that that was called Death.

She poked her finger into the well of her belly-button, which she now knew was called navel. Nanny Bridget once told her that Mummy had a belly-button, too, and that she, Sarah, and her baby brothers, had all come out of it, and one day she'd have little baby boys and girls of her own who'd come out of her belly-button, but not out of Guy's and Toby's because boys' belly-buttons were useless — only for show, as you'd expect.

Now, at last, she understood why Nanny Bridget had been dismissed so soon after saying that — because it was a fib. All Sarah knew at the time was that when she giggled the secret into Daddy's ear, Daddy got very cross and shouted at Nanny Bridget, who cried and packed her things and went away and sent a postcard from a munitions factory in Woolwich a year later, where she got thirty shillings a week, which made Mummy smile and say, "So there!"

But now she was grown-up enough to know the truth. For months and months she'd been *inside* Mummy — and so had Guy and Toby, but later than her. And all the food to make her tiny baby body grow had got into her through a hosepipe. And that's where her navel was. As soon as Mummy said it she got a nice warm tickly feeling round her navel and she could almost sort of half-remember lovely meals pouring into her there, better even than Aunty Lorna's meals. Or no. Just as good but in a different way.

And now Aunty Lorna was giving meals to her own little baby just like that — through a little hosepipe down in her own tummy. But we have to be very grown-up and remember it's a grown-up secret, just between the women in the house, and not to be talked about outside at all. Because usually ladies waited until they had a husband who could be a Daddy to the baby. But Aunty Lorna, bless her, had been just a teeny bit impatient and hadn't waited, and then poor Philip had died before he could agree to be the baby's Daddy. And *some* people in the town were going to be very angry when they knew about it because they think it's very naughty of a lady not to wait until she gets that agreement.

She explained all this again to One-Eyed Teddy because, although he'd heard Mummy say it all, he didn't always understand things the first time. So she hugged him tight against her heart and whispered, "But *we* aren't going to be angry with Aunty Lorna and *we* aren't going to stop speaking to her, because we love her too dearly, and she's so good-hearted and kind, and the little baby when it comes is going to be so sweet and adorable. So there, Teddy — d'you understand it *now?*"

She gave him an extra-hard hug and a kiss, to show him he'd still be loved and wanted even after the baby came. And then she tickled her navel until it made her giggle all over again. And at last she fell asleep, quite assured she had the tickliest tummy and the softest Teddy and the nicest Mummy and the dearest Aunty of any little girl in the world. And two quite nice brothers at times. But she still didn't find the pattern of the baby in the chaos of light and dark on her bedroom ceiling.

*J*essica telephoned Marcus Corvo a short while before they set off for the party. "We made a new friend last Sunday," she said. "In fact, I parked Doctor Carne's car across his drive, rather thoughtlessly, and he was terribly nice about it. He's a terribly nice man altogether. His name's Theodore Foster. He's a retired emeritus professor of moral philosophy — does retired mean the same as emeritus? — never mind — that's what he is. And to tell you the truth, he came to tea today and we can't get rid of him."

She bared her teeth at Foster, who beamed back at her.

There were tinny noises in the earpiece and she went on, "Mister Corvo, you're an absolute angel. You'll adore him, too, I'm sure. Say?"

More tinny noises.

"Oh no," she replied. "Don't worry about that. Apparently it has very little to do with what you and I understand by the word 'moral.' So ... we'll join you in about half an hour?"

She put the instrument down and said grimly to Foster, "Though what *that* man understands by 'moral' I dread to think."

"I can hardly wait to meet the fellow," the doctor told her. "I have heard so much."

Out in the passage, where they had been watching Jessica through the half-open door, David murmured to Lorna, "Now *there* is a Jessica I have never seen before. Have you ever seen her flirt like that?"

"Oh come!" Lorna went off into the kitchen to assemble the breakfast crockery on a tray. "It's hardly flirting."

"What are you doing, dear?" Jessica called from the drawing room.

"Getting the breakfast things ready. I'm sure neither of us will feel like laying it up by the time we get back."

"I say! D'you think it's going to be *that* sort of party?" Jessica shouted excitedly.

"Better safe than sorry!" Lorna lowered her voice to a normal pitch and said to David, "You could get out the cutlery if you want to help."

"If it's not flirting, what is it?"

"Full-blooded courting, of course!" She watched the horror fill his face and then laughed. "David! Relax — she just enjoys the prof's company. So do I, I may say. If he were twenty years younger, I'd be fighting Jess for a bit of his attention."

"Really?" He was curious but baffled.

"I know," she said soothingly. "There is a certain kind of man who's very attractive to women — and other men just can't see it. Theo Foster is a perfect example."

"Well" — he dropped the cutlery collection beside the plates on her tray — "he certainly has perked up dear Jess. Did you discuss the figures I gave you last night, by the way? I'd hate to think the night was *totally* wasted."

"There, there!" She patted the back of his hand by way of consolation. "Actually, I'm rather glad nothing else happened last night. I think it's best if we just remain good friends, don't you?"

He sniffed haughtily. "You only raised my hopes so as to get your hands on those calculations."

She nodded merrily. "Mata Hari's the middle name. What were we talking about? Something important. Ah yes — did I discuss them with Jess? Indeed I did. In fact, we spent the whole morning poring over them and trying not to get *too* excited. I've copied them out in my own hand."

"Why, for heaven's sake?"

"To impress Mister Curnow at the West of England Bank."

"Ah. Good idea. How did you explain things to Jess?"

"What things?"

"Yesterday night you had no figures. This morning — six pages. She must have wondered."

"Well, she didn't. I told her you were hiding them from Estelle, so I went over at midnight to get them."

His eyebrows shot up at this rash confession. "And even then ... not a glint of suspicion?"

"She *trusts* us, David. That's why I think we must just be good friends from now on. I couldn't enjoy going to bed with you again. I'd feel such a traitor." She smiled weakly. "To be so utterly trusted by someone you love and admire! It beats the locksmith every time, eh?" Her eyes twinkled at a sudden new thought. "Perhaps *that's* what they mean when they say love laughs at locksmiths!"

Later, as they were all walking down the garden path on their brief excursion between Rosemergy and the hôtel, Theo Foster asked, "Did I hear, a little while ago, someone saying that love laughs at locksmiths?"

"That was me," Lorna confessed. "I was saying that perfect love implies perfect trust — and *that* is why love can afford to laugh at the locksmith — rather than the usual interpretation, you see."

"Not entirely, Miss Sancreed," he replied. "What d'you understand to be the usual interpretation, may I ask?"

You imagine you can embarrass me! she thought and drew herself up to meet the challenge. "When bold Sir Brian Brassbound goes off to wage his campaigns, leaving Lady Brassbound bound in brass and unable to wage hers, young Captain Standish — the upright Member for Hairyfordshire — will make short work of the locksmith's most elaborate efforts. So, at least, the archbishop told me last time we were discussing it."

The old fellow chortled. During Lorna's reply he had fallen back to be at her side. Now he linked his arm in hers and said, "I know the very archbishop you mean."

David, who had hastened forward to join Jessica, murmured, "What *is* it about that fellow? He brings out the very worst in both you and Lorna."

She laughed delightedly. "D'you think so?"

"Yes — what's the secret?"

She gave a little sigh. "It's something I don't think one could explain to another man. He's just such *fun!*"

"And not entirely harmless," David warned.

"Exactly! You do *half*-understand it, anyway."

"Your comparison implies," Foster said loudly enough for the two in front to realize they were included in his remarks, "that love is a prison far more confining than any locksmith's gaol. What a shocking thought to find in the head of one so young and so lovely!"

"Come, Doctor Foster!" Lorna chided. "I'm sure it's not the first time that same shocking thought has occurred to *you*. Why, I'd be willing to bet a small fortune that it's crossed your mind several times during the past century alone!"

"Lorna!" Jess giggled nervously. "Doctor Foster is a very distinguished emeritus professor ..."

"... of moral philosophy, I hear!" Marcus Corvo stepped from the shadows beside the front gate. "I was about to lock up — and then I heard you coming after all. Good evening, dear lady." He kissed Jessica's hand with jovial mockery — performing the action, she was surprised to see, with punctilious correctness. Then it was, "Carne — good to see you can get away from your blisters and leeches." Then, "Miss Sancreed! When are you going to come and take command of the kitchens in *my* humble little establishment? Say the word and old Salford's out on his ear." And, without waiting for Lorna's response — which was just as well, since his excessive bonhomie had taken them all slightly aback — he said, "And you, sir, must be Professor Foster."

"I *must* be!" Foster agreed. "Though I am never quite sure whether it is an immanent necessity or merely a contingent one. Am I a nominal Foster or a real Foster? People once burned their fellow man at the stake — and fellow woman, too — for getting the answers to such questions wrong."

Corvo chuckled and patted the two men on the back, turning them toward the brilliantly lighted foyer of his "humble little establishment." The two ladies went a pace or so ahead of them. "I was just wondering," he said, "what a professor of moral philosophy actually does. I can't say I'm any the wiser."

"Oh, that is a much easier question to answer," Foster said at once. "My principal duty at Edinburgh was not — as I supposed when I accepted the position — to go about with two iron bars, prying into corners and prising the students apart. My duty was to keep absolutely regular hours." They began mounting the steps of the hôtel. "I made it a point of principle, for instance, to bicycle from my mistress's lodgings back to my wife's house at precisely six o'clock every morning. Not a minute past. Not a minute to. People used to set their watches and clocks by me. I am told that since I left the city, even the noonday gun has been firing at irregular hours."

They burst, laughing, through the swing doors. Foster was still speaking as he advanced on Petronella Trelawney, who was waiting rather nervously to greet them. "My successor," he said, "has reached the extraordinary — and to my mind quite untenable — conclusion that no man with a wife should simultaneously have a mistress. Mark my words! He will bring university life down around his ears — like Sampson with the pillars of the temple." He smiled genially at Petronella and waited for Corvo to introduce them.

Then he shook her warmly by the hand and complimented her on the superbly redecorated foyer; he patted one of the marbled pillars as he passed and murmured, "We're safe enough here, anyway!"

For the next five minutes Corvo watched in astonishment at the way Petronella hung on every word the old fellow said — though every syllable passed far over her head — and how concerned she was to see him seated comfortably, and the care with which she mixed his cocktail, exactly as he said he liked it. At last he turned to David and murmured, "What *is* it about that old geezer, Carne? He's got her eating out of the palm of his hand."

"One of life's big mysteries, Corvo, old chap," he replied.

"But I don't think you understand," Corvo persisted. "You don't know that gel. A bloke came in here last summer — asked for a champagne cocktail. All haughty, like. You'd have thought he was royalty. Well, that's like a red rag to the darling gel. Besides, she's not going to crack a whole bottle of bubbly for one measly sale, is she?"

"I don't know. Is she?"

"No, listen — this is good. She goes behind the bar there, sticks her finger in her cheek and goes …" At that point he stuck his own finger in his cheek and produced a very creditable impression of a champagne cork popping.

Everybody stopped talking and turned to look at him, so he repeated the gist of the story so far — without saying why he was telling it to Doctor Carne — and then continued, "So, when his nibs has heard the cork go pop like that, she pours him out her own patent mixture of Tio Pepe and tonic water, which I'd challenge anyone to tell apart from a true champagne cocktail, and serves it him. He drinks it down, follows it with two more, tells her it's the best he's ever tasted, and leaves her a half-crown tip!"

When they had finished laughing — and Petronella had done preening herself — Corvo said to David, "So, to get back to my original point — what makes a gel who's as savvy as *that* go and behave like *this!*" He gestured toward her and Foster.

David longed to tell him what both Lorna and Jess had replied in answer to that same question, but it occurred to him that Corvo himself was in a somewhat similar category — in fact, he was in an even more exclusive one, since David knew at least two women who could *not* understand what Petronella Trelawney and Betty Corvo saw in the man.

*T*he opening of the redecorated bar at the Riviera-Splendide called for a little ceremony. There were in all some thirty people present; the party from Rosemergy had been the last to arrive. Marcus made rather a pompous speech, for him; he had planned something lightly amusing but the unexpected presence of an emeritus professor led him, unwisely, to add a serious thought or two. Fortunately it was also brief. He spoke of the enormous social changes caused by the upheaval of the Great War, which had brought about the downfall of the great landowning families and had ended their long stranglehold on English life. What it boiled down to was that a great new Age of Democracy and the Common Man had arrived. And what *that* boiled down to, in turn, was that — while the dying remnant of the "nibs and nobby persons" might still go to the *French* Riviera for their holidays — John Bull, having inherited his own land at last, was beginning to discover it had its own Riviera, too. Soon the trickle of summer visitors to Cornwall would swell into a flood. Well, the Riviera-Splendide would be ready for them. Voilà!

He flourished a showman's hand at the curtains that had, until now, concealed the refurbished bar. A chambermaid, hidden beneath the counter, switched on an electric knife cleaner to provide the sound of a motor. Simultaneously two other concealed maids with fishing rods reeled in the lines, whose hooks were connected to the curtains. Petronella, who had spent an hour that afternoon rehearsing the effect with the three maids, clapped her hands with childish delight and looked to Marcus for approval.

"Better than anything I ever saw at the London Palladium, darling," he assured her.

Nobody laughed unkindly; in fact, they found it rather touching. Even when the knife cleaner continued to whir after the curtains had come to rest, no comment was passed.

But that was because all eyes were now riveted on the transformation that had overtaken — indeed, *overwhelmed* — the bar itself. Those who remembered it at all now discovered that they remembered it only vaguely, for it had been the epitome of all that is nondescript in interior decoration. Take away the counter and the bottles and it could have been anything — a storeroom, a railway waiting room on a small branch line, an outer office where people who are owed no favours must sit and hope. But no such vagueness hung around what it had since become.

"D'you like it?" Marcus asked eagerly of those nearest him, and then widened the inquiry, guest by guest. "What d'you think? Takes the breath away, eh! Guess what it cost?"

These questions and ejaculations gave way to more informative remarks: "A friend of Betty's got us the gold paint. Her husband's in the trade. It's not real gold, of course. And an old mate of mine makes the wallpapers in a factory down the Mile End Road, but it's good, eh?" And so on.

"And the stuffed monkeys?" Jessica asked, touching one gingerly. "They're real enough, surely?"

"Yeah," he said ruefully. "Cost real money and all. But they add that touch of class, don't you think? Them and the bamboo."

"Is it *real* bamboo?" David put in.

Lorna pinched him surreptitiously.

Corvo was puzzled by the question. "It's not *growing,* if that's what you mean. It's from China. And the bamboo in the wallpaper," he added, "I mean, obviously that's painted. Or printed, or however they do it." He turned to Ben Calloway. "What do *you* think, old man?" he asked, professional to professional. "I've still got the pattern book for the papers. I can get you anything you want — very cheap."

Jessica watched in amazement. The man who had greeted them so suavely not fifteen minutes earlier had been full of assurance; he knew how to handle people and how to assert himself without offending them. But set him down in a world where style and taste were what mattered and he turned into … *this* — a man who has just walked off the edge of a cliff under the impression he still has solid ground beneath him.

Theo Foster was obviously thinking along the same lines. "The importance of culture, eh?" he murmured in her ear.

Corvo saw him and said, "What does our perfessor think, then? Does my little piece of tropical jungle bring forth any moral or philosophical condemnations?"

Foster toasted him solemnly. "The moral law of the jungle, Corvo, can be stated in a single word: *Thrive!* If *this* doesn't help the Riviera-Splendide to thrive in the zoo of tomorrow's tourism — which you described so vividly in your prefatory remarks — then Cornwall itself is doomed."

Petronella put down her glass and clapped; then everybody followed suit, without quite knowing why. It certainly relieved the tension.

"Approval all round!" Corvo exclaimed, slightly surprised that it hadn't been immediate and spontaneous.

Ten minutes later, people were looking about them with new eyes and saying to one another, "Actually, once the surprise wears off, it really is rather jolly, don't you think?" And: "One can't imagine bringing one's friends here, but one can think of several friends who'd have no hesitation in bringing one here." And: "We're so used to hôtels that try to look as if they go back to Roman times, it's rather refreshing to find an interior that's obviously going to fall to bits inside two years!"

Petronella put a record on the gramophone — a bunny hug — and cultured critics became orgiasts at a stroke — all except Theo Foster, who picked one beat in four and led Jessica round the floor in a slow and stately foxtrot.

"That was a most diplomatic reply," she said. "I couldn't tell whether you approved or disapproved."

"University training," he told her. "And to think I imagined it would be wasted once I retired!"

"Is it a crime in university circles to like or dislike something — openly, I mean?"

"Oh no. It is essential to have strong opinions on absolutely everything. The crime is to express them so clearly that people get to know where you stand. There are no friends in Academe, you know — only enemies."

Jessica sighed. "It sounds like the world of business to me." And that led her to tell him of her present preoccupations with the future of Rosemergy.

Ben Calloway had meanwhile cut in on Lorna, who had begun the dance as David's partner. "I still haven't returned that *Saturday Evening Post*," she said apologetically.

"Oh, I meant you to keep it," he replied, embarrassed she should mention it at all. "I'd have said so, only it seemed so cheap to make you a gift of something I'd found abandoned."

"Ah — scruples!" Lorna chided gaily. Then her tone became serious. "Talking of which — did you think any further about our last conversation? That also touched on a matter of scruples. I believe that when this little cocktail party is over, we are invited to a buffet supper at which your joint bid with our host will be revealed."

Calloway cleared his throat awkwardly. "It's a bit difficult to talk about the man when one is his guest," he muttered.

She laughed. "Corvo's well aware of that!"

"May I ask — has he done as you suggested?"

"What was that?"

"You know — has he made a separate bid for Rosemergy?"

Her bewilderment increased. "Of course not! We have to be fattened for the slaughter, first. But I'm quite sure he will. Actually, Mister Calloway, what I was really suggesting was that where a man of honour finds himself up against an unscrupulous opponent, he had better have an unscrupulous response of his own in reserve."

"Ah ..." He stared uncomfortably over her shoulder. "That sounds like ... like ..."

"Good advice?" she suggested.

He nodded glumly. "I'm afraid so. And Corvo, you say, hasn't yet ... I mean, he hasn't actually ... you see, I wouldn't want to be the *first* to act in an unscrupulous way."

"I imagine he'll wait a day or two — while Mrs Lanyon comes to terms with her disappointment over the measly size of your joint bid — and then he'll come out with an offer she'd leap at."

"Leap at?" he echoed nervously. "You mean she'd say yes to him on the spot?"

"It would be very human. You know what shallow-minded creatures of impulse we women are! And of course, having said yes, no matter how rashly or impulsively, she would find it very hard to go back on her word."

The prospect suddenly seemed so bleak that he faltered in his dancing, which had been surprisingly polished until then. "What can one do?" he asked in anguish.

"Find a friend at court?" she suggested.

He stared at her. "You?"

She pushed him into picking up the rhythm again. "Unless you know anyone better? You could give me a bid in a sealed envelope, marked, 'To be opened only in case of a solo bid from any other party' — something along those lines."

"Yes! Of course!" he exclaimed, filled with relief and gratitude. "I'll do it now. Will you excuse me?"

"Oh, come! I think there's time to finish this dance. Dear Ben!" She butted his shoulder playfully. "Always so impetuous!"

After half a circuit in stunned silence, she said, "I'm so sorry! Did I call you Ben?"

"Yes," he replied in a daze.

"Oh *do* forgive me! It just slipped out. It's how I often think of you. But it won't happen again, I promise."

"Oh, please!" he begged. "You didn't ... I mean, I wasn't affronted by it. But it's just that I never ... "

"Call me Lorna if you want your revenge," she suggested.

"Oh my! I was friendly with Miss Lessore for four years before I called her ..." He hesitated, as if he were unsure of her Christian name.

"Before you dared call her 'Miss Lessore'?" Lorna offered helpfully.

"No!" he laughed. "Maude, of course."

"Well, this is nineteen-twenty and times have changed, Ben. You wouldn't have seen all these respectable burghers doing the bunny hug before the war!"

On the far side of the room, Corvo took one of the maids aside, as if they were discussing catering arrangements. "Well?" he asked eagerly. "Did you get near enough?"

"I was trying not to spill the tray, boss," she grumbled. "It's hard when everyone's jigging ..."

"Yes, yes! But did you hear anything? Even one or two words?"

"*She* said something about a sealed bid," the woman admitted. "An envelope and a sealed bid."

She saw the boss stifle the beginnings of a smile, but there was no doubting the joy in his tone. "Good gel!" he said solemnly. "You can take tomorrow morning off. You can have the whole day if you come up with any more. Only" — he reached out and plucked her sleeve as she turned away, eager to earn the rest of the promised bonus — "don't let any of them rumble you. Else I shall take it all away off of you again."

Lorna, who had seen the girl hovering near, noted this tête-à-tête with grim satisfaction. It confirmed all her worst suspicions — which were also, as it happened, her best hopes. When Ben went off to write out his sealed bid, she sought out Wallace Curnow, Manager of the West of England Bank in Market Jew Street.

"Hallo." She gave him a welcoming smile and held out her hand. "I'm Lorna Sancreed — staying at Rosemergy next door with Mrs Lanyon for the moment. Are you a visitor, too?"

He chuckled at the thought and set her straight.

"Not *the* Mister Curnow?" she asked excitedly. "Manager of the West of England?"

"I don't know about the *the*," he answered modestly. "But I do, indeed, have the honour to ..."

"Oh, but I've heard so much about you, Mister Curnow — from my Uncle Thomas and Aunty Gerty, of course. I'll spare your blushes but they speak most highly of you."

"Oh ... ah ... how very kind." He was taken a little aback by her effusiveness, she saw, but he recovered quickly. Also, he didn't entirely believe her; not that there was any actual suspicion in his disbelief. He simply considered it the exaggeration of a girl not long out of school and not quite at ease in social gatherings.

He was a short man — in his early fifties, she guessed. His cherubic face was dominated by a pair of pouting, baby lips. His baldness was ornamented rather than disguised by the long strands of side hair he had larded with macassar oil and combed up over it. Behind his pebble glasses, she noticed, his bright little eyes kept straying toward her breasts, where they lingered for a longer spell of admiration than most men would have risked.

"To be candid with you, Mister Curnow," she went on in a confessional tone, "I'm only saying that to butter you up! I *have* heard my uncle say pleasant things about you but I cannot claim you are an object of daily veneration."

He laughed at her frankness and readjusted his glasses several times. "I can't imagine why you should wish to butter *me* up, Miss Sancreed," he replied — in a tone that forgave her ten times over for the offence.

"You'll laugh, I know," she told him, "but if I were a man, I'd give my eye teeth to be the manager of a bank, especially of an important bank like yours."

"Really?" He showed the first spark of a more-than-social interest. "I can't imagine why." His eyes strayed again, making it clear how glad he was that she was *not* a man.

"It's such a godlike position, I've always thought. I don't suppose there's a single business in the West Country that isn't represented on your books?"

"Oh, well, there are other banks, Miss Sancreed — even if their names escape me for the moment, ha ha!"

"I mean *types* of business, of course. You must lend to farmers, wholesalers, retailers, publicans, hôteliers, manufacturers ... fishermen ... everyone?" He nodded confirmation at each suggestion. "You must spend half your time *legitimately* poking your nose into other people's business — it's every woman's dream, don't you see!"

He laughed at her pleasant fantasy and disabused her of the notion that it had anything in common with his actual daily life.

"Well?" Corvo muttered to the maid — who shook her head and replied, "She's just buttering him up — making fun of him."

"Well, which?"

"Bit of both, boss. He can't take his eyes off her tids, and she don't seem to mind."

"Good gel. Okay, go and see what the other one's up to with that perfessor geezer."

Lorna, meanwhile, was shaking her head stubbornly. "There must surely be something in my belief, though," she insisted. "I mean, if a farmer comes to you for a loan, d'you mean to tell me you don't even drive out for a quick peep over his hedges? I'll bet you've spent many an hour in the market, listening to the talk, seeing how prices are moving ... wondering if your loans to this or that farmer aren't turning a little risky?"

Curnow was at last beginning to suspect she had a serious point to make. He went so far as to acknowledge that there was something in what she said.

"You're like a doctor, in a way, aren't you," she continued. "You're never *really* off duty. Every occasion is social and business — a bit of both, as they say."

He decided to call her bluff. "I'm beginning to feel decidedly *on* duty all of a sudden, Miss Sancreed," he said with a solemn smile. "Are you working around to asking for an appointment?"

She dipped her head in agreement. "Even more than that," she confessed. "I was working round to asking you to dine at Rosemergy next Thursday — a week tonight — with Mrs Lanyon and me."

"And would that be business?" he asked. "Or social?"

"A bit of both," she replied, "as they say."

"I'm intrigued."

"Good. We dine rather late, I'm afraid. Eight o'clock. So if you came around half-past seven, we could sip a cocktail or two and ... chat about this and that?"

"I'm grateful for the invitation — and sensible of the honour, Miss Sancreed. But may I write and confirm it?"

It was pure flannel, of course. His eyes, lingering for the last time on her bosom — at such delightfully close quarters, anyway — offered all the confirmation she required.

And in any case, she would be writing to him before then, too.

*J*essica had her eye firmly on Lorna, who seemed to be in very earnest conversation with Mr Curnow, the bank manager, so she did not see David's rather guilty jump when she asked him, "Did you and Lorna do anything more than simply pore over figures last night?"

But Theo Foster saw it. His eyebrows twitched; he pursed his lips in a silent whistle; he studied the ceiling; he leaned a little closer to be sure of catching David's reply.

And David, aware that his guilty start had not gone unobserved, decided to make a joke of it. "Good heavens, Jess!" he exclaimed, putting his hand to his chest in a parody of wounded innocence. "What *are* you suggesting?"

Her mind's ear recalled her question and she turned wearily to him, a mild rebuke ready on her tongue. But then she hesitated. Behind his attempt at humour — his boyish head-lolling and his hurt expression — she sensed a genuine panic. A frightened man was watching her out of his clowning eyes. Her hesitation was brief enough to pass off as a momentary incomprehension. Then she pretended to let the penny drop; she pursed her lips in a smile that said, *Men! Don't you ever think of anything else?* and punched him playfully in the side. "I mean, did you hatch plots to set Calloway and Corvo at each other's throats and *rig* (I think that's the word) Mister Curnow?"

He played the part out by pretending to collapse with relief. "Oh! Is *that* all you meant! Well, let me tell you, Jess, by the time Miss Sancreed had finished quizzing me over every last financial detail, the only thing I wanted was a couple of matchsticks to prop up my eyelids." He turned to recruit Foster. "Don't let that young lady talk you into any project whatever," he advised solemnly. "She looks such a frail and fragrant young thing but I tell you — she's solid armour-plate steel driven by the sort of mind that Prussian generals would sell their grandmothers to possess."

"She is certainly making herself busy tonight," Foster replied neutrally. He had seen Jessica's hesitation but could not be sure it had been for the right reason.

"It's worrying," Jessica said, though she did not sound as if Lorna's behaviour worried her, personally.

Foster turned to her in surprise and said, "Oh?"

"She's such a born conspirator."

"Born or made?" the professor asked at once.

That gave Jessica pause for thought. "I suppose," she said at last, "it could have been 'made.' We've talked and talked and talked — and yet there's so much she hasn't told me about herself." She turned to Foster suddenly and said, "But you speak as if you know something about her, yourself?"

His hands circled an airy denial. "Only what I've seen on the two brief visits I've paid. What d'you think she's holding back?"

Her gaze lingered on him a moment, accusing him of being less than forthcoming; but she answered his question. "I don't know what has 'made' her such a conspirator." She glanced briefly around and lowered her voice. "You remember what I was telling you about earlier — our hopes for the future and so on? Well, *she's* the real drive behind it, not me."

He flashed a brief grin at David, as if to suggest he, too, would find her words amusing.

It made her snap at him. "Did I just say something funny?"

His attitude was at once apologetic. "You complain you know so little about Miss Sancreed! I smiled at how little you know yourself, Mrs Lanyon."

She thought of telling him she didn't follow, but realized that could be seen as confirming his accusation. "Tell me, then," she said, still piqued.

"Oh dear!" He ran his hands through his hair as if distraught. "You are asking me to peddle a very dangerous commodity — truth. I would far rather give you opium?" He raised his tone questioningly and looked at her with hope.

She relaxed and gave his arm a friendly squeeze. "I'm sorry I snapped, Professor. Please be the dear, kind man you are and tell me what it is I don't know about myself. It can hardly be worse than what I *do* know."

"Hoo-hoo!" Foster's eyes gleamed and he rubbed his hands avidly. "What a bargain she suggests, eh, Carne! To trade what I think she doesn't know for what she thinks she does!"

"Seriously!" Jessica insisted.

He came to heel. "Seriously, my dear? Well ... seriously, I think that if Miss Sancreed had not dropped into your life the way she did, you might now be doing all the things she is now doing on your behalf."

"And hers, too."

"And hers, too. There would be a difference, I think. You would be doing them with some reluctance, whereas she is obviously doing them with zest. But you, too, would be fighting your corner with every weapon in your arsenal — which, if you ever chose to unlock it, is every bit as formidable as Miss Sancreed's let me assure you. Or do I mean *warn* you?" He turned to David as he asked this last question, which left the 'you' ambiguous. To Jessica again he continued: "You, too, would be trying to set A against B. You would be conjuring figures and plans out of" — he smiled again at David — "let's call him C, shall we?"

"Carne, Calloway, or Corvo? All three victims have names beginning with C," David pointed out.

"All *four*," Foster corrected him, with a tilt of the head toward Curnow, the bank manager, who was just shaking hands in his farewell to Lorna — and not hurrying about it, either.

"I shall change mine by deed poll tomorrow," David joked, mopping his brow as if he had just survived a close shave.

Jessica grew tired of their foolery. The implications of David's moment of panic in response to her innocent question were just beginning to organize themselves in her mind. She said, "You're implying that I'm quite happy for Lorna to 'do my dirty washing,' as they say, so that I can launder my own conscience by going about, saying, 'Dear me, I'm not too happy about some of the things that young lady gets up to!' Is that the gist of it?"

"Keep your voice down, Jess," David murmured.

But it was too late. The chambermaid was already on her way back to the boss, eyes bright with the promise of revelations. "They'm falling out good 'n proper, boss," she confided breathlessly. "You know what that Mrs Lanyon said? 'I'm vurry unhappy 'bout what that Miss Sancreed's been and gone and got up to!' Her vurry words!"

She earned her promised day off. And at last Corvo saw what he must do.

Women! How could they ever be trusted? You'd see them walking arm in arm, laughing, heads together, all lovey-dovey — and inside it'd be knives out and they couldn't wait to slip the blade between the ribs! Well, if Jessica Lanyon was starting to get "vurry unhappy" at Miss Lorna Sancreed's antics — and who could blame her? — that was all a clever man needed. If Marcus Corvo couldn't turn that chink of daylight into a ten-mile gap, he must be going soft in the head.

As Foster watched the maid depart — which he did with undisguised satisfaction (and with eyes that had watched a thousand senior common room conspiracies unfold with academic slowness and grace) — he replied, "To put a different gloss on it, Mrs Lanyon, I'm suggesting that you are as implacable a warrior for your children's interests as Miss Sancreed is for her own. Further, that you are restrained by conventions in a way that she is not. Further still, that she is unencumbered with responsibilities that inevitably hold you back. And, finally, that in your heart-of-hearts you are perfectly aware of all this. I also suspect — and this is where I stray from certainty (in my own mind, at least — but where else can certainty find its first foothold in the world!) ... where I stray from certainty to surmise — I suspect that Miss Sancreed is perfectly aware of it, too. In short, you are, together, the right and left fists of a common will and purpose. I would not care to go into the ring with either of you. But let you combine in some enterprise — as you have combined in this — and I would not even be your *sparring* partner!" Again he turned to David as he made this concluding remark, but this time there was no softening smile.

David shivered.

Jessica, too, felt a prickling of the skin up and down her spine. And when Foster turned back to her and asked mildly, "Do my clumsy gropings after truth awaken the faintest echoes of recognition in you, Mrs Lanyon?" — all she could do was nod.

*W*hen the cocktail-party guests had gone, Corvo led the party-within-a-party down to the billiard room, where the table had been covered over with boards and a splendid buffet awaited them. No Oriental pasha was ever more solicitously attended to than Theo Foster. Jessica rearranged the chairs, putting the most comfortable one in the central position, where he could lord it over his court; Lorna brought a cushion from a sofa out in the foyer; and Petronella buzzed back and forth with the dishes from which the other guests had to help themselves.

"And he wasn't even invited!" Corvo murmured to David as they helped themselves. "What's the secret? You couldn't *buy* service like that, not even at Claridge's."

"We are like the poor," David said.

"Speak for yourself," Corvo responded dourly.

"No, I mean we are with them always."

Corvo vaguely remembered a bible story in which the disciples ticked off a girl for paying too much attention to Jesus. In fact, it had been the lesson in church only a week or two ago — but he had been too busy pondering his Rosemergy Plan to pay much attention. Rather than risk his hazy learning he said, "They think he's *safe* — that's what it is. They think he's retired from *everything* — know what I mean?"

David chuckled as they went off to a card table in a corner of the games room. "And you think he hasn't?"

"Not from *that*! Men never retire from *that*, do they. You watch his eyes when a bit of skirt walks by — or bends over him, like now. They rest where any man's would rest. But that's enough of him. The best of luck — that's all I can say for him. We only live once. Me, I'm glad of this chance for a chat, Carne, man-to-man — if you follow my drift?"

"You want to talk about Rosemergy?" David speared a small, cold sausage and used it as a platform for some pickle.

The hôtelier laughed and put on a Jewish-joke accent: "Shtumm! Shtumm! The fire's not till *next* Thursday!"

David frowned in puzzlement.

The other waved a hand at him. "No matter — private joke. You're quite right, though. It's no secret that I'd be interested in acquiring the land for expansion."

"It's certainly been no secret since you shouted it from the rooftops — immediately after old Lanyon's funeral. What splendid pickle! Is it home-made, I wonder?"

After a brief parody of shame, all smiles and winks, Corvo said, "A little contribution from Miss Sancreed, as a matter of fact."

"Oh, don't talk to me about that woman!" David furled up his waistcoat until he could pinch a tiny roll of fat from his waist. "See that!" he exclaimed with feeling.

"I fancy the lady herself will be showing a lot more than that in a month or so," Corvo replied evenly.

David's hesitation confirmed his suspicions — which was all they had been up until then. "But let's talk about Rosemergy, eh? I want to do the best I can by Mrs Lanyon, see? I'm not like some spec builder from up in England — come breezing in here — charm the land off of her for a song — tear the house down — put up some eyesore in its place — and then vamoose! I've got to go on living here. My business is here. And very *bad* business it would be if Penzance got to whispering that I'd cheated a poor widow and her three little mites. It wouldn't do. The pennies I might save would never balance the pounds I'd lose in goodwill. See?"

David smiled tolerantly. "You're saying there's no one else in all the world who wants to do better by her than you!"

"*And* for the soundest possible commercial reasons, Carne. Don't overlook that. I'm a businessman to my fingertips. I *know* the value of goodwill. I'm also a bit of a rough diamond — which is another thing I also know. If I wasn't in this trade, I wouldn't have a clue which knife and fork to pick up. But even I — hairy ape that I am — even I find it hard to bargain with a woman. It goes against my innate decency — know what I mean?"

David looked alarmed. "I think I'm beginning to. You're hoping I might act as go-between?"

"Yes!" Corvo smiled hugely with relief. "You being such a close pal of the squadron leader's, God rest him!" He raised a hand in benediction, like an Old Testament prophet, as depicted on a Sunday School attendance stamp. "If he's somewhere up there now, looking down on us ..."

"Yes, yes," David said impatiently. "Spare me that!" He chewed in thoughtful silence awhile and then said, "What if I myself were interested in acquiring the property?"

"Ah!" Corvo's eyes twinkled. "Now we come to it — man-to-man, like I said. It's a real pleasure to talk to you. No blind horses here! I'd rather sweat through ten deals with men than one with a woman — God's truth! That's where we ought to begin. Is this a boxing ring with three corners — or just the usual two?"

"Well now, what if it's a ring with *four* corners?" David asked, watching him carefully.

To his enormous surprise he saw that Corvo had not once considered the possibility. Even now he was having some difficulty grappling with it. "Who else, then?" he asked, bristling with dark suspicion. "Not that Bennett?"

Bennett was a local builder, widely regarded as more than a bit of a scamp in matters of business.

"No, I mean the two ladies themselves," David said. "Perhaps they have ambitions of their own. Who knows?"

Corvo's eyes narrowed as the notion at last took root. "*You* do!" he accused. "Come on, tell me! What's their game?" Then reaction set in. He still could not bring himself to believe it. His face split in a slow grin. "You're testing me, you old fox! Two ladies — three kids to look after and one on the way — what could they do that would bring in half as much as what I'm willing to offer? No, Carne — you're pulling my leg. Besides, they are *ladies*."

"I'm only saying you shouldn't discount the possibility, Corvo. Ladies get up to all sort of things these days, or hadn't you noticed?"

"*One* of them's been up to something, anyway!" the man muttered.

David knew he ought to step in and threaten the cad with rapiers at dawn or something. Carriages for two, breakfast for one. Only the thought that Corvo was probably hoping he'd lose his temper in precisely that way enabled him to keep it.

When he saw his ruse hadn't worked, Corvo went on. "I won't ask you if they *are* hatching schemes of their own, Carne, because I know for a fact you're too much of a gent to divulge. But I'm sure they've mentioned *something* — what would it be, I wonder? A seaside boarding house? An old folks' home? A nursing home, even — yeah!" He grinned. "With the doctor next door. That would keep you out of the bidding, too. But I'll tell you this: You'd be a fool to believe them! Don't you see?"

David drained his beer glass and said, "I'm afraid I don't, old chap." Peering into the dregs he added, "I'm also afraid you're about to tell me!"

"For your own good," Corvo assured him. "And free, gratis, and for nothing. Take a tip from an old and ugly warrior. Women may have their pipe dreams — that's their nature, God bless 'em. The Eternal Eve. The Garden of Eden was a castle in Spain. I know! But they'd never carry it through. Not them two. They're *ladies!* They know their limitations. They know the world is full of sharks like me who eat small fry like them for breakfast — or just to work up an appetite for breakfast proper! No, they'd never do it. It's just a clever trick to make me offer even more than what I'm going to offer — that's all. They've got that much business savvy — I'll grant them that. Fair dues! No hard feelings! I'd do the same myself. Well, you can tell them I *will* go higher. A lot higher, 'cause I never was one to do things by halves." He took an envelope from his pocket and tore it dramatically in two. "That's my old bid. I'm being a fool to myself, I know," he said lugubriously. "But my good name is worth far more to me than a mess of potage."

He rose and went off toward his office, contemptuously — and demonstratively — dropping the torn-up envelope and its contents into the waste-paper basket as he passed.

*J*essica came bustling into the kitchen, intending to ask why the kettle was taking so long to boil. She found it was, indeed, already boiling — and Lorna was standing over it, gingerly poking a brown manilla envelope into its steam. "What on earth are you ...?" she asked.

Lorna put a finger to her lips. "I don't suppose our professor of moral philosophy would approve of this," she said.

"What's in that envelope? Where did you get it?"

"It's Ben Calloway's sealed bid. I promised on my absolute honour not to open it unless Corvo went behind his back and tried to outbid their joint offer."

"Which he hasn't done," Jessica pointed out.

"No. So now we know what my absolute honour's worth!" She went on steaming the flap.

Jessica went on, "I asked David if they discussed it at all and he said only briefly. And all that happened was that Corvo tore up his bid."

"Those bits of paper he threw away?"

"Probably. Listen, if you don't mind my saying so, that isn't the way to steam open a long envelope. That bit's going cold and re-sticking itself again, see? Let me show you." She took the envelope from Lorna and squashed it under tension so that portions that came unstuck remained unstuck. "Also you can keep your word and retrieve your absolute honour."

"You've done this before!" Lorna accused merrily.

"I steamed open every letter that came for Ian, especially the Air Force ones. They always sent him into a blind fury."

Lorna stopped smiling and nodded. "I wonder what David and Corvo were talking about all that while, then," she said. "If they only discussed the bid briefly. Did he say?"

"They talked about the prof," Jessica replied. "They were wondering if he was past it."

"Past what?"

"It — you know. *It.*"

"Oh!" Lorna chuckled. "*It!* And what conclusion did they reach?"

"He didn't actually say. But they probably think the same as ..." she hesitated.

"As you and I think?" Lorna asked. "Well, I wonder if even our conclusion agrees?"

"I'm inclined to think he's *not* past It. What d'you think?"

"Most *definitely* not!" Lorna's eyes flashed. Then, with an impish smile, she added, "When you were pregnant — did we not discuss this once? Or am I just imagining it?"

"I don't know. Finish the question." A little voice was urging Jessica to bring it all out into the open — to ask the only question that mattered now, ever since David's strange behaviour had sown the suspicion in her mind.

"Did you feel an almost overwhelming desire for ... you know — It — at that time?"

"Not all the time — not for nine solid months. Thank God!"

"But sometimes? Or often? I mean you *did* feel like that?"

Jessica nodded reluctantly and then asked in an accusing tone: "You don't mean the prof awakens such feelings in you, surely?"

She asked the question purely as a peg on which to hang the *real* question later: "If not the prof, then *who?*" But, to her surprise, Lorna nodded and said, "Why not?"

"Why *not?*" Jessica echoed, aghast. The envelope was open by now but she held it, forgotten, at her side.

"Yes — why not? He's good-looking, for his age. Well preserved. I'll bet he knows a trick or two. Older men can keep going longer, too. I wonder what his mistress was like? And is she dead, too?"

"I'll bet he wore them both out!"

"Oooh! Stop or I won't be answerable!"

"Lorna! Do try to control yourself!" Jessica tried to make it sound like a joke.

But Lorna could see she was genuinely shocked. "I'm sorry, darling!" She raised a hand to Jess's shoulder and massaged her neck briefly. "I forget so easily. I get carried away. You don't like these feelings to erupt and burn themselves out, do you. You prefer them to smoulder away for ever. Really, we're not well matched at all, when you get down to it."

Or down to It? Jessica wondered — and then went on to marvel that even now she didn't ask the question uppermost in her mind. Instead, she said, "You're joking about the prof, surely? You couldn't ... seriously ...?"

"Not seriously, no. But I could *lightly* ... how does it go? 'Unadvisedly, lightly, wantonly, ... satisfy men's carnal lusts and appetites ...'"

"Lorna!" The cry was even sharper this time.

"Sorry!" she giggled. "It's getting late and I did have one too many of Petronella's champagne cocktails. Aren't we going to look at that bid now you've opened it?"

"Jess?" David called from out in the hall.

"Ssssh!" both women hissed from the kitchen.

"You'll wake the children," Jessica chided as he came in.

He was holding out a white envelope. "Extraordinary thing. Petronella Trelawney just tapped at the drawing-room window and handed this in. She said it's for you." He looked at it. "Got your name on it, too."

"How amazingly uncontradictory!" Jessica said sarcastically, holding out her hand for it.

He, meanwhile, was staring at the envelope in her hand, a slow smile spreading on his lips. "Snap?" he guessed at last.

"I think so," she replied. "Let's go and share this with the prof. He must be feeling rather left out."

"All this tender solicitude for his nibs!" David murmured to Lorna as he stepped aside to let her out of the kitchen.

She brought the kettle with her, for her original purpose had been to boil it up for a whisky toddy. "Diddums feel jealous!" she said, parodying the solicitude he complained about and pouting her lips in a kiss. "Diddums want ickle Jess and ickle Lorna for umself!"

He took a dramatic pace back from her. "Leave me out of it!"

"Besides," she continued as they trooped up the hall, speaking now in an entirely matter-of-fact tone, "if a girl's virtue isn't safe with a professor of moral philosophy, what *is* the world coming to?"

"To Porthgwarra, I hope!" Foster called from the drawing room.

Lorna, standing just outside the door, bit her lip in remorse and whispered to David, "He heard!"

As if you didn't intend him to! Jessica thought. "You're a regular scandal, Professor," she cried gaily as she entered the room.

"He already confessed to that," David reminded her. "They used to set their clocks by him, remember?"

"Eeny meeny miny mo ..." Lorna raced through the counting rhyme to see which bid they should look at first.

"Wait-wait-wait!" Jessica shrieked, just in time to stop her. "Make the whisky toddies first, so we'll have something to drink in celebration. I have a feeling it's going to be a celebration, too."

The two women made short work of the preparations; meanwhile David arranged the envelopes on the mantelpiece. Then he took out a coin and said, "Heads we look at Corvo's first, all right?"

"What if it's tails?" Lorna asked — so anxiously that for a moment he was taken in.

"Then obviously we read ..." He stopped and kicked his own shin. "Aargh!"

He spun the coin and grinned at Lorna. "Tails it is."

She gave two skips to the fireplace and whipped Ben Calloway's bid out from under David's nose.

She lifted the flap, took out the sheet of paper, unfolded it with maddening slowness, and read it — in silence. A smile parted her lips.

"Well?" Jessica asked impatiently.

Lorna hid both paper and envelope behind her back. "Guess!"

Jessica raked the ceiling with her eyes and said, "Two thousand?"

Lorna shook her head.

"More?"

Lorna nodded vigorously.

"A lot more?"

The nod was even more vigorous.

"Four thousand?"

"Higher," Lorna said.

"No!" Jessica caught the spirit at last and a wild glint began to shine in her eyes. "Five?"

"Almost there!"

"Five-three?" She held her breath.

"Five thousand, three hundred and fifty pounds!" Lorna threw both arms in the air, letting the paper and envelope fall where they would, and brought them down round Jessica's neck, hugging her like a lost sister. "Five-three-five-oh!" they shouted, time and again, dancing round in a clumsy little circle. The men looked on, amused and slightly embarrassed.

When they had calmed down a bit, Jessica said, "It hardly matters what Corvo offers now. That's more than we need for the first phase of our sanitarium."

"I still want to see, though." Lorna turned again to the mantelpiece.

"Of course!" Jessica raced past her. "But you opened the last one." She snatched the remaining envelope and fled to the farther corner of the room.

David laughed and turned to Theo Foster. "Isn't that exactly what the monkeys do in the zoo, when you throw a nut and one of them catches it! Off it beetles, just like that."

Jessica gave a shriek of delight — or disbelief — and then just stood there, staring at them open-mouthed.

"What?" Lorna asked.

Jessica came toward her, pale as a sheet, and slipped the paper into her hand. "I simply can't believe it. Tell me I'm not seeing things." She walked on to David and raised his hand to her brow. "Is this some kind of delirium?" she asked.

"My God!" Lorna's words were almost a whisper. She stared at the two men in turn, as if she, too, could no longer believe in their reality.

David raised his eyebrows; Foster just went on smiling, as if he were seeing all this for the second time.

"Ten thousand pounds!" Lorna said.

Jessica let go of David's hand and came back to her. "I didn't dream it, then. Oh, Lorna! What on earth are we going to do?"

"Decide, of course," David replied. "You never believed you'd get enough to make the sale worthwhile. You only ever wanted these bids so as to have something to show Curnow at the bank. Now you have a real choice."

The two women stared at him balefully.

"What now?" he asked. "Didn't you *want* a choice?"

Foster burst out laughing beside him. "Of course they didn't, Carne!" he said. "Don't you understand — they're *women!* They wanted their backs to the wall!"

"Well, I'm *sorry!*" he exclaimed sarcastically. "I'll go and tell Corvo to come down to six — if that's what you really want." A further — more serious — thought struck him. "Actually, I wonder what was in his original bid?"

"Was that the thing he tore up so dramatically at the conclusion of his conference with you?" Foster asked.

"Yes." They all turned to him, for his tone promised something.

"Which he then discarded in the waste-paper basket?"

"Yes!" they shouted.

"Well then, let's see, shall we?" he asked. And, with a slowness that made Lorna's earlier tease seem amateurish, he fished out two crumpled bits of paper from his pocket and assembled them into a single sheet.

"Well?" they chorused.

"Well, indeed!" he exclaimed mildly. "Well-well-well!"

He scooped it in his hands and held it up for their inspection. The paper was blank — on both sides.

uy wrote a five-act play, chiefly about smugglers, though it also included a wrongfully imprisoned governess who was finally rescued by someone called the Prince of Whales. Toby was disappointed that none of the smugglers owned a parrot, because he had lately learned to turn the tables on that species of bird and imitate it to perfection — several hundred times a day. He did not know it but there *had* originally been a part for a parrot; it had been eliminated at his mother's insistence. Sarah had suggested that some of the devices for moving the story between its three locations (a cave near Penzance, a house with a turret in a foggy quarter of London, and a castle in Whales) were a bit awkward. A fight had ensued, which Uncle Theo reduced to an armistice by offering to let the three children, and the four friends they had co-opted into the cast, iron out their production difficulties in the barn behind Porthgwarra Cottage. David rounded up the four friends and he and Jessica hazarded all nine lives, and the springs of her car, over the eight bumpy miles to Porthgwarra.

Lorna stayed behind in the hope that Ben Calloway might look in. When the car had been gone a full five minutes and he still had not come calling, she thought she might remind him of her existence by going out and doing a bit of dead-heading along the flower beds. But no sooner had she looked out her gumboots than it came on to rain — not enough to discourage a keen gardener, but more than enough for one whose motives were ulterior. Her excuse for wanting to see him again was that she hoped to discover whether he would raise his offer at all; but the reality was that he had awakened her interest during their outing the previous Sunday — not in any romantic sense, but she could imagine their becoming good friends. At least, that was all she would admit to herself before impatiently thrusting him from her thoughts entirely.

For a while she wandered disconsolately around the house, not wanting to start anything in case the rain passed over. She wished the family hadn't had dinner at midday, for then, if the rain did persist, she could spend the afternoon preparing something really elaborate. She recalled that she had promised to write down some recipes for Sarah — perhaps she should go and do that? Or there were letters to write to the bank and the War Office — and to Philip's solicitor about the will. He had left everything to her "in trust for our child" or to her absolutely if "our child" did not survive. Probate was ready to be granted if she'd just sign one or two papers, but she didn't want the will to be published yet, not with that damaging revelation in it. She would write a not-yet letter to postpone the day. And a wet Sunday afternoon was an ideal time to get such chores over and done with.

So why didn't she go and do it?

She stared out at the rain-sodden back lawn, where the birds were hopping round for an orgy of earthworms, and told herself she certainly ought to go and get on with it. But a terrible lethargy overcame her, making it easier just to stand and stare than to move even one pace.

Go, she told herself. *Get away from this window. There's nothing to see!*

Away from the window but toward ... what? What was the point of anything, any more? Why was she standing here in this alien house, paralyzed, void of all feeling? She pinched her forearm hard enough to hurt. It did hurt, too, but in a muffled, remote sort of way. Was some wasting disease creeping over her — some undiscovered temperate-zone variation of sleeping sickness? She felt a twinge of alarm, but even that was oddly muted.

She forced herself to move — one finger at least; she made it draw a line across the window sill to divert a tiny trickle of rain running across it. She knew she ought to lift her arm a bit higher and close the window tight, but there was something fascinating about that slow seepage of pure water and its refusal to cross any line she drew with the natural grease on her fingertips. The pure water, distilled in heaven, refused to mingle with the impurities from her body.

Her impure body.

An *Impure* was an old-fashioned euphemism for a prostitute. Canon Walmsley in Yeovil still used it. He'd tell her that what she had done was little better than what Impures did. She'd tell him that in her opinion it was quite a bit worse, because at least Impures knew what they were doing and why.

Why had she ever gone to live "in sin" with Philip? To thumb her nose at her parents, of course. That was the easy answer, anyway. There were others that made her less comfortable, though her mind did no more than skirt the edge of them. She did not wish to face them now. In any case, they were all aspects of the one basic thing, which there was no escaping.

At rock bottom it was because Philip had flattered her — not like some moustache-twirling Don Juan, but with an adoration she could do nothing to diminish. Scorn, sarcasm, coldness, indifference — all had failed to stem his outpouring of love and worship. She had been able to do nothing to hinder it in the slightest degree. In the end he had convinced her that the most wonderful thing that could ever happen to a girl had happened to her, though she had been sure it never would: She had fallen in love.

And she truly had fallen in love, too. She did not doubt that. It had changed everything while it lasted — from the colour of the sky to the taste of her food, from the thoughts that swam in and out of her head to the way she felt when she saw herself in the looking glass. It had transformed her and her life and the world in which she moved. But even at the dizziest heights of that wonderful and unlooked-for experience she had been aware that it was not quite reciprocal. Philip's adoration was not the mirror-image of hers. He was far more obsessed with the physical sensations of love than she was. When she wished to be with him, he wanted to touch her. When she wanted just to hold him, he desired to caress her. When she desired merely to *be*, he longed to *do*.

And that overwhelming craving of his had been the subtlest flattery of all, for it offered her the prospect of almost limitless power over him. His obsession with her ineffable beauty (in his eyes), her "charms" — all those euphemisms — was like putting a loaded weapon in her hands, especially when she could give him no such power over her. Power was such a seductive thing. Wasn't it only human for her to use it? After all those parental and schoolmarmy voices telling her she must find a man, a dependable man. Men knew how the world worked. Men understood, as no mere woman ever could, what a harsh, unforgiving place it was. Men could protect a girl from all that. And then along came one of these fabulous creatures, who made her a gift of almost unfettered power over him! Wasn't she only human?

He said she bewitched him, and it did seem a kind of witchcraft to her. It seemed that she controlled forces she did not begin to understand. This lucky arrangement of anatomy — which he called "Lorna," but which she knew was merely a cage that imprisoned her from moment to moment — this accidental grouping of flesh and bone, skin and hair, somehow radiated the sort of power that had once frightened men into burning women at the stake. She understood that, because in the end it had begun to frighten her, as well.

And that was when the whole mess had started to unravel — when love itself ceased to be the harbinger of life and hope and became the force that was driving Philip inexorably toward his death. His adoration dwindled with his fading vitality. Then she slowly emerged from the stupor of his worship and understood that her love could not survive its final withdrawal. Love itself would perish along with him.

And so, indeed, it had proved.

Now, though she no longer hoped for love, she still craved the power it had conferred upon her. It had become like a drug whose brief ecstasy cast the raging devils out of her and made her feel pure again — good in the sense of innocent; for how could she be guilty of anything she did not fully understand?

Something within her had hoped to exercise her power over David; but since that day at Land's End she realized it would never be. Every man, she supposed, had a certain capacity to become the slave of that particular bewitchment. In men like Philip it could not be divided into so many pieces and doled out to an equal number of women; in men like David, by contrast, it could not be bound together and offerred entire to one woman and one only. Like his gift for healing, he had a bit of it ever-ready for one and all.

She could feel Ben Calloway waiting there in the wings of her mind, ready to volunteer himself as the next candidate. Dare she cry, "Come in!"? Would the miracle happen a second time? She had no doubt but that she could arouse an admiration in him that would dwarf even Philip's in time, if it had not already done so. But would that rekindle in her a love of equal grandeur? As yet she felt not the faintest stirrings of it within her.

Perhaps the baby — whose stirring she could most certainly feel! — was crowding them out? Yes, she reminded herself bitterly, let the baby be born and *then* see how bewitching she would be to the worthy Ben Calloways of this world!

She gazed down at her belly and let all her muscles go slack. The resulting bulge shocked her — and made her aware how much effort she was devoting, quite unawares, to holding it in all the time. Perhaps that was why she felt so exhausted by the time evening drew on. God, just think how jaded she'd feel when she was almost to term!

Better go and write those letters. There was no point in delaying probate much longer; soon it would merely confirm what everyone already knew.

She was on the point of turning away from the window when she saw a woman standing out in the rain, over in the garden at Trevescan. At first she had the ridiculous idea that David must have bought a piece of garden statuary, for the woman was standing utterly still, and was scantily clad in a long white robe that clung to her figure in the way beloved of flashy sculptors.

Then she realized that it was a soaking wet nightdress.

Then she realized it could only be Estelle Carne standing there. She flung open the window and shouted, "I say?"

It was as if she had not uttered a sound; the woman went on staring at Rosemergy. She was just too far distant to let Lorna see her expression clearly.

"Are you all right?" Lorna called out, even louder.

Still there was no response.

Galvanized to action at last Lorna left her post at the window and ran into the hall. She threw on her coat but did not bother to struggle with the gumboots. She ran out by the kitchen, slamming the scullery door behind her, and slopped, squelching at every pace, across the lawn to the fence, which she cleared in a single-handed vault like a true steeplechase runner. While she was in the air it crossed her mind that she would not be vaulting again like that for many months. It sobered her enough to ensure that she landed on the balls of her feet, ankles and knees together, flexing her muscles to ride with the shock. Then, with some care, she walked the four or five paces to Mrs Carne, who was now staring at her with a curiously — or, rather, *incuriously* — glazed expression.

"I know you," the woman said in a dead-flat voice. "I know what you want."

"You'll catch your death out here," Lorna told her.

Estelle Carne laughed bitterly. "Snap! Now you know what I want, too."

"Let's get you back inside." Lorna slipped off her raincoat and draped it round the woman's shoulders. "You don't *really* want to die, do you? Not when there's so much *fun* to be had!"

The bitterness in her voice surprised even Lorna herself. It certainly shocked Mrs Carne into allowing herself to be thrust homeward without protest or dumb resistance. She turned to look at Lorna, who was pushing her in a shoulder-to-the-wheel fashion, and said, "You're an odd one."

Lorna, still bearing her relentlessly forward, stared her in the eye and replied, "Coming from a woman standing out in her nightie in the pouring rain — that's praise indeed!"

Mrs Carne smiled feebly and Lorna had an inkling that the woman had intended all this to happen. She had seen Lorna standing at the window and had gone out in the rain to provoke this "rescue." They reached the french windows that opened from the drawing room. Lorna tried one and found it unbolted. She pushed the woman inside and saw with relief that a healthy fire was burning in the grate. "Are there any servants in?" she asked.

Mrs Carne stared at the fire.

Lorna led her to it, calling out, "Anyone at home? Coo-ee!"

The silence was broken only by the murmur of the flames and the quiet drip of water from Mrs Carne's sodden nightdress.

Lorna checked all the windows and saw that they were overlooked only from the now deserted Rosemergy — and a couple of attic rooms in the Mouse Hole, but they were rather too far off to matter. "Better take that soaking wet nightie off," she advised. "No one can see. I'll go and get you a dressing gown or something. May I — d'you mind?"

The other just stood and stared into the flames.

"Come on, off with it!" Lorna stooped and lifted the hem.

She offered not the smallest spark of resistance — but nor did she make the slightest effort to help, either. Lorna had to fight it over her head and unpeel it inch by inch down her arms. It came away with loud, sticky noises, as if she had smeared herself in thick starch before venturing out into the rain. "I thought you were completely bedridden," she said. "I didn't even know you could stand."

Mrs Carne went on staring into the fire. She had the body of an athlete, Lorna thought. She must have been getting up to do exercises when no one was around. She was willowy, slender, with boyish hips and scooped-out buttocks like a young man. Her breasts were scarcely developed at all. Only the graceful angle of her arms, which hung at her sides, and the svelte curve of her thighs, showed any trace of femininity. All this, Lorna saw in a single backward glance from the door — where she repeated, "You don't mind, I hope?" Even as she spoke she knew she might as well have saved her breath.

The house was not at all as she had pictured it — and it was certainly not the sort of house in which she imagined David would be at ease. But then he wasn't, was he! Everything was white — marble white, alabaster white, eggshell white, quartz white, paper white, angora white, plaster white, glossy white. Without seeing it, Lorna could never have imagined such a symphony of whites. It was so surprising, so staggeringly beautiful, that her pace slowed to a crawl and she came to a halt on the half-way landing and just stared about her in amazement. Then she noticed a spot of colour here and there. A restrained bit of stained glass over the window at the far end of the landing ... the escutcheons over the keyholes, which were of coloured cut crystal ... a single fine thread of scarlet in the white stair runner ... a grain of palest caramel in the white maple parquet.

And then she noticed Estelle Carne's eyes upon her, peering up from the open drawing-room door. She was smiling enigmatically — a smile that made Lorna feel suddenly trapped. She raced on up to the landing and went through the first door she came to.

The room was dark brown — David's room; she knew it even before she registered the microscope, the dusty skull, the motheaten fox in a glass case. How she would have loved to stay and explore it!

She tried the room next door. A man's dressing room. With a bed in it. The bed ruffled. She would have loved to explore that, too.

The next room was beyond doubt Estelle's bedroom — indeed, her boudoir, one could call it. Except for golden tassels on the bed head and a golden sash for the bell pull, everything here was also white — and in the same breathtaking variety as in the rest of the house, or that bit she had seen.

The first drawer she opened was filled with nightdresses — all, of course, white. A white towelling dressing gown hung behind the door. And there were gold slippers with white powder-puff pompoms underneath the dressing-table stool. Lorna gathered each to her and then hastened to the door.

There she paused and closed her eyes and breathed a little prayer that whatever guardian spirit had seen her through the previous twenty-two and a half years of her life would not desert her now. As to what might happen when she returned to the drawing room she had not the first idea. But that it would be something significant she had not the least doubt, either.

By Lorna's guess Estelle Carne had not long turned thirty. She had dark hair, lustrous now that it had dried, though it was straight and lank from her soaking. She must once have been quite pretty, Lorna thought, and might be yet again; but her features were marred by the scars of ten thousand frowns and the feeling that any big bright smile which cracked those lips would pay for it dearly.

She had obviously decided to behave as if she had done nothing out of the ordinary by standing out there in the rain; one would have supposed that she had simply locked herself out by some stupid oversight and Lorna had come along and rescued her. Now she cradled the cup of hot, sweet tea Lorna had brought her and, looking her benefactress up and down, said, "You are not at all as I imagined you, Miss Sancreed."

Lorna remembered one of her headmistresses addressing her in precisely those tones, after her first or second expulsion. "Imagined me?" she echoed. "Have you not seen me from your window, then, Mrs Carne? I'm in the garden often enough."

"I don't mean in appearance. I mean in manner."

"Ah." Lorna gazed into her own cup and said no more. To go further with this conversation would raise the question of who was the woman's chief source of information, and she didn't want to get involved with all that.

"Mine is not a common illness," Estelle Carne continued.

"Clearly not," Lorna agreed.

"Why d'you speak in that tone?" she asked sharply.

"I wasn't aware of speaking in any particular tone, Mrs Carne," Lorna responded soothingly. "What I meant was that the few women I have known who suffer a chronic but happily not fatal complaint have all … how may I put it? Gone to seed? No one could accuse you of that."

Mrs Carne bit her nail and was not soothed in the least. "What could they accuse me of, then?" she asked.

"Jumping to conclusions all the time?" Lorna smiled sweetly. "Jumping down my throat at every other word? Some kind of jumping sickness, anyway."

The other had the grace to smile, if only thinly.

Lorna decided her best course was to seize the initiative and turn the spotlight round. "Did you really hope to end it all by standing in the rain, Mrs Carne?" she asked.

"Why d'you ask?" She was wary now, rather than sharp. When Lorna merely smiled she added, "D'you suppose your own grief has given you some special understanding?"

While the question was still coming at her, Lorna assumed it was intended sarcastically; but when she heard its echoes in her own silence she caught the smallest hint of ... something else there. Not strong enough to call it a cry for help, but a small, hesitant step in that direction. She quashed the angry reply she had already half-assembled and said instead, "What a very perceptive question! I believe it has, you know — because mine is not a simple grief, you see?" She smiled encouragingly. "And perhaps your words to me, out on the terrace there, Mrs Carne, were also ... not simple?"

Estelle Carne returned her gaze to her tea and murmured under her breath, "It's like trying to climb a glass mountain!"

Lorna said nothing.

At length the other was compelled to ask, "In what way was yours not a simple grief."

"*Is* not," Lorna corrected her. "It is still unfolding, you see. In fact, I was standing at the window over there in Rosemergy, not half an hour ago, trying to puzzle it all out. I presume you know the bare facts — that I was the fiancée of Philip Morvah ... injured in the same accident as Squadron Leader Lanyon ..." She hesitated.

Estelle Carne did not seem to notice. Her face had gone as pale as anything in her house at the mention of his name; the tea in her cup shivered from the exhalation of her breath. "I know," she murmured when she became aware that an answer was expected of her.

"Good. I fell in love with Philip in nineteen-seventeen. I was then nineteen years old — God, it seems a lifetime ago already! I was living at home at the time, near Redruth."

"I know your home," the other said. Her tone was so flat she might have meant anything, from "I have seen it from the road" to "I went to dances there when you were in pigtails."

"The accident happened a year later."

"The eighth of September, nineteen-eighteen," Estelle Carne said flatly. "At fifteen-thirty hours."

"That's right." Lorna did her best to hide her surprise at this pedantic accuracy. "Philip came out of hospital the week before Christmas — the same week I quarrelled fatally ... I mean for ever ...

with my parents. I left Cornwall, took a house in Yeovil, and brought Philip there to convalesce."

"Why Yeovil?" Mrs Carne asked suddenly, and rather surprisingly.

"Because I went to school near there." Lorna smiled at the memory. "One of my many schools! And I still knew a few people locally. Anyway — to cut to the discovery scene at once — Philip died in that same house. And on the day he died my love for him perished, too. The day before, I had *that* much left!" She held finger and thumb a split hair apart. "Next day — pfft!"

Estelle Carne was staring at her now, mouth open.

"It was nothing he did," Lorna explained. "Nothing he said. Nothing he *was*. It just happened." She frowned. "I've lost the fox now. Why did I start telling you this — oh yes! I was saying it's no simple grief. I mourn the loss of a lover who became a mere friend. And I grieve for my own loss, too — the capacity to love as freely as that. It never happens twice, does it."

Mrs Carne shook her head slowly and stared again into her teacup, which was now almost drained.

"Dear me, what an awful hostess I am!" Lorna said with sudden arch gaiety. "Do let me top that up for you."

Mrs Carne handed over her cup with the first truly warm smile she had given since Lorna had brought her in from the rain. It looked as if it hurt her to do it. "You are certainly not as I was led to expect ..."

"Let's not go into that!" Lorna busied herself with the milk-in-last ritual to let that conversational bud wither.

"Am *I* at all as you expected me to be?" Mrs Carne asked as she took back her cup.

"You're beginning to look flushed," Lorna said. "Perhaps you should move away from the fire. I'll sit over here." She moved to a chair facing the sofa.

"*Am* I?" the woman insisted as she settled herself in the place Lorna had vacated.

"Yes and no," Lorna replied judiciously.

"Well! That's hardly an answer."

Lorna gave an embarrassed laugh. "Does it really matter?"

"I suppose you thought me bitter and lonely?"

Lorna tilted her head awkwardly. "I wasn't kept awake with the loud music and the cars and carriages coming and going at all hours," she confessed. "But that's a long way short of bitter and lonely. Anyway, I think *I* am bitter and lonely at times — so it would hardly be a damning indictment of you, would it!"

Mrs Carne set down her cup and sprang to her feet. She began to pace about in such agitation that Lorna became alarmed for her once again. "What is it?" she asked earnestly.

"You're no good!" The woman made the remark more to herself than to Lorna. "I thought you could help. I thought you *would* help. I've watched you on and off for weeks."

Lorna set down her own cup and came to her. "I'll help in any way I can." She took her by the arm and gave her a reassuring squeeze. "That's a promise! Now do please come and sit down — and try to calm yourself."

She glanced desperately at the clock and saw that she might expect three or four more hours before David would return.

"I am lonely," Mrs Carne admitted as she returned to her seat. "But that is by choice. I am bitter, too. But that is not my choice. It has been forced upon me by … another."

"Mrs Carne." Lorna cleared her throat in a cautionary manner. "Doctor Carne has made only the most oblique and fleeting references to your marriage …"

The woman cut her short with a laugh, harsh and brief. "You think I mean him, don't you! You think *he's* the one who has filled me with bitterness! Ha!"

"That isn't the point I was about to make," Lorna said patiently. "In fact, I was hoping to make two points — one openly, the other I expected you to twig … to read between the lines, as it were. The open point is that no matter what your husband had told me, whether everything or nothing, I should not repeat a word of it to you — and the same goes for anything you might say to me."

"That's the one you hoped I'd twig, eh?"

"No! The point I hoped you'd grasp without my making it is that — since he has made only the most oblique and passing references to your marriage …?" She let her tone rise and raised her eyebrows — as teachers encourage pupils to finish a sentence.

"It's no use my trying to claw the information out of you!"

"Bravo!"

The smile soon faded from Estelle Carne's lips, however, as she returned to her earlier theme. "I was saying that if you thought David is the one who has made me so bitter, you are quite wrong. It's *her*." She gazed into the fire so as not to have to meet Lorna's eye. "You know who I mean."

"I know who you mean," Lorna echoed affably. "I disagree with you, of course. But I will listen — and, as I said, I will carry no tales."

"You think a mere listening post is all I want?" the other sneered.

"No. I think you want to poison my mind against her. I think you wish to destroy her. I think you spend a large part of each day having daydreams — all about bringing her world down around her ears. For all I know you make wax dolls and stick pins in them — perhaps you want me to bring you her toenail clippings or a lock of her hair?"

Mrs Carne could think of nothing to say — but the venom in her stare said it all.

Lorna shivered, and her spirit sank as she realized that no mere chat over a cup of tea was ever going to dislodge so vast and so all-embracing a hatred. "Let's talk of other things, then," she suggested.

"She destroyed one of the finest men who ever lived," Estelle Carne snapped. Her hand began to tremble — and her lip — and her voice. "One of the finest ... noblest ..." Suddenly her eyes were awash with tears. "You can have no idea! No idea!" she whispered in a thin, strangled voice.

"I can." Lorna did her best to steer a middle way between coldness and anything suggesting sympathy. "I can because I am the butt of similar accusations about Philip — not only from his father but from my own parents as well."

They were probably the only words that could have dented Estelle Carne's antagonism at that moment. Indeed, it was hardly so much as a dent — but it was enough to bring her back from hysterical collapse, and just in the nick of time. "Your own parents?" she echoed in a slightly bewildered manner.

Lorna nodded. "What is worse, I have to live with the thought that they may, indeed, be right. Not absolutely right, of course." She stared the woman directly in the eye as she added: "*Nobody* is ever *absolutely* right. But there may just be a grain of truth in it." Then some imp for which she was unprepared made her add: "But his father will come round when he hears about the baby." She stretched a protective hand across her belly. "I'm sure of that."

If she had not been watching Estelle Carne so intently she might have missed it — the fleeting emotion that passed across her features, too swift for her to be sure, yet she was *almost* sure it was jealousy. Not the mild, self-righteous jealousy of the childless wife for the pregnant spinster, but the raging fire of one who knows her chance has gone forever, though she did nothing about it when it was there. Then she knew, with that same near-certainty, that Estelle Carne had loved Ian Lanyon with every fibre of her being — and had longed to bear no man's child but his.

Mrs Carne was quick to mask it, of course — it was, after all, something she had long practice at doing. "You?" A delighted smile spread across her features; it seemed a little forced at first but soon appeared quite genuine. "You're expecting a baby?"

Lorna nodded.

"She'll throw you out then."

Lorna shook her head.

The woman frowned. "Does she know about it?" Her tone expected the answer no.

Again Lorna shook her head — not so much in denial as in refusal to discuss the matter, or that aspect of it. She said as much and then added, "You realize how much it shocks me to find you so absolutely set in your condemnation of Mrs Lanyon. It hurts me, too, I have to confess. So I'd prefer to say nothing more about it *this* time" — the promise of a next time was implicit in her stress — "because you'll only think I'm lying in a good cause. Or what *I* would consider a good cause. The fact is, Mrs Lanyon does know — and she will take up cudgels against all the world in my defence."

"It's easily said now," Mrs Carne jeered. "She has ... what? ... five months to go back on her word?"

Lorna shook her head. "Three and a half at the most, according to Doctor Carmichael. Talking of going back on words — that's not the only thing one can do with them, you know. Whenever we complained at school about the *awful* puddings they served, Miss Rix, our housemistress, used to tell us it was good practice for the most dreadful diet of all — being forced to eat our own words!"

Mrs Carne nodded pensively but said nothing.

Well, Lorna thought, *it's a start!*

Sarah drank dry ginger ale with ice. She didn't like it much but Petronella had once told her it was a safe drink for a girl because the lads couldn't tell whether there was whisky in it or not, and you could always tip the barman a wink to make sure it was not. Sarah felt there were one or two logical steps absent from that line of reasoning, but that was often the case with discussions about lads and girls — also with *any* line of reasoning from Petronella. So she swallowed her mild aversion *and* the dry ginger — and pretended it contained whisky. The ice made a merry clink, anyway.

Jessica glanced again at her watch. "He's late," she said for the third or fourth time.

"He's nervous, that's all," Lorna told her soothingly. "He's only a common or garden bank manager. He's not used to dining in high society." She grinned at David, immaculate for once in a dinner jacket. "Isn't that so, Doctor? Bank managers, clergymen, and doctors — they're only just beginning to be considered invitable to dine in their own right. Before the war they had to be good conversationalists and sing for their supper as well."

He smiled at her and laid a reassuring hand on Jessica's arm. "One late night will do no harm, Jess," he said.

"If they're only just being admitted to society, they ought to pay more attention to its rules. And Sarah has school tomorrow — a history test."

"Mum-mee!" Sarah said cajolingly. Then she did an extraordinary thing, in her mother's view, at least. She simpered at the other two as if begging them to humour her poor dear mamma. Then she said to Lorna, manager-to-manager, "I'll just pop out to the kitchen and make sure I salted the potatoes."

It was a trivial enough piece of social manipulation but a woman three times her age could hardly have managed it with a lighter touch. It made Jessica realize how much her little girl had matured these past … well, since Lorna had joined the household. Only two months! Two months ago Sarah would simply have begged and wheedled like any child of ten.

Part of Jessica felt proud of her daughter but the rest felt cheated. She wanted to hold on to the earlier Sarah, who did not know how to manipulate people in that effortless way.

There was the sound of a car grinding its way up the drive, pinking and straining in too high a gear. She looked at her watch yet again and said, "About time, too."

Lorna smiled at her, a smile that said, "Now it begins!"

Jessica nodded and smiled back. Her heart missed a beat and a voice said inside her, "You can still turn back." It had been saying the same thing for days but it was getting really insistent now.

The car came to a halt and then, inexplicably, there was a crashing of gears. Lorna looked accusingly at David and said, "You've opened a school of motoring on the side!"

They all laughed, a little too heartily. Sarah returned in time to take up her glass and join in the laughter. Their eyes were still full of merriment when Daisy, who had stayed on for the evening, showed Mr Curnow in.

"Dear ladies!" He advanced upon them, showing a pair of oily hands. "Do forgive me — though I shall never forgive that wretched death-trap I drive, if it has spoiled your dinner."

"*Our* dinner, Mister Curnow," Lorna corrected him. "And rest assured, it won't have spoiled in the slightest. Let me introduce you to some soap." She held his sleeve between a tweezer-like thumb and forefinger as she led him back out again. His eyebrows flagged apologies over his shoulder.

"That was rather daring of her," Jessica said in a tone not overburdened with approval — though, for Sarah's sake, it was not too critical, either.

"It broke the ice very nicely, I think," David replied. "We're off to a good start."

"As the Gadarene swine must have assured one another at the top of the slope!"

It was not the only "rather daring" thing about Lorna tonight. Jessica wished she had had time (otherwise known as courage) to talk to her about her dress, or "my little black thing," as she called it. It was one of the new "backless" evening gowns — and pretty nearly frontless, too. Not that it would have served any purpose. Lorna had gone to call on Curnow the previous morning, wearing an angora-wool sweater which, though it covered her right up to the neck, left not a scintilla of doubt about *what* it was covering. Her own tactful remark that something slightly less *anatomical* would be more appropriate for a visit to a bank manager brought the reply, "Ah, I'm leaving the bank manager to you and David. *I'm* going to call on the man!"

"Gadarene swine!" David laughed. "Is that how it feels to you?"

"No, but I'm sure this is how it felt to them!"

"Anyway," Sarah said. "It's on the Roman villa, and I built a model of one, so the test will be easy-peasy. So there!"

She did not understand why her mother looked down at her with such relief in her eyes, and tousled her hair so affectionately, and said, "All right, darling. Just this once. But mark my words now, if those vegetables aren't perfect ...!"

Sarah went out, loudly chewing the remains of her ice, just to set her mother's teeth on edge. For revenge Jessica called after her: "And it's up to bed you go the moment they're served!"

No business was discussed during the dinner, of course. Jessica watched with amusement to see Curnow going through the same agonies that had beset her and David on Lorna's first night at Rosemergy. In their small circle Lorna's almost magical skills with quite ordinary food had become a legend. Tonight, for instance, it was a "simple" steak-and-kidney pie; yet it was already clear that it was *the* steak-and-kidney pie of Curnow's entire life — the one he would remember hereafter whenever the conversation turned to all that was best in "good old British scoff and none of your foreign muck." But how to say it aloud? Fortunately, what with Lorna's new evening gown, he had plenty of distraction from his perplexity; but Jessica could see that, when he was not enjoying the view, he was savouring his food and trying hard not to speak of it.

Poor man, Jessica thought — trapped between two social taboos. And which of them, she wondered, would be the first to be overthrown in the years to come? Would it soon become more acceptable for a gentleman to compliment a woman on her physical charms or on her cooking?

At last, she took pity on him. She waited until just before they rose from the table and said, by way of an easy link to the discussion that must now follow: "If our project ever amounts to anything, Mister Curnow, we shall lay great emphasis on the value of a simple but appetizing diet."

He shot her a look of gratitude and said, "If tonight's offering is any guide, Mrs Lanyon, I'm sure people will be breaking legs and faking heart attacks merely to be admitted." He smiled at her and bowed at Lorna.

But as they strolled up the hall toward the drawing room he became a different person; it was a move from their territory to his.

Jessica had set out the papers on a card table by the sofa. He took one look at it and, lifting it bodily over the sofa, set it down behind. He said, "I doubt we'll be needing that just yet. That's not what this meeting is all about."

"Oh?" Jessica's tone was surprised and a little hurt. "I thought it would be quite important."

"Paper!" he exclaimed dismissively. "On paper, Mrs Lanyon, the *Titanic* was unsinkable. Tonight it's not figures that are important, but people." He manfully avoided Lorna as he spoke of figures — but in any case, she had unwittingly prepared the way for his remark by draping a gold-lamé stole about her shoulders — a highly symbolic first step from the black of mourning.

"People?" David echoed nervously. He handed round the coffee cups as Daisy poured them.

"The three of you, to be precise, Doctor Carne. How well you get on together. Which of you will be doing what. How much stomach you have for what may be quite a struggle at times — and how much stamina, too. What you really hope to get out of it. That sort of thing. Any plan can be made to work on paper." The two men sat down as he concluded: "Who, for instance, would you say is the real driving force behind this entire project?"

He kept his eyes fixed on David. David looked at Lorna. Jessica looked at Lorna.

Lorna looked alarmed at each of them in turn. "Me!" She sat bolt upright and only just managed not to slop her coffee.

"Yes." Curnow chuckled. "I thought so."

"I don't agree at all," Lorna came back stoutly.

The chuckle became a laugh and he rubbed his hands gleefully. "Good, good! I always like to start with a blazing disagreement. Modesty, politeness, and even propriety have very little commercial value." He leaned forward like a boxing promoter with two of his own boys in the ring.

"For my part," Jessica reminded her, "I was all for selling the place to the highest bidder."

Curnow leaped in before the point was lost. "And in your heart-of-hearts, Mrs Lanyon, you'd still prefer to do that?"

"No!" She tried not to flinch under his challenge. "It's just that I would never have had the courage to even *think* of trying to open our own sanitarium. In fact, it's only because it's *our* own — between the three of us, I mean — and not *my* own that I'm willing to contemplate it at all."

Curnow nodded. "Actually, I'm surprised the idea didn't come from Doctor Carne."

He shrugged. "I had something of the sort in mind, but on a much more modest scale — a simple nursing home … a few elderly patients … convalescents … shell-shock victims … mustard-gas victims … that sort of thing." He darted an awkward glance at the two women for they could all see what was coming.

The nursing-home project was, indeed, far more suited both to their capital and to the present state of Rosemergy. The sanitarium called for a great deal more outlay, considerable rebuilding, and a much larger staff, to say nothing of medical equipment. True, it would repay the outlay within the usual commercial term, leaving them with a considerable asset, but, most important of all — and the only reason as far as Jessica was concerned — it would make David independent of Estelle, which was something the nursing-home project would not achieve. But they could hardly say as much to Curnow!

Lorna was in a kind of double-bind, for she could hardly tell the others — even if Curnow were absent — that she was sure Estelle could be won around to the nursing-home project in the end. And that the means to achieve it lay in *their* hands. Something had happened under this roof — many years ago, perhaps — to turn that poor woman into the angry, bitter, reclusive invalid she had become. Yet, during their bizarre meeting the previous Sunday, Lorna had caught the merest glimpse of another Estelle, trapped inside the one who hated Jessica with such insane power that she almost scourged her own husband into Jess's arms, hoping, no doubt, to ruin them both in this town.

But Curnow was no fool. He was onto the point like a terrier. The project Doctor Carne described was so eminently sensible, he said, and so easily within their grasp — why did they not pursue it instead? It would hardly set them back a thou'. He'd authorize the loan on the spot, if they needed it at all. "Then," he concluded brightly, "we may all settle down to an enjoyable rubber of bridge!"

As before, both Jessica and David turned to Lorna.

"Oh, so now it's me again!" she exclaimed with jocular pugnacity. "I wish the pair of you wouldn't keep doing this." But she saw no way forward, except to grasp the bull by the horns. "We abandoned that project, Mister Curnow, because — although Doctor Carne does not, of course, *treat* Mrs Carne — his responsibilities toward her would make it hard for him to dedicate himself to a one-doctor nursing home as well."

"And you would not think of taking up the venture with another doctor?" Curnow asked at once.

"Of course not! It's Doctor Carne or no one."

She was so emphatic that he felt it would be pointless to ask why. Instead he raised an inquiring eyebrow at Jessica.

"I absolutely agree," she told him.

He turned his gaze — which was now admiring and slightly envious — on David, who felt goaded into saying, "We stand revealed as amateurs, Mister Curnow. I'm sure you hard-headed men of business do not think like that."

The banker shook his head in rueful agreement. "Don't lump me in with the hard-headed men of business, Doctor Carne! I try to avoid them like the plague." He stared around at their surprised expressions. "Yes indeed! The trouble with them is that they have an unerring instinct for that moment when the ship begins to sink. They desert it without a second thought — and certainly with no regrets for chumps like me who lend them money. No, give me *soft*-headed people with moral obligations to one another every time!" He waved a happy hand promiscuously at the three of them. "They have no idea when the ship is sinking and they often set to with a will and bale it dry again. However" — a rueful note returned to his voice — "a sanitarium, which is a small hospital in effect, would be quite a *large* ship, I can't help feeling."

"In fact," Lorna said in a slow, thoughtful voice, "I think we may have overestimated the degree of Doctor Carne's responsibilities toward his wife."

The other two stared at her in amazement; in Jessica's case it was tinged with suspicion, too.

"His future responsibilities, anyway," Lorna added.

The amazement — and the suspicion — increased.

"What on earth makes you say that?" David asked.

Lorna drew a deep breath and said, in as matter-of-fact a tone as she could manage, "I had a little chat with Mrs Carne the other day — last Sunday, in fact, while you and the children were ..."

David interrupted her. "You spoke to Estelle? She never said a word to me about it."

"No," Lorna agreed. "She asked me not to mention it, either — so please don't tell her I've done so. But this is too important." She turned apologetically to Jessica and added, "I'm sorry, darling! It's awful for everyone when there are secrets like this among friends. But Estelle was so insistent that I ..."

"How did it come about?" Jessica asked. Her suspicions were still running high.

"I was writing a letter and I happened to glance out of the window and saw her standing on the terrace, outside the drawing-room window, in the pouring rain. So, naturally ..."

"Eh?" David did manage to slop his coffee.

Curnow cleared his throat delicately and said, "Er ... should I, perhaps ..."

Lorna waved him back into his seat, though he had made not the slightest move to vacate it. "It concerns this business," she said before turning again to David. "She'd stepped out of doors for some reason — I didn't cross-examine her. And she thought she'd locked herself out. Actually, the door was only jammed. All it required was a bit of the Sancreed brawn." She flexed a muscle — invisible to them under her stole. "I suppose she didn't want anyone to know how stupid she had been." She smiled around as if to say, 'Surely we can all understand that, can't we?'

Both Jessica and David guessed there was far more to this "trivial incident" than Lorna was telling, but they each admired the ease with which she belittled it and led on to her conclusion: "Anyway, I got her into some dry clothes and made us a cup of scalding sweet tea, and we had a cosy little chat by a roaring fire." She smiled at David. "And none the worse for it!"

"As a result of which," Curnow summed up, "you concluded that Mrs Carne's health will soon improve enough to release Doctor Carne from his present obligations and make the smaller nursing-home project possible?"

Lorna raked the ceiling with her eyes. "Oh, if only the real world could be so cut-and-dried, Mister Curnow!" There was no actual rebuke in her tone — but then there hardly needed to be. "Until five minutes ago I had not given our abandoned project for a nursing home a second thought. It is just one more 'if' among the many we must now discuss." She smiled and added, "... the *three* of us, that is. Did you mention bridge just now?"

They played two rubbers before Curnow, who won three shillings and fourpence, bade them a tactful goodnight and left them to the really difficult part of the evening. His parting words were: "I shouldn't entirely overlook Marcus Corvo's offer, if I were you. You could buy a substantial mansion for twelve hundred — far away from public houses and hôtel ballrooms — but not too far for a doctor with a motor car! But I'm sure you've thought of these things!"

"The beast!" Jessica said when, with a crashing of gears, he had left. "He sees every weakness in everything. And everyone." Then without more ado she rounded on Lorna and said, "You might have told me, dear!"

"Us!" David said.

The two women ignored him. They both knew that the ferocity of Jessica's accusation was part of a women-making-it-up ritual. It was supposed to prompt an apology from Lorna, sincere or not, whereupon Jessica would say that perhaps her anger had been a bit hasty, which would be a platform for a brief orgy of "my-fault — no-*mine*," ending in smiles and warmth all round.

For a moment Lorna even toyed with the idea of going along with it. But every thought she had had on the subject since last Sunday's encounter with Estelle had warned her against putting things off. So, after a brief silence, she fixed her eyes in her friend's and said evenly, "Do you really think so, Jess?"

Jessica felt a sudden heaviness in the pit of her stomach.

"Lor-na," David said nervously, making two words of her name. She trained that same unblinking gaze on him.

"Drop it," he said quietly.

Jessica turned to him in surprise, opened her mouth, but thought better of it and said nothing.

"Now?" Lorna asked. "Or for always?"

"Certainly for now."

"Why? So that you can ..." Her voice trailed off. There was such a powerful entreaty in his gaze that she could not go on. She concluded with a shrug. "If you say so." She turned back to Jessica. "I was probably wrong not to tell you, dear. I had no choice but to go to her — standing out in the rain like that — but ..."

"Did she really think she'd locked herself out?" Jessica interrupted.

"No, she was standing there quite deliberately."

"In the rain?"

"In her nightdress, in the rain."

"But why?"

"To attract attention, of course," David sneered.

But for that Lorna would not have said, "To end it all."

They both stared at her aghast. "Those were her exact words," she assured them.

"Oh, David!" Jessica closed her eyes and shook her head.

"But actually David could be right," Lorna admitted. "She seemed sincere enough when she spoke like that but I noticed that she made a jolly swift recovery!" She smiled wanly at David. "I think I gained a little insight into the difficulties you must battle with daily, old chap."

"Well, there you have it," he intoned lugubriously. "I have made my bed. Now I must lie in it."

It was such a bathetic statement, and so unlike him, they ought to have laughed. In fact, nobody smiled. Lorna gained the distinct impression that it had been a narrow shave for them all.

Part Two

Flights of Fancy

*T*he track to Porthgwarra branched sharply from the main Penzance—Land's End road (or lane, actually) at Poljigga; from there it snaked its way southward for the best part of two miles to a dead end at the head of the cove, a hundred yards or so beyond Porthgwarra Cottage. The final mile, from Ardensaweth by way of Rôskestal, was steep and winding — and, Lorna soon discovered, it was liberally spattered with cowpats, too. She milked the steering wheel from side to side and prayed. The skies had rained almost solidly all that first week in December, and several times she almost failed to make one of the turns. By the time she drew to a halt in Theo Foster's drive, she was shaking like a blade of dry grass. She switched off and sat at the wheel for a moment, listening to the ping of the cooling metal and the hiss and pluck of the sea, while she gathered her nerves and thoughts. It was going to be a difficult little chat — or so she hoped, or it would be no use at all — and she didn't want to start it all in a flutter.

"Hallo, Jess!" Foster called from his front door. It was an understandable error on his part, since the car was Jessica's and Lorna had never come alone before.

"Only me, I'm afraid!" She heaved herself from the driver's seat and gathered the basket of goodies from the back. His chest medicine, the ostensible purpose of her visit today, was in her handbag.

"Oh, you are all so kind to me," he called. Then, when he saw her coming up the side path, looking decidedly pregnant by now, he beamed and raised his hands in priestly benediction. "Ah, fecund Mother Nature!" he intoned.

Lorna grinned wryly. "That's pretty close to what *I* feel like calling the old girl at times," she said.

"My dear young lady!" He pretended she had embarrassed him; his gasp degenerated into a hacking cough.

She put down the basket and helped him with a hearty slap on the back. "You shouldn't be standing out of doors like this," she said.

She admired his dressing gown, all the same, and would have had to agree, if pressed to the point, that its heavy silk brocade was more than adequate for this mild, if damp, Cornish day. And his head was sensibly covered, too — by a smoking cap of black velvet, richly embroidered, and embellished with a gold tassel. "No Jess?" he said as he followed her indoors.

"Are you heartbroken?" she teased. "Won't I do?"

"Admirably, admirably," he replied.

Mrs Pengilly, his housekeeper, came from the kitchen and relieved Lorna of the basket. She was a large, square-bodied countrywoman with a weatherbeaten shine to her face. "There's a cold starry-gazey pie on top," Lorna warned her. "You could heat it up for the professor's supper tonight." She took the cough mixture from her handbag as the housekeeper returned to the kitchen.

"Starry-gazey pie!" Theo cried happily. "The astronomer's delight, I presume? I can't wait to see what it is."

"It's fish," she began.

"No — don't tell me. When I say I can't wait, I mean, of course, that I can. Quite easily."

He ushered her down a short passage to his den. Porthgwarra Cottage was a "cottage" of the artistic rather than the humble-peasant type; in fact, it was a substantial little granite farmhouse with outbuildings and a barn. But, like many a genuine cottage, it had a privy in the back garden and a zinc bath hanging on a nail outside the scullery door. So the name was not a complete fiction. "Indeed," Theo was wont to say, "like everything Cornish, it is, in fact, half true."

As he closed the door behind him he said, "I see you cannot help admiring my dressing gown."

"Not to mention your smoking cap," she added, handing him the cough mixture.

He gazed at it with distaste and slipped it into his pocket. "Can you have a little tipple without turning that … *thing* in your tummy into a chronic alcoholic? What would it be at this stage — a little fish with gills? An amphibian? An early land vertebrate? One *shudders* to think! What's the rule? Ontogeny recapitulates phylogeny, I believe. But you young people these days know all that sort of thing backwards."

"A small madeira would probably do no harm," Lorna conceded.

"Take you at your word," he said, pouring her half a glass. As he passed it to her he rubbed his other hand over his magnificent dressing gown and said, "It once belonged to Friedrich Nietzsche, you know …" His voice trailed off. He suffered a moment of seriousness and stared out of the little window.

It was very dark in the den, which made his dressing gown seem even more magnificent. It almost glowed.

"Poor fellow died twenty years ago," he went on as he turned to her once again. "Yet it seems like only yesterday."

"You met him?" Lorna asked.

He nodded and fished out his bottle of cough mixture, which he then uncorked and held up to her as if it were a hip flask. "Cheers!"

He downed a good half-mouthful while she took a dainty sip of her glass, not knowing how long she would have to make it last. He pulled a face. "It's worth getting better not to undergo a 'cure' like that! You know of Nietzsche, Miss Sancreed?"

"Not his philosophy," she told him, "only his private life. I looked it up once to confound one of our teachers — an odious man." She shuddered theatrically. "The teacher, I mean. Nietsche was rather sad, I think."

He sat down, recorked the medicine, and took up his own glass, which was generously filled, and said, "Tell me more about your odious teacher."

"What is there to tell? He said there can only be one master in any household — that when we girls grew up and married we should be dutiful wives and defer to our masters — that we must not be surprised if our masters smacked us on our botties from time to time, enough to sting and make us cry but never enough to hurt. It was a sure sign of their love. And we would find the bodily glow which followed such chastisement would transform itself into the glow of love in our own hearts, too — and so, you see, all was for the best in the best of all possible worlds."

He chuckled. "I take it such instruction did not go down too well among you?"

"Oh, some of the girls thought it was wonderful. They couldn't wait to be chastized and come out with glowing hearts and botties. Some women will do *anything* for love."

"And what became of him, I wonder?"

"Actually, he was carted off to an asylum. They caught him running naked down Lemon Street in Truro at two in the morning."

There was a faraway smile on her face — rather savage — but he could not even guess whether it was at some contribution of her own to the man's fate or simply at its poetic justice. "Nietzsche also ended his days in an asylum, you know," he said. "He made the mistake of living with a young Russian girl half his age and almost twice his intelligence — which, in his case, is saying something."

"That's right!" Lorna sat up, her interest suddenly kindled. "Lou … something. I've forgotten …"

"Lou Andreas-Salomé. And yes, I did know her, too. But not when she was with dear Friedrich. She became Rilke's mistress and then Freud's — or his close friend, anyway. I met her in Paris before the war. She was practising as a psychoanalyst then. She probably still is. Rilke's there, too, living with some little orphan-waif. He plays father to her one day and lover the next ..."

Lorna stood up abruptly and shook both fists at the ceiling. A strangulated cry of frustration escaped her lips.

"Are you all right?" he asked in alarm.

"Yes!" she insisted. Then, "No! I don't know. Oh God — all those bright, intelligent people ... *out there*" — she waved her hands vaguely southward — "living their wonderful, chaotic, *packed* lives! What's wrong with *me*? Why aren't I there among them? Why did I tie myself to a man I hardly loved and make him give me a baby I didn't want ... and why am I now ... aargh!"

Her cry of baffled rage drew forth echoes from an old upright piano in the corner. When they, too, had died, Theo said, "You seem to find it difficult to frame an actual question about your present acts of lunacy. I take it that was the general drift?"

She sat down and laughed, not entirely humorously. "It *heaps* me," she said simply. "I just couldn't bear to hear of all those rich and complicated lives going on out there. I'm sorry."

"Don't be. Speaking for myself, I wouldn't give the steam off my shaving water for any of them. And I'd rather face a thousand years in purgatory than exchange lives with a single one of them. Whereas you ... may I call you Lorna?"

"Please!" His suggestion filled her with pleasure though she could not have said why.

"And do call me Theo — think of it as a concession to my second childhood. Where was I? Oh, yes — you and Jess and David could easily fill me with rage."

"Rage?"

"At the thought that you'll outlive me and I shan't know how it all turns out between you. Are you a little more composed now?"

She grinned, slightly sheepishly, and nodded.

"Composed enough to have another go at lifting the lid on your present dilemmas for me?" He smiled accusingly. "I presume that's why you came here today."

She dabbed an embryonic tear from her eye — a tear of gratitude, really — and launched into an account of all that had happened since her arrival at Rosemergy. She left out nothing, not even her single adultery with David at Land's End that day. Her account concluded with the Curnow dinner at which all their projects had been thrown back into the melting pot.

"But that was almost a month ago," he protested. "Something must have happened since then, surely?"

"Nothing of importance."

"I presume you told Corvo you wouldn't be selling the property? What did he say?"

"He took the news calmly enough. He said 'All's fair in love and war' — whatever that means."

"It means war."

She frowned in disbelief.

He nodded to assure her. "It means he'll stop at nothing."

"What a fool!" she said dismissively. "And Ben Calloway has twice told me — oh, I forgot to say — I've been an acting barmaid at the Mouse Hole since then! Twice. Which is why he told me twice — that he's very glad we're not selling up to either of them."

Theo's eyes twinkled. "And you have the cheek to sit there and envy poor Lou Andreas-Salomé her dreary succession of inadequate lovers and her even drearier succession of neurotic patients! Shame on you, Miss! Your life is ten times richer than hers."

"Yes, shame on me!" She hung her head in penitence. "Anyway. That's all that's happened."

"Have you seen Estelle Carne again?"

"Several times. Several times a *week*, in fact. She's taken to her bed once more. I bring her little snacks. We discuss interiors, decorations, and recipes. She quite likes me, I think."

"So you are slowly gaining her confidence. That can do no harm. *Slowly* is the operative word, of course. Have you asked David why Estelle should hate poor Jessica so?"

"He avoids me like the ... no, he avoids being alone with me in situations where I might be able to ask him."

"And Jess herself? She has said nothing?"

"It intrigues her that Estelle has apparently taken a liking to me."

"Yes — how does that make you feel? There you are, sitting at the bedside of a woman whose husband you have ... *known*, let us say. D'you ever think about it?"

Lorna's shrug was almost one of guilt. "Of course I think about it — but it arouses no feelings in me whatever. Am I morally dead? I mean, it was fun ... I suppose? No, I mustn't downplay it. It *was* fun. But it wasn't a step in any particular direction. It wasn't the first step of *anything.* D'you see what I mean? That's why I don't feel particularly stirred by the memory of it when I'm with Estelle. God!" She suddenly grasped handfuls of her hair and pretended to tear them out. "Listen to me!"

"What?" He laughed.

"If *I* ever really loved a man — the way I truly loved Philip at the beginning — but if I loved a man like that for *ever,* and I had to sit and listen to some other woman telling me she'd ... *known* him like that — and really, darling, it didn't mean a thing! — I'd tear her limb from limb! I'd understand her — because after all that's just how I feel about my one time with David — but I'd still want to kill her very, very slowly. That's not sane, is it."

He laughed again, as if he thought her outburst had been no more than an interesting digression. "D'you think Estelle might feel like that if she ever found out?" he asked.

Lorna leaned toward him, eyes bright. "I think she *does,* Theo. Not about me but about *Jess!*"

"You think she suspects there's some hanky-panky between Jess and David?"

"No." Lorna shook her head and swallowed heavily. "It's something to do with Ian. You should see her twitch when his name is mentioned!"

"Ah — hanky-panky between Estelle and Ian, then!"

"Theo," she said solemnly. "Don't."

He grinned, for he knew very well what she meant. "Don't what?"

"Trivialize it like that. This is something much deeper than mere hanky-panky. I don't know what happened between them — or whether anything happened at all. Physically, I mean."

"Spiritual canoodling?" he suggested.

"You're determined to belittle it, aren't you!" she said crossly.

He chuckled. "No, my dear. I simply see these dreadful cross-currents and murderous emotions for what they are. It's *you* who are in the dock — all you young people."

"On what charge?"

"You are charged with giving your passions an importance they cannot possibly bear. You are building houses on sand. Even worse — for the sand is in the top chamber of an hour-glass." He smiled sadly and said, "There now!"

N ow that Lorna's condition had become obvious, it posed a delicate problem to the worthy citizenry of Penzance. In the dear dead days before the war such a situation had been managed discreetly, so that people were never actually confronted with it. Pauper and indigent females were incarcerated in a home for wayward girls; if they were dimwitted into the bargain, they could be certified and held in a lunatic asylum — where many lived on into their old age, becoming steadily more demented until at last they justified the original certification. Girls from better-off families were sent to "convalesce" abroad or to visit their relations in the Celtic fringes of the kingdom. Many a gamekeeper's lodge or ploughman's cottage had its little cuckoo, dressed and educated out of a weekly dole from the lawyers to the shamed family. Girls in that "interesting condition" were thus kept out of sight; and if they were also half out of their minds most of the time, they were wholly out of mind to the populace at large. They certainly did not parade their condition about the town, day after day, as if nothing were amiss, greeting all and sundry with a shamelessly cheerful, "Good morning!" and ever-ready to issue a brief medical bulletin.

But that was Lorna's way.

It was not easy to know how to respond to such behaviour, which, though never provocative, was always provoking. One could not forget that the father of her baby-to-be was a war hero in a minor way — nor that he had died as a result of the same accident that had killed one of the town's greatest war heroes, the much-revered Squadron Leader Lanyon (whose name had at last been added to the war memorial). Also, Miss Sancreed herself was staying under the roof of that same hero, the dearest friend, it seemed, of his widow. Also, the Sancreeds were a respected local family, even if they had quarrelled with their daughter — and who could blame them? Also, she was rich enough in her own right not to care, one way or the other. It was very hard to cut somebody who was, in any case, not in the least bit dependent upon your continuing goodwill. Also (and one should not forget the fact) it was even harder to cut a person who might one day be in a position to take her revenge for it.

Yet, on the other hand, if one returned her greetings and offered sympathetic small-talk, just as if she had that all-important ring on her finger, what sort of example did that set to the other nubile spinsters in the town? How long would it be before one heard the dreaded words: "Miss Sancreed did, and nobody seemed to object very much!" Young girls these days! One could no longer tell them that they simply didn't know what they were talking about and that their father knew best; they *did* know what they were talking about, alas (often in distressing detail, though God knows where they picked it up), and their father was usually the very *last* person to know — best or worst.

In Lorna's case the resultant force of all these fine-tuned arguments was a good old British compromise, acceptable to all but satisfactory to none. Few actually cut her stone dead — walked past her as if she were not there, or spoke to Jessica as if Lorna were invisible at her side. A slightly greater number were willing to acknowledge her formally — with an unsmiling nod of the head or even a murmured "herrm-herrmph!" — but they refused to engage her in any conversation and would ostentatiously leave any group that she joined. But the greatest number by far maintained a cool reserve, putting her, as it were, on social probation. They wished she would do the decent thing and hibernate until it was over (and, of course, make arrangements with the wife of an obliging ploughman or gamekeeper); they did not enjoy having to choose between apparently supporting her or openly cutting her; but, since she remained in the community, making the choice inevitable, they grumbled and put up with it. Worse things happen at sea.

A brave few went out of their way to be cordial. They, in Lorna's view, made up for all the rest. But there was also a zealous fringe of Sister Annas (as she called them, because they were always wanting to "carry the bannas") who took her up as a Cause. She had sufficient strength of personality to freeze them out in a matter of weeks, however; and they, as is their wont, soon adopted another Cause to champion to death.

The greatest surprise was Ben Calloway. Lorna looked out of her bedroom window one morning and saw him with a surveyor's tape, measuring between various points in his car park. Then she realized that he was measuring some of them for the third time, and it suddenly struck her that he was, in fact, waiting for her to come out — as she often did at around nine in the morning, after helping the children get off to school. There was always something in bloom in Rosemergy's gardens (at the moment it was winter jasmine and some old sweet william that had been thrown out of a window box to die and hadn't), and she like to pick a sprig or two to brighten her dressing table.

So out she went, secateurs in hand, so as not to disappoint him. She noticed that the laurustinus, which had been putting out little white blossoms fitfully ever since her arrival, had now, in the week before Christmas, decided to cover itself in snow. Since it was growing right against the fence by the Mouse Hole car park, she made straight for it.

"Good morning, Ben!" she called out. "I think this is the only white Christmas we're likely to see this year, eh!"

He dropped his tape, picked it up, dropped his notebook, picked that up, wiped it across the seat of his trousers, and tried to stuff it in his breast pocket, though even at a distance she could see it was far too thick. All this he attempted while he walked toward her. His face was even paler than his trade had bleached it. He kept licking his lips and trying to smile. Time and again his eyes met hers, conveying a mute plea of some kind, and slid away into vacancy. No child forced onto the infant-school stage to speak his recitation ever looked less willing than Ben as he closed the twenty or so paces that separated them.

"Good morning, er, Lorna." His voice stabbed at the musical scale like a singer hunting for the right key.

"Re-planning your extension?" she asked.

"No. Or rather, yes. That is, there won't be an extension."

"But that's no reason not to plan one, eh?" She laughed.

"Lorna ..." He spoke while attempting to swallow, and then tried again. "Miss Sancreed?"

Her heart went out to him. How could she help? If humour didn't calm his agitation, what else was there? Something direct. "Calm yourself, Ben. It's only me!"

"May I ... that is, please take this in the spirit in which it is ... I mean ... oh dear!"

"You'll be needing a relief barmaid over Christmas?" she suggested, thinking she was being humorous again — but quite prepared to learn she had guessed correctly. One never knew what Ben might find embarrassing.

"No. I mean, yes, it would be very ... you would always be very ... but that's not the point I'm ... er ..."

"... struggling to make? Then stop struggling, Ben. Just make it. The very worst that can happen is that I'll never speak to you again — which is a promise that half the people in Penzance would love me to make to them!"

"Ah!" His eyes lit up. "That's it. That's my point, you see. And the thing is, it must be pretty beastly for you. I've been thinking about it. Honestly — I could go out and shoot some people!"

"Ben!" She was half amused — and half alarmed, too, for there was an odd sincerity in his words.

"I could," he asserted more boldly.

"Well, bring me a list and I'll see. There are some I wouldn't miss. We'll take a vote on it. That'll make it legal."

He laughed and she saw his eyes water a little. He looked out to sea and sniffed. "Oh, you are so brave! You smile through everything, Lorna. You make a jest of every adversity. But why should you have to? They aren't worth the dust you walk on."

She snipped a delicate white panicle, including two dark, glossy leaves, and handed it to him. "Have a buttonhole," she said. "You can out-vulgar Marcus Corvo now."

He took it as if it were gold — and frankincense and myrrh; he pretended to sniff it but she saw him brushing it against his lips, too.

"You didn't walk all this way just to tell me about this week's murders," she said accusingly.

"How *can* you be so cheerful?" he asked.

She shrugged and said, "Needs must ... you know."

"Well, that's really what I wanted to say, Lorna. Needs mustn't — at least, they don't *have* to." After briefly achieving a measure of calm, he was now becoming agitated again. Before it could rise and overwhelm him he gabbled, "So may I humbly offer you the protection of my name?"

For a stunned moment she couldn't believe he had actually spoken those words. They echoed on in her mind ... the protection of his name ... the protection of his name ... until they suffered a curious reversal of meaning and it seemed he was asking her to protect *his* good name.

"I know I'm only a publican," he was mumbling, "and many would say there's little enough protection in ..."

"Ben," she said at last.

He stopped and waited.

"Are you proposing marriage to me?"

He closed his eyes and nodded. "In name only, of course." He flushed bright red and his voice began to tremble. "I would not expect you to ... I mean *us* to ... I'd not demand ..." His eyes pleaded with her through two shimmering pools of tearwater, though no tears actually rolled as yet, and his voice was all over the place.

"Oh, Ben!" It broke her heart to see him so distressed. "My dear! You are such a *good* man. If only you knew how unworthy I am of this ... this ..."

"You'd have your own room," he said. Desperation added the boldness that had been lacking earlier, for he could hear her working around to a refusal.

"That's not ..." She hesitated, caught between her original intention, which was to say that that wasn't what she was talking about, and a new one — to say it wasn't important.

He leaped into the gap. "I know. It's not the point. It's like discussing the wallpaper when you haven't built the house. The point is that here beats the truest heart in England, Lorna, and the most loving heart for *you* that you will ever meet. There is nothing I will not try if you ask it, nothing I will not do to win you to me ..."

"Stop, Ben, please!" She put her hands to her ears. "You don't know me. You honestly do not know me. I have already destroyed one good man ..."

"You don't know what you're saying," he interrupted angrily.

"Very well." A weariness crept into her voice. "I exaggerate. I'm trying to turn you against me. I didn't actually destroy Philip. But I certainly didn't help him by bringing him to live with me, by making him my idol, my god almost — just as you are trying to do with me ..."

"But I'm not ..."

"Listen! Just hear me out. I'm sure I hastened his death by forcing him to give me this baby."

He flapped his hands as if he could swat her words in the air. "You don't know what you're saying. You're still trying to turn me against you. But you can't, Lorna. It would be like" — he looked about desperately for inspiration — "like the sea trying to dry the sand!" He laughed that he could come out with anything so poetic and at the same time so apt. In case she did not grasp it, he explained: "All my adoration comes from you. How can anything you do diminish it?"

"Don't tempt me!" she said ominously.

"Impossible!"

That smile of supreme confidence tipped the balance for her. "Listen," she said again. "I *know* how great an honour you do me with this mad, absurd, *noble* offer. I'm sorry if I've stirred these feelings of love within you, but I *know* how unworthy I am of receiving them. I know, too, that I should ruin your life if I accepted your proposal, so be assured now that I never shall — just as I am sure you will one day find a woman who is truly worthy of you." Then she drew a deep breath and added, "However ...!"

New hope kindled in his eyes, so that she had to steel herself to go on: "If you'd like to go to bed with me from time to time ..."

He turned on his heel and strode away.

But, after no more than ten paces, he reversed himself and came back. His face was white with rage. "I am not shocked!" he barked.

"Good," she said. "You'll think it over then?"

"I am not shocked," he repeated.

He said it a third time: "I am not shocked. I know you are still trying to turn me against you. What terrible cruelties have given you so low an opinion of yourself I cannot even guess. But I know you are wrong. I know you are one of the finest, rarest, most beautiful women who ever lived — beautiful inside as well as outside. I shall never cease loving you. Nor will I ever withdraw my offer. Every time you see me, Lorna, think of that. My very existence renews my pledge to you." He turned and walked away, all his anger quieted again.

"Well, my offer remains open, too," she called after him. "I'd enjoy it — and I'm sure you would, too."

"I am not shocked," he repeated in a thin, tight voice.

*J*essica watched Lorna cutting her morning nosegay and talking with Ben Calloway in the Mouse Hole car park. His stance and the intensity of his gestures made it clear to her that this was no ordinary over-the-garden-wall chat; and the manner of their parting filled her with foreboding. By the time Lorna returned to the house, however, she was back at her writing desk trying to look as if she had not gone within a mile of the window. "You were a long time, dear," she called out. "I hope we're not running short of blossom — what with Christmas upon us?"

Lorna came and leaned against the doorjamb. "I'm just a piece of fluff," she said.

"I beg your pardon?" Jessica laid her pen down in some disquiet.

"Just anybody's piece of fluff — that's me!" She smiled and came into the room. "I think I'll traipse along to Estelle's and have my hair bobbed and shingled, too."

"Oh no!" Jessica rose to her feet in alarm.

Lorna chuckled. "That's very emphatic, Jess. Does that mean you want to be the only woman of fashion in this house? Or that you have come to regret your rash sacrifice of woman's crowning glory? How symbolic that the woman who sheared you should have chosen the name Estelle!"

"Sit down, dear. Did Ben Calloway say something to upset you?"
Too late she recalled that she had intended not to have noticed.

"He proposed to me."

"*What?*" Now it was Jessica who sat down. "What?" she repeated less emphatically.

"He offered me 'the protection of his name,' as he put it."

"Out of pity?"

Lorna shrugged. "Who can say? Probably even Ben himself couldn't tell you."

After a pause Jessica said, "Forgive my asking, darling, but — not wishing to pry, and all that ..."

Lorna shook her head. "No, I never gave him the slightest encouragement — if that's what you mean." She sniffed, for she felt her nose becoming blocked. The emotions she had managed to suppress at the time were reclaiming her in retrospect. "But that was because I knew that if I so much as fluttered one promising eyelash at him, he'd be down on his knees before you could say pax!"

"Since when? I mean, how long has he ..."

"I have no idea. From a sneering remark of Marcus Corvo's, which I wasn't supposed to overhear — or maybe I was, I don't know — I gather it was that first night I came here. You remember? I went out and did a spot of weeding — after David took me to collect my things. Apparently, Ben lost his heart to me then."

"You shouldn't mock him, dear," Jessica said hesitantly.

Lorna lowered her eyelids and a large hot tear rolled down her cheek. "I don't mock him," she said in a voice that was little more than a whisper. "I just feel so desperately sorry for him — for anyone who is so stupidly deluded."

Jessica moved until she could put an arm around her. "Deluded?" she echoed. "To be in love at all? Or to be in love with you?"

Lorna merely shrugged once more, implying that it hardly mattered.

"What did you say to him?"

Still she made no reply.

"I hope you told him you'd think it over — even if you haven't the slightest intention of accepting."

Lorna realized that Jess meant the words kindly, and sincerely, too. But they were so exactly what her own mother would have said — making a thoughtful little social grace out of what ought to be a kindness straight from the heart — that her hackles rose and she blurted out: "I told him that if all he wanted was to go to bed with me, he needn't blather on about ..."

"Lorna!" Jessica was shocked into standing up — which had the unfortunate effect of reinforcing the wise-old-woman-versus-stupid-little-miss atmosphere between them.

"He needn't blather on about the protection of his name and shooting Colonel Paget and his pals and ..."

"Lorna!" she cried again, now more agitated than shocked. "Dear me — are you pulling my leg? Was this a serious conversation?"

"I don't *think* he was serious about shooting Colonel Paget and Co. — though he did offer. The trouble is, he's so intense that you just can't tell. But he was quite serious in his offer of marriage — even *I* could see that."

"Then why on earth did you say such a cruel thing back?"

"Cruel?" Lorna collapsed in a fit of weariness. "Oh, Jess! We might as well have been born in different centuries — you and I. Cruel?"

Jessica stared at her in utter bewilderment. "But it *was* cruel, dear. One has to point that out."

"One has to point that out!" Lorna repeated mockingly. "One has to go about on tiptoes! One has to hide one's own feelings! One has to think of others, morning, noon, and night! One has to *kill* oneself in the end, I'm sure — just out of respect for others!"

"You're not yourself this morning ..." Jessica began.

Lorna looked up at her and laughed harshly. "On the contrary! I'm the only one who *is* myself ... herself ... himself, today. *You* haven't been yourself since ... since you were born, I shouldn't wonder. You couldn't find yourself inside a locked broom closet! You wouldn't even *know* yourself if you did! Who *are* you, Jess? When did you last look at one of your own emotions and say, 'I *know* you!'?"

Jessica's lips vanished in a thin line of compressed white skin. "I think you've said quite enough for one day."

"Then smack me all soundly and send me to bed."

"I would if you were half your age — which you are, up here." She tapped Lorna's forehead.

Lorna burst out laughing. "Go on, Jess!" she encouraged. "There's hope for you yet! Oh God!" Her anguish reclaimed her once again. "To be the one-eyed woman in the valley of the blind! I think I'll go out to Porthgwarra Cottage and be Theo's housekeeper. Good old Theo! I'll say one thing for him — *he* wouldn't turn down the offer I made to Ben Calloway!"

Jessica spun awkwardly on her heel and went over to the window. Never in her life had she felt as inadequate as she felt then. The trouble was that through all Lorna's harsh, disjointed outpourings she had caught a glipse of something important — a truth that had always eluded her. It seemed that Lorna spoke of — or hinted at — things she had always felt to be hovering at the very margins of her, Jessica's, awareness but which she had never been able to drag out into the light. "I realize there's no point in offering you a sedative and suggesting you go and lie down," she said in as composed a voice as she could manage. "The only other way to calm down, I suppose, is to talk it over. You said some very hurtful things just now …"

"I'm sorry."

"No, don't be. That's not why I mention it. The strange thing is, they didn't really hurt me all that much. It's as if I *almost* see what you mean — especially when you say that about being sighted in the land of the blind, or something. I've often thought you see things so much more clearly than I do — especially things about *me*. The trouble is, you're also consumed with such dreadful bitterness, so that you say sensible things in cruel ways — like telling poor Ben you'll sleep with him if that's really all he wants." She began to laugh at that.

Lorna tried hard not to join her but eventually succumbed. Soon they were both howling hysterically, but into cushions for fear that Daisy might overhear them — never mind Ben Calloway and half the Penzance esplanade.

When it passed and they had both recovered their breath, Jessica said, "I don't know about you, but I am going to have a sherry. I have never once touched strong drink before evening — except on my wedding day, of course — but … let's, eh?"

She smiled at Lorna, who said, "Gin for me. But just dip a finger in it and wipe it round the rim. Then splash in a bit of soda. Petronella says they do that with all the drunks at the hôtel."

For some reason each woman, quite spontaneously, downed her glass in one — though they had both intended to sit and savour it. Lorna licked her lips appreciatively and said, "D'you know, I'm going to save an absolute fortune on gin from now on. I'd swear that was fifty-fifty!"

"Let's put up some oilskins and go out for a walk?" Jessica suggested.

"To Estelle's!" Lorna crowed at once.

"To Newlyn," Jessica said firmly. "We'll buy some lobsters for tea."

They both knew they were really going outside so as to make it harder to shout insults at each other — so each was careful to stress how much she needed the exercise and fresh air.

Five minutes later they turned right at the front gate and sauntered past the Mouse Hole; they peeped in at all the windows but saw no sign of Ben. They crossed the road and went to stand awhile at the railings that marked the western end of the esplanade, where the Lariggan Rocks reached their stubby tails out into the sea.

"Toby once said they're like a heap of lizards," Jessica murmured. "I can't see it, I must confess."

The seas were mountainous, but the tide was low and the westerly wind carried the spray parallel to the waveline. Lorna, feeling nothing to wet her cheeks, loosened the chinstrap of her sou'wester and pushed it backward, shaking her long, auburn hair loose and free. "There must have been a storm down Biscay way," she said, closing her eyes and facing into the wind.

"Oh, if I were an artist now!" Jessica said admiringly.

"You'd paint me all in bright scarlet, I know. Hard luck, Jess! I got there first."

They set off, walking at a comfortable pace. It made conversation more comfortable, too.

"Did you *really* go and say an awful thing like that to poor Ben?" Jessica asked.

"Was it so awful? I just said the crudest, vulgarest thing that sprang to mind because I ... I mean, I wanted him to stop putting me on a pedestal and thinking I'm sugar and spice and all things nice. Anyway, he can't *possibly* want to marry me. What does he know about me? What do I know about him, come to that? Except that he's ..." Her voice dried up in reluctance.

"What?"

"He should go down and pick up one of those women round the harbour and ... stop fretting himself to death. Oh! Why do we make such a *thing* about it!"

Jessica decided it might be wiser to hold her peace.

After a while Lorna began again. "I know *exactly* the way his mind works. I spent a whole year curing Philip of the same affliction. It's so disheartening, Jess."

"What is, dear? You've left me behind, I'm afraid."

"He's one of those men who thinks that decent women aren't troubled by feelings of ... of *that* kind at all. *He's* troubled by them, of course! Slugs and snails and puppy dogs' tails! And the guilt! Oh God, the guilt! He needs me to be the pure, sweet angel because otherwise ... pfft! His whole world dissolves in chaos! Why can't we *do* something about it? Read a book! Just be honest! Something ... anything ... I don't know. Jessica? Say something, please — for God's sake?" She gave a hollow laugh.

Jessica cleared her throat hesitantly and asked, "Why did you take such umbrage when I said it was cruel of you?"

They reached a point where the dunes dipped down to open up a larger prospect of the sea. The gray winter light fell upon the shivering waters and emerged as a pale, luminous green, shining out of the heart of each wave. As they stood and watched — and Lorna assembled her answer — a large four-masted clipper scudded clear of the point at Mousehole. It was a rare enough sight these days to make them cry out with delight and linger awhile. She was carrying the bare minimum of canvas — t'gallants, a spinnaker, and a mizzen staysail — enough to let her steer when running straight before the wind.

"The last of the line," Lorna murmured.

"D'you remember when that Dutch three-master went ashore at Praa?" Jessica asked. "Were you around then?"

"I heard about it. The teetotallers in the Helston Band of Hope leading the drunken revels ... men and women gulping themselves into a stupor below the high-water line, where the Excise men couldn't lay a finger on them! Why do we lurch between abstinence and excess all the time?"

"Back to that!" Jessica laughed.

"Back to that," Lorna echoed despondently.

"You were about to tell me ..."

"I know. When you said cruel just now, you meant cruel *to Ben*, didn't you."

"Of course."

"Of course! Don't you see the implication, Jess? Damn *my* feelings in the matter! Damn the cruelty that's been inflicted on *me*! I'm only a woman — one of those quaint, self-effacing little things, you know — so sweet! That's part of my natural burden in life. But whatever I do I mustn't be cruel to dear Ben!" She laughed. "I'm sorry. I've lost the sharp edge. You should have asked me when I was angry — I could have told you then. Let's not talk about it any more."

"No — go on! You implied that you know things about me that I'm too blind to see — and I *almost* understood you."

"Oh Jess!" Lorna threw an arm around her and gave her a quick, sideways hug. "Look at me! I fondly imagine I know things about *myself* that you don't — and just *look* how happy all that knowledge has made me!"

"Ignorance is bliss?" Jessica asked.

"Something like that." She stepped out at a more sprightly pace. "Let's be constructive. Talk about our nursing home. Or sanitarium."

For a moment Jessica debated with herself whether to insist on their former line of conversation or to accept Lorna's new suggestion. At last she gave in. "I can't seem to make David talk about it. It's as if he's shut the whole idea out of his mind."

"To hell with him then!" Lorna said. "Forget it! Let's just you and I go ahead together."

"With Doctor Carmichael or someone, you mean?"

"Perhaps no doctor at all."

"But the bank wouldn't advance a penny without ..." She hesitated, realizing that Lorna's last words had a teasing ring. "What are you suggesting?" she asked.

"To hell with the bank, too. I'm suggesting a partnership — a true partnership — I mean a legal one. You and me. You throw in the house, and I'll put in the working capital. Enough to buy the beds and sheets and cutlery and kitchen equipment ... the advertising ... the staff. A thousand pounds, say ..."

"A thousand!" Jessica was shocked. "It couldn't possibly require that much!"

"Indeed it could! I'm not talking about your average seaside boarding house with kippers for breakfast and chamber pots under the bed. I'm thinking of a small private hôtel-de-luxe. We have to make two livings out of it, remember. Two families!"

"A private hôtel ..." Jessica began nervously pulling her fingers, one after the other. "D'you think we'd dare?"

"It'd be fun, Jess."

Jessica looked at her and laughed. "Yes! That's the way to look at it. *Fun!* Oh, Lorna! Why didn't we think of this in the first place? Why did we ever think David would be free enough to come in, too?"

Lorna, who had her own ideas on that subject, thought it best not to answer.

On Christmas Eve, while finishing off some quick last-minute shopping, Jessica met Lorna's mother at the corner of Causeway Head and Market Jew Street. Though Edie Sancreed was at least ten years older and now lived near Redruth, she and Jessica were no strangers. In fact, she was a Penzance girl and had taught nine-year-old Jessica at a Bible class in 1900, when Lorna had been only two. "Hallo, Mrs Sancreed," she cried out gaily. "My, you *are* looking well!" The woman stared straight through her and passed on, down the hill toward Chapel Street.

For one awful moment Jessica felt she was going to burst into tears. Realizing she had to do something fast, she thought, *What would Lorna do?* It surprised her slightly to realize that Lorna had become her standard for quick, positive action, but there was no doubt about the answer: *Attack, of course! Never stand still long enough to let them get you in their sights.* She could almost hear Lorna saying it as she stepped out to close the dozen paces that now separated her from Edie Sancreed. The woman turned and stared in alarm as Jessica fell in at her side.

For one who wished to walk fast, Mrs Sancreed had made an unwise choice of skirt and footwear, so Jessica had no difficulty in keeping pace and simultaneously talking, all without becoming breathless. To a casual passer-by they must have seemed like any two women out shopping, the older taciturn and preoccupied, the younger talking ten to the dozen.

"Perhaps you don't remember me, Mrs Sancreed," she said. "I'm Jessica Lanyon, Ian Lanyon's widow. I was Jessie Fields. You taught me Bible studies here in Chapel Street when I was nine."

She had expected the woman to break down and say *something* by now — anything at all — even a crushing, "Go away!" But not a glance did she give, not a word did she utter.

Jessica was beginning to see where Lorna's determination came from — her ability to set all convention aside when her own passions were ascendant. Then it occurred to her that she knew exactly where Mrs Sancreed was headed. Lorna had once mentioned that her father had friends in the Trinity House office down by the dock; he had most likely driven down there for a chinwag. So his wife was now a virtual captive for the full length of this street — the best part of half a mile!

"I suppose you know Lorna is staying with us now?" she went on. "At Rosemergy, down on the esplanade. You remember the house, of course." By way of deliberate provocation she added, "Two young widows together!"

Mrs Sancreed's lower lip trembled with anger but stoically she held her peace.

"She is *such* good company — I can't begin to tell you. In fact, keep it under your hat, but the two of us are thinking of turning the place into a small private hôtel."

The older woman's pace faltered and then picked up again.

"We think it will provide a modest but acceptable income for the two of us — and our families, of course."

Mrs Sancreed actually stopped dead this time — and then pretended it was to look into the window of a second-hand bookshop. Too late she realized it was *that* bookshop — the one with a rather seedy reputation. She set off again, more angry than ever — but still determined not to engage in a public brawl.

Jessica realized what had just happened. Mrs Sancreed must have thought the words "our families" could only refer, in Lorna's case, to her as daughter to *them*, not as the mother of their grandchild-to-be. But surely they knew of it by now? Some damned good-natured friend or other must have told them?

"To tell you the truth," she went on, "I'm rather glad I bumped into you like this." Her tone now had a conspiratorial, mother-to-mother edge. "Lorna puts such a brave face on things but I know how keenly she feels her isolation from you and her father — and especially from you. Her baby isn't due for two or three months yet, but I know it would mean so much to her if some sort of reconciliation could be achieved by then?"

So they did know about the baby. No mother could have responded to that news so stonily if it had come as a surprise. Mrs Sancreed did not even falter in her stride. Anger entered Jessica's heart and she began to understand something of the isolation the poor girl must have felt — the sense of friendlessness that had enveloped her that Sunday afternoon as she paced the esplanade, trying to pluck up the courage to knock at Rosemergy's door.

They were passing the old Sunday School now. Jessica said, "D'you remember those classes, Mrs Sancreed — or Miss Matthews as you were when I started there? What carefree times, eh! The old queen still on the throne and the whole world at peace. I can still run through the roll-call in my mind. But where are they to answer now? Fourteen girls, twelve boys. Now we're a dozen women and only seven men. Arthur Holman, Charley James, Frank Pask, Harry Smart, Clifford Tregembo — all gone! And Willy Sampson blind for life. I can see little Franky Pask going up for his attendance prize now — he was your favourite, we always thought. What wouldn't John and Dora Pask give to have him home for Christmas *this* year, eh!"

They had reached the dock by now, and there, sure enough, stood a car grand enough to belong to the Sancreeds. A moment later Mrs Sancreed herself put its ownership beyond doubt by grasping the rear door handle. Then for the first time she spoke. "Very clever, Miss Fields," she said. "But you always were an inattentive child. I remember standing you in the corner for it once. You only ever grasped half of anything you set your mind to — and I see you have not changed. Mister Sancreed and I have no surviving connection with the young person you have invited into your home. And that is the end of the matter. Good day!"

The only feature to mar this speech was the fact that she kept glancing at the windows of the Trinity House office, almost as if she were seeking her husband's approval for what she was saying.

Jessica laughed, for the woman had unwittingly given her the perfect riposte; until that moment she had quite forgotten being stood in a corner by Miss Matthews. It was something every teacher in her life had done to her more than once. But now she not only remembered it, she also remembered why.

"You may laugh ..." Mrs Sancreed began.

"I do, indeed!" Jessica interrupted. "For I am not the only one to grasp only half the essence of the thing. You recall standing me in a corner but you have clearly forgotten why — you have forgotten the topic for your lesson that day." She saw the woman hesitate, torn, probably, between a dismissive response and an attempt to bluff it out. "It was the Parable of the Prodigal Son, as a matter of fact!" Jessica called back over her shoulder.

When she arrived home she couldn't wait to tell Lorna of the encounter. However, from the moment her mother's name was mentioned Lorna looked as if she would gladly turn Jessica to stone. She refused to laugh at any of the funny bits — which caused poor Jess to stumble and correct herself and generally turn into the world's worst storyteller.

The moment she had finished, Lorna leaped in with: "Goodness me, Jess, that was a crushing reply and no mistake! How clever you must feel!"

"Well, what was I to do?" Jessica was stung into saying. "I've known her since I was in knickerbockers. I have no cause to cut her in the street."

"Oh? That's a sentiment which she clearly does not reciprocate!" was the cold rejoinder.

"Yes, I know that now. I didn't know it then. Anyway, I shall go on being pleasant to her whenever our paths cross because — as someone *very dear to me* has revealed recently — in a small town like this, people cannot hold out against charm and pleasantness forever!"

It put Lorna back-to-the-wall.

"Besides," Jessica said, "it's Christmas!"

Lorna had to laugh at last. "Bah, humbug!" she cried, taking up Jessica's hand and brushing it briefly against her cheek. "I know you meant well, dear, and I know you weren't doing it for their sakes but for mine. But don't, eh? You have no idea what you're stirring up."

Jessica was about to reply that *that* wouldn't stop *some* people she could name, but — as she had just pointed out — it was Christmas.

The incident, however, produced a sequel the following morning, Christmas Day. They arrived home from matins to find a plain brown paper parcel on the seat in the front porch. It was addressed simply: Miss Sancreed. When Lorna saw the handwriting she threw it to one side in disgust and went indoors to put the dinner in the oven. Sarah went to help her and the two boys asked if they could go and play bowls on the billiard table at the Riviera-Splendide because Mr Corvo said they could. Jessica, alone for the moment, picked up the discarded parcel and felt its contents through the paper. It was a garment of some kind, not very large — a blouse, perhaps ... a chemise? Or ...

A thought struck her, bringing a smile to her face. "Heigh-ho — interfere for a penny, interfere for a pound," she murmured as she carried the parcel upstairs.

It was, as she had begun to suspect, a baby's christening gown — a beautiful creation in Honiton lace embellished with some of the most exquisite needlework she had ever seen. There was no accompanying note but Jessica had not the slightest doubt it was the gown in which Lorna herself had been baptized, some twenty-two years earlier — and who could say how many generations before that, for it was clearly a garment of some considerable antiquity.

She admired it for several minutes, holding it up to the light and turning it this way and that; every angle revealed some new wonder of the long-dead embroiderer's skill. At last she took out some tissue paper and re-wrapped it, enclosing it in fresh Christmas wrappings and coloured ribbons. She glued a small ticket to it on which she wrote: *From little baby Lorna to Lorna's little baby.* In place of a signature she drew a sprig of holly. When she looked at the result she wished she had not made the spiky bits so long and sharp, but it was too late now. She carried it downstairs and slipped it among the other presents under the tree.

And then Sarah rang the dinner gong.

The traditional goose, the old-fashioned capon, the new-fangled turkey — these were not for grand mistresses of the kitchen like Lorna and Sarah. They were content with nothing less than guinea fowl — three of them — their plump little bodies stuffed with yams and saffron rice, and all sent down from Fortnum and Mason's in London at Lorna's expense. It was, she said, her thankyou to her new-found family. By the time they were brought to table the aroma had made everyone, even the two cooks, mad with hunger and the boys' hard-learned manners were put to the severest test.

The wine was an '08 Montrachet just at its peak. At Lorna's suggestion, and against some resistance from their mother, the boys were allowed a thimbleful at full strength — so that they should learn the taste of a fine wine.

They pulled the most wretched faces and Lorna told them that's what was meant by "an acquired taste."

Sarah was allowed two thimbles, to drive the lesson home; then it was diluted four to one — to teach them to be grateful they weren't little French boys and girls, who had to drink it like that every day of the year.

They toasted Absent Friends, which was the only solemn moment of a meal that otherwise steered the usual course between boisterousness and anarchy.

When he saw the rice stuffing being ladled out of the birds, Guy recalled a story Mr Salford had told him about when he'd been a night-chef at the Savoy and had served up some quails stuffed with rice, prepared by one of the day-chefs. The compliments simply flooded back from the dining room all evening, so Mr Salford had come on duty early the following day to ask the day chef what his secret might be. "And the day-chef was horrified," Guy concluded with relish, "because he'd put the quails out for throwing away. The little white things weren't rice grains, see, they were ..."

"Guy!" Jessica shouted, getting the point of the story in the nick of time. "How *can* you tell such a disgusting story in the middle of such a wonderful dinner! I simply do not understand you!"

She could not understand Sarah, either, who had certainly grasped the unspoken point of the story and had accepted it with a sort of amused tolerance. Of course, it was a *chef's* story, so she'd have to be all professional instead of all girlish about it!

Guy giggled happily, for to him, naturally, his mother's words were high praise.

"What?" Toby complained. "What was it? I don't understand."

"No!" Jessica roared, levelling a finger at Guy as if it were a twenty-inch gun. "You *dare!*"

"What?" Toby went on whining.

"He'll tell you later, dear," his mother said firmly, not taking her eyes off Guy.

Lorna waited until they started clearing the plates for the main course. Then she said, "We used to have the most dreadful names for dishes at school — mostly puddings, for some reason." She glanced briefly at Jessica, who saw a certain devilish glint in her eye.

"Like toad-in-the-hole and spotted dog?" Jessica suggested heavily. "I *hope* that's the sort of thing you mean, dear?"

A moment later she saw her mistake, for she had given Lorna precisely the peg she needed — it was as good as permission, in fact.

"Exactly that sort of thing," Lorna replied cheerfully. "There was Mishap-in-the-Alps — that was strawberry jam on semolina. Then there was The Boers' Last Stand, which was chocolatey sort of lumps. And a really *frightful* suet-and-jam-roll, boiled in a cloth, which gave it just the right sort of g r a y, s l i m y skin." She dragged the words out with relish. "Guess what that was called!"

She avoided Jessica's eye all this while, but Jessica knew this was some kind of obscure punishment for speaking to her mother the day before. *She is just a child,* she thought sadly. *She hits out at the world, just like a child.* After that she could no longer be angry with her.

"Drowned Man's Leg!" Lorna said with piratical relish.

The children rewarded her with all the expected cries of happy horror and then drew the curtains for the ritual of the flaming plum pudding — or *pouding au raisins de Corinth flambé,* as Sarah called it.

When it was all over, and they had pulled the crackers and put on the funny hats, they left the wreckage of the table exactly as it was and went through to the drawing room for the best of the day's rituals — the opening of the presents.

It had always been Jessica's habit — or, rather, Ian's — to untie the ribbons carefully and gather the coloured paper wrapping in neat piles so that they could be ironed flat and used again for birthdays or for Christmas the following year. Today Guy, as the man of the house, sat cross-legged beneath the tree and handed out the presents, beginning, as always, with one for his mother. "For Mummy with love from Sarah," he read.

Jessica said all the usual things as she took it — "Why dear, how lovely! I wonder what it can be?" — rattling it and feeling it through the paper. Then, without pausing for thought, she tore the wrapping off and found, to no one's surprise, a handkerchief with a beautifully embroidered JL in one corner. Her exclamations of amazement and gratitude fell on deaf ears; the children were all staring at the scrabble of paper as if *that* had been the real present and she had wantonly destroyed it.

"Don't you understand?" she asked them, flicking her fingers at the torn paper. "This is its brief hour of glory. Beautiful, frivolous paper like that *hates* being ironed flat again and stuck away in a drawer for months."

She grinned a challenge at Lorna — and only then did she fully understand that she had done it to spike Lorna's guns, feeling sure that if she had insisted on sticking to Ian's rules, Lorna would have subverted them anyway. It occurred to her then to wonder which of them would win a most-like-a-baby contest.

Toby got a fort and some lead soldiers. Guy got a clockwork car with front wheels you could steer — "And if you put sand in the works, you can make it sound *just* like Uncle David's," Lorna assured him. Sarah got her first set of real artist's water colours and a block of real John Sell Cotman paper, which looked like bleached elephant hide. These were from their mother. To Toby, Lorna gave a war-surplus periscope, as used by our gallant boys in the Flanders trenches. It had a cross-hair in the sight lens so he could pretend to be a sniper, singling out his victim; he spent the rest of the afternoon killing off his family and its pets while himself remaining out of sight round corners and behind the sofa called Hill 61. To Guy she gave an old-fashioned stereoscopic viewer and a bundle of fifty-year-old views of "the Orient," which turned out to be Egypt and the Holy Land; he spent the rest of the afternoon giggling at the stereoscopic illusion and the extraordinary things people used to wear, which had never seemed real to him until now. To Sarah she gave a first edition of *Mrs Beeton*, published in 1861; the girl spent the rest of the afternoon reading, perversely, not about crimped salmon and beef à la mode, but about the duties of a lady's maid, a between-maid, a mistress ... and the proper organization of a coach-house and stables.

Jessica could hardly contain her impatience for the moment to come when "baby Lorna" was handed the puzzling present — apparently from herself to her baby. The effect was dramatic. Lorna twigged at once that this was the parcel she had tossed aside so contemptuously in the porch after church, but it was obvious to Jessica that she had no idea what it might contain.

When she opened it she was visibly shaken. She gave out a little gasp, swallowed heavily, and blinked rapidly, several times. She lifted it out and held it up with an air of disbelieving reverence. Sarah declared it was the most beautiful thing she'd ever seen and even the boys were slightly in awe.

"Well?" Jessica prompted.

Lorna breathed in deeply and her whole attitude and expression hardened once again. "Call *that* a fatted calf!" she said in disgust.

All the same, Jessica saw her creeping downstairs to iron it just before midnight — when she must have thought the rest of the household fast asleep; and she had never seen Lorna with an iron in her hand before.

*B*oxing Day was gray and still. Lorna said it would make you feel you had a hangover though you knew you'd drunk nothing. Even the sea had a hung-over look — dead calm, slick, and oily. The six-inch wavelets it flipped lethargically at the rocks and sand were mere tokens — the ocean on tiptoe, trying not to wake anyone who might be hung over. The steady background roar of the waves was so constant at Rosemergy that it was taken for silence; thus a rare, genuine silence like that was unnerving. The milkman's horse clip-clopping along the esplanade, and the clink of his bottles when he drew to a halt, jangled the nerves. A dog's sudden bark made one jump. The shrieking gulls, always savage and deceitful, seemed bent on a raucous vendetta to drive every last human out of their world.

So when Jessica suggested a mid-morning walk to the Jubilee Baths and back there was none of the usual "Do we have to?" and "Can't I just finish this?" with which children try to sabotage the arrangements of the grown-up world. It was as if they each unconsciously realized they had to see the sea whose voice was so unnaturally stilled. When they reached the esplanade the boys took off their shoes and raced down the steps to make Man Friday marks in the unbroken sand; Bunyan went with them. Their sister and the two women stayed above, on the asphalt. Every now and then the sun made a fitful appearance — miles out to sea, or beyond St Michael's Mount, or above Mousehole, and once, tantalizingly, over the salt-water swimming baths, their still-distant goal — but never where they were. There was no pattern to those sudden stabs of lemon yellow; it was like strolling across a vast stage where a novice electrician was trying out the spotlights at random.

As they passed the Riviera-Splendide, Betty Corvo opened a window and coo-eed a greeting. She shook out a large yellow duster and, as if to justify her presence there, began polishing the glass. "Pop in for a drinky on your way back," she cried gaily.

Jessica called out their thanks and acceptance with a zest she did not feel. "What else can one do?" she sighed. "We can hardly claim to be busy today."

Tarquin and Augustus Corvo — two chubby city lads with white knees — slipped out of the main entrance and trotted down to join Guy and Toby at the water's edge.

"Look! They're shaking hands!" Lorna said in amazement.

"And so another of life's important little milestones is passed," Jessica commented.

"That was our first Christmas without Daddy," Sarah said abruptly.

After a brief silence her mother said, "What made you think of that all of a sudden?"

"The Corvos," she replied. "Being all together."

"D'you think about your daddy very often?" Lorna asked. She lifted an eyebrow at Jess as if to ask permission.

Jessica nodded eagerly.

"I do now," Sarah told her. "More than just after he died. I was angry when he died."

"Angry?" the two women repeated in surprise.

"You know. Like if anything gets taken off you. Also that made me ashamed, so I tried not to think about it at all. But now I can."

"I've been wondering ..." her mother said hesitantly. "Shall we all go and visit his grave on our way to Porthgwarra this afternoon? D'you think it would upset the boys? I've been avoiding making a special trip up there — but if we just dropped by on our way to somewhere else ... what do you think?"

Sarah was silent awhile and then said, "At first I thought you never went there at all. You never said you did."

Her mother found it an odd sort of answer. "Then how d'you know I *do* go there?" she asked.

The girl turned her face away, staring out to sea. Lorna, who was on that side of her, saw her lips tighten, as if she wished she had never opened her mouth on the subject. She reached down and took her by the hand. "Have *you* been going up there too, then?" she asked.

Sarah looked up at her gratefully and nodded.

"Darling!" Jessica exclaimed. "You didn't say."

"I saw the roses you planted," Sarah told her. "And those spotty-leaved things."

"Lungwort," Lorna said.

Jessica looked sharply at her. "You too?" she asked.

Lorna laughed mildly. "What a secretive threesome we are, eh!"

They all laughed, then, not quite wholeheartedly, for each in her own way knew that a certain degree of guilt lay behind their unmentioned visits to Mount Misery.

"That settles it!" Jessica said. "We'll go up there this afternoon on our way to Uncle Theo."

"Mrs Carne was there, too, once," Sarah put in.

The two women stopped dead and stared at her, then at each other.

"Mrs Carne?" Jessica repeated in disbelief. "Are you sure?"

"Quite sure. She didn't see me. It was almost dark. I waited until the taxi took her away again. Then I was afraid of ghosts."

They resumed their stroll.

"When you say she was *there*," her mother went on, "d'you mean actually at Daddy's grave? Or someone's else?" To Lorna she added, "There are several relatives of hers up there."

"No, she was at Daddy's grave. She left some flowers there, and a card. I took an empty jamjar off an old grave — full of rainwater, I mean, but no flowers — and put them in it."

"Flowers and a note — I never saw them," her mother said, more in puzzlement than disbelief.

"No, next time they were gone."

"*Next* time? How often d'you go up there?"

"I go in dinner hour from school. Don't tell them, please!" she begged. "I can squeeze out through a hole in the hedge behind the groundsman's hut."

"Every day?"

"No. Every week. Sometimes twice."

"What did the note say?" Lorna asked.

The girl shrugged. "I don't know. It was too dark."

"Pity!" Lorna grinned over her head at Jessica, as if to hint it might have been scandalous — a suggestion so absurd that Jess would never seriously entertain it thereafter. She did not explain that it was she who had moved the jamjar — after reading Estelle's note, which, though not exactly scandalous, had been a rather incautious quotation from *Julius Cæsar*: "Thou art the ruins of the noblest man that ever lived in the tide of times — Estelle."

"*Are* there ghosts?" Sarah asked.

"People who want there to be ghosts often see them," her mother replied diplomatically.

"Have you ever seen a ghost, Aunty Lorna?"

"Every day!"

"No, honestly — have you?"

"Honestly — every day. Look up there — that bright patch where the sun's trying to break through. See it?"

"Yes."

"Now close your eyes. Can you still see it?"

The girl tut-tutted wearily. "Of course I can — but only a ... shape of it. What's the word?"

"A ghost!" Lorna said. "That's a ghost of the sun. I think human ghosts are like that, too. Some people burn a strong impression in our minds so that we go on seeing them after they've died."

"Ah! Yes, I see!" The idea appealed to Sarah so much that she laughed and clapped her hands.

They had reached the bottom of Alexandra Road, where the "esplanade," without undergoing any outward or visible change, became the "promenade." Down on the beach the sands reached their arms seaward to embrace the outcrop known as Wherry Rocks. There two young girls and their mother were gathering shellfish from the intertidal band. The girls had seen the four boys approaching them along the beach and had slowly edged their way to the point where rock and sand met. They stood barefoot in the pools, their long lean legs splayed confidently out of ballooning skirts, which were tucked up into their knickers.

"Does your mother know you're out?" the taller girl shouted with jocular contempt.

"Does yours know you can talk yet?" Tarquin Corvo fired back. At ten he was two years older than Augustus and Guy and the natural leader of the group.

"Bet you've never kissed a girl in all your life," the shorter one shouted scornfully.

The three younger boys all looked to Tarquin to uphold their honour. "You're right enough there, young lassie," he replied, nonchalantly tugging at his earlobe. "But plenty of girls have kissed me. I can't keep 'em off."

The boys laughed in triumph and began drifting down the slope of the beach, narrowing the gap between the two parties.

"Smug little devil!" Lorna said.

"But polished," Jessica added in reluctant admiration. "What'll the girls say to that, I wonder?"

The girls grinned at each other and decided they had met a worthy opponent. "Got any smokes?" the taller one asked.

The four boys, fascinated by these slender, nut-brown creatures who were showing so much leg and smiling so boldly, stood in a semicircle and stared. Because they had their backs to the road, the watchers by the railings did not hear Tarquin's reply, but it involved a certain amount of pointing in the direction of the hôtel and other gestures signifying "behind" or "round the back." The exchanges finished abruptly when the girls' mother awoke from her daydream and called them angrily to her side. Tarquin saw them off with an elaborate bow which he had just perfected as one of the three wise men kowtowing to Herod in the school nativity play.

"He's his father's son, all right," Lorna murmured.

"Plus a coat of shellac!" Jessica put in. "Did you see the way he tugged his ear when he was boasting about fighting the girls off him?"

"Mister Corvo does that," Sarah commented.

"Yes," Lorna agreed, "when he's not quite sure whether ... how shall I put it? When he has cause to suppose you may not utterly, utterly believe him!"

They stood and watched the boys awhile. Tarquin had led them a little way up the beach, where they were now engaged in an animated discussion that involved scratching diagrams in the sand, laughing, punching one another, falling over in grotesque parodies of violent death, roaring in pain, and glancing furtively back at the two cocky young cocklepickers from time to time.

"I wonder why Estelle Carne went to visit Ian's grave?" Jessica mused as they set off again.

"Did they not get on?" Lorna asked. "When he was alive. Actually, when *did* she become a semi-permanent invalid? Did you ever tell me? I forget."

"They got on fairly amicably I suppose?" Jessica canvassed Sarah's opinion with a lift of her eyebrows. "Not that we mixed very much in those days. They played bridge with us twice, I think. But we were in different circles. Of course the war changed all that."

Lorna saw that Sarah had something to say, on the tip of her tongue, but then thought better of it.

"David didn't enlist in the war?" Lorna asked. "Did that have anything to do with Estelle's illness?"

"He tried to enlist but they told him to stay put. He was called away quite a lot, though. Whenever there was a big push on, we always knew beforehand, because he got called away to Basingstoke. That was when they needed extra doctors at the base hospital. Estelle wasn't at all ill in those days. In fact, she was one of the queen bees of the comforts-for-the-boys circles." She laughed dourly. "Hark at us — talking about it as if it were back in the days of Good Queen Bess! It's less than three years ago, for heaven's sake!"

"So she's only been an invalid for the last three years?"

"Less. Since just before the Armistice — sometime in the summer of nineteen-eighteen. Why?"

"Oh, I don't know. I just got the impression it was much longer. Of course, the Chief was away from the very outbreak of war, I suppose?"

Jessica nodded. "He was one of the few people in Cornwall with a pilot's licence. Naturally he came home on leave — at least once a year — and he managed quite a few passes."

Again Lorna saw Sarah draw breath — and once more decide not to speak. "So!" she said, keeping half an eye on the girl. "The mystery remains. If you and the Carnes didn't mingle much *before* the war, and the Chief was away almost all the time *during* the war, and if she took to her bed in 'eighteen ... before or after the accident?"

Jessica had to think. "More or less the same time as far as I remember. I *was* rather preoccupied with other things!"

"In which case, they can't have exchanged more than half a dozen howdedos over the garden wall. So why the flowers and the note — unless you were mistaken, angel?" She smiled at Sarah.

"There was that time you were in Scotland, Mummy," Sarah said. "Daddy's last leave before his accident."

"When he got a surprise fourty-eight-hour pass you mean?"

The girl nodded.

"What about it?"

"Mrs Carne gave us all our meals that time."

"Of course!" Jessica laughed apologetically at Lorna. "That must be it — I'd completely forgotten that." She tousled Sarah's hair. "She was very kind to you, wasn't she."

"She read us the *Just So Stories* and gave us hot milk and honey before we went to sleep."

"Yes, I remember. Shall we turn about now? We shall have to leave a bit earlier if we're going to stop off at Mount Misery *and* have Betty Corvo's 'little drinky'!" She pulled a face at the word, but made no open comment on it.

The boys had already turned about and were half way home by then. Lorna made a quick detour down to the beach to see what they had been sketching in the sand.

"Well?" Jessica asked when she returned.

"Boys!" Lorna exclaimed. "Lots of shapes like *that*." She drew a zigzag in the air.

"Lightning?" Sarah suggested.

"Something like that."

The girl stood and stared wistfully at the cocklepickers. Behind her back Lorna touched one of her own breasts to show Jess what the sketches had really shown. "And so yet *another* of life's little milestones is passed," she said.

*B*etty Corvo now had short frizzy hair, blonde for the most part, though it was redder at the roots. Her flat freckled face was dominated by a pair of bright turquoise eyes and an endearing snub nose. Her lips were thin and her daily attempt to enlarge them by drawing a different outline in lipstick was not successful — unless her purpose was to make an extremely determined mouth and jaw look indecisive; in that she succeeded absolutely.

"Drinkies!" she exclaimed as Jessica and Lorna entered the foyer. "Come on up to the Monkey Bar where it's nice and warm. We've got all the windows open down there because of the paint. Doesn't it look nice though?"

"It looks sumptuous, Mrs Corvo." Jessica took a tentative step into the transformed ground floor.

"We can look at that later. Come and get a hot toddy inside you. I gave the boys sodas before they went over to Rosemergy. What's my darling Sarah going to have?"

Jessica introduced Lorna as they mounted the stairs. Mrs Corvo said, "Charmed, I'm sure," and shook hands as soon as they arrived at the top. Then she said, "Just a mo!" and went to write something on an order pad in the bar — the one word *sumptuous*. "I like the sound of that word," she explained to Lorna. "Only it's one I always forget."

"De luxe?" Lorna offered. "Luxuriant — or luxurious, rather, opulent, palatial, stately ...?"

"Ooh!" Mrs Corvo squirmed with delight. "Write them down, there's a duck! While I pour drinkies."

Lorna obliged.

"I do envy you, Miss Sancreed," she said as she put the rum toddy on the counter beside the order pad. "I know all those words but they go in and out of my brain like butterflies."

"They've been on my mind a lot lately," Lorna confessed. "I've been writing advertisements in my head for the establishment that Mrs Lanyon and I are thinking of opening at Rosemergy."

"Eh?" Betty threw etiquette to the winds and stared at her with wide, pale eyes.

Jessica rested her drink on the bar and kept her hand around it, to hide the sudden shakes.

"A de-luxe private hôtel?" Lorna mused. "An opulent private hôtel? A sumptuous private hôtel? It's not easy to choose, is it." She smiled disarmingly.

Mrs Corvo looked from one to the other. "You're definitely not selling, then? Corvo thinks you're playing games with him."

Lorna nodded solemnly — and so did Jessica when she, in her turn, was canvassed.

"Ha!" Betty Corvo gave a single cry of delight, set down her drink with such force that half of it spilled on the bar, and clapped her hands. "I warned him! But he would do it. Men don't understand us, see? Not like the way we understand them. He thought you'd bring the deeds over next day, in case he changed his mind."

"You don't sound disappointed, yourself," Lorna prompted.

"Not a bit, pet! To me it was a barmy idea. The Riviera-Splendide is too big as it is. We're spending a small fortune on this refurbishing, I can tell you! Let's get that back before we get infected with even grander notions. Penzance is never going to be year-round, is it. Not before we're pushing up daisies — begging your pardon." She saw the spillage then and said, "Oops!"

While she went behind the bar for a cloth Jessica said, "Have you persuaded your husband to this same point of view, Mrs Corvo?"

She answered with a belly laugh. "Won't need to now, will I! Speaking personally, I blame that Petronella Trelawney. She tried to talk him out of it, too — and that's a mistake. Me on the phone and her beside him, both saying no. If you want to get a man to do something, get two women to argue against it. That's a man's instinct, isn't it, angel?" She chuckled at Sarah and pinched her cheek gently. "Love her!" she added. "She's getting so pretty."

Sarah giggled happily and said, "I'm acting in a play this afternoon."

"Yes, by heavens!" Jessica became suddenly brisk and businesslike. She finished her drink, set it on the bar, thanked Betty Corvo, and said she and her husband must come over for a cocktail one evening.

Betty said, "I meant to say — excuse a personal remark — but I like your hair like that."

Jessica thanked her, said *hers* looked nice cut short, too, and then turned inquiringly to Lorna. "Shall we be off?"

"I haven't quite finished my drink," Lorna told her. "I won't be long. Everything's ready-carved in the meat safe in the pantry. Take the lump of coke out of the potato saucepan and set them to boil. I'll be there in half a jiff."

"You know all the tricks!" Betty said as mother and daughter trotted back downstairs.

"I just want to be sure where we all stand, Mrs Corvo," Lorna told her. She took her half-filled glass and walked to the window at the back of the building.

Betty joined her and they stared out at Rosemergy for a contemplative moment or two. "You do need a car park," Lorna pointed out.

"Not for ten thousand smackers, we don't. Anyway, we could get the Richardses' place next door for a few hundred. Suit us better with the road on two sides. Don't mind my being personal, pet, but are you still going to want to go shares in a private hôtel after that swelling goes down?"

Lorna jerked round and looked at her in surprise. "You're very frank, Mrs Corvo," she said.

Betty smiled and Lorna noticed how set and determined her mouth could be, despite the misleading warpaint. "It's what you stopped back for, isn't it, Miss Sancreed? A frank look at where we all stand in this business. So I'll tell you — I'm not trying to pull the wool over your eyes. If you *really* want to start a private hôtel over there, I'm a hundred percent with you — wish you luck."

"You speak as if you doubt that we *do* really want to, though. D'you suspect we're just trying to push your husband's offer a little higher? Has he put you up to this little talky over a little drinky — to tell us not to bother?"

The woman's expression was a mixture of admiration and surprise.

It was quite clear to Lorna that no such thoughts lay behind this morning's meeting.

Betty licked her bottom lip thoughtfully; the wet scarlet pigment screamed as she surveyed Lorna coolly, weighing her up. "You won't believe me, I can see, unless I tell you why I doubt you really want to start a hôtel over there."

"It would help," Lorna agreed.

The other sighed and said reluctantly. "Because what would Doctor David Carne have to do with a hôtel, eh?"

"Why should he have *anything* to do with it?"

Betty laughed. "If you want to dig a trap to catch me, my pet, try and make it less than a mile wide, eh! You don't need me to answer that one."

Lorna smiled ruefully and yielded the contest to her. "I'd best be going," she said. "Thanks for the toddy. It was just …" She grinned and said, "… just what the doctor ordered."

"I won't offer your baby another. When is it due? Roundabout March, by the looks of things?"

"Thereabouts."

"And no wedding ring, I see."

Lorna stared at her coldly before she replied, "No."

The woman broke into a broad smile. "Good for you, pet. I admire your spirit."

Lorna, though still annoyed, could not suppress an answering smile. "Don't bother to come down," she said. She felt sure Corvo was hidden somewhere nearby and had been listening to the entire conversation. Such crass duplicity annoyed her and she wanted to hit back without seeming crass herself — for instance by saying she was sure Mister Corvo must be feeling *rather cramped* by now.

Her chance came when, as they reached the top of the stairs, Betty said, "I hope you're satisfied now, Miss Sancreed?"

"Completely, Mrs Corvo. However," she turned to her with a disarming smile, "since we are all being so terribly frank and open, may I ask *you* a rather personal question?"

"Yes?" She was on her guard at once.

Then Lorna's courage began to desert her. So, before she could dry up completely, she blurted out, "Petronella Trelawney — you mentioned her just now. How do you cope with that situation?" She patted her own breastbone. "In here, I mean."

For a moment she thought the woman was going to hit her. And, she had to admit — now that the question was out in the open — she thoroughly deserved such a response. Then, to her amazement, Mrs Corvo burst out laughing and said, "You think Corvo's been eaves-dropping on all this, don't you."

Lorna blushed.

"Listen!" She raised her voice and screamed, "Cor-vo!" pushing the two syllables almost an octave apart.

"What?" came a cry from the far end of the ground floor.

"'S'all right, I just thought you was dead."

"I bloody nearly am!" he yelled back.

"Company!" she called.

"I'm up a ladder."

"Stay there, then!" She turned back to Lorna and laughed. "Happy now?" she asked.

"Ashamed." Lorna bit her lip.

"You shouldn't be. Come and have a cup of tea." She went back to the bar without waiting for a reply.

"Just a quick one," Lorna replied, having little other choice.

"This'll boil quicker than your spuds." She drew instant boiling water from the geyser teamaker, which ignited and expired with a small explosion each time. "Every home should have one," she chanted. "Anyway, they won't start lunch till they send my two boys back here. You shouldn't ought to feel ashamed, gel. You're *thinking* — that's what. No one should ought to be ashamed of that. You're thinking the way I do — which is why I cottoned on so fast." She swirled the teapot round and left the tea to draw a minute or two. "D'you really want to know how I cope with Miss Petronella Trelawney?"

"No, honestly ..." Lorna began to splutter in embarrassment.

"Go on! You do, don't you!" Her pale eyes danced merrily and Lorna could see she was dying to tell. She shrugged.

"In the first place," Betty explained, "what would happen if she wasn't in my bed every night I'm not? D'you think it would lie empty? Not with my darling Corvo in it, it wouldn't! He'd be sniffing round every bit of convenient skirt that walked through that foyer — chambermaids, guests, guests' *daughters!* It'd be Sodom and Gomorrah up there every night. But my lovely Petronella 'ud claw his eyes out if he so much as pinched another woman's backside. I bless the day she said yes — because he never guessed what he was letting himself in for, poor lamb! We're the two jaws of a nutcracker, her and me — and we've got his ... no, let's keep it ladylike. The other thing is, she knows her place, God bless her. The day I arrive — fssst! — she's solo again. All right?" She poured Lorna's tea. "Sugar?"

"No, thanks. I think that's marvellous."

"Do you? I call it pathetic. Men! Can't go two days without it, some of 'em. Pathetic!"

"Do you ever talk to Petronella about it?" Lorna asked.

Betty poured her own tea. "What's to talk about?"

"You never compare notes?"

The woman stared at her as if she had suggested something unspeakably vile.

"I would," Lorna said defensively.

Betty shrugged. "I was wrong. You don't think at all like what I do. Still" — she grinned cheerfully — "it takes all sorts, eh? It'd be a dull old world if we all thought the same."

Lorna sipped her tea and wondered what to say next.

"There's a thing I should tell you," Betty went on. "Corvo's got lads out all over Penzance, this minute, putting up bills to say we're having a Grand Gala Ball here on New Year's Eve. Free — all welcome. I s'pose you can guess why?"

"To show off the new decorations, perhaps? Get the year off to a good start?"

She chortled. "That's what he'd tell you if you asked. Really, he's hoping for a calm night so's he can throw the windows open and show you what racket your nursing-home patients would have to put up with. He still thinks that's your game, see?" She sniffed and added, "Mind you, it'd be even worse with private hôtel guests. You can't bung them full of laudanum and thumb your noses at us! Still, it's not going to *be* a private hôtel, is it." She smiled knowingly. "That's just your cleverness."

"You saw Mrs Lanyon confirm it," Lorna replied.

The woman merely laughed.

Then her two sons returned, bursting with a peremptory message that lunch was about to be served at Rosemergy. The way Tarquin, the older lad, stared at her made her pull her coat more loosely about her bosom.

"We're going to see Guy's play this afternoon," they told their mother excitedly.

uy had seen an article in the *Illustrated London News* showing how the smartest theatres and picture palaces of the day dispensed tickets to their patrons by means of an electrical machine that thrust a ticket of the correct denomination out through a little slot in the metal counter of the ticket booth. He determined that where London led, Porthgwarra should not lag far behind. So, with a bow-drill and a padsaw, he cut a slot in the side of an old teachest; then with the help of his brother, his sister, and his mother's sewing machine — and inspired by tales of Petronella's "automatic" curtain-opening mechanism at the ceremonial unveiling of the Monkey Bar — Guy produced the equivalent for the Porthgwarra Theatre's single day of glory.

The tickets said *Received with Thanks* in violet ink on one side and *Past Due* in green on the other — stamped by courtesy of the Riviera-Splendide; they would have said PORTHGWARRA THEATRE but Guy's home-printing kit was down to only three little indiarubber Rs. Toby squashed himself into one half of the teachest, between Guy's knees and the sewing machine, and slowly fed one ticket through the slot every time Guy nudged him; he, in turn, nudged Sarah, squashed into the other half with the sewing machine, whose handle she simultaneously cranked for five slow turns.

"Goodness me!" Theo Foster exclaimed when it was his turn to buy a ticket from the wonderful machine. "After such a dramatic opening scene, the play can hardly fail, young Guy. I confidently predict, here and now, that it will enjoy a full house for the entire length of its run."

It was, too, a great success. The pirates were caught but promised to reform at the very moment when they were to walk the plank. The Prince of Wales, having at last discovered how to spell his own name properly, went on to rescue Miss Montmorency, the governess, from a house in a foggy quarter of London — also in the nick of time. By then the bemused audience — David, Jessica, Lorna, Theo, Mr and Mrs Cardew (the parents of the remainder of the cast), and the two Corvo boys — took in its collective stride a handful of extra scenes set on a South American Slave Farm. These, tacked on at the end for no other purpose than to fill out the time to thirty-five minutes, involved some gruesome whipping of wayward slaves and lots of bloodcurdling yells for a rousing finale. By then everyone was ready for the tea and saffron cake that Theo had ready for them in the cottage. The excited cast, still showing traces of burnt cork, relived its moments of glory until its mothers told it that enough was enough. And then came "blow away the cobwebs" time — a brisk, half-hour walk to generate an appetite for party games, followed by high tea. When Lorna realized that Theo was going to stay behind to lay the clues in the Treasure Hunt and other games, she volunteered to help him.

The silence that descended on the house the moment they had all gone was almost eerie.

"Children!" Lorna exclaimed with theatrical weariness.

He laid his hand briefly on her belly and laughed. "And to think — you have it all ahead of you!"

She looked down and thrust it out. "Literally!"

"See this?" He handed her a little stack of cards, fanning out the first two — on which he had written CNOAB and GEG. "They're anagrams of well-known foods — right up your street."

"Bacon and egg?"

"Proper job! They're all pairs like that. HISF and SPICH ... PRETI and INSNOO — see? Distribute them here and there around the room. Prop them up, pin them up, stick them up — just do whatever's handiest. Remember Toby has to be able to see them, too. We're not trying to hide them. They have to go round and make lists like 'Clock and Vase equals Tripe and Onions' — if that's where you stood those two cards. Got it?"

"What are you going to do?"

"Don't worry. I shall be busy, too. I always pull my weight."

"I didn't mean that!" She butted his arm with her forehead. "I meant will you be around to talk to?"

"Ah — yes, indeed! I shall be placing twelve identical thimbles in such a way as to make them visible but hard to spot. That's for the second game. So talk away!"

"Oh, Theo!" she laughed. "You're loving it, aren't you! Childhood all over again."

"Nonsense. We played games like this every day in the Senior Common Room. Hunt the thimble was a favourite." After the barest pause he went on, "It must be marvellous to feel a new little life growing bigger and bigger inside you like that. But doesn't it also frighten you sometimes?"

"David Carne says an unborn baby is really just a naturally occurring tumour of the self-healing variety."

Theo pulled a distasteful face. "They're a human sub-species, all right — doctors. Medical students are even worse. Sub-sub. But enough of this! You obviously don't wish to talk about babies — so what's next? Are you any forrarder with the mystery, or mysteries, of the Carnes and the Lanyons?"

"Oh!" she exclaimed wearily.

"Ah!" he responded happily. "I gather that means you are?"

"It gets more and more involved, Theo. Only this morning I learned that there was an occasion during the war when both Jess and David were away — when Ian came home on a forty-eight hour pass — and guess who looked after him?"

"Estelle Carne?"

"Who else! She was quite the little athlete in those days. But does that mean anything, Theo? Or ... is it just my dirty mind? I mean, am I *looking* for niggers in the woodpile?"

He pulled a distasteful face at the expression. "Must you use these awful Americanisms, woman? What's wrong with good old flies in the English ointment?"

"All right — am I just looking for good old flies in the ointment? Or is it ..."

"I presume you heard this from Estelle herself?" he interrupted. "What sort of expression did she have?"

Lorna explained how the story had come out; he listened in fascination. "What's amaremdla and stoat?" she asked inconsequentially as she finished.

"Toast and marmalade."

"Of course! Some of them you can look at for *ages!*"

"How fascinating, though! You mean Sarah let all this information fall, and Jessica was there, and ... no reaction?"

"Not a flicker. I can't fathom her at all. I'm suspicious of absolutely *everything*. Someone says to me, I love your hair like that, and I think, oh yes, what's coming next? But not Jess. The butcher overcharges her and she says, dear me, beef's gone up again!"

He chuckled. "You're a well-matched pair, then."

She did not share his good humour. "We would be if it weren't for this secret — if it *is* a secret — hanging over everything. I didn't tell you the worst yet. This forty-eight hour pass of Ian's was in the summer of nineteen-eighteen."

He saw the point at once. "Just before the accident!"

"Yes. And just around the time when Estelle Carne became the neurasthenic invalid she now is. Of course it could be all coincidence.

There may be no deep, dark secret at all. But if not, then why was David so insistent I drop it that time?"

His long silence forced her to say, "That was not a rhetorical question, Theo."

"I know. Unfortunately I can't answer you. Human affairs were so much easier before the war — before we had all these psychologists and alienists around to confuse us. In the good old days if someone said, 'I'm doing this for reasons A, B, and C,' then we jolly well knew that was why they were doing it. But now, according to all these experts on the mind, if someone says that, then the only thing we can say with any certainty is that A, B, and C are *not* their reasons at all. You see, you're a post-war person — you believe nothing and trust nobody. Jess is a prewar person — she even believes the butcher's bill! However..." He saw the exasperation in her face and went on hastily: "I realize that this doesn't help. The point I'm making is that old-fashioned speculation about events — the Sherlock Holmes approach to human behaviour — is no longer of any value to us."

"You mean we have to accept situations exactly as they are, warts and all?"

"No. That would be like going back to prewar simplicities — pretending that people meant what they said, said what they meant, and remembered every unpleasant experience. We can't do that."

"What then? God, I thought it might *help* to talk it over with you!"

"Rash female!" He pointed a tragedian's finger at her and beetled his brows. "We have to become jugglers, dear. We have to juggle five or six alternatives all the time — and be ready to pluck one of them from the circuit as and when its time has come. Or throw it aside when its time has gone, of course. Suppose, for instance, Ian Lanyon and Estelle Carne *did* enjoy one wild night of passion ..."

"Or forty-eight hours of it!"

"Steady!" He clutched at the sideboard. "At my age I can't keep a supposition up that long! One night? One hour? It makes no difference to the argument. You know what sort of man Lanyon was — a stickler for absolutely everything. He wouldn't put the marriage vows and the Sixth Commandment aside ..."

"I thought adultery was the Seventh?"

"Ha-ha!" He chuckled as if she had fallen into an elementary trap. "Are not the first two Commandments really one single Commandment? Might there not be a Missing Commandment — the True Tenth — which it is our duty to seek here on earth to the end of our days? But I stray from the point."

She stopped distributing the anagrams and fixed him with an accusing gaze. "You don't stray at all, do you! I've just realized that whenever you want to make a truly important point, you disguise it as a red herring. There *is* a Missing Commandment, isn't there — that's the lack we all feel in our lives these days."

"What's missing in *your* life, young lady, is any desirable alternative to some kind of partnership with Jess at Rosemergy. This hôtel, sanitarium, or whatever it's to be — you need an alternative to that."

She stuck her belly out again. "This?"

He shook his head. "That's not an alternative. It's a complication."

She nodded ruefully. "It's that, all right. It makes the prospect of any *other* sort of partnership rather remote."

She stared at him evenly and said, "Well?"

At length he smiled and shook his head — knowing just what sort of offer she was making. "It would work for me," he said, "but not for you. Or not for long."

She inhaled sharply and squared herself to the decision — his decision. "The trouble is, I feel myself being drawn more and more to Ben Calloway." Then, while she placed the last few anagrams, she went on to tell him of the offer Ben had made before Christmas. "Wasn't that a quixotic thing to do?" she concluded. "He really is a very good man. A very *good* man."

"Hmm." His agreement was less than avid. "Another of them! Ben — from all I hear — is a man very much in the same mould as Ian Lanyon. Lacking his quality of leadership, perhaps, but with the same moral convictions and rigid backbone."

"Is this another aside?" she remarked with an accusing smile.

"Guilty." He raised his hands in a kind of benediction as he surveyed the room. "Well now! I think we're ready for anything life may care to throw at us, eh? Even the children."

*T*he thirtieth of December that year brought one of the worst storms of the winter to the whole southern coast; it was so dark inside Rosemergy that the lights were kept on all day.

By nightfall, however, it had blown itself out and New Year's Eve dawned bright and cold, with scarcely a cloud in the sky. Half an hour later the sun rose upon a spectacular sea, as waves that had been whipped up over Biscay hurled themselves at the stone ramparts of the esplanade and promenade and rose in explosive plumes of white along the entire seafront. At times you might imagine that three or four dozen depth charges were exploding in unison, creating one long wall of white to screen the bay.

Loud as it was, it did nothing to spoil Marcus Corvo's little demonstration of the disruptive power of a modern dance orchestra. He walked across to Rosemergy at around nine that evening, half an hour after the ball officially started, on the excuse of escorting his two guests of honour back to the hôtel; his true purpose was, of course, to gloat over the racket. The band, playing in an almost empty room, was at its cacophonous worst.

"Oh! You *did* get a band after all!" Jessica said, pretending to hear it for the first time when they stepped outdoors with him. But it didn't work. "Is it local?"

"London," he replied offhandedly. "I never thought they'd kick up such a din. Thank God it'll be only twice a week in the season, eh!"

The two women realized by now that, if they did open a private hôtel at Rosemergy, the dances at the Riviera-Splendide would, indeed, pose a formidable problem. However, they weren't going to give him the satisfaction of showing it — especially when they were both looking forward to the dancing themselves.

"If only we could be sure you mean to continue, Mister Corvo," Lorna said.

"Eh?" he replied.

"If you could *guarantee* us this gaiety twice a week, we could advertise for the sort of bright young things who'd adore it."

"In a nursing home?" he asked incredulously.

"Ah ... yes," she stammered. "Stupid of me."

It left him with a thoughtful look in his eye and a smile that suggested his teeth were glued together. Clearly Betty Corvo had said nothing to her husband about the private hôtel.

There was nothing forced, however, about their expressions of amazement as they entered the ballroom — this being the first time they had seen it since its redecoration. What had formerly been a rather plain, functional sort of space had been transformed into an Egyptian palace, with fantastical columns, heavy entablatures, palm fronds, peacock feathers, and pampas-grass plumes all over the place. Spotlights over the orchestra made every instrument sparkle; elsewhere imitation flambeaux shed a discreet radiance that took five years off any woman and hid the five o'clock shadow on any man.

"Who did you get to paint murals like that?" Jessica asked in awe.

"It's all wallpaper, Mrs L.," he said with quiet pride. "I told you — like in the Monkey Bar upstairs. My pal in the Mile End Road does them. We could have had anything — Tyrolean Villa, Greek Temple, Roman Baths, Moorish Hareem, Taj Mahal ... That's the one I almost did choose, Taj Mahal. Only it had monkeys in some of the little windows, see, and I thought the monkeys upstairs was enough."

"Oh!" Lorna's voice was heavy with disappointment.

"You think I should ought to of got that?" he asked anxiously, biting his lip.

Yet again they were amazed that a man so confident and thrusting in all other departments of life should show such conspicuous hesitation in matters of taste.

"We've done up the restaurant like a Venetian Palace," he said, brightening. "You'll see it when the buffet starts. We're giving every room a different style, see?"

"Why," Lorna rejoined, "this place will be a living catalogue for your pal in the Mile End Road."

He chuckled craftily and tapped his nose. "I couldn't say there's no percentage in it, Miss Sancreed. But trust *you* to think of that!"

"The trouble with that sort of statement," Lorna complained later to Jess, "is that — on his lips — one isn't sure whether it's a sneer or a compliment. He's so ..." Her voice trailed off as she saw Jessica's eyes stray toward the foyer — and then go wide with shock.

"Wonders never cease!" Jessica murmured. If looks carried an electric charge, there would have been a blinding flash of lightning clear across the ballroom and a clap of thunder that would have obliterated the orchestra.

Lorna turned round and saw Estelle Carne on the arm of her husband. She was in a dark blue ballgown with a feather boa around her shoulders. Lorna had time to take in no more than that before Jessica said, "I shall have to go."

"Don't be absurd," she told her lightly — as if she thought Jess was, in any case, joking.

"But I thought that he would ..." Jessica broke off and sighed. "He didn't say a word about it, and I saw him only this afternoon."

"Which can only mean that Estelle has staged a miraculous recovery since then. You don't suppose he'd have kept it from you if he *had* known, do you?"

"No," Jessica admitted reluctantly. "God, they're coming this way! Don't look! Let's dance — will you partner me?"

"Jess!" Lorna gripped her wrist and squeezed hard. "Your next-door neighbours have come to the same ball as you. That's all. I'm going to *have* to be sociable. I mean *I* have no reason not to be. I don't know why you have, but that's none of my business." She turned and exclaimed in happy surprise. "Mrs Carne! How lovely to see you up and about again! That *clever* Doctor Carmichael!" She favoured David with a teasing grin.

Poor David looked even more distraught than Jessica. "I'm not sure it's wise," he said warily.

Lorna cut him short with a laugh. "He's not such a dunce himself, is he! Make dubious noises every half hour and he'll provoke you into seeing the New Year in. Isn't that the idea?" The orchestra struck up a new number. "Ah!" she cried happily. "The tango! The dance I've been waiting for. Come on, man — let's not waste it." She grabbed the surprised David by the arm and dragged him onto the floor. Over her shoulder she grinned at Estelle and said, "Just this one. You don't mind, do you?"

"I can't do the tango," he complained between his teeth. "Anyway, we daren't leave those two there."

"Kill or cure," she said. "I'll teach you. Look, all you do ..."

"You've no idea what you're interfering with."

"That's why they'll take it from me, David. They'll each be saying to themselves, 'She has no idea.' And the next thought will be, 'And she mustn't *get* any ideas, either!' And then they'll be nice as pie to each other."

"Is that the kill or the cure?" he asked glumly, though his lack of argument showed he accepted hers.

"Can you cure an infection without killing the microbes?" she asked. "Now look — you take each step as if you're going to do the splits — like so. But then you change your mind at the last minute and sort of glide into the next. And then on those staccato notes — boom-boom-boom — you imagine you're at the back of the crowd and can't see what's going on — make a long neck and spin your head the opposite direction ... like so. Stop grinning! This is fiery Latin-American stuff, David. Grim of face and staring of eye. Pretend you're fighting a passion you can only just control."

He halted in mid-stride and burst into laughter. "You're unstopp-able!" he complained, as if it hurt him to show any gaiety at all.

"Aren't you even going to try?" she asked.

"I'm an English country doctor, love. Not some Latino poodle faker." Despite his protests, however, he was allowing his feet to make an effort of some kind, and then, finding it all rather easier than he had feared, the effort became more commendable with each repeat of the basic steps.

"She's got him to do it, by God!" Estelle exclaimed — rather more loudly than she had intended. In fact, she had not intended speaking aloud at all.

It was the first remark of any kind between the two women since Lorna had danced off with David and left them marooned, side by side. It prompted Jessica to say, "She could get anyone to do anything!"

She had intended the comment in a spirit of pride, as a child might say, "My daddy can bend horseshoes straight!" But her nervousness added an unintentionally petulant edge to the words — which caused Estelle to stare at her in surprise.

Jessica forced herself to smile, then. "I'm also glad to see you up and about again, Estelle," she said. "Are you quite recovered from ..." She left the affliction unspecified.

"That has yet to be seen," Estelle replied cagily. After a pause she added, "I was sorry to have missed Ian's funeral. What a dreadful loss he was — and continues to be."

"Your letter ..." Jessica began to give her stock answer before she remembered that Estelle had written no letter of condolence. Committed now, she made her voice deliberately vague and continued: "... was a great comfort. How long ago it seems already! Four months, all but a week. Ah, well!" She sighed.

As castaways scan the horizon, their eyes sought out Lorna and David, now on the farther side of the floor.

"But for *her* I probably shouldn't be up tonight," Estelle mused.

"Really?" Jessica's surprise was twofold — first that it might be true, secondly that Estelle would admit it, true or not.

"Really," Estelle assured her. Then, with a little laugh, "Isn't it absurd — the lengths to which jealousy will drive us?"

Jessica was so busy trying to reconstruct the improbable train of thought that had led from her own white lie about a letter that was never written to Lorna's rôle in Estelle's recovery that she missed the word *jealousy* for a moment. When it did finally register she was too perplexed to respond at all.

Estelle tried again. "But then jealousy itself is an absurd emotion," she murmured.

Jessica became aware that, for some reason, Estelle wished to harp on this one point. It alarmed her, though she could not have said why — except that it always alarmed her when people tried to bend conversations into paths they had prepared well in advance. "I wish you'd convince Sarah, Guy, and Toby of that!" she said in the traditional tone of the war-weary parent. "She gets jealous when everyone keeps telling Guy he's 'the man of the family now,' because, in point of fact, she's got ten times more common sense than he has — which makes him, in turn, jealous of her. Toby's jealous of both for being older and they're equally jealous of him because his drawings and paintings are so much more admired than theirs."

And that, she thought with satisfaction, *has drawn the sting out of that word very nicely!*

The glum expression on Estelle's face confirmed it.

"At least they're talking," Lorna commented. "No, don't turn round and stare! Something much more extraordinary happened over this side of the room a few moments ago."

"What?" he asked, keeping his head fixed for fear of annoying her but swivelling his eyes about eagerly.

"It happened when I spoke aloud what I imagined Jess and Estelle must be thinking."

"What happened? I don't remember anything."

"Precisely, David! *That's* the extraordinary thing: You didn't question it at all. I hinted at dark secrets — shameful secrets? — and you behaved as if you knew exactly what I meant. Oh, damnation!"

"What?" This time the staccato beats allowed him to turn his head and he saw Dr Carmichael asking Estelle onto the floor for what was left of the dance.

"Your esteemed colleague!" Lorna said in disgust. "I'd like to steam his head!"

Jessica, meanwhile, had spied Petronella Trelawney and went over to speak with her. Petronella was back at the hôtel for one night in charge of the catering.

The dance came to an end shortly after that. David thanked Lorna and then looked about awkwardly. "There's no one to take you back to," he said.

"I'm a big girl now," she assured him. "And getting bigger every day, come to think of it! You just run along and work out with Jess and Estelle what answer you're going to give to the question you know I'm going to ask."

"You have no right to ask it," he replied.

"On the contrary, I not only have a right, I have a duty." She pointed surreptitiously at her stomach and then laughed. "Oh, you convenient little thing!" she said to the unborn child. Then, serious again: "If I'm to put money into a sanitarium with you and Jess as partners, I think I have a right to …"

He stared at her, wide-eyed. "Did you say 'sanitarium'? But I thought that idea was over and done with? What about your scheme for a private hôtel?"

She looked at him wearily. "You know very well 'what about our private hôtel'! It's a wonderful idea for keeping the vultures at bay until the three of you have resolved your differences — whatever they are. Then we can get down to some …"

"Does Jessica know this?" he interrupted again.

She shook her head slowly. "It wouldn't help." She smiled and took his arm, leading him among the dancers who were waiting for the next number to begin. "I know I must seem dreadfully machiavellian to you, but believe me, I'm not. If I thought: *Sanitarium at all costs!* and if I …"

"And don't you?"

"Not a bit. If the three of you can't resolve your … what's the word? Not 'differences.' You don't really have differences. Difficulties? Anyway — whatever it is between you — if you can't sort it all out, then that's the end of it as far as I'm concerned. Whatever scheming and plotting I may be involved in is purely to keep the world of decisions at bay — to give you three a little time to sort things out. And *you* particularly, David — to give you the incentive — which is what I hope I'm doing at this very moment."

They passed Estelle and Dr Carmichael, just as the next dance began. David smiled at his wife, who, somewhat surprised, smiled feebly back. Carmichael frowned at Lorna.

"No complaints yet," she told him brightly, patting her stomach. "I think he's going to be a dancer."

David, missing the gesture, heard only the words. Thinking they referred to him, he laughed and said, "I'll teach you to tango, Carmichael."

"I'll teach you the one-man highland fling if you try," he answered. Then, to Lorna: "Don't overdo it, now."

"That man knows all my weaknesses," she sighed to David as they walked off in search of Jessica.

"Whereas I know all your strengths," he commented ruefully.

"Just don't put them to the test," she warned.

*I*t stood to reason — to three reasons, in fact — that practically everyone at the Riviera-Splendide ball knew everyone else. First, the fly-bills had gone up only in Penzance. Second, there was hardly a tourist in the whole of West Penwith at that time of year, and the few there were tended to be bird-watchers, feminists, vegetarians, or amateur painters — people on the awkward perimeter of society, unlikely to be interested in bourgeois events like dances. And third, evening dress was *de rigueur* — which cut the likely comers down to the tail-coat-owning class.

It was therefore a very different affair from the average municipal ball, where the classes mingled promiscuously and each felt obliged to set a good stiff-upper-lip example to the others. This was more like a hunt ball or the exclusive ball of a private club, where, since there was no one to set an example *to*, people could actually unstiffen the lip and enjoy themselves for a change. It all went far better than even a born optimist like Marcus Corvo had dared hope; his pleasure at managing the Walls-of-Jericho trick with Rosemergy was augmented by his pleasure at being the popular man of the town for once.

Even Lorna, after only four months in Penzance, was pleased to realize how many faces she recognized — though the eyes in those faces did not always recognize her. She scanned each new batch of arrivals to see how many of them would let the start of a new year mark the start of a new attitude toward her — by admitting that the game of looking straight through her had become too tedious to play any longer. It did not amount to many, but at least there were none who decided to travel in the opposite direction.

The buffet was due to open at around ten, at which hour everyone would get to see what a Venetian Palace looked like, as viewed from the Mile End Road. Lorna was standing at the edge of the dance floor, chatting in a desultory way with Mr Curnow and his wife — his good lady wife, he called her, without provoking any obvious squirming on her part — when a small band of young men entered from the foyer. The sight of them, or of one in particular, gave Lorna a start, for he wore the undress uniform of an officer in the RAF. Though Philip had not been an officer, the sight of any air-force uniform always stirred her slightly.

To her surprise she saw one of the other young fellows pointing her out to him. The officer caught her eye, smiled at her as if to say, "Don't go away!" and turned to make the obligatory gestures of gratitude to the Corvos.

The banker and his wife drifted away toward the restaurant; clearly they were intent on being first at the trough. Lorna stood alone and waited.

Marcus kept up his conversation for a minute or more, though she could see from the young fellow's gestures that he several times tried to get away. From her present location he was three-quarters turned from her; she moved a dozen paces or so, to where she could at least see him in profile.

It was quite an attractive profile, she decided, with a firm chin, an intelligent brow, a wide, clear eye, but a rather flat nose. The nose was the one feature she would have changed.

When Marcus finally released him he hunted for her with his eyes, growing increasingly anxious until at last he spotted her where she had moved. He smiled then and made a beeline for her. Did that smile imply he understood why she had changed her position? The thought alarmed her slightly. She didn't want him to go leaping to all the wrong conclusions; in her experience men in uniform were vain enough already.

"Mrs Lanyon?" he asked, giving her a smile that made her forget the nose entirely. And her qualms.

She grinned. "I'll take you to her."

"Oh, I'm most frightfully sorry. Do forgive me. I was told you were Mrs Lanyon."

"You were probably told I'd know where she is to be found — which I do. But it's hard to hear oneself think in here — it is a *very* good band, isn't it! I'm Lorna Sancreed, by the way. I'm staying with Mrs Lanyon. Her house is next door."

He nodded. "I saw it. A beautiful place. And you're right — it *is* a very good band. Are you allowed to dance?" He indicated her protruding stomach with his eyes. It was a gesture few men would have dared to make. Even fewer would have been able to carry it off so easily and naturally.

"On very special occasions," she told him, lifting her arms and stepping into a gap among the other dancers.

He joined her as if the movements had been choreographed for him and led her — rather more sedately than she would have wished — into the easy steps and gyrations of the foxtrot. "I'm Bill Westwood, by the way," he said.

"Is your business with Mrs Lanyon urgent?" she asked.

"Oh, not at all, Miss Sancreed. I merely wish to pay my respects."

"Were you ever in Ian Lanyon's squadron? Is that why ..."

"No. I was in two-oh-four, but we messed together a couple of times and shared the same airfield at Vimy. I know about his death, of course. Dreadful thing. Dreadful."

"Yes." Lorna wondered how much to explain.

He saved her the bother. "I also know about Philip Morvah, Miss Sancreed. I'm so sorry."

"Thank you, Mister Westwood. I'm sure you lost many good comrades-in-arms, yourself."

He nodded. "My brother among them." After a pause he added, "And life goes on!"

She gave an involuntary gasp and danced to a halt. "I think he heard you say that!" She laughed, letting her eyes flicker briefly toward her midriff so that he alone should understand who the *he* might be.

He grasped her meaning at once. "I see the buffet is now open," he said, offering her the crook of his arm.

"And *we* are ravenous," she replied, taking it gladly. "We'll probably find Jessica Lanyon in there, too. She was near the orchestra just now but I see she's gone. Are you still with two-oh-four, Mister Westwood? Or ought I to call you Pilot Officer? I never know."

"Mister is perfectly correct. In fact, it is *entirely* correct in my case, for I was demobilized last week. These are the only glad rags I have."

"You could be arrested for impersonating an officer," she joked.

"*That* could have happened at any time during the last four years," he replied in the same vein.

"Well, never mind. I shall bring you nourishing meals to the prison every day if they do."

He looked at her sharply, first in surprise, then with pleasure. "By George, but it'd be almost worth it, Miss Sancreed!"

"And are you staying in Penzance? I'm afraid I didn't recognize any of the party you came with."

"Well, I didn't actually come with them, you know. They showed me the way. I don't know them, either — except for Frederick Jenkins."

"Councillor Jenkins's son?" Their progress came to a halt in the general crush at the restaurant door.

"Yes. I'm negotiating to buy a couple of fields from him out beside Penzance Green — on the road to Long Rock, you know?"

"I know it. It's where people see if their cars can do sixty miles an hour or if the salesman was lying."

He laughed. "Because it's so flat and straight, you see. That's why it interests me, too. I have an idea for a racing monoplane and I need a landing field with a barn for a hangar and workshop."

Lorna saw several people around them beginning to take an interest. For no reason she could name she felt angry with them. Such inquisitive busybodies! *She* was doing all the hard work ... well, easy work, actually — but *she* was getting all these interesting details out of him. Why should they eavesdrop for free? "Oh dear!" she murmured, "If the crush is like this out here ..." She left him to surmise the rest of her meaning.

Again he twigged immediately. "Thoughtless of me," he said and led her back across the ballroom, where they took two empty chairs by a card table. "Now we're thinking like good soldiers," he added approvingly. "First secure your base, then coordinate with neighbouring units! Are you willing to coordinate with me, Miss Sancreed?"

"Only if I know the objective, sir," she replied in a clipped, mock-military style.

"To put two full plates of grub on this table, of course."

"Ah!" she said. "Well, that would make a good start."

"I thought so, too. Is there anything you *dis*like — onions, fish, sausages ... that sort of thing? I have no idea what the boards are groaning with in there."

At that moment Mr and Mrs Curnow crossed the ballroom floor toward them; she was carrying her own plate, he had an extra one for Lorna. "I took the liberty," he said, placing it in front of her. "And I brought this for our gallant aviator." He set the other down before Westwood's chair — or the chair whose back he was holding.

Mrs Curnow's surprise, though swiftly masked, gave him the lie.

"Very kind but wouldn't dream of it, sir," Bill said as he left them.

Over his shoulder he called, "I'll be back in a brace of shakes. We'll do the introductions then."

Lorna watched him all the way to the restaurant door, which was now free of the throng. "I'll do half the introductions now," she said to the Curnows. And then, while they ate, she told them what little she had gleaned about Bill Westwood and his plans. "He might need a man of vision as his banker," she concluded.

Curnow closed his eyes and smiled. Mrs Curnow leaned forward and said teasingly — at least, Lorna hoped it was teasingly — "You are a wicked and shameless young woman, Miss Sancreed!"

"I beg your pardon?" Lorna asked in surprise.

"You *know* my husband is an incurable romantic — so you dangle one alluring financial disaster after another before him. It is very naughty!" She grinned so convincingly that Lorna could not tell how much steel was hidden inside the velvet.

Her husband opened his eyes and, still smiling, patted her hands. "Marjorie!" he murmured affectionately.

"Well, just you be careful," she replied, and this time there was no doubting the steel.

It was something that had never crossed Lorna's mind before — that there were degrees of romance in such a cut-and-dried business as banking. She had always thought of it as a trade governed by the strictest rules, where you calculated profits and shaved percentages so that all risks balanced out and left you with a little margin over. The idea that one banker might leap in where others feared to tread was worrying, for it made them as hazardous a haven for her money as all the other places she might put it.

Westwood returned and Lorna completed the introductions. When he heard Curnow's profession he said, "Ah, I may be calling on you, sir — on a less social occasion than this."

It was all the excuse Mrs Curnow required. With zest she set about *her* trade, which is bred into the bones of each new generation of English matrons — the unpacking of a young man's character. Whether the young man is seeking a hand in marriage or a loan from a bank is immaterial, for, in the circles where such matrons do their hunting, those two goals have almost everything in common. Marriage is a business or it is nothing. Their motto.

Within five minutes she had mined the lode to exhaustion. Bill Westwood was twenty-four years old, the only surviving son of a pharmacist in Gloucester. He had three sisters; two older and married, one of eighteen who "had hopes." He was schooled at Uppingham and had started a degree in mechanical engineering at University College London but had left in 1916 to enlist in the Royal Flying Corps. He was now too deeply in love with aeroplanes and the future of flying to resume his studies. In any case, his sole interest was the racing aeroplane and he could already teach the professors at UCL more than they were ever likely to know on *that* subject. He thought the Air Ministry had fallen into the hands of fools — a bunch of conservative old nannies who believed a hundred miles an hour was fast. He had no time for them. And marriage? He had no time for that, either — nor money. In fact, he had hardly any money at all.

This final admission was accompanied by a brief smile in Curnow's direction, as if to say, "Over to you!" — for Westwood knew well enough what game the banker's wife had been playing.

But there he was only half right, for, in turning to the banker, he missed the wife's glance toward Miss Sancreed. That also said, "Over to you!"

*J*essica sat between Estelle and David Carne, fuming at Lorna's desertion — as she saw it. The girl was nothing more than a tart! In walks a handsome young air-force officer and she battens onto him like a limpet — all other obligations forgotten. It was too bad of her. *She* was the one who got on so famously with Estelle. She should be here now, easing the tension instead of allowing it to fester like this.

Estelle spent some time sizing up Jessica before she said, "That's a very presentable young fellow sitting with Lorna Sancreed." She smiled sweetly as she added, "Freddy Jenkins said he was asking for *you* when he arrived."

The reply was cool. "He probably knew Ian, though I'm sure he wasn't in six-oh-four."

"No," Estelle said meaningfully. "I'm sure one would have remembered him if he had been! He's getting on with Miss Sancreed like a house on fire, though. I wonder why the Curnows moved away from their table? Nobody else has joined them, I see."

"Tskoh, really!" David exclaimed.

The two women looked at him in surprise.

"Well, I ask you!" he protested. "The poor girl has been practically starved of the company of young men ever since she came here ..."

"What about Ben Calloway?" Jessica asked.

"Calloway was middle-aged at fourteen. That young fellow is the first one she's had the chance to talk to since ..."

"*She's* mostly to blame for that!" Estelle pointed out. "Letting herself get in that condition."

"And you two can't *wait* to get out the knives!" He leaped directly to his conclusion before either of them could interrupt him yet again.

Jessica wondered why she found herself on Estelle's side rather than David's — an unprecedented situation for her. It was that worrying word *jealousy*, which Estelle had trailed before her earlier. Why jealousy?

The suggestion behind it ... no, it was not a suggestion, not even a hint — it was an innuendo. Its purpose was to fill her mind with worries about Lorna and then to poison it against her. But jealousy over what? Lorna had been dancing with David at the time. To imply that *that* might make her jealous of Lorna was frightening, for it implied, too, that Estelle suspected David was carrying on with *her*, Jessica. A chill settled on her stomach.

How could Estelle suspect anything? Until that brief incident at Porthgwarra, it had all been daydreams (and what woman did *not* have impossible daydreams about all sorts of men — some of whom were mere flickering images on a silver screen!); she had never once given Estelle the slightest cause to suspect it. So the woman was simply fishing. And anyway, David was her doctor, and, as Estelle should know better than anyone, it was more than a doctor's life was worth to start any sort of romance with a patient.

But there her thoughts came stumbling to a halt — or, rather, started out abruptly along a new line. For it suddenly occurred to her that David was not *Lorna's* doctor. From the very beginning, come to think of it, he had insisted that Jeremy Carmichael should be her doctor. *He* had insisted? Or had it been Lorna's choice? She couldn't remember. Either way, it was a strange decision — especially when one recalled that Carmichael often looked to David for a second opinion in his more difficult obstetric cases; when it came to obstetrics, David's reputation was among the highest in Cornwall.

Angrily she put this new line of thought from her. There must be a perfectly simple and reasonable explanation for everything. But how typical of Estelle to pick on that one weakness and work away at it!

"Well!" David said in surprise. "That brought a welcome hush! Can the two of you honestly find no other stain in her character to launder in public?"

"Heavens!" Estelle's good humour sounded very nearly genuine.

"You're defending the poor woman almost as if she were one of your patients, David!"

Jessica saw the woman glance in her direction — just to make sure she caught the hidden significance of the jibe. She decided she'd had enough. She beamed at Estelle and said, "I still can't quite believe you're up and about again — it's *wonderful* to see! There are so many things we ought to have been talking about ... so many arrangements we should ..."

David pressed her foot beneath the table.

"Really?" Estelle's mood was divided between curiosity and suspicion. "I'm sure I can't think of any."

"Well, this is hardly the proper place." Jessica spoke as if Estelle understood very well what she was driving at — which only increased the woman's curiosity and suspicion still further.

"He's going for second helpings," David interrupted.

They looked across the room and saw Bill Westwood rising to his feet and, obviously, consulting Lorna's preferences.

"Well, she *is* eating for two, after all," Estelle murmured.

Jessica caught Lorna's attention and smiled broadly, beckoning her across to join them, patting the one empty chair at their table. Lorna said something to the young man. Then, instead of returning directly to the buffet, he picked up his chair and carried it across to Jessica's table. About half the eyes in the room followed him surreptitiously. The remainder looked studiously away and waited to be told about it.

"Mrs Lanyon?" he asked as he drew near.

She nodded. "You have the advantage of me."

With a murmured apology he set down the plates and shook her hand. "I'm Bill Westwood," he said. "And you must be Doctor and Mrs Carne, I take it? How d'you do? I'm delighted to meet you. May Miss Sancreed and I join you?"

All three indicated their pleasure at the thought. He turned and nodded across the room to Lorna but went directly to the buffet instead of going back to escort her across.

"Now that's something that would never have happened before the war," Estelle remarked.

"I think Lorna would have cut him dead if he'd dared escort her across," David told her.

Estelle smiled at Jessica and, with a nod of her head toward her husband, said, "He's become quite the specialist on what your young friend likes or dislikes — and will or will not do!"

Jessica smiled back — having found the perfect way to show Estelle that her scheming little habits were exploded. "We must *both* try to put a brave face on it," she said dramatically. To her satisfaction it wiped the grin off Estelle's face at once. "Lorna!" she went on. "How good of you to join us. I thought you might not have noticed us, stuck away over here."

Lorna chuckled. "All right, Jess! I have to admit he *is* a very interesting young man."

"Is all well?" David asked as he slipped the chair in under her.

"Spoken like a doctor!" Estelle said. "Almost."

"All is exceedingly well," she assured him. "How about you, Mrs Carne? Is it not all rather too much for you?"

In that moment Jessica forgave her everything. If there was any jealousy left within her toward Lorna it was for her ability to seize a situation and make it run her way. Jessica remembered girls at school who, with the merest flick of a hockey stick could turn a ball in mid-flight and send it unerringly onward in whatever direction they desired. In the game of life the situation was far more complex, for in life there were as many hockey balls, so to speak, as there were players; but Lorna still had the knack of turning them all to her advantage. "Do tell us about him," Jess urged after Estelle had been forced to say that all was exceedingly well with her, too.

"He was in two-oh-four at Cherbourg but he knew the Chief quite well — and Philip, too, slightly. They shared an absorbing interest in aeroplane engines."

"And what is he doing in Penzance?" Jessica asked.

Estelle chimed in: "One might almost ask what *on earth* is he doing in Penzance!"

"He'll explain all that. While we're waiting, do tell me about Venetian Palace. Is it as breathtakingly lovely as Egyptian Dynasty, or whatever we're in now?"

They laughed, slightly annoyed that she was so unforthcoming, and told her it was even more beautiful than she could possibly imagine. She then began a discussion as to whether some kinds of decoration could be so utterly appalling that they achieved a strange, perverse sort of beauty all their own. They were deep in debate when Bill returned.

His subsequent interrogation at the hands — or tongues — of Estelle and Jessica followed almost word for word the one to which Marjorie Curnow had submitted him not twenty minutes earlier; and his answers, of course, were even readier the second time around.

David told him that if secrecy were important, the fields at Penzance Green might not be the cleverest choice of landing strip, for they were overlooked on two sides by houses and lanes and on the third by the railway embankment; he recommended an equally flat, upland area out at St Buryan, three or four miles from Land's End.

Bill laughed at his fears and assured him that the country was infested with cranks and crackpots like himself, all beavering away in garages and blacksmiths' forges from Land's End to John o' Groats, hoping to make the world's fastest aeroplane. "I'd just *love* my rivals to waste precious time spying on me!" he concluded. Such disarming modesty endeared him to them all.

After the meal there was a set of slow waltzes and foxtrots. He invited Jessica onto the floor and they talked and laughed with great sparkle, circuit after circuit.

Lorna watched nervously, trying to ignore a childish voice in her head, telling her it wasn't fair and she saw him first — and trying to forget that his opening question had, after all, been about Jessica.

Estelle watched Lorna during this time and then, when David excused himself awhile, she said, "Jessica's always gone rather *well* with air-force officers. To look at them now you'd never believe she's five years older than him."

"It'll do her the world of good," Lorna replied evenly. "It takes remarkably little to buck Jess up, you know. One smile from David can keep her happy for days. She's so lucky. I, on the other hand, require a constant *shower* of flattery, fun, and furs." A subtle arcing of her brows framed an unspoken question as to what Estelle might need to keep her sweet.

Estelle ground her molars a time or two and said that perhaps the women who needed neither smiles nor flattery were the happiest.

"Nuns," Lorna said.

Estelle drew breath to protest that that was not what she had meant — but then saw that Lorna was leading her any way she wanted to go. Her gaze returned to young Westwood. "I wonder if he has money?" she mused.

"Nothing beyond his war gratuity, I should think," Lorna said. "Aren't men *alien*! They think in such alien ways. Can you imagine what it must be like to be consumed with a passion to build the world's fastest aeroplane? It's quite incomprehensible to me." She chuckled at a sudden memory. "I looked out of the window the other day and saw Guy and Toby by the potting shed — competing to see who could urinate the farthest! It's in them from birth, you see."

After a pause in which Estelle tried her best not to laugh — and only just succeeded — she said, "Which of them won? Just as a matter of interest."

"Toby — which left poor Guy rather shaken. But then he challenged him to a return match that evening, for which he saved up all day — he was in utter agony. And then he won — because Toby just rested on his laurels and thought that what he'd done once he could easily do again. It really does matter to them, you see?"

"But we women like to win, too," Estelle objected.

"Of course!" Lorna's eyes sparkled as if the other had just thrown down an open challenge. "But the things *we* like to win can't usually be measured in miles-per-hour, or inches from some starting line. We go after more interior satisfactions. Look at Betty Corvo over there! Every woman wants to throw the party that the guests are going to be talking about long after rival hostesses' parties are forgotten. And Betty knows she's done that tonight. Look at her! No one's thinking about Petronella Trelawney — except Petronella herself, of course."

"How do men and women manage to live together at all?" Estelle asked — adding glumly, "The answer, I suppose, is that we don't!"

"Oh, it can be done," Lorna replied. Her eyes strayed back to Bill Westwood. "If that man did manage to build his dream areoplane ... and if there were a woman in his life who could say to herself, 'Without me he'd never have managed it.' Well ..."

Her smile hinted at all sorts of interior satisfactions.

*I*t was, Bill Westwood assured Lorna, as safe as a stroll on Sunday. He had taken the aeroplane to pieces, modified it, and put it all back again with his own hands, so he could guarantee every last little bit of string and elastic that was holding it together. The engine was from Armstrong with the crankshaft specially balanced by James Curtiss; he could push her to five thousand revs a minute and she'd *probably* stay all in one piece. The only thing that worried him was the baby.

"Oh, if *that's* all," she replied — for she was determined to fly that afternoon — "let's go. You couldn't possibly do worse than the Cornwall County Council Highways Department did to us on our way here. Do you have a spare helmet?"

"Well ... if you're quite sure," he said, still unhappy about it. "We could go back and ask Doctor Carne."

"In the first place he's not my doctor. In the second place, Doctor Carmichael, who is, would be bound to say no because he's a Scots Covenanter or something and he says no to every amusement on principle. If medicine tasted nice, he'd stop prescribing it. Aren't we wasting valuable sunshine?"

He shrugged and reached into the passenger cockpit for a second helmet. "It won't be very amusing, I'm afraid. It'll be fifteen minutes to a thousand feet and two-mile-radius turns with no banking. You'd better put a parachute on, too — just in case some bit of elastic breaks. Where would you like to go? Conversation will be very basic once we're aloft."

She wriggled excitedly into the harness. He showed her how to fasten the buckle over her belly if need be but said she should leave it undone meanwhile. She told him she'd like to go all along the south coast to Land's End, then up the north coast to Hell's Mouth, then back across the peninsula to Penzance.

"That's just about the length of one Schneider Trophy circuit," he said as he helped her in. "Nothing to it."

To her surprise, the passenger cockpit was the one in front — then she remembered he had explained how he had modified the "kite," as he called the 'plane, to take people on aerial trips around the bay in summer — to make enough money to keep him all year. That was also why he had bought a parasol monoplane — so there was no bottom wing to obscure the view. It was not, however, the 'plane to beat world records. That was still no more than a gleam in the eye.

Sitting there in the front cockpit, she found herself almost wishing there *was* a lower wing. The distance to the new-mown grass of the landing strip already seemed frighteningly great — and he hadn't even started the engine yet.

He put his hand to the propellor and swung it once. The engine gave a single bark and died. "Look down to your left," he shouted up at her, "and you'll see three or four cables running through pulleys. Grab the top one and give it a few tweaks when she starts to fire."

"What is it?" she asked.

"The throttle."

"Ah, got you!" She grasped the wire firmly and gave him the nod.

The engine fired on his second swing and, by dint of skilful tweaking, she managed to nurse it into a full-throated roar. In fact, she revved so hard that the plane actually moved forward an inch or two.

He leaped to one side and made frantic gestures at her, which changed to a happy thumbs-up when the roar died back to a purr. She understood what he meant about a balanced crankshaft, for there was amazingly little vibration. She inspected the cockpit more closely and saw cables running on both sides, and in the gap between the panels under her feet, too. She wondered if, by pulling at them, she could actually fly the "kite" from where she was; she enjoyed a brief fantasy in which he passed out at the controls and she landed the machine safely and won his undying gratitude.

"It's a good thing *I'm* not expectant," he shouted in her ear as he climbed in. "You'd be rushing me home by now! I thought you were all set to fly solo to France."

"Is that possible?" she asked.

"Easily," he replied — then, catching the gleam in her eye, added, "But not today!"

He checked she was fastened in properly — all but the belly strap — and then seated himself. The cables to her right and left slid back and forth over their pulleys and she saw flaps on the wings move up and down and vents into the engine housing open and close. There were steel ribs along the top of the housing with naked bolts sticking out of them. Had he forgotten to fix on some vital part? A reserve fuel tank, perhaps? She turned round and mimed a worrying-questioning face at him and pointed to the bolts.

"Machine-gun mountings!" he shouted, just managing to make himself intelligible. He mimed that she should lower her goggles now.

The world was suddenly transformed. It was not simply the fact that she now saw it through two private portholes, as it were — this was the world she had last seen when she had put on Philip's flying helmet. And *this* was precisely the view Philip had had when *he* wore that helmet in action. The gun mounts made it easy to imagine the weapons themselves bolted there. It was as if she had been transported bodily back to a time and place she had pictured so often in her waking nightmares of war. She had to force herself to look out, across the airfield, to the road, the railway, to St Michael's Mount and the bay, in order to dispel those sudden visceral memories.

And then at last the engine rose from tickover to a roar and they began to move forward — in earnest this time. And then the present moment was too full of sensations and excitement for the past to linger with her.

It surprised her that, despite the noise of the engine, she could still hear the rattle and thump of the undercarriage as it coped with the minor unevenness of the grass beneath them. The grass itself was now a green, streaky blur. Crisp white cottages turned to linear smudges, all parallel, and there was a fiery serpent in the air where the sun glinted off the dark shadow of the propellor sweep. She was so absorbed in these fascinations that she missed the actual moment of take-off. A second later she became aware that the rattling thrum of the undercarriage had ceased.

He meant what he had said about climbing slowly and turning gently. They skimmed the barn roofs at Long Rock and only just cleared the hundred-and-fifty-foot cliffs at Marazion, two miles out. Chickens fluttered wildly in back gardens; women clutched their laundry as if they feared some act of aerial piracy; wind-wizened faces stared up and grinned, salt-tanned arms waved back at her. She could count the fingers on their hands. And then they were out over the sparkling January sea. St Michael's Mount seemed no more than a jewelled toy as they made it the pivot of a long, slow arc from southeast to southwest. Everything was toylike. She understood at last how pilots – fine, decent men – could return to squadron and boast of the bombs they had dropped on those toy houses, toy railways, toy factories, and all the little toy people inside them.

There were surprises wherever she looked. She was used to the vee of a bow-wave spreading out from a ship; but from up here, looking directly down their funnels and masts, she could see that each had a second vee, spreading out from the stern. And Penzance was so *small!* And how did those toy motor cars manage to drive past each other in top gear along those miserable little lanes? And how *big* Rosemergy's garden was – bigger even than it seemed during an afternoon spent raking up leaves!

He throttled back to attract her attention and then, by shouts and pointing, managed to ask her if she wished to go down and make a low pass over the house. She shook her head vigorously. Jessica would have a fit if she knew anything about this jaunt. A moment later it occurred to her it would be a wonderful way of paying Marcus Corvo back for the noise of his dance orchestra.

Another surprise was the speed at which the well-known places slipped by. From over a thousand feet the land seemed merely to drift past; but the familiar landmarks, each ten minutes or more apart by car, practically trod on each other's heels – Newlyn, Mousehole, Lamorna Cove, Cribba Head, Porthcurno … and suddenly, after only six or seven minutes in the air, they were over Porthgwarra Cottage! And there was Theo, cutting back the ramblers round his door!

"Theo!" she yelled at the top of her voice. "Yoo hoo!" She waved frantically to attract his attention.

But they were over Gwennap Head and out of sight before he had time to respond — if, indeed, he had heard her at all.

And then there was Land's End, still shuttered and forlorn — just a flock of sheep looking around in bewilderment, unable to equate such a landlubber's noise as a roaring engine with anything in the heavens.

There was no doubt from up here which headland was most westerly — the one immediately south of *that place*. She gazed down at its desolation and let her mind's eye people it with two little toy lovers, lying half naked in the grass, locked in that most ancient clasp of all. How thoroughly unimportant it now seemed! Theo was right — as always; that bit of sand had already fallen through the hourglass. It made her regret that she had struck David so violently as they walked away from there. He would remember it. It would make him believe the whole episode was far more important to her than it was.

The north coast was less familiar to her. She viewed it more as a tourist might — whereas the surprise of the south coast had been to see familiar places from an unfamiliar angle. The towering cliffs, some of them rising sheer, two hundred feet or more, were especially impressive. She gazed down at the rolling Atlantic swell and shivered at the thought that tin miners were at that very moment drilling and blasting for the mineral, miles out to sea and hundreds of feet beneath its surface.

Only moments later the landscape changed again, from one of the bleakest moorlands in the country to the palm-infested toytown of St Ives with its picturesque beach, its picturesque lighthouse, its picturesque harbour ... and no hint of the centuries-long poverty that had gone into making it so delightfully quaint. Lorna saw the briefest flash of it before the fading Victorian splendours of Tregenna Castle and Carbis Bay replaced it.

Somewhere down there, in one of those gardens, Ben Calloway had seen a vision of loveliness he would never forget — a loveliness whose possessor had died before he suffered the pain and disillusion of learning how frail and human she was.

Then Hayle was beneath them — the smallest industrial town (or largest industrial village) in the country. From here it was tucked away between the massive sandhills that guarded its estuary. To the northwest they stretched for several miles, forming a long expanse of smooth white beach — a favourite place for people to race their cars, though none were there today. She turned round in her seat as well as she could and pointed it out to Bill. He, thinking she was suggesting they land there, grinned and shook his head. He rubbed his fingers and thumbs together, trying to suggest that he would have to feel the firmness of the sand before he'd risk it. She thought the gesture meant "Shekels!" and that he was saying, "I wouldn't do it for all the money in the world."

A few minutes later they did a lazy sweep round the lighthouse at Godrevy and there before them was Hell's Mouth, a giant's bite into the massive face of the cliff. The clarity of everything when she raised her goggles and shielded her eyes from the slipstream still amazed her. She could actually count the gulls, wheeling around in that mighty amphitheatre — and doubtless shrieking in protest at the lack of wind today. They were such tiny dots of white you could not even call them pinpricks.

Bill began a full right-angled turn onto the last leg of their flight. It kept Hell's Mouth at the centre of her view for longer than Lorna would have liked. Again she found her mind returning to that day — Sunday the seventh of November, 1915 — when Maude Lessore had drowned in those cold, gray waters. Or had drowned herself? That was the question which never ceased to nag Lorna whenever she thought of the woman — which she did almost every time she thought of Ben Calloway, of course.

Suppose it had been deliberate? Had Maude been unable to face the knowledge that, sooner or later, Ben was going to discover the awful truth that she was just another common-or-garden mortal? Had she allowed his adoration to become so important to her that she would rather die than disillusion him? She shuddered at the thought that illusions could have such power — and even more at the thought that Ben himself might now be redirecting that same set of illusions toward her, despite all she had done to dissuade him. What if *he* woke up to the same truth one day? Would he then understand why Maude had done it — and think it almost a duty to follow her?

She emerged from her reverie with a jolt, realizing they were back over Hayle again, though now on its southern side. From here on they followed the railway line, descending slowly as they went. If there were guns on those mountings still, they would have pointed at the landing field all the way. By this time mere height held no terrors for her at all. She had grown quite used to a godlike view of the world in miniature. Indeed now, by contrast, their ever-decreasing altitude and the ever-burgeoning size of the houses, trees, cows, cars, and people grew evermore alarming until, just before they cleared the hedge and touched down, she had to close her eyes at the gargantuan size of the thistles and nettles rushing up to meet them.

"Don't touch your face," was the first thing he said as he helped her descend to grass again. "Oil in the slipstream. We must do something about that before we make it a business."

She could only smile in reply, being still too awestruck for words. The spell was not broken until they had walked across the grass to the barn and she saw her face in a piece of cracked looking glass he had wedged in the barn door. It was white where the flying helmet had covered it, black all across her cheeks and from the bridge of her nose to the bottom of her lower lip — and much worse on her left than her right. "You can tell I spent almost all the time looking landward," she said. "It's black as pitch here."

"Yes." He pulled a rueful face. "Sorry about that."

"Oh no, Bill! Don't apologize. It was wonderful — the most thrilling ..." She looked at her watch. "Good heavens! We weren't even gone an hour. The Land's End peninsula will never be the same again for me." For *two* reasons, now, she added to herself.

He gave her a bar of engineer's soap and a handful of clean shoddy, again apologizing for being so thoughtless. He, being farther back and behind her, had much less oil on his face.

They washed side-by-side, stooping over a rainwater butt at one end of the barn, passing the soap carefully from hand to hand for fear it might fall in and sink out of reach. The touch of his soapy fingers was pleasant and she noticed that his grasp lingered, too. For his part he noticed that she did not pull away from him.

"How's that looking now?" she asked, for they had left the mirror wedged behind the door still. "You've got it all off you."

"You're almost there," he told her and, making a lather between his hands he began to remove the last of the oil from her face.

She closed her eyes for fear of the suds and the next she knew his lips were gently pressed to hers.

Time stopped. Her heart stopped — or, if it beat, she was past feeling it. Indeed, she seemed to have turned completely hollow inside. Only her lips were real — and his, of course. The whole wide world, which she had just seen from the grandest viewpoint ever, had narrowed down to that tiny portion of space in which their lips touched ... and grazed ... and explored.

"Well!" he murmured when they separated at last. "Now I shall *have* to buy this field!"

*J*essica clenched her fists and said, "No!" She tried to stop shivering — though whether it was with anger or fear she could not have said. Fear, probably, because when Lorna wanted something she usually got her way. "No," she repeated. "A thousand times no!"

"Once is enough, dear!" Lorna smiled nervously and held up her hands as if to ward off the waves of emotion radiating from Jess.

"I should jolly well think it is, too!"

Lorna was turning to leave when the oddity — and venom — of this rejoinder struck her. She turned back again. "Meaning ...?" she asked brusquely.

Jessica, who immediately regretted letting the remark slip out, made several placatory noises and said, "Nothing."

Now it was Lorna who had to bridle her anger. "No, come on, Jess — that won't do. This has been brewing up ever since the New Year ball. You've got it in for me, somehow, and ..."

"Don't be absurd! Got it in for you! I admit I was annoyed — mildly annoyed — at being left to cope with Estelle all on my own ..."

"David was there, too. Anyway, the crowds ..."

"And a great help *he* was! But we've been over all that. I told you, you absolutely redeemed yourself when you said to her ..."

"Yes, all right! So it's not that. It's something else. What did you mean by saying, 'I should jolly well think so'? It's to do with Bill Westwood, isn't it!"

"It's really none of my business," Jessica said airily.

"There you go again! That tone ..."

"*Where* do I go again? I wish I knew what you were talking about."

"Off on your high horse! 'It's really none of my business!' you say. But that's only half the sentence, isn't it! The unspoken thought is:'It's really none of my business if you make an idiot of yourself all over again with another boy in blue!' That's what you're really driving at."

Jessica closed her eyes briefly and sighed, for the truth was that her unspoken thoughts had been a great deal harsher than that; words like *tart* and *wanton woman* would have replaced Lorna's *idiot*. She replied, "I can honestly say that that was *not* what I had in mind. If you think it was, it's a comment on the state of your own conscience. Do *you* believe you're 'making an idiot of yourself' with young Westwood?"

"Of course I don't. If I did, I'd stop seeing him. You think I have no self-control at all, don't you."

You have a huge capacity for self-delusion, though, Jessica thought. *And that makes self-control seem easy!* She said, "I yield to none in my admiration of your powers of self-control ..."

"You're talking like Theo!" Lorna interrupted. Her eyes narrowed. "Have you and he been discussing me?"

Jessica smiled thinly. "Of course we have. He asked how you were. I gave him an obstetric summary. He stopped his ears ... d'you want the whole conversation? It was extremely shallow. We also discussed David and Estelle — equally shallowly. Also the oddly respectable *ménage à trois* next door. Oh — and Ben Calloway."

"Hardly a soul was left unscorched!"

"Don't tell me you haven't had conversations with Theo about all those people — and about me. He's become the regular father-confessor to us all."

"We're straying from the point," Lorna said uncomfortably. "All I asked ... in fact, I didn't even ask — I merely *suggested* that, as Bill is staying in some rather wretched digs in Lanoweth Road, listening to the trains shunting farm produce all night, it might be a good idea to let him lodge here, et cetera, et cetera. Then you'd have his rent as well as mine. And you stamp your foot like Rumpelstiltskin. I thought it might be rather nice for us to have a man around the place — to shoot burglars and mend doorhandles and all those other little things that men are useful for."

And we all know what that *means!* Jessica said to herself. However, a deeper instinct for self-preservation kept the lid tightly screwed down on all such opinions. She smiled at her in a conciliatory fashion and said, "So it would, dear. I assure you I'm not blind to the many advantages of the situation ..."

"You don't need to explain, Jess." Lorna felt suddenly afraid of a kiss-and-make-it-up scene; for some obscure reason she needed the sense of righteousness and mistreatmeant this minor tiff had given her. "It's your house. You have a perfect right, an absolute right ..."

"Darling!" Jessica reached out across the table and squeezed her arm. "D'you think I'd brandish my *rights* under your nose? Especially when you have even better reasons than I have for being wary of letting Bill stay here?"

Naturally Lorna could not leave the matter there. It distressed her to realize how good Jess had become at manipulating conversations lately — or rather at manipulating the emotional thrusts and parries, usually unspoken, that lay behind them. Who had she learned it from? "I don't follow that," she answered warily.

"Think, dear! Burglars are a *very* remote possibility. The back door has never been capable of being locked. The original builder lost the key and no one ever got around to replacing the lock. But I admit it would be nice not to have to fight the broken spring in the spare bedroom door. However, the price you and I would pay for these little blessings would be too ..."

"What about his rent?" Lorna repeated. "Ten shillings a week is not to be sneezed at."

"It simply wouldn't work." Jessica pronounced the sentence as mildly as possible.

"I don't see why it shouldn't. I'm proposing a perfectly respectable arrangement. Or perhaps you think my reputation is too tattered to give yours much shelter!"

Still Jessica preserved her smile. "If I've learned anything from you, Lorna dear, it's how to ignore social demands of that kind. No — it wouldn't work for the same reason that small mixed schools don't work. Can I be rather frank?"

"Please," Lorna replied reluctantly.

"We both know there are certain elements missing in our lives. I think we both find it a struggle at times. We indulge in daydreams that could not possibly become reality. But we manage — by the skin of our teeth, somehow, we ... get by. Now just imagine how our lives would change if we suddenly invited this handsome, charming, unattached (as far as we know) young man to share our house. Imagine yourself lying alone in your room, in the dark, listening to the roar of the sea and fretting endlessly over the question, 'Is she?' Imagine me, alone in my bedroom, starting up at every stray noise in the landing, wondering, 'Is she?' And imagine poor Bill Westwood, alone in *his* room, wondering, 'Would she?' — about either of us. Or both! We're not schoolgirls any longer. We know the power of these emotions. We know how things can ... fester. It would end in some almighty eruption. You know it would. *That's* why I say no. I'm not some Victorian chaperon saying 'Tut-tut!' I'm a woman of flesh and blood who sometimes cannot bear the *waste* of me." Her voice cracked on the word and she fell silent.

Lorna drew a deep breath and held it. She gazed down at the polished rosewood table, at the remains of dinner, at the guttering candles — at anything that would stop the tears behind her eyelids from swelling to the point where they might roll.

"I shan't ask whether you agree," Jessica concluded, "but do you at least see my point of view?"

Lorna nodded. Her lip trembled. The baby stirred.

It was all the fault of the baby, of course. She never used to give way to her emotions like this.

"I'm sorry, darling!"

Jessica's tender squeeze on her arm was all it took to set the tears rolling. Once they started there seemed no way to stop them. She did not sob. Her body did not tremble. She sat as still as a carving, staring at her empty coffee cup, while the tears traced a hot-to-chill streak down her face, round the edge of her jaw, down her neck, and blotted themselves in her collar.

Jessica, finding her young friend in a rare moment of vulnerability, let the weeping almost run its course and then steeled herself to say, "Can I go further, dear, and be absolutely devastatingly frank? Or have you had enough?"

Lorna shrugged.

Jessica took it for consent. "After all, let's remember we only met him five days ago — or *you* only met him five days ago — so perhaps there's still time."

Lorna gave a gluey sniff and muttered, "Time for what?"

Jessica passed her a clean hanky but she waved it away and took out her own. "Time to take an honest look at the situation — as it is and as it might become."

"From *your* point of view, of course." Lorna swallowed hard and forced several big breaths to fight the after-tears hiccoughs that were threatening her.

"You think that might therefore make it worthless?"

"No-o-o." She drew the word out wearily, jutting her head forward in a gesture she must have picked up unconsciously from Sarah.

It made it easier for Jessica to adopt the maternal rôle. "Bill is, as I say, a handsome and charming young man, attractive in every way. But ..."

"Attractive enough for you to warn me we'd be duelling for him if he lodged here!" Lorna said coldly.

"Exactly! But since we've agreed it would be unwise to take that risk, let's look at the situation that follows if Bill Westwood remains at his present ..."

"No!" Lorna said suddenly. "We haven't agreed. You ... you bamboozled me into ..."

"Bamboozled!" Jessica was outraged.

"Sorry! Not bamboozled, then. I don't mean you tricked me. But you *rushed* me with arguments. You overwhelmed me. If I'd been able to think straight, I'd have ..." She hesitated, eying Jess warily in case she were still too angry to accept an unpalatable truth.

"What?" Jessica made herself smile, though her actual mood was more cautious than jovial.

"Well, darling, I'd have pointed out that *I'm* the one who's falling for Bill, not you."

"Ah! You admit it, then!"

"I'd rather not. As you say, I've known him less than a week, so it's not something I could say with any confidence. But if you force me to the point where I have to come down on one side or the other, then that is the most likely. I probably do ... I'm on the *way* to loving him ... how else can I put it?"

"And how d'you know *I'm* not in the same boat?" Jessica asked — to her own surprise as much as to Lorna's. The moment the words were out she could have bitten her tongue off. There wasn't a shred of truth in it, of course. She had no idea why she'd said such a thing — especially as Lorna's admission that she was merely on the brink of falling in love with Bill Westwood was the perfect opening for her to say what was really on her mind.

Lorna stared at her as if she, Jessica, had just slipped a knife between her ribs. "I see!" she said quietly.

"Oh, Lorna! Of course I'm not. Don't be silly."

"Why d'you say it then?"

"I don't honestly know. Perhaps I was just resentful of your blandly assuming I couldn't possibly be in the same boat — that I'm past falling in love, I mean. *But*" — she insisted as Lorna drew breath for a further protest — "since you confess that you *are* in that boat, just *starting* to fall in love, all I'm saying is that it may be the ideal moment to take a cool and reasonable look at the situation. Before it gets too hot." She smiled encouragingly. "If you'd rather close your eyes to it, say so — and I'll shut up."

Lorna sniffed the last remnant of her tears away and said, "I wouldn't be the only woman in these parts to be closing my eyes to a developing situation, would I!"

"What d'you mean by that?" Jessica asked icily.

"Nothing. It's like your saying 'I should jolly well think so!' when I remark that once is enough. It's just a little pebble tossed into the pool of conversation so that we can watch the ripples spread in silence." She smiled bleakly. "We're just going round in circles, aren't we."

Jessica smiled again, still rather coldly. "I'd say we are being pushed in circles with some determination! To get back to my question — *do* you want to look dispassionately at the situation with Bill ... before it's too late?"

Lorna yielded to her will at last. "If it pleases you." She sighed.

"It ought to please *you*. To have at least one good friend willing to try it. Think what you'd have been spared if there had been a conversation like this before you went off like a madcap with Philip!"

Lorna raised both hands feebly and let them fall limply to her lap. "So be it!"

"Let me play devil's advocate, then. Forget it's you and Bill — let's imagine we're sitting in the Falmouth Repertory and the curtain goes up for Act One. It's a play by Pinero, say, or Galsworthy — someone very skilled at fleshing out the situation in one crisp opening scene. So that when the curtain falls we know there's this devastatingly handsome, charming young bachelor burning with some costly ambition. He's penniless, of course — but wait! Glory be — our heroine has money! She is lovelorn and pining. They meet at a local ball. He makes a beeline for her (though *apparently* he doesn't know her from Eve) and they remain inseparable for most of the evening. Curtain! End of Scene One! I turn to you and say, 'Well, dear, how d'you think *this* little drama is going to end?' And what do you reply?"

Lorna simply stared at her, face void of expression.

"Well?" Jessica prompted.

"Oh!" Lorna exclaimed sarcastically. "You actually want to hear *my* answer, do you? You're not going to put that into my mouth like everything else?"

"Prevarication won't help, dear," Jessica said.

Lorna pushed everything away from her — plate, coffee cup, table mat, napkin and ring. She placed her elbows in the space thus created and rested her face in her hands. "I should tell you," she said wearily, "that if Galsworthy knows his stuff — which he does — our heroine understands only too well what's going to happen. To the last teardrop and the last broken heartstring, she understands only too well. But alas it'll make no difference to what happens in Act Five! If women insist on behaving sensibly, dramatists leave them to buy the tickets!"

Jessica felt cheated. "You know I'm not really talking about tragedies on stage," she said. "They have their own rules and ..."

Lorna gave out a despairing laugh. "I'm not talking about stage tragedies either, Jess. I'm trying to tell you what I know about *me!*"

*E*stelle had a small relapse after the night at the Riviera-Splendide; she took care to see that it remained small in case her interests demanded a swift recovery. Lorna went over to see her one Saturday morning, about ten days after the ball. It seemed clear to her that, left to themselves, David, Jessica, and Estelle would drift on forever, wrapped up in their discontents — but also finding the status quo quite useful, in its way.

She understood David well enough by now, she thought. He was yoked to Estelle in a loveless marriage — a miserable situation on the face of it. In fact, it suited him rather well, for it freed his conscience to indulge his two genuine passions — a love of dangerous, exciting adventures with every likely lass that came his way and a pure, unsullied (and undeclared) love for Jessica. Like all successful Casanovas, he had developed the most remarkable antennæ for ferreting out a willing woman; also certain mannerisms for reassuring them that they were *special* and that all would be well. He cocooned them, so to speak, in a little hothouse of esteem and appreciation, where a woman's normal inhibitions had to struggle to be heard.

She did not for one moment believe he sat down and worked out his strategy in a calculating, cold-blooded manner. Quite the contrary. He was the least thinking, most haunted man she had ever known — a helpless prisoner of his own desperate need to conclude an affaire with every woman who caused his antennæ to buzz. It was a relentless hunger that drove him, day and night, even in the depths of physical and mental exhaustion. He told her once that, during the war, when he had been called up to the big army hospital at Basingstoke, when the casualties were heavy, he used to go round the nurses at the end of a long duty and ask them discreetly, one after the other, if they'd like to go to bed with him. He'd often get a yes from the first or second nurse; he never had to ask more than six. And these were respectable women, some of them from the highest families in the land — and the married nurses were worse than the spinsters!

He had told her the story, not to boast of his prowess, but to comfort her, to reassure her she was no trollop merely because she had experimented with more men than most. He could not understand why it depressed her to hear that sexual hypocrisy — and the female duplicity on which it thrived — was pretty well universal.

The situation was almost as congenial to Jessica. She had been brought up to believe that marriage was a natural tyranny of husband over wife — benign, one hoped, but natural in any case. On the face of it, Ian had been an ideal husband — handsome, gregarious, a born leader, idolized by many, admired by all. Ignorant of the world and swept up in that general opinion, Jessica had only lately come to realize that their marriage, which had been the whole world to her, had been no more than a base for Ian; Rosemergy had been like an airfield where he rested, fed, and serviced his machine before taking off into the great blue yonder where the *real* adventures of his life awaited. The pain of that discovery was sugared by the realization that it was over. An arm's-length affaire with a safely married man — with the occasional embrace to keep it alive — probably suited her very well.

So two of this eternal triangle had cause to keep it in existence. The unknown quantity was Estelle. Lorna hoped to lift a veil or two that Saturday morning.

She laddered her stocking climbing over the fence to Trevescan. She would have gone back to change had not Estelle thrown wide her bedroom window and called out, "Come on up, Miss Sancreed. The french windows are unlocked. You're just the tonic I need!"

By the time Lorna reached the bedroom door Estelle had realized she should have said, "You're just what the doctor ordered!" — so she said it now.

"Does it make any difference?" Lorna asked.

Estelle, looking as healthy as a woman could, was sitting up in bed, toying with a jigsaw puzzle of *The Fighting Temeraire*. She glanced up expectantly. "Does what make any difference?"

"What the doctor orders."

Her smile faded. "That's unkind, dear. If you're going to be unkind, you can leave your hot broth, or whatever you've brought for me, and go whence you came. No uplifting tracts, though, please."

"You may relax your guard. I didn't bring anything today. I came to invite you to lunch."

Estelle's lips almost vanished. "At Rosemergy?" she snapped.

"No. At the Mouse Hole. Ben Calloway has decided to serve light luncheons on Saturdays. It'll be strictly meat-and-two-veg, I'm sure, but I thought we ought to support local enterprise. D'you feel up to it? *I* need some moral support, anyway."

She added that last statement to see whether David had told his wife anything about Ben's proposal, or even his interest in her.

Obviously not, for Estelle immediately said, "Why so?" She also began to rise, reaching across the bed for her dressing gown.

"It's quite disgraceful," Lorna said in an envious tone, looking at her lithe body and nimble movements; the woman must be indulging in secret exercises.

Estelle searched her nightdress for coffee stains or something she might have missed.

Lorna went on, "There are women who swim miles through ice-cold water, and run up and down mountains, and even do without chocolate, just to have a figure and complexion like yours."

Estelle relaxed and giggled happily, her question forgotten.

"Still, it's just as well," Lorna concluded. "Just think! If you got up and did all those things, too, none of us would get our toe in the door."

Estelle settled at her dressing table and started to brush out her hair — which hardly needed such attention. "Is this the start of some rather unsubtle campaign to get me out and about again?"

Lorna chuckled and took the brush over. "I don't think it would require much of a campaign, do you?" She felt the woman grow tense and said, "Sit still!" She gathered all the hair into one thick tress, which she held loosely in her left hand and brushed vigorously with her right — so vigorously that it took up a huge static charge. She let it go suddenly and laughed to see how many wisps stood out in a shock, like Struwelpeter.

"Oh, you *pest!*" Estelle exclaimed and grabbed the brush back. Her hairs followed it round and made juicy crackles whenever it touched them. "That's you all over, isn't it — offer to help and leave everything in a mess!"

"That's what we always did at school to girls who went on brushing their hair long after there was any need for it."

Estelle stopped brushing and stared up at her venomously; she knew full well that Lorna was making some kind of equation between girls who went on brushing their hair long after the necessity had passed and women who stayed in their sickbeds long after there was any need for it — if, indeed, there ever had been a need in the first place. But she could say nothing without referring to it, which would be like admitting she had a conscience about it.

"How simple life was in those days," Lorna added pitilessly. "How elementary every problem seemed! Miserable though we were at the time, they really were the happiest days of our lives."

"I think I'll go back to bed," Estelle muttered.

Lorna went over and plumped up the pillows invitingly.

Estelle made no move to carry out her threat. "Where is your landlady today?" she asked, picking up a lipstick.

"She's gone to call on Mister Westwood. She feels responsible for me. She wants to see if he is suitable." She spoke with a superior detachment that angered Estelle. "A suitable suitor."

"That's what *she* says," she snapped. "You watch out! She'll pinch him off you if you're not careful."

Lorna smiled. "She could even pinch him off me if I were. Being careful doesn't help in matters of the heart, does it!"

Estelle's words were distorted by the need to keep her lips still while she reddened them, but Lorna managed to make out: "You pretend to be so aloof about it but you don't deceive me, Miss Sancreed. Tell me what *does* help in 'matters of the heart'?" The question was clear enough for she stopped her painting to ask it — adding, "What an awful phrase!"

"The knowledge that I'd kill her if she even tried," Lorna replied sweetly. "May I lay out moddom's things? What'll you wear today? It's only the Mouse Hole, remember." She opened one of the wardrobes — and gasped at the rich array of clothes it contained. What mighty forces, she wondered, could have kept a perfectly healthy woman in bed, feigning minor illness month after month, when she had all *this* to play with? Grimly she wondered, too, about the even mightier forces that might be needed to get her out of that state.

Estelle showed some restraint in her choice, a tweedy town-and-country suit with a pale gray silk blouse and chiffon scarf in charcoal gray. "It's only Ben Calloway, after all," she remarked.

"A dark horse," Lorna said; it still fascinated her that Estelle knew nothing about Ben's interest in her.

"If you say so. I hardly know the man. To me he's always seemed the quintessential bore — meat-and-two-veg is just about his mark! But then there are so many men like that, don't you find?" She threw Lorna a pair of stockings. "Here! If you ladder those as well, it'll cost you three-and-sixpence."

They decided to walk the long way round, to work up a bit of an appetite. When they reached the junction with Love Lane, which ran down to the Mouse Hole, Estelle gave a cry of disappointment. "Look what they've done — the swine!"

She seemed to be pointing to the street nameplate, fixed to the garden wall opposite: LOVE LANE. It was of the common municipal pattern, freshly painted.

"That's rather nice, isn't it?" Lorna suggested.

"The lane itself is rather nice," Estelle replied angrily. "It always has been rather nice. But there's no need to go sticking ugly great signs like that up at every junction. We all know its name round here."

"Motorists don't, perhaps?"

"Then they've no business here. It's like those gardens where every plant has a fussy little label. I *hate* them."

"Mrs Carne!" Lorna laughed in surprise at this outburst. "Steady the Buffs!"

"Or *laryngitis* when you have a sore throat, or *syncope* when you're feeling faint, and *tinnitus* when you've got singing in the ears. Everything has to have a ticket these days or it can't travel with us. Is it any wonder I prefer to stay in bed when I have to face *that* sort of ugly monstrosity the very minute I get up?" She flung a despairing gesture at the offending nameplate.

Lorna placed herself between it and Estelle. "We can creep out tonight and deface it if you like," she promised.

Estelle yielded to her humour and they set off toward the esplanade. "That's always the first thought with you, isn't it, Miss Sancreed — wait till it's dark and then break the law. Rules are there to be broken — that's your motto. Would you really kill your landlady if she made sheep's eyes at Mister Westwood?"

The skin prickled at the nape of Lorna's neck. Estelle Carne was trying so hard to be brittle and witty — the very picture of someone to whom only trivial things mattered. But underneath it all, Lorna was suddenly sure, her mind was working flat out. They were drawing close to something that was of cardinal importance to the woman. "What do *you* think?" she replied cagily.

"I'm asking you, dear. Does the man already mean so much to you? Because if he does, then you ought to take my warning more seriously than you seem to."

Lorna realized that if she paused to think out her responses — first trying to decide what was really behind each of Estelle's provocations and then deciding on her own best rejoinder from this point of view and that point of view ... the momentum would be lost. Trusting to instinct, then — and feeling like someone leaping from log to log in the middle of a rushing torrent — she replied, "How d'you know that? You talk as if you've seen her do it to others?"

Estelle gave a contemptuous snort but volunteered nothing.

Lorna pressed on. "Yet to the best of *my* knowledge — I mean from all I hear — she married the Chief practically out of the nursery and never *looked* at another man."

Now came the test, Lorna thought. Would the woman say something disparaging about her husband — "If you don't count Doctor Carne as another man — in which you'd be fully justified ..." — something along those lines. Or would she follow the other hare — the Chief? She had not long to wait.

After only the briefest pause Estelle said, "She was the greatest disappointment in *his* life, I'll tell you that."

"Oh come!" Lorna chided jovially. "Be fair! That's an easy judgment that anyone can make from outside. Not many marriages would escape it."

Estelle knew very well which other marriage Lorna had in mind but the accusation that there were no grounds for saying such a thing about the Lanyons' marriage was more than she could leave alone. "That was no *exterior* conjecture, let me assure you," she said severely. "Ian told me so himself."

Lorna held her breath and then let it out on the single, rather embarrassed word, "A-a-h!"

Estelle realized where her emotions had led her. Lorna's lack of challenge — indeed, her failure to ask any kind of question at all about this amazing revelation — left her, Estelle, free to make any response she liked. But it also compelled her to respond in *some* way; she could not simply leave it as it was.

Fortunately they had reached the lounge bar door of the Mouse Hole by now, so the business of taking off hats and coats, stamping feet, and rubbing outstretched hands toward the fire occupied a little time. Marje, the waitress on duty, asked, "Was it for lunch?" in that strange, depersonalized grammar that is peculiar to restaurants in England. On being told that it was for lunch, she informed them there was a ladies-only dining room upstairs, with a view over the bay, if they preferred.

On hearing Lorna's voice, Ben Calloway left the bar and came through into the ladies' room just in time to hold out Estelle's chair. They had chosen a table at the side of the room, by a window overlooking Love Lane.

"Are we the first?" Lorna asked.

He nodded. "I'm very grateful for your support."

"Mrs Carne rose from her sickbed to do her little bit," Lorna assured him.

Estelle looked daggers at her and smiled encouragingly at Calloway. He crossed the room to the sideboard and returned with two hand-written menus for them.

"What beautiful writing," Lorna murmured. She was sure it was not his for it bore no resemblance to the hand that had scribbled his bid for Rosemergy.

"My Sunday best," he replied to her surprise.

Estelle was experiencing a surprise of her own, not at the handwriting but at the decor. She had expected reproduction Jacobean with distressed shellac masquerading as three centuries of beeswax and elbow grease. Instead it was all unashamedly modern, in limed oak, with pastel wallpapers and pale chintz curtains. "You've absolutely transformed this room, Mister Calloway," she said admiringly.

"No point in half-measures, Mrs Carne," he replied.

Lorna saw that the same principle applied to the menu, which was far more adventurous than her sneering "meat-and-two-veg." It was a three-course table-d'hôte with more than a dozen dishes. For hors d'œuvres alone they had a choice of onion soup, terrine, smoked salmon, or dressed crab. "Ben!" she exclaimed. "This is wonderful!"

Estelle looked up sharply at her use of his first name.

Ben accepted the compliment gravely and said, "There are so many meat-and-two-veg establishments in Penzance now. I saw no point in competing with them."

The two women exchanged glances. Lorna smiled ruefully up at him and admitted she had maligned him. She and Estelle chose, respectively, terrine and smoked salmon followed by mackerel and Irish stew.

"He's certainly competing on price!" Estelle murmured when Ben had gone. "One shilling and elevenpence for a table d'hôte like this! How can he do it?"

"Ask him when he comes back."

"I shouldn't dream of being so vulgar." She grinned. "However, you may ask him."

He returned at once, in fact, with two tumblers and a jug of water — a practice unknown in English eating establishments. "The American who left that magazine advised me to do this," he said.

Lorna asked him the vulgar question. Estelle prepared to die of shame, but abandoned it when he answered without embarrassment. He said he expected to make no profit until the summer trade started — when he would also begin a daily luncheon. He was using this slack period to train the cook and waitresses, to make all his mistakes, and to gain a reputation among the residents, second to none. He added that all the boarding-house landladies — who offered no midday meal to their boarders — would be getting a voucher for one free luncheon, so that they could recommend the Mouse Hole with absolute confidence.

He would not normally have been so free with his information but the look of frank admiration in Lorna's eye led him from one point to the next. His final words were, "Of course, if the few who *do* patronize us today are sufficiently impressed to spread the word ..."

"Well well well!" Lorna murmured after he had left them again. "Did I call him a dark horse? I'd never have believed it. He's starting to take his own trade seriously."

Marje brought their first courses.

"Did I hear you call him Ben? I'd never have believed that, either."

"Oh well ... you know what we young people are like these days!" Lorna smiled cattily.

"Now see here! Just for that you shall call me Estelle, young lady — I mean, old girl."

Lorna chuckled delightedly. "There's a streak of vanity in you after all, Estelle," she said. "Is that your Achilles heel?"

"Oh, is that what you're hoping to find?" Estelle replied at once.

"Aren't we all?" Lorna asked lightly. "Shall I tell you mine? Men in light blue uniforms with stars in their eyes!" She saw Estelle freeze — caught between frivolity and seriousness. She went on. "But enough of this badinage! To weightier matters! You were telling me something the Chief once said about ... my landlady — if that's what you prefer to call her."

"I shouldn't have said it," Estelle came back at once. "Ian never told me such a disgraceful thing."

"He was too ... *noble*?" Lorna suggested. Her emphasis left Estelle in no doubt but that she referred to the impulsive note she had left on Ian's grave.

She closed her eyes and nodded. "You saw!" she murmured.

"Saw it and removed it."

Estelle heaved a sigh of relief and, reaching across the table, gave Lorna's arm a squeeze. "Thank God! I cannot think what possessed me. Did *she* see it?"

Lorna shook her head.

"And you said nothing about it?"

Lorna put her head on one side and stared back accusingly. "If you don't know me better than that by now, Estelle, we'd better go back to using our surnames. I would never betray one of your confidences to her — nor, let me stress, any of hers to you."

"This was hardly a confidence."

"An accidental confidence is still a confidence."

"I cannot think what made me do such a thing."

"D'you want me to supply a few guesses?"

Estelle's eyebrows shot up but four other ladies entered at that moment — all known to her and two known to Lorna. They exchanged some rather embarrassed hallos and made for a table overlooking the esplanade, where they settled to an animated discussion about someone referred to only as *she.*

Marje took their orders and cleared away the remains of Lorna's and Estelle's first course.

Lorna repeated her question and popped the last little square of toast and terrine into her mouth. When Estelle did not demur, she went on, "Is it possible that you were trying to provoke a crisis? Did you want *her* to come storming over to Trevescan, demanding to know what on earth you meant by it?"

"Why should I do a silly thing like that?" Estelle was more guarded than uncomfortable.

"So that you could be provoked into letting drop to *her* the little nugget of information you let drop to me just now?"

"And then?" She was beginning to appear uncomfortable.

"Who knows? Do you think that far ahead? I never do."

Estelle laughed grimly. "If I could be sure you'd never repeat what I say ..." she mused.

Marje brought their main course and served them the vegetables. Ben hovered anxiously in the shadows until they had tasted a mouthful and then dashed forward to ask what they thought of it so far. When they told him it was excellent he seemed disappointed, especially with Lorna. "I expect to be told of at least one improvement each time you come here," he chided.

"We must get together sometime, Ben," she replied. "I can see improvements in all sorts of directions."

"Lorna!" Estelle exclaimed under her breath when he had gone.

"What?"

"That man is in love with you!"

Lorna shook her head. "Only with what he thinks he knows about me — which is quite another matter."

"So, it's no surprise to you, at least. Has he said anything?"

Lorna grinned. "I'm the one who does not pass on other people's confidences — remember?"

"Oh but he's a man. That's different." Estelle laughed, trying to coax something more out of her.

Lorna just shook her head. "Well!" she said briskly. "Now that you *are* convinced I can keep a secret — I hope — what was it you were going to tell me?"

Estelle became serious again. "I was lying when I told you I only guessed at Ian's true feelings about ... her. His wife."

"It's Jessica, Estelle. Just say the name."

"I heard it from Ian's own lips."

Her eyes searched Lorna's eagerly — right, left, right, left — as if one of them must surely yield a clue. Lorna said, "That could mean everything and nothing, Estelle, unless I also know the context."

"The context doesn't matter. He said it. 'Jessica is the greatest disappointment to me.' His very words. She ruined his life. What more d'you need to know?"

"I told you — the context. Did you just answer the phone one day and he was on the other end. 'Hallo, Mrs Carne. Jessica is the greatest disappointment to me. D'you want to hop over the fence and make something of it?' Was it like that?"

For a moment she feared Estelle was about to upend the table. But she pressed on relentlessly, for it was make or break, now or never. "Or did he lick the crumbs of one of your bakewell tarts off his fingers and say, 'Best I ever tasted, Mrs Carne. Jessica is a great disappointment to me — in the bakewell tart department, of course!' Could it have been like *that?*"

Now she saw Estelle was trying not to laugh. Still she pressed on, this time in earnest. All the flippancy went out of her voice as she asked: "Or were you lying close beside each other in the dark? Did he whisper those words in your ear, perhaps?" To prevent an eruption of anger she reached out and squeezed Estelle's hand, adding without a pause, "I do hope so. It would be wonderful to know *that* was what really happened."

The shock of these additional words, implying approval where any woman would have expected condemnation, had the desired effect. Estelle's eyes moistened; her mouth fell slack; she stared in a kind of baffled happiness at her inquisitor — who was suddenly an inquisitor-turned-friend.

One of the women at the other table noticed that something fairly emotional was going on and nudged her companions. But by the time they felt it safe to turn and stare, all they saw was Marje gathering up the plates and asking if they wanted any pudding.

Estelle chose spotted dick; Lorna asked for cheese and biscuits without even glancing at the list of puddings. "I seem to have gone off sweet things," she told Estelle when the waitress had returned to the kitchen. A pat on her stomach offered a probable cause.

Two women and a little boy came in — strangers to the six who were already there. They also chose a table overlooking the esplanade.

Estelle glanced over her shoulder at the other four women before she turned back to Lorna. "What you said just now — did you really mean it?" she asked.

"Every word."

"Why?"

"Because!" She laughed. But when she saw it did not satisfy Estelle she added, "I don't know why. Would you prefer me to throw up my hands in horror and tell you to wash yourself all over, seven times seven, in carbolic?"

Estelle gave a baffled laugh. "You are certainly the strangest young woman I've ever ... and the most" — she smiled awkwardly at having to use the word — "likable, too."

"D'you believe you ought to be whipped through Penzance at the tail of a cart, then?"

"Well, it certainly wasn't the noblest thing I ever did. I swear I had no intention of ... doing that. It's just that he came home for forty-eight hours and his wife wasn't there. The children had their nanny, of course, but she had a terrible cold so he sent her home. The cook had gone to Devon for a funeral, and the poor man couldn't even boil an egg. That's all I intended."

It occurred to Lorna that if that really had been all, she could have sent meals over from her own kitchen, since her cook was not, presumably, also at a funeral in Devon. All she said, however, was, "And the rest was up to Mother Nature — fecund Mother Nature, as Theo calls her."

"I *beg* your pardon!"

"Fecund." She enunciated the word extra-clearly.

"Ah! Well, fortunately not on that occasion! One is not a doctor's wife for nothing!"

"It only seems like it at times."

Estelle stared at her coldly. "Yes, well, that's another story. Don't you wish to hear this one?"

"The incandescent details? No thank you."

She was about to explain her refusal in kindly terms when Estelle rushed on anyway. "Oh but they *are* the context. I don't want you to think we were two ... two ... two *animals*. It was so natural. So easy. So inevitable. So ... beautiful." The tears were back in her eyes when she spoke the word. "It's what I shall ask to be judged by when they sound the Last Trump. I may feel shame for it here below, where it is called adultery, but" — she raised her eyes skyward briefly — "He will surely understand. Otherwise why did He let it happen at all? Why put these feelings in our breasts?"

Marje brought their puddings and went on to take more orders. Ben came up again and canvassed opinions at the other tables. "Better than I'd hoped," he murmured to Lorna as he passed by on his way out again.

"Same here," she agreed.

"Ears like beetroot," Estelle whispered as he went back downstairs. "It's not fair of you unless you intend doing something about it."

"Who said I don't?" Lorna grinned.

"I thought you'd kill any woman who came between you and Mister Westwood?"

"That's also true." Lorna chuckled. "You keep asking me to explain things that I can't, Estelle. Actually ..." She became thoughtful again. "There's one thing about *you* I don't quite understand."

"Only one?" Estelle pretended to be disappointed.

"Yes. You claim you hate Jessica Lanyon so much, but really I think you have a bit of a soft spot for her."

"For *her!*"

The cry brought all conversation in the room to a halt. Estelle blushed and apologized to the four she knew, including the strangers with a brief sweep of her eyes. "How can you say that?" she asked in a vehement whisper when the others had resumed their babble again.

"You speak and behave as if David has blighted your life — isn't that so?"

"What of it?" she answered uncomfortably.

"And you hate Jessica Lanyon with a loathing one can almost touch — or so you try to pretend."

"It's no pretence — believe you me!"

"But it must be. Otherwise why not give him his freedom, Estelle? Doesn't she *deserve* to have her life blighted, too? And isn't he — from your own experience — the perfect man to do it?"

At the West of England Bank, the "incurable romanticism" (of which Marjorie Curnow accused her husband) proved remarkably curable that January. All it required was fifteen minutes with Bill Westwood — during which time the young idealist managed to convince him that "the world's fastest aeroplane" was the nearest thing to a bottomless pit he had ever encountered. During the brief interview Lorna completed her shopping in Market Jew Street. It was now the third week in January, some six weeks off the earliest date Dr Carmichael had given her, and movement was becoming laborious. She was browsing in the bookshop opposite the bank when Bill emerged; she knew the outcome the moment she saw his dejected figure in the doorway.

She went outside and yoo-hooed to him. He barely managed a smile as he crossed the street.

"The man's absolutely obsessed with money," he complained as he took her arm and relieved her of her only parcel. "Where's the rest?" he asked.

"They'll deliver it. I've changed my mind about a cup of tea." She smiled wryly. "Somehow I don't seem to have the capacity I used to! Let's walk down to the dock and along the seafront."

"Are you sure you can?"

"It's good for me."

They set off up the street, past Sir Humphrey Davey's statue, to the little square at the top. "Tell me what he said," she prompted.

"Oh ... he wasn't interested in the glory of the thing — the honour it would be for Britain ... the universal interest it would focus on Penzance ... the sheer exhilaration of pulling it off. He brushed all that aside. The only thing he wanted to know was how much would it cost and when it would start paying back."

"And what did you tell him?"

"How much it would cost? I said I didn't know, but we could give it a jolly good shake for five thou'. When it would pay back? Never, probably. But that isn't the point."

"No. The point is, Bill, he's the wrong man. A banker will only lend you money if you can prove to him you don't really need to borrow it. What we've got to find, my lover, is another looney like yourself — only one with money." She broke off and exclaimed, "Good lord!"

He turned to her in surprise but she was staring straight ahead, across the edge of the square, which they were now entering. "Seen a ghost?" he asked.

"The next best thing," she answered. "I think I saw my mother going down toward Chapel Street. Come on!"

"This cannot be good for you." He puffed as he struggled to keep up with her.

"It *is* my mother. This is providence at work, Bill. I don't know whether my father is quite looney enough, but it's up to you to infect him." She grinned over her shoulder at him. "I'd say you're pretty infectious. It was just your bad luck today — to meet someone immune. Wait a mo!"

She halted abruptly and drew into a shop entrance. He almost bowled into her. "What now?"

"She's going into Cargill's. That's even better. We can get ahead of her and you can buttonhole my father."

He laughed at her enthusiasm and pointed out that he didn't even know the man. She said they were wasting breath and set off again, though not at such a cracking pace this time. Five minutes later they emerged onto the Trinity House Quay, where, as she had expected, her parents' Daimler was parked outside the offices, with the chauffeur-groom at the wheel.

A swift survey of the quay revealed no one who resembled her father. Lorna went up to the car. "Hallo, Ricks," she said cheerfully. "She's looking pretty impressive still — the old bus."

"Why, Miss Lorna!" Pleasure and guilty fear were equally mingled in his face.

"Don't get out, for God's sake," she told him.

"Fancy meeting you!"

"Yes, fancy! Is his nibs up in the office?"

The chauffeur darted his head toward the quay, which was littered with huge buoys brought in for maintenance. "He's admiring the new customs cutter."

"Ah!" She glanced hopefully at Bill before she turned back to Ricks and asked, "Anything special about it?"

He nodded. "New Thorneycroft engines — six hundred horse-power, or so they claim."

Bill leaned forward with interest. "The vee-eights with counter-rotating twin screws? Really?"

Lorna laughed with delight and pushed him away toward the quayside. "That's your buttonhole, man. He must be behind one of those buoys. His name's William, too, by the way, so perhaps that's a good omen. I'll be waiting back there, round the corner."

As Bill hastened across the quay, she murmured, "See if Bill can get Bill to foot the bill — and the best of luck!" Then, with a wink at the chauffeur, "I'll go and ambush my mother. We can't have her barging in on the start of a glorious partnership!"

"And the best of luck to you, too, Miss," the man called after her.

The moment she rounded the corner Lorna saw her mother coming toward her, about two hundred paces up the street. She withdrew into a doorway, to get what little shelter she could from the raw southeasterly blowing in off the bay. There she waited until her mother's footsteps came close; then she stepped out and said, "Hallo, Mummy. D'you want a screaming fit or would you prefer a chat?"

Mrs Sancreed looked for one fraught moment as if she would walk straight on by.

Lorna added, "Thanks for the christening shawl, by the way. It's even more beautiful than I remembered it."

That tipped the balance somehow. Mrs Sancreed did walk past her daughter but only for a pace or two, so that she could scan a larger portion of the quay. "Your father ...?" she inquired.

"He's lost in love," Lorna assured her. "Seduced by a wily Thorneycroft vee-eight of six hundred horsepower with counter-manding twin screws all over the place."

Her mother frowned. "Have you been speaking to him?"

"Of course not. I make for the exit the moment I hear the words 'balanced crankshaft' these days. He's with a friend of mine who comes out with things like that all the time. Daddy wouldn't thank you for interrupting them, though. My friend's called William, by the way, so Daddy will be extra-pleased!"

This taunt raked over an ancient bit of family history that Mrs Sancreed preferred to forget. Her eyes narrowed. "You're up to something. You can't deceive me."

Lorna smiled at her. "D'you know, I could almost swear I heard you say, 'Darling, how wonderful to see you! How well you're looking in spite of everything! When is the baby due? What arrangements have you made?' Or didn't I?"

"All right!" Her mother stamped her foot. "Of course I want to know all those things. It's just ... meeting you out of the blue — and with your father just round the corner. He'd cut me dead for a week if he even saw me nodding at you." She smiled wanly. "And you *are* up to something — I know jolly well!"

"If you mean something underhand — absolutely not. I'll tell you everything. The friend I mentioned is Bill Westwood, ex-flight lieutenant. He knew Philip and the Chief. And he's come down to Penzance to start an aeroplane company. We're beginning to be quite keen on each other."

Mrs Sancreed's eyes strayed to the swelling in her daughter's belly.

"Yes, Mummy, despite all that. Can you understand it? I suppose *you* can't."

"No, I can't!" her mother agreed vehemently. Then, more gently, she added, "Still, I'm glad for you — for your sake."

"Not to mention the sake of your grandchild."

"Yes." Mrs Sancreed bit her lip and looked about her unhappily.

"The only grandchild you're likely to get — unless *someone* takes me on and gives you more."

"Yes, dear! I am aware of all these ... these implications."

"So it's no great shock to the system to talk about them."

Mrs Sancreed closed her eyes. "You are relentless."

"Weren't you when you were expecting me? Someone has to be."

octor Carmichael pulled down Lorna's nightie and said, "It could be a false alarm, of course, but if I have to put the proverbial penny on the drum, I'd say it's well on the way now." He shook his head reproachfully as he drew the bedclothes up over her again. "You should never have gone out in that cold wind."

"It was only a breeze," she told him.

"Well!" He rubbed his hands cheerfully. "We are a *little* premature, but not alarmingly so — not these days." He picked up his bag and headed for the door. "I'll go and make the arrangements. Don't hesitate to send for Doctor Carne if the contractions change markedly before I get back, but I shouldn't be more than half an hour."

Outside he confessed to Jessica that he'd be happier if she were up at the hospital. Forty days premature was quite a lot, even in these days, but he thought it too late to move her now. "Liven up the fire in her bedroom," he said. "Get the temperature up."

"And a rubber sheet below her?"

"Yes, well, you know everything that's needed, Mrs Lanyon. I'll see about the midwife, too, in case it's a long haul and I get called away. I have two more mothers-to-be who come to term today. Isn't it always the way!"

"It never rains but it pours," Jessica agreed.

"Let's hope it pours with Miss Sancreed before too long!" he called back as he went down the stairs.

Guy and Toby came out onto the landing, wanting to know what was happening. She told them that Auntie Lorna was going to have her baby at last; when they saw her tomorrow, her tummy would be flat again. They wanted to know if they could help. The question so baffled Jessica for a moment that she almost asked for suggestions; then she said, "If you really want to help, you can just stay *quietly* out of sight until it's all over. You may play with your toys — *quietly!* — read, write your next play for the Porthgwarra Theatre ... anything. Just keep out from under our feet. All right?"

They knew when not to look a gift bribe in the mouth and returned to their room without another word.

Jessica went in to Lorna, with a broad smile of encouragement ready. "Well, my lass! The Big Push is on for tonight — as they said in the trenches."

"For Hill Sixty One!" Lorna exaggerated her belly. "We'll flatten it! It *looks* full term, wouldn't you say?"

"D'you know, I believe it is," Jessica replied. "I was like that with Sarah. She hardly showed until about eight months but she was over seven pounds. I'll bet that's the same with you."

"Talk of the devil!" Lorna nodded toward the door — and then winced as another contraction gripped her.

"Are they getting closer?" Jessica asked.

"No!" Lorna gasped. "Or I don't think they are. Come on in, Sarah, darling. But they're certainly getting stronger." She turned her head and flashed a welcoming smile at the girl, who was approaching her in a kind of reverent awe.

"Can I stay?" she asked nervously.

"Well ..." her mother began.

"Of course you can," Lorna put in before Jessica could say otherwise. "As far as I'm concerned, that is." She glanced at Jess then. "No reason why not, is there?"

Jessica shrugged, annoyed to realize that Lorna was right, though she herself would instinctively have denied the request. "As long as she helps."

Lorna grinned at the girl. "Of course she'll help. She can begin now. Read me that drivel." She nodded toward the book on her bedside table, *Chéri* by Colette. "Take my mind off this ... oh, it's such a relief when it stops!"

Jessica went off to gather things and make arrangements, telling Sarah to call immediately if anything happened. At the bottom of the stairs she glanced toward the front door and thought that Dr Carmichael must have forgotten something; through the hammered pattern of the glass she could discern someone standing out there. She opened the door to find Bill Westwood pressing the bell button. "I rang several times," he explained apologetically when their greetings were done. "Is Lorna ready?"

"You could call it that!" Jessica laughed. "Come on in. There'll be no picture palace tonight, I'm afraid — or not for her, anyway."

He closed his eyes and leaned his forehead against the jamb. "Oh God!" he murmured. "No!"

"Why d'you say it like that? It's not a tragedy. Do come in — you're letting all the heat escape." She repeated the question as she shut the door behind him.

"She met her mother today," he explained — or began to.

"Did they fight? They're pretty much ..."

"No. On the contrary, it was fairly amicable."

"Were you there? She never said a word about it to me. Mind you, this business started almost as soon as she got home."

"I was talking to her father round the corner at the time — oh, it's too complicated to explain."

Jessica turned and headed toward the kitchen. "Tell me while we assemble this and that."

Bill followed her and described what had happened that afternoon.

"Well, what's done is done," she said when he had finished. "Carry these up for me, will you? There's a dear."

When they reached the landing, Bill hung back.

"Go on!" Jessica urged. "She's only lying in bed. Stay and talk with her a bit. Keep her mind off things. Just dump that lot on the chair." She poked her head in the door. "Here's a visitor for you, love. And Sarah — come and help me make some sandwiches, eh? We may not have much time later."

As they went downstairs she asked the girl if she really wanted to stay and watch. "It can be a bit messy, you know — blood and water and ... all the afterbirth things."

Sarah went pale but stuck to her guns.

"As long as you're prepared, darling," her mother concluded. "The moment you turn green or look the least bit distressed — out you go! Is that understood?"

"Yes," the girl replied wearily.

Jessica tousled her hair. "Go on, I'm just preparing you for the worst. It's actually a happy occasion, despite the pain and the gore. Don't look so worried!" She set a pan of eggs to hard boil.

"It's not that." Sarah brought the butter from the larder and began mashing it softer while her mother cut the bread as thin as it would go.

"What then? Why that furrowed brow?"

"Does Mister Westwood truly *love* Auntie Lorna?"

"What a question! Why don't you ask her?"

"I did."

"Oh." For a moment Jessica did not know what to say.

"She says she isn't sure. When a woman has something a man wants very badly and he tells her he loves her, she can't always be sure he's speaking the truth."

For a moment Jessica thought Lorna had been trying to tell Sarah something of the facts of life, but then she realized it was a conversation about money — that other fact of life. She agreed ruefully that such was, indeed, the case.

"How can we test him?" Sarah asked.

"We, dear? It's not really our business, you know," Jessica said — and then realized her daughter was thinking of a fairy story she had read to the boys the night before; Sarah was too old for such stories herself, but she didn't mind eavesdropping. "Oh! You mean like the Prince of the Eastern Empire, where they sent him off and told him not to return without bringing a golden apple! We could try that."

"Or we could tell him Auntie Lorna's lost all her money. Then see if he'd still stick by her."

Jessica laughed. "You spread those slices while I chop the parsley. The eggs'll take a while yet." After a while she added, "Actually, you've given me an idea, though. A little test might not come amiss."

When Sarah had all the slices buttered, her mother went on, "Just slip upstairs and ask Mister Westwood if he'd come down and carve the ham for me, will you?"

"I can carve ham," Sarah replied scornfully.

"I know, dear. In fact, even *I* can carve ham. But it's the sort of appeal to which men cannot help responding — and I would like a little chat with him. You stay and read to Auntie Lorna. Tell her I'll be up to put the rubber blanket in the bed by and by."

The girl's eyes danced merrily as the penny dropped. She ran to obey. A few minutes later Bill was at the kitchen door, saying, "Where's the carving knife, then?"

He tut-tutted at its bluntness and honed it for more than a minute on the back doorstep before he was satisfied.

"Mrs Carne is up and about again I see," he remarked as he returned indoors.

"Mmm," was all Jessica replied to that. "How was Lorna when you left her?"

"Quite cheerful — unless she's putting a brave face on things." He swilled the blade under the tap and wiped it on the curtain.

Jessica clenched her fists but said nothing. "I expect she *is* cheerful," she said. "I know it's a worrying time — but at least all the worrying will be over by tomorrow — unless it's going to be one of those marathon labours. *Then* we'll be able to get on with our real business in life." She smiled as if to say she was sure Lorna must have talked about it to him.

"Your boarding house," he suggested.

"Well that was one of our ideas. Personally, I always thought it a bit of a stop-gap notion. It wouldn't really keep us in the style to which we have, alas, become accustomed. Our real ambition ... has she told you about it?"

He shook his head.

"Our real ambition is to turn this house into a sanitarium — employing a couple of doctors and quite a large staff, you know. It'll take every penny we've got between us, but the prospects are very bright." She cracked the shells and started peeling the eggs. "Of course, we haven't been able to give it much thought — I mean what with the uncertainty about her baby and so forth. But now that's all over — the uncertainty part, anyway — we can really get down to it."

"Planning it," he said.

"Bless me, no — it's all planned. Right down to the very last bottle of mercurichrome." There was a knock at the front door. "I wonder who that could be?" she murmured as she slipped off her apron and went out.

It was Ben Calloway. "I did ring," he said.

"I know. It doesn't work — I think the battery's flat but I can't find where the electrician hid it. Come in."

He entered far enough to let her shut the door but would not come farther. "Is everything all right?" he asked. "I saw Doctor Carmichael leaving in a bit of a rush. Is it ...?"

"It is, Mister Calloway. But don't fret yourself. So far everything's going swimmingly."

"I thought it might have started." He fumbled with a paper bag. "Give her this, will you?"

"What is it?" Through the paper it felt like a short wooden twig, slightly green.

"Liquorice root," he replied. "She can bite on it to stop crying out if the pain gets ... you know."

"Liquorice root?" Jessica repeated in amazement.

"It's a clean piece, brand new," he told her. "It's what the sailors used to bite on in naval floggings. You will let me know the minute there's any news."

"I promise." She flexed the root inside its paper bag. "It really works, does it?"

"Even if it happens in the small hours — wake me up. I don't mind. Anytime! I'll leave the back door open and the landing light on. Yes, it really works."

"Very well. Bless you, Mister Calloway, I'm sure she'll be touched at your concern."

"It's more than concern, Mrs Lanyon. Lorna means absolutely everything to me."

"I'll tell her that, too."

He turned to go. "Tell her my offer still ..." He hesitated. "No. Tell her *Calloway is willin'* — say that to her."

She returned to the kitchen to find Bill standing at the quarter-open back door, talking in a low voice to someone beyond it. "More visitors?" she asked.

He stood aside and opened the door to reveal a somewhat startled Estelle Carne, standing on the back step and blinking at the sudden flood of light.

"Am I welcome here?" she asked hesitantly.

Jessica went to her, holding forth both hands. "You have *always* been welcome at Rosemergy, Mrs Carne," she said. "Do come in. You must be frozen stiff out there."

"I've only just arrived," she replied, by way of excusing Bill for not asking her in. "I gather it's started. I just took a call from Jeremy Carmichael. How is she?"

"Go up and see her if you like. I'm going to bring up a cup of tea in a moment."

Estelle pulled a face. "I couldn't. It frightens me. I'd only make her feel afraid, too."

"There is that, of course," said Jessica, who had been about to cajole her into going up.

The kettle boiled and Jessica set about making the tea. "If you want to do something, you could finish peeling these eggs and chop them and fill the remaining sandwiches. Mister Westwood will help."

Bill came out of the pantry holding something diseased-looking in his hand. "That's why your bell doesn't work," he told her as he dropped it in the waste bin.

"Splendid fellow!" She lifted the tea tray and made for the door. "I'll be back in ten minutes. Go through to the drawing room when you've finished the sandwiches."

After that, nothing happened for a couple of hours, except that the contractions became more frequent, the waters burst, and Lorna discovered that the liquorice root — so efficacious in naval floggings — was a great help against the pains of labour, too.

Jessica made several visits to the drawing room as the evening wore on, each time with a new progress report, all of them vague but encouraging. David came over at around half-past nine, shortly after Dr Carmichael had returned — having successfully delivered one of his other patients in the meanwhile. They agreed Lorna would not be long now. David gave her shoulder a manful shake and said, "Bear up, old thing!"

"Or down," Jessica corrected him.

She took him off to the kitchen for a bite to eat. The moment they were gone, Carmichael snatched *Chéri* from Lorna's hands and flung it across the room. "None of that, my lass," he said sternly. "You've got work to do." He looked inquiringly at Sarah.

"She's staying," Lorna told him firmly.

"With her mother's approval?" he asked.

"Full approval. She's going to be a nurse when she grows up."

His attitude softened. "That's in the lap of the gods." He was about to add a remark to the effect that, after tonight, Sarah would think very hard indeed about what she'd allow to happen in her *own* lap, but he realized it might not be the most tactful start to the evening's proceedings — what with the general lack of wedding rings in the room at that moment.

On their way downstairs Jessica mentioned to David that she had left Estelle and Westwood playing a round of two-handed whist in the drawing room.

"I knew she had come over here," he replied, turning directly toward the kitchen door.

She lifted the damp cloth and let him take a generous selection of sandwiches. "Westwood says Lorna walked rather fast down Chapel Street this afternoon — in pursuit of her mother. He got very worried by it but you know how headstrong she is."

He shook his head. "I doubt if that has anything to do with this." He nodded at the ceiling. "I think the dear girl got her dates muddled. This has all the hallmarks of a natural, full-term parturition so far." He bit a large mouthful and ate with relish.

She suddenly realized he'd had no dinner. "Listen!" she said. "I can easily rustle you up something."

His eyes bulged in theatrical fear. He gestured frantically at his full mouth and patted his stomach reassuringly.

"You!" She pulled a punch on his arm. "I'm not as bad as all that!"

He chuckled when his mouth was empty again. "At least you no longer burst into tears, Jess."

She had almost forgotten the occasion. She was about to remark on what an eternity ago it seemed when she heard someone open and close the front door.

"Only me," Mrs Hughes, the midwife, called out as she went upstairs. She had visited the house twice since New Year, so she knew her way. Seeing Jessica at the kitchen door she called out, "If there was such a thing as a nice cup of tea …? This is my third delivery today!"

Jessica went to boil the kettle yet again. "Are you going up to join them?" she asked David.

He shook his head. "Midwives and doctors just don't mix. I'll leave the pair of them to it. The mere sight of Mrs Hughes rolling up her sleeves strikes terror into me."

"More sandwiches?"

He shook his head.

"Are you going home then?"

"D'you want me to?"

"I ought not to neglect my two guests in the drawing room much longer — uninvited though they may be."

He ignored the point. "I'd only bite my nails to the bone. Anyway, I asked Doris on the exchange to put my calls through here. I hope you don't mind."

"Not at all," she replied airily. "I always wondered what it'd be like to be a doctor's wife." Then she realized what she'd said, and blushed. "I mean …" she stammered.

To rescue her he resorted to humour. "Had you any particular doctor in mind?"

She raised her apron and fanned her face, parodying a servant girl, so as to make a joke of it.

"Sit down, Jess." He pushed a chair out with his foot. "Eat something yourself. You look as if you need it."

With some reluctance she did as he suggested, dithered over the sandwiches, and eventually selected egg. "D'you realize, David, this is the first time you and I have been alone since the day we met Theo Foster at Porthgwarra?"

"Yes," he said.

"Was that deliberate?"

"Yes. And so is this." He pointed at her and then at himself. "We ought to talk, Jess."

"With Estelle in the house?"

"Can she hear us?"

A loud peal of laughter from the drawing room answered him.

"I don't know what Lorna's purpose has been," he went on. "Encouraging Estelle to get up and about again."

"Aren't you happy? You never seemed happy when she was bedridden all the time."

He shrugged and grinned ruefully. "One got used to it."

Jessica sighed. "Yes, I know what you mean."

"In an odd way it suited both of us," he said. "Our consciences, that is. We could say, 'Oh well, if she *wants* to cut off her nose to spite her face, what can we do to stop her?' And we didn't bother to try all that hard."

Jessica laughed bleakly. "And now the dear girl's messed it up for us! Is Estelle starting to make ... demands on you again?"

He looked surprised; for her it was an amazingly frank question. Jessica realized it, too, and, blushing, added, "On your time, I mean."

He smiled. "I know what you mean, love. The answer is no — to both questions. She is as cold to me as ever. The only difference now is that I run the risk of bumping into her more often — and in more places — than before."

Jessica stared at the kettle, praying for it not to boil just yet. "Would she let you go, d'you think? Ever?"

"Not out of ... kindness. You see! I find it almost impossible to use the word in any connection with her!"

"Not even to get her own freedom?"

"She has all the freedom she requires as it is. A divorce would only restrict her — when you think of how many doors would automatically close against her."

"And against you."

"I'd happily go through with it if every door in Penzance was barred against me. Except one, of course." He reached across and squeezed her hand.

The kettle began to sing.

"We've never spoken like this before, David," she said.

"We've never had to. But don't you feel things are coming to a head somehow?"

"Just because Lorna has managed to persuade Estelle to pick up her bed and walk?"

"She's behind it all. She can't leave us be — any of us. She's got some scheme in her mind and she's pushing and pushing ..."

There were noises from above — not exactly a cry but a loud grunt of exertion followed by a long-drawn-out "a-a-a-gh!"

Jessica laughed. "You never spoke a truer word, David. I'd better go and see if it has worked. When the kettle boils, make the tea in that pot. Five measures."

At the foot of the stairs she hesitated, half-inclined to go to the drawing-room door. It was odd that neither of them had come out. Surely they, too, had heard Lorna's outburst?

There was another cry from upstairs. She raced up the flight, three steps at a time.

*S*arah's near-whisper was almost drowned in the orgy of grunting, heaving, exhortation, and exultation that was going on, both in and around the childbed. "It's the baby's *head!*" she exclaimed to her mother, who had joined them at that moment. Various kindly but sarcastic responses occurred to Jessica but all she did was smile; she was too amused at the thought that her own ten-year-old daughter was giving her a birds-and-bees lesson.

Sarah yielded her place at Lorna's side and went across the room to watch the business end of things; that bit about the baby being fed through a kind of hosepipe to the tummy button had her really puzzled now that she saw where it was emerging. At this, Mrs Hughes and Dr Carmichael exchanged glances, but they, too, passed no comment. Jessica grasped Lorna's hand and squeezed it hard; she took up a dry cotton towel and mopped her brow. Lorna grinned feebly up at her and pulled a face. She took the liquorice root briefly from between her jaws and gasped, "It's like the worst constipation ever."

"I remember. Does that thing of Ben Calloway's help at all?" Jessica asked.

"I don't know. But it was kind of him. Kindness helps."

"One more heave," Mrs Hughes said. "The last, I think."

Lorna closed her eyes, drew a deep breath and held it, clenched her teeth tight on the root, and pushed for all she was worth. The baby came out in a wet, slithering mass. Carmichael reached for it but Mrs Hughes got there first. "A boy," she said. A small, silent battle-of-the-eyes raged between her and the doctor.

Jessica began to see what David meant when he claimed to be frightened of the woman. "It's a boy, Lorna!" she repeated.

Lorna just lay there gasping, a tiny smile on her lips.

The midwife, having wiped the baby's mouth and nose and made sure he was breathing, lifted him no farther than to lay him on his front on his mother's now deflated belly.

"D'you feel him?" Jessica asked.

Lorna nodded and opened her eyes. "My God!" she exclaimed, blinking uncertainly at the gory bundle. She stirred and the placenta came away. Mrs Hughes grabbed it as if it were the true prize for all this labour. Holding it up, she massaged the umbilical cord toward the baby, three or four times — and at last Sarah understood that business about the hosepipe.

"Now, Doctor!" said the midwife triumphantly as she laid the placenta down again.

Dr Carmichael assumed the sort of face important men assume when they have humoured a woman's foibles long enough. He bound the cord and severed it. "Has he a name?" he asked.

"Philip," Lorna replied.

"Touch him," Mrs Hughes commanded.

With a look of distaste Lorna laid her fingertips hesitantly on her baby's head. The moment she made contact, however, and felt him stir, she gave a little gasping laugh and said, "Hey!"

This seemed to satisfy Mrs Hughes for she at once removed the baby and took him across the room to be washed. He began to cry the moment he felt the water.

Ten minutes later, with everything cleaned up and fresh sheets on the bed, mother and baby were reunited. Carmichael went to have a word with David.

"Do I feed him now?" Lorna asked.

"If he'll take it," the midwife said. "Otherwise wait till he cries."

Lorna, who was now wearing one of Ian's voluminous pyjama tops, unbuttoned it and put little Philip to her breast. He began to suckle at once. She watched in fascination, shared by Sarah and her mother, too.

"How do they know what to do?" Sarah asked in amazement.

"He's had weeks of practice. Look." Mrs Hughes pointed to a small white callus on the baby's thumb.

"In there?" Sarah asked incredulously.

"My dear, he's been swimming and crawling and climbing trees and swinging through branches — and walking — for months. The busiest period of his entire life has probably just come to an end."

"The real mystery," Lorna put in, "is where all this milk came from. I'll swear it wasn't there this afternoon."

"You felt nothing?" the midwife asked.

"A little tenderness, perhaps."

"A-ha!" Mrs Hughes exclaimed as if Lorna had just confirmed some theory of hers, which she held in the face of orthodox opinion. "Swap him over," she advised, "or you'll end up lopsided."

Sarah began to giggle, slightly hysterically. It galvanized Jessica to action. "Right, Miss!" she said. "It's all over. Beddy-byes for you — and not before time."

The girl reached over and tried to shake hands with the baby. "Such a grip!" she said to Jessica as she was led away. She was still babbling with wonder when she laid her head on the pillow. She wanted to know why little Philip's face was all squashed and his head so long and thin — but she was fast asleep before her mother could answer her.

Jessica leaned over and kissed her tenderly. She sat and gazed at her for a long time, thinking that, really, they were a wonder at any age ... and had she done the right thing in allowing her to be there and watch it all? ... and how could any parent ever answer a question like that? It was all an experiment. You'd be old and grey yourself by the time the results were known. At least she cared enough to ask such questions; she didn't think her own parents had ever worried about such things at all.

She rose to find a yawning Guy standing in the doorway. "Is the baby borned yet?" he asked.

She scooped him up and carried him back to bed. "Yes, indeed," she told him. "It all went smoothly. It's a darling little boy and we're going to call him Philip."

She tried to pull the bedclothes back over him but he struggled free and raised his fists over his head like a boxing champ. "Y-e-e-a-h!" he cried. "A boy!" — and then he, too, fell asleep as quickly as his sister had done.

Out on the landing she met David, carrying the tray laden with all the tea things.

"That'll be stewed by now," she said.

He grinned. "I've only just made it."

"Is Lorna allowed tea?" She held the door open for him.

"Whether she's allowed it or not," Lorna cried, "she's going to have a cup — hot as hell and sweet as love, please!"

"You made *me* drink glucose water," Jessica grumbled as she set down an occasional table for the tea tray.

"That was back in the Dark Ages, old girl," he told her. "Medicine's come a long way since then." He set down the tray and went over to kiss Lorna on the brow. "Well done, bonny lass!" He glanced at Philip, now a snoozing, dribbling bundle between her breasts, and said, "Seven pounds, two ounces, eh? Hardly six weeks premature!"

"So-rry," she replied in an insincere dying fall.

He arched his eyebrows and included Jessica in his surprise. "No arguments?" he asked. "Where's all that fighting spirit?"

"David!" Jessica scolded. "She's just been through ..."

"It's all right, Jess," Lorna interrupted. To him she answered: "I'm saving it for a worthwhile cause, see?" and she laid a demonstratively protective hand over Philip's swaddling.

"Good heavens!" Jessica exclaimed suddenly. "I quite forgot — Bill and Estelle! Surely they've ..."

"Gone," David put in.

After a moment of perplexed silence Jessica said, "Gone?"

"Bill?" Lorna added. "Was he here?" Then she remembered he had come to her bedside earlier. "Oh yes! We were going to see *Pollyanna!* Poor man."

"I'm sure he understood, dear," Jess said sarcastically. Then, turning back to David, "Where have they gone?"

He shrugged. "How do I know? For a walk along the seafront? To prop up the bar in the Mouse Hole? Even back to my place — or perhaps the lure of Mary Pickford and Douglas Fairbanks was too much for them after all!"

She shook her head slowly as if she still could hardly believe it. "What an extraordinary thing to do, though — just to wander off without a word to anyone."

"And Estelle was with him?" Lorna asked. "D'you mean Estelle was *here*, in this house?"

He nodded. "Quite the gadabout, isn't she!"

"She wanted to be near Lorna," Jessica said reproachfully. To Lorna she added, "Pay no attention to his sneers — she was very concerned for you. But I can't understand Bill going off like that. Especially not saying a word."

"Some men simply can't bear the thought of childbirth," David pointed out.

Jessica fell silent at that; she knew he was referring to Ian, who had always gone out to the club when she had given birth to their children. True, he had sat by the telephone and drummed his fingers, but he couldn't stand being in the house while it was happening. Perhaps Bill was like that, too.

"Estelle calling at Rosemergy, eh!" Lorna murmured.

Jessica came out of her reverie to find Lorna staring up at David with a truculent sort of smile on her lips — a smile of petty triumph, almost. After all she'd been through tonight — she was still capable of all the old obscure battles! Where did that frightening energy — and the implacable will that it fed — come from?

And David was staring back at her with one of the coldest expressions she had ever seen on his face.

It made no sense to her at all. It merely served to reinforce her feeling that, no matter what was going on around her, she would always be the last to know of it.

*M*rs Sancreed sent her daughter a silver christening mug with the name William already engraved upon it — a crude hint that naming the baby after his grandfather might be seen as an olive branch. A conciliatory note accompanied it but there was no visit in person.

Lorna was not allowed to rise from her "sickbed" until the middle of February, for, though it was becoming unfashionable to treat pregnancy itself as an illness, nobody saw any reason to forgo the accompanying convalescence — certainly not the young mother who was the chief beneficiary of the indulgence, nor the women around her who had similarly benefited in the past and might, who knows, do so again.

If anyone had been so crass as to seek her absolutely honest opinion, Lorna would have allowed that she was sufficiently recovered from the ordeal after a week. The next seven days were sheer indulgence — and why not, for it was wet and miserable outside with not a glimmer of sun from dawn to dusk. Several times she said she knew why Estelle had taken to her bed and stayed there despite every appearance of blooming health. It was absolute bliss and well worth all the pain. But during the third week her understanding had worn thin and by the time Dr Carmichael gave his consent to it she was actually chafing to be up and about again.

David's earlier fears that she might not appreciate the difference between an animated toy and a live baby proved unfounded — which was a measure either of his poor judgment or of the maturity she had gained in the meanwhile. Little Philip was, for those three bedridden weeks at least, the centre of her life. Her questioning nature, which had earlier led her to look for ulterior motives in everything people said or did, now focused entirely on the baby. If he curled his toes in a way she had not observed before, she'd wonder if some parasite might not be eating at his nerves, or could it be the wrong sort of cotton in his swaddling? Everything was called into question, or so it seemed to a casual observer.

But when David — who had no other choice than to be a casual observer — commented on this to Jessica she pointed out that Lorna was, in fact, rather selective in the things she allowed to worry her. If Philip cried for no obvious reason (no wind, no hunger, no nappy pins inadvertently pushed through the skin of his tummy … et cetera), she usually remained quite calm. She would pick him up, comfort him, murmur, "There there!" and go on reading her latest romance. It was only his involuntary little acts that set her worrying — little shivers, random movements of his features, and so forth. "In other words," Jessica concluded, "if he deliberately *demands* her attention, she'll have none of it. She won't be bossed about, not even by him. It'll be interesting to see how quickly she trains him to catch her attention without apparently meaning to. Did *I* do anything like that?"

He rolled up his eyes and consulted some oracle in his head. "You were rather over-protective of Sarah, I seem to recall, but you were quite brutal with the boys."

"That was Ian's rule," she said. "Let them cry twenty minutes before you go near them. D'you remember when Toby got stung by a wasp — and how *awful* we felt afterwards? I didn't hear so much about those rules after that!"

Lorna's long period of enforced idleness had one unexpected outcome. Her idea of heaven had been to stay in bed three weeks reading nothing but light fiction. Somewhere around the middle of the second week, however, when she was halfway through the latest novel, she discovered she had read it before — and not years ago, either; in fact, it was the first one she'd read after having Philip, a mere ten days earlier! From then on she took to "eating plain brown bread with my blancmange," as she put it — that is, *Pear's Cyclopædia, The Races of Man,* an eighty-year-old *Flora and Fauna of the Land's End Peninsula,* and anything else that came to hand.

In *The Races of Man* she saw how all the backward peoples of the world tied the baby to the mother during the first months of life. What struck her most was that all the babies were smiling. True, the photographs were heavily retouched — especially in the case of naked female breasts, which often needed enlargement to make them conform to the reader's expectations; but the mouth of a bawling baby (as she knew very well by then) fills about ninety per cent of its face — well beyond the retoucher's skill to transform it into a smile. And, retouched or not, she had never seen babies smile like that in their English cots and bassinets. Her memory of English babies, among friends of hers who had married early, was of ranks of selfish little homunculi, set out to ripen in the sun on the terrace of some country house — and all yelling their heads off. It thereore seemed to Lorna that the world's backward peoples might, in this one respect at least, be rather more forward than the distinguished professor of anthropology who so named them.

At all events it was worth a try. Anything was worth a try if it alleviated this boredom and cut down the howling. And so the last days of her convalescence she spent sewing large linen squares into a sort of papoose cradle, as she called it, which would allow her to "wear" little Philip like a rucksack.

When Bill Westwood saw the result he laughed until he cried — hugging her and kissing her and telling her she was priceless. He never volunteered any tale of where he and Estelle had gone that night — not that Lorna asked him but he must have known she'd wonder about it. Nor would he tell her much about what had passed between him and her father, beyond saying he was a cagey old bird who would never invest in rash new ventures without a great deal of thought. Meanwhile he, Bill, had put his plans for building the speed-'plane to one side and was concentrating on preparing his old "crate" for commercial work during the coming tourist season. Already he'd had several commissions for aerial photographs of various properties — factories, harbours, country estates, and so forth — and he was discussing an idea with the printers of the *Falmouth Packet* for a calendar using photographs of all the well-known Cornish beauty spots as seen from the air.

He thought these signs of an honest, sober, and upright life would impress Lorna, and she wondered why they didn't. It forced her to confront the fact that she did not actually *want* Bill to be an honest, sober, upright sort of fellow. The most endearing thing he'd ever said to her was his outburst on crossing Market Jew Street after his interview with Curnow: "That man is obsessed with money!" Such wonderful, childlike naïvety! Such utter self-absorption on Bill's part! She wanted him to go on being like that; it depressed her profoundly to hear him talking of printers and commercial calendars; and the fact that he was doing it — partly, anyway — to impress her only made it worse.

By contrast Ben Calloway not only failed to laugh at her "papoose sling," he failed altogether to notice it; at least, he did not remark upon it as anything out of the way. When he saw her wearing it — or, rather, wearing Philip — for the first time, he merely said, "Hallo, young fellow-me-lad, how's the grip today?" and offered the baby his finger over Lorna's shoulder. That depressed her too, in a different way. If anyone else had carried a baby like that, Ben would have remarked upon it at once. "Good lord! Look at that idiotic woman — what *does* she think she looks like!" and so forth. But because she, Lorna, had done it, the action was above criticism. If she came to him wearing gold slippers on her ears, he'd probably finger them gently and tell her the effect was charming.

What a choice! she thought gloomily: on the one hand a handsome, charming, idealistic rogue determined to behave like a conventional man of commerce — at least for her sake, and, on the other, a handsome, thoughtful, profoundly conventional man determined to play the bohemian — at least for her sake!

At moments like that she thought of Theo Foster.

ill had redesigned the exhausts in his "kite" so that a fine spray of waste oil no longer bathed the passenger. As a mark of his confidence in the improved design he provided Estelle with a brand-new flying helmet. The reek of freshly worked leather reminded her of every saddlemaker's shop she'd ever been in — a comfortingly familiar sensation at that moment, since everything else was so utterly novel.

At least, it ought to have been novel, for she had never been within a hundred yards of an aeroplane before today; in fact it was eerily familiar because Ian had once described to her the wonder of taking to the air for the very first time. She had often re-lived it at second hand in her waking dreams — in which, of course, *she* was in the second cockpit. The fantasy had become especially poignant after his death, when he had, in a way, "taken to the air" for the very last time.

And now it was about to come true; she would be doing in the flesh what Ian's reminiscence had allowed her to do so often in spirit. She was glad the pilot's cockpit was behind her, so that she could pretend that *he* was at the controls.

Bill climbed in and leaned over her to check her straps. Satisfied, he strapped himself in and then revved the engine several times, testing whether he could push in the choke just yet. He decided to let her tick over a while longer. He was excited, too, for he was not going to give Estelle Carne the sedate sort of flight he had given Lorna; this outing would be packed with all the flying tricks and sensations of which his robust little machine was capable. But there was one trick he was still unsure whether or not to play on her. He resolved to leave the decision to the very last moment, when the flight would be drawing to an end; at least he was loaded with enough of the right materials to carry it out.

Conversation was a great deal easier now that the exhaust outlets were relocated beneath the kite; one could shout actual words at last. Also, he had moved his seat forward to shift the centre of gravity to the neutral flying position; now, apart from gusts and air pockets, he could take his hands off the stick in level flight and she'd look after herself. As a result, Estelle's seat was now actually between his knees and her head was only twelve inches or so in front of him.

"If you knew exactly where Doctor Carne's gone this morning, we could fly there and give him a buzz," he suggested.

She turned round and was startled to see how close he was. "No thanks!" she said vehemently. It was David's free Wednesday; he had said he was going to visit the Iron Age ruins at Chysauster, north of Penzance, and then walk over Tonkin's Downs to the ancient hill fort at Castle-an-Dinas. The last thing she wanted was to see him enjoying himself — from any angle. "I want some aerobatics."

"You asked for it," Bill replied ominously. "Check your straps again." A few moments later he shouted "Ready?"

She held up both thumbs in the ritual as Ian had described it and shouted "Chocks away!" (Nothing to do with chocolates — how they had laughed at that!)

"I say!" he exclaimed admiringly. "You're quite the seasoned airwoman, aren't you!"

He raised the revs and the kite began to nose down the mown strip across the field. He pushed the throttle to maximum and took off at the earliest possible moment. Turning seaward at once, he kept her at full throttle and rose at just below the stall angle so that they had gained a thousand feet by the time they were over St Michael's Mount, a mere eighty seconds after take-off.

The rush of the air and the sense that a giant hand was lifting her up, up, up forever was so exhilarating that Estelle did not at first notice the discomfort in her ears. Then she remembered what Ian had told her — no, not Ian. Bill, of course. Bill had told her to swallow hard to clear the trapped pressure. She tried it and the relief was immense. She felt slightly guilty at confusing Ian with Bill — but then, in their flying helmets, they became almost interchangeable. "Down!" she shouted, pointing toward the esplanade. "Fly low!"

"Bomb Rosemergy?" he suggested.

"Yes!"

He banked sharply and dived on a steep trajectory between the Mount and the Trinity House dock, levelling off with a sickening force over the Jubilee Baths. Estelle's cry of elation was the final proof for Bill — if proof were needed — that she was no invalid. They raced along the seafront about a quarter of a mile out to sea. It was a bright morning in late February with an almost cloudless sky, but it was also cold and there were few people about.

"Go closer!" she urged.

"Mustn't frighten the horses!" He pointed out a coal merchant delivering to a house near the Riviera-Splendide.

However, when he saw the man get back on his cart and trot off along the promenade, he decided to risk a frontal atack on Rosemergy and Trevescan. He pulled sharply up and to port. Estelle was amazed that the land had vanished so suddenly; it seemed to have no connection with the fact that her weight also appeared to have doubled. She hunted around for it and discovered it dead astern, beyond the goggled leather sphere that was Bill's head. The tailplane was swinging round across the Riviera-Splendide ... Trevescan ... Tolcarne Beach ... Newlyn ... a blur of green and brown countryside ... and then nothing but sky behind them! The land had vanished entirely this time.

"Up!" Bill shouted. "Look up!"

And there it was — Penzance and Newlyn revolving slowly overhead. It was impossible, because *down* — the pull of gravity — was still toward her seat. She was falling toward the sky, and the town had somehow been liberated to float above her!

It did not last long. Land, sea, and sky continued to slide round the 'plane and soon resumed their natural positions, except that now they were approaching Penzance at a right angle to the beach, with Rosemergy dead ahead.

"*Pwch! Pwch!* Rat-a-tat-tat-tat!" Estelle gripped the aiming handles of an imaginary Lewis gun and raked the house with a deadly hail of fire. "Oh Ian!" she yelled ecstatically — and then, realizing what she had said, quickly exclaimed, "E-e-e-h ... e-e-e-ah ..." several times, getting close to "Ian" without quite finishing the name.

Just before they pulled up and away she saw a face at one of the windows — though whether Lorna's or *hers* she could not tell. It could even have been Daisy's. The car was standing on the drive and there were two seagulls on the ridge tiles — what funny little details could freeze in the mind's eye as one flashed overhead in a roar! Trevescan was a blur behind bare poplar branches; the garage door was open and there was no car.

Then suddenly there was no land, either — only sky. Again she felt her weight increase. Her fists pressed hard into her lap. Laboriously she turned her head round and this time was slightly less surprised to see the town spread out behind Bill's grinning mask and the shivering tailplane. Sunlight flashed off his goggles. He pointed ahead. She turned again and saw they were climbing almost vertically toward a little fleecy cloud. She had seen it earlier and had been struck by its resemblance to a cauliflower; now, as they drew closer, she saw it was really quite ragged and wispy. And by the time they clipped its edge, it was no more than a drifting patch of misty vapour.

"Hold tight!" Bill pulled the 'plane into level flight, upside down.

At once the centrifugal force that had enabled her to go on feeling that down was down — that is, toward her feet — vanished and the truth dawned on her: She was held in place by four straps of webbing and one brass buckle! Her fingers locked tight round the rim of her seat and clung there for all she was worth.

She looked down beneath her head — and now it truly was down beneath her head — and saw the comforting sparkle of that stretch of Mount's Bay known, for some reason, as Gwavas Lake. If a person fell into it from this height, would the impact kill her? she wondered. Or would her parachute open in time? Or would it open at all?

Before panic had time to set in, Bill began the second half of the delayed loop. Soon "down" was once again toward her feet and the world reappeared ahead of her, the right way up at last. It was a measure of her rapid acclimatization to the ordeal of flying that she no longer turned a hair to realize they were approaching the ground at quite a steep angle and a fair old rate of knots.

Again they made the sort of run over Rosemergy which, if they had been carrying bombs, would have let them obliterate it from the map of the town. This time there was no seagull on the roof and the face at the window had become a figure at the door. It was *her*. She waved up cheerfully and watched them climb for yet another loop and then yet another "bombing run."

On their third approach Estelle saw the unmistakable figure of Marcus Corvo trotting out of his hôtel to stand in the middle of the road and shake his fist at them. Looking back she saw him flailing his arms like a cricket umpire. His meaning was plain and could not have been repeated in polite society.

Bill waggled his kite's wings in a gesture of triumph and began a long climbing turn westward toward Land's End. To Estelle's relief Castle-an-Dinas, clearly discernible by the mock-medieval folly that crowned it, slipped away to the rear.

It took them only minutes to reach their destination. And there, over the mile-wide stretch of Atlantic between the last of Cornwall and the Longships Light, Bill did every aerobatic manoeuvre of which he and his machine were capable — loops, stall turns, falling leaves, corkscrews, and more. Estelle, her terror blunted by the foretaste over Rosemergy and Gwavas Lake, went through every other emotion from stark fear through nausea to elation — and, finally, to satiety. Bill, who began by feeling proud of his machine, ended up being vastly more proud of his passenger.

He throttled back and began a long, anticlockwise turn, gliding more than flying, on a path that would bring them back over the coast at Porthgwarra, at just a few hundred feet of altitude. In the rushing slipstream, with the engine just ticking over, something like normal conversation became possible, though they still had to shout.

"Are you okay?" he called.

"Say?"

He gestured: R U O K ? and throttled even lower.

"Never better! Thrill of a lifetime!"

"You'll make a good pilot!"

"Really?"

"Really! Want some more?"

"Not today. But soon."

"I want to try some sky writing. Understand?"

"No."

"Writing letters in the sky with smoke. Big letters."

"Must we loop the loop? Fly upside down?" She gestured the manoeuvres with her hands.

He laughed. "No! All level flying, but quite tight turns. Shall we try? I'll stop if you can't take it."

"Okay!" She gave him the thumbs-up again.

By now they were down over the little cove of Porth Loe, which lies on the western side of Gwennap Head, half a mile from Porthgwarra, which lies to the east. He gave it some throttle, levelled out and began to climb again. Looking ahead and south she could see the familiar outlines of the Logan Rock, whose vast bulk is so finely balanced on a slender pedestal beneath it that a person can make it rock — thus giving two meanings to its name.

The 'plane was climbing over Rôskestal Cliffs, which rose to a trig point at over two hundred feet. The moment they cleared it she saw before them the whole of Porthgwarra, and Porthcurnow beyond it. But that was not all she saw. Immediately beneath them, in the field near the coastguard cottages, was a courting couple, walking hand-in-hand across the still-frosted meadow. The moment they saw the aircraft they let go of each other's hands and sprang apart. Had it not been for that guilty gesture Estelle would probably not have looked at them closely enough to recognize them — or, at least, to be almost sure of recognizing them. A moment later the sight of David's car parked beside Porthgwarra Cottage confirmed her identification of him, at least. So much for Castle-an-Dinas! The female had looked amazingly like Lorna Sancreed.

David and Lorna Sancreed hand in hand! And leaping apart so guiltily the moment they recognized the 'plane!

Hand in hand — that was what gave them away. It would be quite reasonable — well, not totally *un*reasonable — for the two of them to meet at Dr Foster's place and discuss this and that. Estelle couldn't think of an innocent topic, offhand — but nor, having seen their guilty behaviour, did she particularly wish to now.

Had Bill recognized them, too?

She turned round and pointed back down toward the coastguard cottages, then gestured a circle for the 'plane to follow. He shook his head and pointed onward and up. She did not insist. Anyway, even if he did see them, and recognize them, he'd probably think it no harm. He'd have to see them actually holding hands and then jumping apart, all full of guilt, to realize what was afoot.

The funny little details that could freeze themselves in the mind's eye as one flashed overhead in a roar!

At twelve hundred feet Bill levelled off and turned rather tightly inland. Estelle was aware of no difference in the sound of the engine but as the turn continued to the point where they completed the circle she saw that they had been laying a trail of white smoke or vapour for the last half mile or more. She put all thought of David and Lorna aside and turned her attention to this new and more exciting mystery.

At first she thought he must be skywriting an o, because of the circle, but as they came up to the point where they would cut across their own smoke-trail she saw a longish tail stretching back toward Porthcurnow. So it must be an e! Then she realized his intentions. Of course! He was going to write her name in letters a mile wide! Only he'd spell it *estelle* because he couldn't do the sharp corners and stops and starts of an E.

But then the next letter was also an e — rather larger, but still an e. And so was the next. *And* the next — which was when she decided that *all* skywritten letters must seem to be an e when you try to guess them from a cockpit in the aeroplane that is writing them. And it was as hopeless trying to look back and read them as it would be for some flat worm buried in a sheet of paper to try to read the words upon it. In the end it just seemed that they flew an incomprehensible number of clockwise circles running from west to east, each one a little nearer Penzance. Once or twice toward the end he shut the smoke-making device off while he did an anticlockwise circle north or south of the line, but by then she was lost in the general dizziness of the exercise and could not even guess what letter he might be attempting.

Maddeningly he flew straight and level away from the word when he had written its final letter, so that by the time they began their descent toward the airstrip, it was just a small white blur in the western sky.

Landing, which in her daydreams had always seemed the most frightening part of the flight, was, in reality, the tamest of all — or at least of that particular flight, even though they had to make a couple of passes over the airfield to move the cows and the sheep off the actual landing strip. Bill taxied off the runway and rolled to a halt before the hangar doors, where at last he killed the engine. In the blessed silence that followed she closed her eyes and luxuriated in her fantasy one last moment. He reached forward and fiddled with the buckle of one of the straps, which was just forward of her shoulder. Her body, rather than any conscious part of her, responded as if the hand were Ian's. She leaned her head against his arm.

He became tense at once, but for no more than a moment; then he let her use his arm in any way she wished. He did not respond. Nor did he caress her cheek in return. He simply allowed her head to rest on his arm.

The entire episode lasted only a second or two but it was long enough to alarm Estelle and make her realize what she was capable of doing once she allowed her guard to slip. Then, resisting the impulse to snatch her head guiltily away — precisely the movement by which Lorna and David had stood self-accused on the cliffs near Porthgwarra — she leaned against it even harder, making a joke of it, and gave out a great sigh of exhausted satisfaction. "What an experience!" she cried. "I'll need a week in bed to recover, I'm sure."

"Go on with you!" He, too, exaggerated his response — the heartiness with which he flipped her head upright again. "You have everything it takes to make another Philip Fullard. Up with you!" He slapped her heartily on the shoulder. "I've known strong men turn into gibbering wrecks after going through only half what you've just experienced. So we'll hear no more of the invalid bed, if you please, Mrs Carne!"

"Aye aye, sir!" she said smartly and, making short work of her buckles, rose to her feet and climbed stiffly from the cockpit. He, already on the grass, made a sling of his hands for her to step into. When he unclasped his fingers to let her fall the last couple of feet it took her by surprise and she stumbled against him. He did not move away, but nor did he take advantage of it; he just stood there, smiling enigmatically into her eyes until she made a move away from him.

"You took a chance," she told him, "if you've seen strong men quail at aerobatics like that."

He laughed. "It's the only way you get anywhere in this life — taking risks — don't you think?" He gazed at her with his frank, blue eyes. "Hang on," he added. "That smoke has made your skin a bit gray. D'you want to wash? I have soap but the only water around here is in a butt up the end of the barn."

"*Your* face doesn't look dirty," she said.

He grinned. "One advantage of the rear cockpit." To her surprise he led her inside the barn but then he explained that he'd moved the butt in there and redirected the water chute inward through the wall because the cows kept drinking from it outside.

While she washed he stood by attentively with the towel. She made to take it from him but the feeling of having her face dried by him was so pleasant, so sensuous, that she just stood there and let him do it for her. It was a second or two before she realized he was kissing her as well. And then she just stood there, letting him do it.

"Estelle!" he murmured after a long while. "What a wonderful woman you are! And what an appalling waste, too!"

"Bill!" She flung her arms around his neck and pulled him tight to her, burnishing her body against his in an invitation he could hardly fail to notice — nor, she thought, resist.

Again, he neither responded nor discouraged her from continuing; he went on kissing her and running his fingers oh-so-gently through her hair.

"Shall I undress?" she whispered.

He kissed her lips in a series of rapid darts, never in the same place twice, as if he would push her question back between them.

"Don't you want me?" she asked.

"Always," he replied. "For ever and ever. But not just once, here, like this."

After that she surrendered to his caresses and did nothing to provoke him to venture further. In a curious way his tenderness moved her beyond the reach of all strong passion; she felt only an aching sort of *goodness* inside her now.

After an eternity he left her to take off her flying suit and get back into her skirt. She would have liked him to stay and watch, although she hated it when David turned his back on her in the bedroom and then tried to watch her undressing in the mirror.

When she joined him at the door he waved a proprietorial hand at the sky and said, "*Voilà!*"

The skywriting had drifted on the wind and now hung over Penzance — somewhat ragged but still clearly legible:

Estelle

Half an hour earlier she would have been overjoyed. Now, because of what had just taken place between them — and even more because of what had *not* but soon might — her happiness was clouded.

ill was anxious to see whether the smoke-making had clogged the exhaust tubes so he stayed on at the airfield to strip them. Estelle drove herself back to Trevescan. She took a luxurious bath followed by an invigorating cold splash — mainly because she could not bear the sight of herself in the looking glass after a long soak in hot water, which made her skin all lobster pink and blotchy. In any case, the last thing she needed today was artificial invigoration of that crude kind. Nerves she had forgotten she possessed were tingling with the remembered thrills of her first flight; feelings she thought were dead and buried up there on Mount Misery had wakened from their long slumber at the touch of Bill's lips on hers.

At last, when the cold water no longer felt cold, she dared to rise and towel herself dry in front of that pitiless mirror-mirror-on-the-wall. The result was a pleasant surprise. Her skin glowed, her eyes sparkled, her figure was seemingly undamaged by her long hibernation … *Yes*, she thought, surveying herself with a kind of restrained excitement, *you'll do very nicely.*

Her vague sense of excitement persisted through a light luncheon of soft-boiled egg and anchovies on toast. It intrigued her, for it had no precise focus. Of course, it was partly the physical elation of the flight and partly — or mainly, to be honest — to do with the fact that a strong, handsome young fellow like Bill Westwood obviously found her attractive. She would have liked to believe that was all, so that she could wallow in his admiration and weave her usual fantasies around it. But a self-protective honesty forced her to admit that this excitement had not been born today; in fact, it had been swelling inside her, from the tiniest origins, ever since that day last November when she had stood outdoors in the rain to attract Lorna Sancreed's attention. Lorna had somehow *challenged* her to do it. There was something about the woman that made one want to call out, "Hey! Look at me!" One wanted her to notice and approve.

Estelle knew she wasn't alone in this feeling. In one way or another it had affected everyone around her. Lorna had changed all their lives, even the lives of people who hardly knew her. Who else could have walked about the place as blatantly pregnant as she had been and yet remained on good social terms with half the town? More than that — many of those who had earlier cut her dead were now coming round to accepting her again. No doubt it bewildered them, too — but there it was. She had that effect on others.

The question was, had Lorna intended it? Was she working to some grand master plan for them all? Pushing a little here, tugging there ... encouraging one strand of thinking, discouraging another ... bit by bit chipping away until their lives took a form that pleased her?

On the whole Estelle thought not. No one could be so calculating, surely? If Lorna *compelled* people's attention and created situations in which they were forced to accommodate her, it was because she, in her turn, was driven by compulsions too deep to control; she was the handmaiden, not the mistress, of her own yearning to *be*.

The last of the anchovy fillets played a swimming game around Estelle's tongue.

Why did she still feel uneasy?

Well, of course, it didn't really matter whether Lorna was deliberately manipulating them all or whether she was the mere plaything of her own compulsions. The effect was the same. She was pushing, and the rest of them were being pushed. In short, then, it was time someone stood up (rose permanently from her sick bed, perhaps?) and *did* something off her own bat!

She went out and told Rogers, their gardener, to remove a small part of the fence between the vegetable garden at Trevescan and the potting shed at Rosemergy and replace it with a gate. She knew no one would quarrel with this decision. It was something David had often talked about, something she had always refused to allow.

The moment it was possible to step over the half-removed barrier with dignity, she did so. She found Jessica doing the weekly household accounts — a chore she was always willing to put off in favour of any distraction ... a passing cloud, a falling leaf ...

"Did you see us?" Estelle asked excitedly. "'That was you at the door, wasn't it?"

"Saw *and* heard!" Jessica answered. "And I wasn't the only one."

Estelle did not follow.

"Half the town saw it. I've just telephoned for an appointment with your namesake — my *coiffeuse* — and she's inundated with bookings for some reason. And as for hearing it — poor old Marcus Corvo was throwing a fit out on the esplanade. I'll bet he thinks I put Bill Westwood up to it."

Estelle did not like the notion that any part of *her* first flight should have been done at Jessica Lanyon's behest — even if only in Marcus Corvo's misapprehensions.

"By way of revenge," Jess explained. "To pay him out for the racket his dance band made at the New Year's Ball. Corvo was trying to scare us off ..." She hesitated, remembering that — according to David — Estelle knew nothing as yet of their plans for Rosemergy.

Perhaps this was the right moment?

Perhaps not. It should be agreed with Lorna first.

"Scare you off what?" Estelle asked.

"Oh ... the idea that Lorna and I might start a guest house or private hôtel here. He wanted us to understand he could make life hell for us if he chose to." She chuckled. "I'll bet he's thinking twice about it now!"

"Actually, it was *I* who suggested it to Bill."

"Bless you!"

Estelle contained her anger that Jessica had unintentionally managed to convert her "bombing raid" on Rosemergy into a conspiracy to teach Corvo a lesson. But it made her injudicious enough to say, "You weren't the only one I saw from up there today!"

"Oh?" Jessica's eyebrows arched in pleasant anticipation.

Estelle cursed herself; she wanted to know a great deal more about what had been going on between her husband and these two women, and how they felt toward each other now, before she revealed anything of what she knew — and felt toward them all. Indeed, until she knew a great deal more about them, she hardly knew what to feel. "Where's Lorna, by the way?" she asked.

"Having a heart-to-heart with our father confessor — Professor Foster — out at Porthgwarra. You know him, of course?"

"And the baby, too, I suppose — in that ridiculous rucksack affair? Hasn't she got a nanny yet?"

Jessica shook her head. "We're still looking. She has to be the best nanny that money can buy, of course. Besides, Theo Foster wouldn't let her through the door without baby Philip. He adores him. He's like a second father."

Estelle sniffed. "The office of the *first* being vacant, of course!"

Jessica did not rise to it; she repeated her earlier question: *"Do* you know the prof?"

"Not really. We've exchanged a few pleasantries over the garden fence. Talking of which ..." And she went on to tell Jessica about the new gate.

Jessica said it should have been done years ago.

"Did she take your car?" Estelle asked. "I thought I saw yours on the drive."

"You did. Isn't it amazing what crystal-clear details one can spot from the air! Ian always said that."

"Oh?" Estelle was surprised. "You mean you've never been up in the air yourself?"

Jessica shook her head. "Ian could never take me up in a service machine, of course, and every time he got his hands on a private 'plane I seemed to be with child."

"Ha! That didn't stop Bill Westwood from taking Lorna up!"

Jessica sat bolt upright. "I beg your pardon? When?"

"Oh, weeks ago — about a fortnight before the baby came. Didn't she mention it?"

Jessica saw how much Estelle was relishing this surprise. "Oh yes!" She patted her forehead as forgetful people do. Guessing, she added, "But it was a very *gentle* flight compared with yours. Hardly worth calling a flight at all." The disappointment in the other's eyes told her she had guessed correctly. "Anyway — you were saying how crystal-clear everything is from the air?"

"Yes, it certainly is!" Estelle replied heavily.

Jessica chuckled. It was becoming clear to her that Estelle had come over here to make trouble between Lorna and her; she felt ready for anything now. "Come on!" she said. "You know something — and you're dying to tell me. I can feel it."

Again Estelle was annoyed at her own lack of self-control; it was so tempting to crow. But this time she felt a contrary urge to tell all — a reckless urge, whispering the seductive thought that, if she was going to toss a pebble in the waters, why not make it a boulder instead ... why not come back to life with a real splash?

She drew a deep breath and squared herself to it. "I suppose I ought to be furious, actually," she said. "Or heartbroken ... or something — *anything* rather than this ... this utter numbness."

"Goodness!" Jessica threw up her hands dramatically. "Are you quite sure you want to speak about it? Would you like a ..." She stared at the drinks cabinet. "Is it too early?"

Estelle waved away the offer with a smile. "No! It's nothing so ... I mean, I'm not in shock or anything like that. In fact, being up in an aeroplane gives one a curiously godlike perspective not just on the actual landscape but on everything. I mean, I saw old Corvo come running out like that and shaking his fists at us and it just looked ... comic, really. Of no account. A mere childish tantrum."

Jessica nodded — and waited.

"Well-well!" Estelle became brisk again. "I'm just trying to account for my lack of ... what's the word? This feeling of being remote from what I saw. Anyway, the reason I asked how Lorna got out to Porthgwarra Cottage was to find out if *you* knew." She bit her lip in a naughty-girl parody.

"Ah! Because you *do* know! You flew over the place and saw David's car parked there?"

"So you do know!"

Jessica eyed her guardedly. "I know she got a lift from him. It's his day off, isn't it? He said he'd drop her off there and go on to do his usual communing with nature — bird-watching, or whatever it is."

"Bird-watching!" Estelle sneered.

Jessica felt the skin prickle on her neck. "Isn't that it?"

"The only bird he's watching today ..." Estelle halted and took a different tack. "Well, decide for yourself. I'll just tell you what I saw." She described how Bill had pulled sharply up to clear the cliffs west of Gwennap Head. "And there below us — strolling hand-in-hand among the daisies — who should I see but my own dear husband and our own dear friend, Lorna Sancreed!"

Why is she telling me this? Jessica thought quickly. *Surely she cannot know of my feelings about David? She cannot be hoping to awaken my jealousy? Quick! Respond like any good neighbour to such news!* "Oh, my dear, I'm so sorry!" she said. But her mind continued to race. Estelle could not possibly suspect that anything was going on between David and her. This was a rather blatant attempt to poison her mind against Lorna — the trollop, the wayward girl ... determined to steal husbands away from their lawful spouses. She could almost laugh, especially when she thought of the glacial state of the Carnes' marriage! "Are you *sure*?" she went on. "Actually hand-in-hand?"

Estelle gave a cold, airy laugh. "I might not even have noticed — if they hadn't sprung apart so guiltily."

Jessica slipped even further into the rôle of consoling neighbour. "You could only have seen them for a flash. I'm sure there could be a thousand innocent explanations, you know."

"I'd like to hear one! What are they doing together in the field in the first place?"

Jessica stared at her a moment or two, as if sizing her up. Actually, she was sizing herself up. Lorna had probably been discussing the sanitarium, but could she explain as much to Estelle? She was sure Estelle knew nothing as yet of their plans for Rosemergy; if she told her about them now, could she live with herself hereafter? Suppose it led to an almighty row between the Carnes, and suppose David walked out on his wife? Apart from the practical effect — that it would be quite impossible for either her or him to go on living in Penzance — could she answer the accusation that she had played the traditional harpy, the widow who stole another man's wife?

With some sadness, she realized she could not. "Well," she said vaguely, "I wouldn't go jumping to conclusions until you've heard David's side."

"Ha! He knows I saw them. He'll have had half a day to invent something good. Knowing that man, it'll be seamless by now."

Jessica decided to divert the conversation to the lesser "crime" of holding hands — which she did not, in any case, believe. "They must have spotted you flying around, you know — long before you saw them. They must have known it was Bill — and I presume at least David knew you were with him. So it's most unlikely you took them all unawares."

"*You* explain it, then!" Estelle was furious, both that her squib had proved so damp and that Jess had managed to focus on the more trivial trespass.

"Well, suppose, for instance, that Lorna got the idea that Bill Westwood was going to come zooming up over the cliffs and then clip the daisies all around her and David — she might have turned to run away. And then David might have grabbed her hand, saying, 'Don't be so silly,' or something like that — and, hey presto! That was the moment you caught them in the act!"

"I didn't claim I caught them in the *act*," Estelle protested. Then, seeing the shock in Jessica's face, she added, "Or perhaps the phrase means something different to you?"

"It obviously does!" Jessica replied.

"Well ... come to that — I wouldn't put that sort of *act* past the pair of them, either!"

"Estelle!" Jessica exclaimed in horror.

"Oh come on, Jess! Face it! *You* know David's ... how shall I put it? His propensities?"

"I'm afraid I don't," Jessica replied coldly.

"Well you must be the only one west of Plymouth who doesn't. It's only out of pity for me that more women haven't complained and got him struck off."

"*More* women?" Jessica asked pugnaciously. "I'll bet there haven't been any."

"Well, I'm not going to name names, but ..."

"Poison-pen letters!" Jessica sneered. "I'm surprised at you!"

"Not at all. I've had my share of those, too, of course, but I ignore them. No, these are girls who've told me in person. Why else d'you think David and I are more-or-less estranged?"

Jessica shifted uncomfortably. "I didn't consider it any business of mine." Then her anger at these unjust accusations against the man she loved got the better of her. "And as for these allegations ... well, what *are* you accusing him of, Estelle? Speak plain! Are you saying he's some sort of Casanova?"

"Oh come on, Jess — don't go on pretending you've never heard a whisper about it yourself!"

"If I had, I would *know* they were lies."

"Lucky you! I don't see how anyone could be so certain, but ..."

"Don't you? Just think! Think of all the chances David has had to make advances or improper suggestions to *me* these past two years. Two and a half years, now. Evening after evening ..." She broke off and stared at Estelle in horror. "My god — that's what you think, isn't it! You think he was over here, philandering with me. You do — don't deny it! That's why you hated me ... oh, how blind I've been!"

Estelle saw that she had somehow allowed herself to be manoeuvred into an impossible situation. She could hardly explain that her "hatred" for Jessica had been mostly guilt for what had happened with Ian on his last brief leave before the accident. She therefore had no choice but to pretend to accept Jessica's explanation for it. "I have never *hated* you, Jess," she replied. "Not as such. But even if I had, would it be altogether surprising? After receiving such visits from all those nurses and ... other women — all warning me about David's behaviour. But I *don't* suspect you — nor have I ever. I suspect *him*, right, left, and centre. But not you. I'm sure he tried something and you very soon showed him the door. He's probably behaved impeccably ever since, but I'll tell you this — he won't have given up hope. Be warned!" She clamped her jaws together and nodded with self-righteous assurance.

Jessica stared back, long enough to count down her rage. "You really believe that?" she asked quietly.

"Unless you say otherwise."

Jessica rose, went out to the hall, and returned with the little Bible she carried to church each Sunday. "I won't merely say it," she told Estelle, "I'll swear it on this." She almost poked the book into Estelle's face. "David has never once, not by the smallest hint or gesture, made an improper advance toward me." She almost let the book fall when she suddenly remembered the moment Theo Foster had surprised them at Porthgwarra. True, nothing had actually happened. But it might have, but for Theo's arrival. So, as a sop to her conscience, she added, "I once put my arms around him — in a moment of extreme misery — which you can probably guess — but he made no improper response to that. Not even to that."

Estelle saw the strength of Jessica's heartbeat shake the soft flesh of her bosom and neck. She knew the woman was speaking the truth; the three finest actresses in the world all rolled into one could not be that good. David had, indeed — despite every opportunity — made not the slightest advance toward Jessica. It left her speechless — until, suddenly, she divined the truth of the situation. "My ... *God!*" She almost whispered the word.

"Whether or not you believe it," Jessica concluded.

"Oh, I believe it." She closed her eyes and shook her head, still trying to come to terms with her new insight. "My God — talk about being blind!"

"I said it first," Jess reminded her.

"No, I mean *me!* I'm the one who's been blind all this time, not you."

"Blind about what?"

Now it was Estelle's turn to size up Jessica. At last she said, "Why d'you think those women took the trouble to come and warn me about David?"

"Why indeed! I trust most other women as far as I could throw them. Perhaps he put in an adverse report on their competence — the nurses, at least. Perhaps the others threw themselves at him and he rebuffed them — and don't tell me a woman wouldn't seek revenge for that! All I know is that, despite *daily* opportunities, David ..."

"Yes, yes! I believe you — truly. But you're wrong about those women who accused him. They wanted revenge, all right, but it was for his *coldness,* you see! His contempt for them after he'd had his fun — the way he simply discarded them." She laughed bitterly. "The odd thing is that I've known all this from the beginning — with the very first woman who came to warn me. That was before the war — so I'm not talking about some recent aberration or some unfortunate consequence of wartime weariness." She glanced away as she added, "We all know that things happened during the war that would otherwise never have crossed one's mind. Anyway, to get back to the girl — that first one. She was a nurse, I grant you that, but David was never in a position to cast any sort of professional slur against her."

"What did she say?" Jessica challenged. "I mean what did she *actually* say?"

"I'll tell you. David saw a man being kicked by a horse in the street. He took him up to the hospital for an x-ray. And while they were waiting for the result, he just asked her if she'd like to go into the stockroom with him and have a bit of fun."

"And she said yes — just like that?" Jessica asked skeptically.

"I don't suppose it was 'just like that,' but she said yes in the end. And that's the point I started to make — why I say I've been blind all this time. When she told me she consented to it, I looked at her and thought, *Yes, my girl, if I were a man with a Casanova itch, you're just the type I'd pick!* She looked ..." Estelle could not think of a word bad enough. "Yeurk," she said instead. "A man couldn't help feeling contempt for such a tart. I felt it within the first minute. But until today I've never realized that the *opposite* is also true. You may not believe that David has this ... this Casanova urge — what my father calls 'the Irish toothache' ..."

"I don't," Jessica interrupted.

"I know you don't — and now I'll tell you why. He'll fight the most fearful odds — fatigue, rebuff, risk of discovery — he'll fight them all to cure his Irish toothache with a woman for whom he feels only contempt. So what's the opposite of all that, eh? The opposite of contempt? What emotion is powerful enough to make even Casanova behave like a saint? Must I name it?"

Jessica felt her mouth turn suddenly dry. "Estelle!" she murmured. "You're talking about your own husband!"

Estelle's lips curled in scorn. "In name only, I assure you. There is no marriage left between David and me."

Jessica shook her head sadly. "I'm so sorry — but why are you telling me this?"

Estelle's gaze did not waver. "Because now we've established that David is in love with you, you realize what my next question will be, don't you?"

Jessica swallowed audibly and closed her eyes, afraid even to nod her assent.

"I'm telling you because this is a moment for absolute honesty, Jess," Estelle added by way of a prompt.

Jessica risked a small, rather reluctant nod; she could see no escape for herself now.

"So — *do* you?" Estelle insisted.

Jessica merely nodded.

Estelle would have pressed her to say it in so many words but when she saw the tears beginning to gather she relented.

*A*t any other time the sight of a young woman with bare breasts in his parlour would have driven the entire history of Western philosophy to the remotest corners of Theo Foster's mind; but the addition of a suckling baby transformed the scene, dousing its incandescence and offering a mere sentimental radiance in its place. It was a moment of rare perfection in his life and he held his peace for fear of shattering it.

Baby Philip broke off and gasped for breath, letting it out again in a tiny, ecstatic shiver.

"What a paradise!" Theo murmured.

"Mmm?" Lorna looked up, her eyes dark and drowsy, a faraway smile on her lips.

"We must all carry some dim, suppressed memory of *that* state of bliss." He gestured toward the baby. "Not the actual circumstances — simply the feeling — the bliss itself. So when we later hear legends of paradise, the Garden of Eden before the Fall and so on, we *know* they must be true. Dimly we recall being there once ourselves."

She smiled at his fancy. "And the Fall?"

He spread his hands wide. "Weaning, of course. Get out into the world, thou sluggard! Stand on your own two feet!" He shivered at the harshness of life outside the gates of Eden, gates that had closed for ever on humankind.

"Well, weaning can't come soon enough for me!" Lorna said. She poked her face down near the baby. "You bloated little ... succubus." She grinned at Theo. "And while we're on the origins of myths and legends, I don't think we need look too far to see where the idea of vampires came from, either!" She gave the baby another indulgent grin. "Do we, eh! Talking of blood, I gave him a suck of tomato soup off my finger yesterday and he seemed to adore it. So I live in hopes of a very early weaning. D'you hear that, Philip? The Fall from Paradise is going to come rather early for *someone* I could name!"

She looked up to see Theo grinning and shaking his head.

"I mean it," she assured him.

"I'm sure you do, my pet. But what you don't realize is that to move from a world in which the only food is mother's milk to one in which all the food is prepared by *you*, is actually a step up. No one could possibly call it a Fall. The little mite will never grasp the meaning of that particular myth."

Philip fell off her nipple into a profound slumber. She hoisted him over the towel that was already draped over her shoulder and weighed the breast he had only half emptied. "Lopsided again," she grumbled. "I never guess it right."

The baby belched mightily and dropped a dollop of curdled milk on the towel.

"Hooray!" she cried with sarcastic disgust. For good measure she poked a finger in at the opening of his nappy. "Wonder of wonders," she said.

"Dry?" Theo asked.

"Not for long, I'll vouch." She settled him in his sling and arranged him over her back. "My little piccaninny," she murmured, rubbing her cheek against his sleeping head on her shoulder. Only then did she remember her open blouse. "Oops!" she exclaimed, buttoning herself up again. "Back to the real world!"

"By 'real world,' of course, we usually mean the most artificial world of all."

"D'you think so?"

"Don't you?"

She shook her head. "I think the most artificial world of all is the one called *marriage*."

"Ah! Well, I'm sure you're right there."

"Were you happily married, Theo? I know it's a dreadful thing to ask ..."

He shook his head. "No compromise can ever be *happy*, Lorna — and marriage is above all a compromise. It is the least-worst answer to all our problems."

"And what are they? No — don't tell me ... of course, I know."

"Talking of problems, what decisions did you and David reach — if any?"

"We decided we'll go ahead with the sanitarium, full pelt — come hell or high water."

"Or both!" He chuckled grimly. "In fact, you can almost certainly bank on both."

"I know."

"Talking of banks, by the way ..." He raised his eyebrows to complete the question.

"No. We'll do it with my money." She counted the three elements off on her fingers: "David's knowledge, Jessica's property, and my money — and the equal dedication of all of us, of course. It seems a fair sort of division."

"You don't sound too convinced of that!"

She sighed. "It's the equal-dedication requirement. I'm not sure I can provide it, you see."

"Because your heart is elsewhere?"

She laid her head to Philip's cheek again. "It's this little man. Before he came along I swore he'd make no difference — apart from the obvious demands on my time, of course. I meant he'd make no difference to my life, to the decisions I'd already made."

"To join forces over the sanitarium idea?"

She nodded. "That was carved in stone. I had resisted every urge to 'give the baby a name,' as the saying goes — in other words to marry for propriety's sake and keep the red ink off his birth certificate ..."

"It can't have been easy."

"It wasn't, I can tell you! But it's done now. The red ink is there. And even if I do marry now, it stays."

"'Nor all thy tears wash out a word of it'!"

"Just so. And yet now, Theo, I feel a terrible urge to agree with what you say about marriage — that it's the least-worst answer to all my problems. The fact that I *could* bring Philip up alone, that I *could* provide for all his wants, put him through a good school, set him up in a profession ... all that ... it just seems irrelevant."

"Because he'll be growing up in a home where there's no father? But that will be true of a great many other boys, no matter what school you send him to. One in five? Something of that order."

She shook her head sadly. "It's not the same, though, is it. Even to *me* — the bold, brave, independent lassie — the picture feels incomplete. I look into his eyes sometimes and I fancy I already see the question beginning to take shape behind them."

He gave a dismissive laugh. "Which is patently absurd — as you very well know."

"Utterly. It's so absurd, it forces me to wonder where the question is *really* beginning to take shape." She tapped her own forehead.

"What a pickle, eh! All my life I've done nothing but break the rules and defy the conventions. Then along comes a baby and my thoughts turn at once toward a nice respectable marriage with a nice orthodox husband. And there's poor Jessica, the very pillar of outward respectability, and yet she's been in love with David for years without once revealing it ..."

Not by the smallest lift of an eyebrow did Theo show that he knew better. "You seem to imply she's about to erupt in some kind of emotional explosion?" he suggested.

Lorna nodded. "She is *so* conventional — and yet so full of passion, too ... I mean, *something* will have to give way. And it won't be her love for David!"

"If you're putting up the money, I suppose there's nothing Estelle can do to stop the project," he said.

She shook her head. "But I'd rather she gave her consent. Why make unnecessary enemies?" She chuckled. "In fact, I'd rather she pushed him into it."

"A bit of a tall order, what!" His expression suggested it was worse than hopeless.

Lorna smiled cannily. "Not if she had some good reason for ending their marriage."

"Even so," he warned, "she'll never do it if she knows that David loves Jessica."

"What if she imagines he loves me, instead?"

His eyebrows shot up. "*Both* of you? What a man!"

Lorna told him what Estelle must surely have seen from the air a couple of hours earlier. She made it sound so casual and accidental on her part, and David's, that he knew there was more to it than she was admitting. "You presumably knew Westwood was piloting the machine?" he suggested. "I mean, the air over Land's End isn't exactly teeming with monoplanes!"

"We had a good idea it was him," she admitted reluctantly.

"And, presumably also, David at least knew his wife would be with young Westwood today?"

She stared uncomfortably past him, out through the narrow window. "We both knew. I mean, he told me on our way here."

"Therefore you could have let go of each other's hands long before they flew close enough to recognize you." He smiled and placed his fingertips together. "Or — let's not speculate about David — *you* could have let go of his hand in good time, eh? And yet you didn't. I wonder why?"

Briefly she hung her head, conceding the game to him. "I felt I had to *do* something to … to break the pattern of our lives. We're all stuck in the mud. I didn't think it all out — one, two, three … just like that. I simply seized the first opportunity that came along. Honestly."

"I believe you. Even so, I go back to what I said: Estelle won't let David go if she even suspects there's anything going on between him and Jess — in my humble opinion, anyway."

Still Lorna refused to believe it. "Surely it all depends on how strong her own reasons are for wanting to end her marriage?"

He continued to insist he was right. "It's a great mistake — and common among people of your tender years — to think that self-interest is at the heart of all human action. D'you know the fable of the scorpion and the frog? The scorpion begs the frog to ferry him across the river. The frog refuses. 'You'll only sting me to death,' he says. 'Why should I do anything so foolish?' replies the scorpion. 'You would die and I should drown.' So the frog is persuaded to ferry him across on his back. Halfway over he feels a searing pain in his neck and he realizes the scorpion has, indeed, stung him. 'You fool!' he cries with his latest breath. 'Now we'll both die.' 'I know,' the scorpion replies through his tears. His bitter, bitter tears. 'But I can't help it. It's my character, you see!'"

Part Three

Swimming
Through a Cliff

*P*hilip was christened "Philip William Benjamin" — so as not to waste the christening mug, Lorna said; also because William Westwood and Benjamin Calloway were his godfathers. When the ceremony was over, Rev. Meecher began to cultivate Lorna in the most effusive manner. His behaviour was all the more conspicuous in that, two months earlier, he had been among those who teetered on the very brink of cutting her entirely; only his respect for Jessica had prevented him from doing so. Yet now he bubbled with congratulations on her baby ... what a *man* he was for not crying at the shock of the water on his brow ... and how mercifully dry he'd stayed throughout the ceremony. Lorna, who looked every gift horse in the mouth, was convinced he'd got wind of their plans for Rosemergy — probably through Marcus Corvo. That would surely have set every cunning brain-cog whirring! And it wouldn't have taken long for him to realize that the sanitarium would require a visiting chaplain of each major denomination. The further equation was obvious: grateful patients plus the power of prayer equals small endowments. And many small endowments add up to one substantial income. She remembered Theo's fable of the scorpion and the frog and it seemed to her that the old boy did not know quite so much about human nature as he supposed.

Yet the contrary theory — that people acted entirely for their own benefit — fell apart the moment she turned away from the font and started across the aisle to the door. For there, slipping out of the farthest pew and trying to make good her escape, she saw her mother; God alone knew what personal happiness she was risking by daring to turn up here. Lorna, hampered by the baby in his voluminous christening gown, could not immediately hurry after her. The occasion was too decorous for her to have carried Philip in his sling; they had, in fact, wheeled him up the esplanade in an old wicker bassinet that Jessica had brought down from the attic — last used by Toby in 1917 — and Sarah, who had special leave from her school for the afternoon, had proudly borne him across the aisle to the font.

Lorna passed the baby back to her now and hastened as becomingly as may be toward the door. She need not have bothered, for when she reached the porch she found her mother bent almost double in agony and nursing the hip she had bruised on the huge and painfully knobbly doorhandle. The bassinet was leaning against the wall, half-overturned. "That wretched thing!" she grumbled as she sniffed away her tears.

"You shouldn't have bolted like a frightened rabbit," Lorna chided. "It's your own fault. Oh Mummy!" Her tone hung uncomfortably between loving and anger. "Bless you for coming, though. You don't know how much it means." She put her arms awkwardly round her mother and gave her a hug.

"Never mind all that," the woman snapped. "I must bathe this bruise or put something on it. It's agony."

"Where's your car?"

"I left it down by the dock — in case anyone saw. I mean, no one would think twice about seeing it there."

The others were by now standing in an awkward little group just inside the opened door.

"Estelle came by car," Lorna said. "She'll drive you back, won't you, dear? You know my mother, I suppose?"

There was a hasty flurry of handshakes before Estelle escorted Mrs Sancreed to her car. "If my husband's at home he can tend to that bruise for you," she said.

Bill Westwood and Ben Calloway, tactfully appointed to be joint godfathers, took up their stations on either side of Lorna, each with one hand on the crowded pushrail of the bassinet. Jessica, joint godmother with the departed Estelle, plucked Sarah back to walk a comfortable distance (that is, out of easy earshot) behind them. "Well, darling," she said when they had settled to their pace, "which of them would you choose for a husband if you were Aunty Lorna?"

Sarah looked up at her in astonishment.

"What's the matter?" her mother asked.

"You've never asked me anything like that before."

"Well ..." Jessica's uncertain tone implied that the past was not really important. "In a way, that's what growing up means, isn't it? Doing things today that were unthinkable yesterday."

The girl pondered this for a moment before replying: "Then I hope I may never grow up — not completely — because then there'd be no new things to do."

Her mother smiled ruefully. "Between you and me, dear, I don't think that moment ever arrives. No one *ever* grows up completely — not if my recent experience is anything to go by! So have no fear of that. Which d'you think Aunty Lorna should pick?"

"I've never thought about it."

"Well, think now."

After the barest hesitation Sarah said, "Uncle Ben."

The safe choice! Jessica was disappointed in her daughter; at her age, she felt, she ought to have plumped without hesitation for the romantic one — the pilot with a dream to chase. "You sound very positive," she challenged. "How can you be so sure?"

"I just am," Sarah replied awkwardly.

Jessica became aware that her daughter knew more about this topic than she was willing to admit. Was it something Lorna had told her or something she had stumbled on by herself? Picking her words with some care she said, "I think you know a secret! If it's one you were entrusted with, say so and we'll talk about something else. But if it's one you discovered all by your clever self, why then … it's altogether different, you know."

She waited.

She watched the waves come rolling in — four or five lines of white, each piggybacking on its predecessor all the way to the sand. There must have been a storm somewhere nearby for the white foam was speckled with broken strands of kelp.

"Well?" she prompted at last.

"It's both, really," the girl replied with some reluctance.

"You mean you saw something secret and Aunty Lorna told you something secret as well?"

"Yes."

"Well you must keep hers at all costs, but the other one belongs to you. What you do with it is for you to decide."

"I don't really like Uncle Bill," Sarah said.

"That's it?" her mother asked. "That's the secret?"

"No. The reason I don't like him is" — she gulped — "he kisses too many people."

Jessica laughed. "Including you?"

"No. I knew you'd only tease."

"I'm sorry, darling. I wasn't really teasing, you know. But without knowing when, where, and with whom, it doesn't really amount to much of a reason for disliking him, does it."

"I saw him kissing Aunty Estelle," Sarah said quietly.

Her mother plucked at her sleeve and they halted; as far as any passer-by might be concerned they were simply leaning on the promenade railings, staring at the waves. After a pause Jessica said, "You are very sure of that, are you, dear?"

"Yes," the girl replied, equally solemnly.

"You actually saw it? You didn't just dash around the corner and see them leap apart rather hastily and smile sheepishly at you so that you *assumed* they'd been kissing?"

"No, I saw them. I *did!*"

"All right, all right! I *do* believe you. But this is something very serious, you realize. We must be absolutely clear about it. Try to tell me exactly what you saw. When did this happen by the way?"

"That day Uncle Bill took her flying — the same day Rogers cut the fence to make the new gate."

"You're sure?"

"Yes, because when I came home from school I went to look at it and that's when I saw them."

Jessica took her daughter's hand. "I don't disbelieve you, dear, but I just want to make sure every detail is right. Now my memory tells me that was the day Aunty Estelle came to call on me — the same day she went flying for the first time." She laughed grimly. "Neither event is so common that I'm likely to forget it! And I also seem to remember that when you came home from school ..."

"Yes — that's the day. Aunty Estelle was having tea with you. And I said hallo and went and changed and took Bunyan for a walk with Toby and fed the rabbits ... do you want everything like this? I mean I do it most days!"

"No, dear." Jessica patted her hand and then, linking arms with her again, resumed their homeward stroll, now some way behind the three with the baby. "What you mean is that you came home, did all your usual chores and things ..."

"And had my tea."

"And had your tea — and *then* you went out to look at the new gate, or the place where it was going to be. So that would have been ... what? Six o'clock? With dusk falling?"

"It was still quite bright. Actually, I went into the potting shed first, to get a bamboo."

"What for?"

"In case of snakes."

Jessica knew when not to pursue her children's logic any further. "Of course," she said. "Go on."

"And then I looked through the knothole in the back wall."

"Dare I ask why?"

"Because you can see birds very close by and they don't see you."

"Ah! And that evening you saw something else — other than birds, I suppose?"

Sarah nodded. "Aunty Estelle was standing there with a tape measure, writing down measurements for the gate, and Uncle Bill's car drew up, and she called, 'Over here, Bill!'"

"She called him Bill?"

"Yes. And you know that clump of bamboo at the bottom end of their lawn? Well, they went in there and that's where they kissed."

Jessica longed to discover how intimate the embrace had become but did not want to alert Sarah to the significance of certain gestures by asking questions about them. Anyway, it was surely enough to know that they had kissed.

"Was it wrong, Mummy?" she asked.

"Not really, darling. I mean, you didn't intentionally spy on them. You were looking for birds ..."

"No, I mean for *them*? Were they doing wrong?"

"Oh! Well, that's rather more difficult, isn't it. The simple answer is, yes, they were both wrong. That's what the vicar would have to say if he were giving a sermon. Aunty Estelle is, after all, married to Uncle David, and married people shouldn't go around kissing other partners. But ... I suppose it's no secret that they don't get on terribly well. Actually, it *is* a secret as far as others are concerned, but not between you and me. So it's not *quite* as wicked as if they were happily married, d'you see? But as for this other secret — what you saw from the potting shed — I don't think you ought to tell anybody else — for your own sake."

"Why?" Sarah asked nervously.

"Because if grown-ups deny something that youngsters say is true, people always believe the grown-ups, and it can cause a lot of distress."

The girl swallowed hard. "I'm afraid I already told Aunty Lorna," she confessed timidly.

Jessica felt a stab of jealousy that Lorna should have been told about this while she herself was kept in the dark, but she gave no sign of it. "Quite right, too," was all she said. She remembered then that Sarah had also hinted at a secret Lorna had told her; perhaps that was the telling moment — in every sense of the word. "I'll bet Aunty Lorna was pleased!" she remarked.

"She said it was exactly what she expected of Uncle Bill," Sarah replied. "People can quarrel and still love each other, can't they? I mean, I love Toby and I *almost* love Guy — sometimes — and yet we still quarrel."

"*Do* you?" her mother asked. "Not that I've ever noticed!"

Sarah punched her playfully. "But it's true, isn't it?"

"Yes, darling." Jessica became serious again. "It's quite true. For instance, I love your Aunty Lorna very dearly. I'd defend her life with my own, I think. But even so, I can feel a quarrel brewing between us one day soon — so don't be surprised if you see the feathers flying, eh?" She hugged her daughter's arm tight. "And don't feel obliged to take sides between us, either. It won't be a final break, but sometimes one just has to clear the air."

"Why?" Sarah asked.

Jessica was intrigued at the tone of the girl's question — not at all anguished — in fact, rather looking forward to it. "Look at her now!" she said quickly.

Lorna and her two escorts had just reached the gate to Rosemergy. They halted and she flung an arm around each of them, clasping them tightly to her side. "D'you understand without my having to say it?" she asked.

"I think so," Sarah replied.

Jessica hoped it was true. Lorna's manipulative behaviour had reduced her to fury so often; yet she realized what a good influence the young woman had had on Sarah and what a bond there was between the pair of them. She sighed. "If only life could be as simple as a sermon, eh!" she said. "Or a war."

*T*he moment Lorna's mother took the weight off her hip the pain abated. She sank into the leather seat of Estelle's car with relief. "What a stupid thing to do!" she said. "I don't know why I was in such a hurry to vanish like that."

Estelle felt she ought to nail her colours to the mast — or at least to make it clear where her own loyalties lay — before Mrs Sancreed said something she might regret. "Lorna wasn't just saying the conventional thing, you know," she told her. "When she said how much it meant to her to see you there. Forgive me, but I couldn't help overhearing."

"You know her quite well, then, Mrs Carne?"

"Very well indeed, Mrs Sancreed. Since last November we have become fast friends. May I ask what you think of your new grandchild?"

"He's a sturdy baby," she replied defensively. "What can one say about babies? They all look alike. And smell alike." After a pause she added, "Nannies are wonderful things in my opinion."

Estelle laughed. "My own opinion, too," she confessed. "But don't say it too loudly while your daughter is around!"

"One of *them*, eh? The New Mothers! Yes, well, she would be, wouldn't she!"

The easy rapport that was now established between them allowed Mrs Sancreed a brief, unembarrassed silence before she went on: "Who were the two godfathers, may I ask? I believe I recognized one of them from somewhere."

"The one with curly hair was Ben Calloway, owner of the Mouse Hole, which is next door to Rosemergy. The other ..."

"He's the one I recognize. Name's Westwood, isn't it? Something-or-other Westwood?"

"Bill Westwood, ex-RAF. He's our local aviator."

"With ambitions to build a racing aeroplane, I believe?" Her tone was scornful.

"That's right." Estelle glanced at her in surprise. "I had no idea his fame had percolated as far as Redruth!"

"It hasn't. The only reason I know anything about him is that my daughter ... *projected* him, I think one could say? Yes, she projected him at my husband one day back in January, down by the Trinity House dock." She was gazing out at the sea while she spoke these words so she failed to notice how Estelle's hands tightened on the driving wheel and how she suddenly sat upright, all ears.

"Really?" Estelle managed to imply that it was an amazing thing for Lorna to have done — an implication that could not help being tinged with polite disbelief.

"I assure you, Mrs Carne!" She turned and addressed her directly now. "The young man had just been refused a loan from the West of England Bank — Mister Curnow. I'm sure you know him. Anyway, Curnow said no thank you — not with a bargepole. So the darling girl sent him to ambush her father."

"For a loan?" Estelle overplayed her surprise in an attempt to mask her anger.

Mrs Sancreed detected an excessive emotion of some kind behind the question and became cautious at once. "Has she never mentioned it?" she asked guardedly.

Estelle sought to mend the situation with a light laugh. "No reason why she should, of course." Her brain, racing ahead of the conversation, homed in on the fact that the woman herself was not at all pleased to think that her husband might part with some money to Bill — which, in turn, meant that the old boy was probably toying with the notion.

But on what conditions? That was crucial. She knew the Sancreeds only by reputation, but what she had heard was enough to assure her not only that there would be conditions but that they would be as stiff as Bill could bear.

The conversation then turned to casual matters and nothing more was said on the subject until after David had looked at the injury and assured himself, and them, that it was nothing more serious than a nasty bruise. He asked Mrs Sancreed if she would like to accompany him over to Rosemergy, where the christening tea was about to be served. Estelle said that *she* would take Lorna's mother across in a moment or two; she sensed a hesitation in the woman the moment David made his suggestion.

She took her upstairs to repair the ravages of the day. As soon as they could both show a new face to the world the older woman said, "Forgive me if I seem excessively blunt this afternoon, Mrs Carne, but time is short and − as is so often the case where my daughter is concerned − I already feel out of my depth. Tell me, did I deceive myself or did I gather that you are not greatly overjoyed to learn that the darling girl sent Mister Westwood to her father − brandishing his begging bowl?"

"Brandishing his *ambition*, I would prefer to say, Mrs Sancreed. But, apart from that, you are correct."

"May I ask why? I do assure you, this is no idle curiosity. In fact − time being short, as I say − allow me to put all my cards on the table so that you will see precisely where my interest lies. The truth is, my husband is half inclined to invest a considerable sum in young Westwood's venture. Of course, he thinks the idea of this speed-'plane is absurd, but he claims to detect a certain canny quality in the fellow. Perhaps you agree? He has the makings of a good businessman, the colonel says."

Estelle conceded the point with a wary nod − enough to encourage the other to continue. "He thinks he'll soon drop his quest for glory and settle for a steady diet of commercial flying of all kinds. The investment will then repay itself handsomely."

Estelle frowned. "In that case, Mrs Sancreed," she said hesitantly, "I don't quite see your objection."

"I would have none − if that were his only condition."

"Ah!"

"I would back my husband's business acumen against a brace of Rothschilds, let me say. But his understanding of *people* ..." She tapped her breastbone and shook her head.

"His other condition?" Estelle prompted, already half-knowing the answer.

"Westwood must, so to speak, join the family."

"Marry Lorna?"

Mrs Sancreed's lips compressed to a thin line. "More than that. He must tame her ... bring her to heel ... break her spirit ... keep her under his thumb. Between you and me, I think the investment in the aviation business is merely a device for keeping him in the district. If Westwood could somehow guarantee to take Lorna off to Timbuctoo and do all those things to her there, Sancreed would give him double the money tomorrow. He is absolutely determined she shall never drag our name through the mud again, you see."

"But it simply wouldn't *work!*" Estelle protested.

Mrs Sancreed smiled at last — and let out a great sigh of relief. "I'm glad to see we are in *complete* agreement over this whole wretched business, Mrs Carne."

"I admit I've only known Lorna for ... what? Not quite half a year. But even so I know her well enough to be sure she'd run circles round poor Bill Westwood. I'm amazed your husband doesn't know her better than that."

"He knows her no better than he knows himself, Mrs Carne — which amounts to the same thing, for they're as alike in spirit as two peas in a pod." She laughed, not entirely humorously. "Not that either of them can see the remotest resemblance, of course. But if you understand the difficulties of — how shall I put it? — of *handling* my daughter, you'll understand at once why I came here today in search of an ally. I trust I have found one?"

Estelle stretched forth a hand. "We may shake on it," she said.

en Calloway, a slave to the draconian licensing hours that had been introduced during the Great War as a temporary measure to keep munitions workers sober, had to leave the christening party soon after it started. Lorna said she'd see him safely home — which seemed absurd to everyone else, since he'd walked hundreds of miles of isolated clifftops in the pitch dark during the war and so could probably be trusted to cover the two hundred paces down Rosemergy's front garden path and along the esplanade all by himself. Just as they were about to leave, Estelle Carne arrived with Mrs Sancreed in tow. But Lorna was not to be deflected from her purpose. She made a few perfunctory inquiries after her mother's bruises, promised she'd only be gone five minutes, and then set off with Ben in tow.

As soon as they were out of doors she took his arm, mainly to slow him down, for she had plenty to say and not much time to say it in. "The most important thing I want to tell you, Ben," she began, " — and I want you to hear it from me before anyone else — is that we've decided to go ahead with the sanitarium. All three of us."

"But that's marvellous!" he replied.

"I hope you'll always think so!"

"You know I will," he said more quietly. "Always. It means you won't be moving on."

"Oh, Ben!" She rested her head briefly against his shoulder. "Do try to keep business separate from … everything else. Anyway, the architect is meeting us, here, tomorrow — David's day off — and if nobody's murdered anybody by teatime, we'll pause for an aspirin or two, and … perhaps you'd care to come over and look at the plans? We want to proceed in a thoroughly amicable fashion, you see — with *both* our neighbours."

"With all three neighbours, surely?"

"Yes, well, the one over our back-garden fence is another matter. She had an odd look in her eye just now, didn't you think? I wonder what my mother's been telling her. Anyway, will you be able to drop by, around this same time tomorrow?"

He cleared his throat awkwardly. "There's just one thing — will you be asking Corvo as well?"

"No," she replied flatly. "He's the other thing I wanted to talk over with you. I'd very much welcome your opinion on the best way to handle him."

"Does he need 'handling'? I thought that with Betty Corvo being dead-set against any expansion of the Riviera-Splendide he'd be out of the picture, anyway."

"Well ..." Lorna's voice wavered uncertainly. "He's still the sort of man who could make trouble. He refused to come to the christening this afternoon. The fact that he's been thwarted by his own wife could actually make matters worse, not better. Anyway, I don't mean I want your advice right this *minute*, Ben. Just give it some thought and let me know. Bill Westwood has offered to mount an aero-engine on a bench in our garage and run it at full revs without a silencer — just to show him how we could hit back if he turned awkward." She felt Ben stiffen satisfactorily at the suggestion that his arch rival might save the day. "I was hoping to arrive at something a little less crude than that but equally effective."

They had reached the door of the Mouse Hole by now. "Did you think over my offer?" he asked in an oddly casual fashion, as if they were discussing some knick-knack she was thinking of selling. "It's three months to the day since I made it."

"It isn't!" she said robustly. "That was the seventeenth of December. Today's only the seventh."

He smiled happily and she saw how he had tricked her. "You beast!" she complained, butting him with her shoulder. "You said that deliberately. Anyway, I only remembered the date because ... because ..." But on the spur of the moment she could think of nothing trivial enough to slap him down with.

And then she realized she was actually quite glad he had discovered her feelings for him by trickery rather than by plodding inquiry (of which he was also quite capable). "I suppose you expect a little reward for your cleverness," she said and, before he could respond, she dabbed a swift kiss on his cheek, just brushing the very corner of his mouth. And then she ran laughing away. "Until tomorrow, then — *à toute à l'heure.*"

After a few paces she slowed to a walk; she did not look behind but she felt the weight of his gaze upon her.

A moment later she was distracted by a figure hastening down the front steps of the Riviera-Splendide. At first she thought it could only be Corvo, for the hôtel would not be open to the public until Easter, which was still three weeks away; also he was clearly making a beeline for her. As he drew closer, however, she saw he was a fair bit older than Corvo — a man in his fifties, in fact — as burly as the hôtelier but much more athletic. He removed his hat as he approached, revealing a dense shock of dark hair; his eyes, too, were dark and their gaze intense. "Miss Sancreed?" he inquired. He was solemn, nervous, seemingly incapable of smiling.

"Yes," she replied guardedly.

"I'm Philip's father — Jake Morvah." He did not offer his hand.

All she could say was, "Oh!" There was a lengthy pause before she remembered to add, "How do you do." She held out her hand but he pointedly refused it.

"I have come to claim the boy," he said. He replaced his hat and patted it firmly.

Lorna glanced behind her but Ben had gone. She turned abruptly and went through the gate to Rosemergy, slamming it shut behind her. At that moment she was too shocked — and too frightened — to do anything else. A moment later she was too enraged.

"Did you hear me?" he called after her. She heard the gate open and close again, then his footfall at her heel. "Did you hear me?" he repeated. "I want my grandson."

Now she did not trust herself to speak at all. She walked on as if he were not there.

Think! she urged herself. But her mind was a blank — more than a blank, a vast, numb emptiness. In any case, what was there to think about? His demand was, quite literally, *un*thinkable.

He took her elbow lightly between his thumb and middle finger.

She stopped dead in her tracks and stared at him. Their eyes locked and he saw in hers the quality of those forces against which he had now pitted himself. She refused to see anything in his. She was dimly aware that something about him might call forth the pity of a disinterested observer, but she quenched the small spark of compassion it roused within herself. He released her elbow and, still silent, she turned and resumed her walk to the house.

Her heart was racing now but that was merely a catching-up with her earlier shock; her mind was cold and clear.

Still at her heels he said, "I was hoping you would yield him up amicably, Miss Sancreed. But if you do not, I shall apply to have him made a ward of court."

She had reached the end of the brick path and stepped out onto the gravel; the determined scrunch of her feet upon it was the only answer he got.

"You should understand that the father's rights over an illegitimate child are greater than the mother's, *Miss* Sancreed," was his final shot.

At the door she turned and spoke to him at last. He was still approaching her. "You're trespassing, Mister Morvah," she said. "Far more seriously than you realize." And she shut the door in his face.

She leaned her back against it and closed her eyes. She heard his feet on the gravel and then — presumably as he reached the path again — silence.

"Aunty Lorna! Are you all right?" Toby was staring up at her in consternation.

"Darling!" She smiled. "Will you do me the most enormous favour? Go as quiet as a mouse to the dining-room window and peep out and see if there's a man in a light-brown overcoat going down the path. Quick as you can."

"A burglar?" Toby asked excitedly.

"I'll tell you afterwards. Quick — before he vanishes."

After a minute or so — and it was the longest "or so" in Lorna's life — the boy returned and said, "He went down the path and along the front and I think he went into the Riviera-Splendide."

"Why?"

"Because he waved at Mister Corvo upstairs and as soon as I couldn't see him any more the light went on."

"Good boy!" She squatted down, put her arms around him, and hugged him warmly.

"Is he a burglar?" Toby asked.

"He wants to steal something from me," she replied. "So I suppose he is."

"Give it me, then," the boy suggested. "I'll keep it safeys for you."

Her reason was beginning to reassert itself over her anger and she saw she ought to play the incident down in the youngster's mind. "I don't suppose he was really serious, Toby. Men and hares go mad in March, you know — men of that age, anyway. But I'll remember your very kind offer and if he makes one false move, by Harry, you're the man for me!"

It was the language of Guy's plays, which made it more genuine to Toby than anything else she might have said; he went off, proud of his augmented stature.

Jessica came from the shadows beside the drawing-room door. "What was all that about?" she asked.

"Trouble," Lorna admitted. "But not immediate. I'll tell you later. Is my mother still here?"

Jessica grinned broadly. "You're going to have a job sending her home, I think. You might have to let her take Philip with her."

"Jess!" Lorna's eyebrows shot up. "You're a genius!"

"I wasn't serious, my dear." Jessica began to be worried.

"You were! You just don't realize it." She gave her arm a friendly squeeze as she went to join her mother in the drawing room — leaving a rather bemused Jessica behind in the hall.

"Mummy!" She gave her the warmest embrace of the decade — too warm, for it left her mother both winded and suspicious. "What about Philip, then, eh?" she went on. "Another little nonesuch?"

That was a family joke. Lorna's great-grandmother in the female line had greeted every child of her own, and every grandchild they, in turn proudly presented to her, with those three dismissive words: "Another little nonesuch!"

Mrs Sancreed both laughed and blinked back a tear or two for she had once, unwisely, voiced the fear that she would never utter the family greeting to a grandchild of her own. "I think the sight of Philip — in *her* christening smock — would have stifled the words even in his great-great-grandmama's throat, my darling. He is *the* most gorgeous baby ever!"

"But of course!" Lorna agreed. "D'you think Daddy might take a liking to him, too?"

"Ah!" A sadness filled her eyes. "If only he could be persuaded to *look* at the little fellow!"

"Well ..." Lorna offered hesitantly.

The sadness turned to alarm. "No, dear! Don't even dream about it. He remains as implacable as ever on that score."

"Such stubbornness!" Lorna said bitterly, adding, on a happier note, "Thank heavens *I* never inherited it!"

Mrs Sancreed's lips compressed themselves to vanishing point but she kept a stalwart silence.

"And yet he's so friendly with Bill Westwood!" Lorna went on. "Although he knows Bill is a friend of mine! It's madness."

"Oh well, dear, as to that — I'm sure he'd behave most cordially to *all* your friends ..."

"... if only to rub the salt in my wound!" Lorna said bitterly, as if she were completing her mother's thought for her.

"That isn't quite what I meant, dear — though no doubt something of that feeling does linger at the back of his mind."

Lorna stared down at her baby, grinning promiscuously up at the world like a baregummed old man. "You don't think that little fellow there might start to heal that same wound?" she asked. "He needs winding, by the way."

She picked him up and was about to put him over her shoulder when she saw the hope in her mother's eye. "D'you remember how?" she asked, arranging the baby over her mother's shoulder.

Mrs Sancreed closed her eyes and hugged her grandson to her with gentle ferocity. She began a slow, semicircular rotation to the left, to the right, left, right ... widdershins, deasil ... that soon became hypnotic; at the same time she began to croon a formless lullaby in a creaky falsetto that Lorna had quite forgotten. In that instant she felt herself transported back to a time that surely lay beyond her earliest memory. She remembered Theo's explanation of paradise and knew that, in his jocular fashion, he had nonetheless hit upon the truth.

Philip belched — a dry one, fortunately — and the mood changed to one of laughing congratulation. Lorna felt it safe to return to her earlier theme. "You don't suppose we could risk it?" she asked, nodding at the baby. "I mean ... he won't eat the little chap, will he?"

"He'd eat *you* a mile off, as Bridey Colquhoun says," Mrs Sancreed replied firmly.

"Well ... if I weren't there?"

For a moment her mother could make neither head nor tail of the suggestion. Then she stared at the baby ... then at her daughter. "You mean ..." Even then she could not put it into words.

"Just for the next two or three days?"

"But ... I mean ... feeding him ...?"

"You can find a good wet nurse, surely? *He* won't know the difference! And I'm sure he wouldn't care, even if he did."

"And you?"

Lorna knew her mother meant, "Won't you miss him?" but she chose to misinterpret the question. "I can use a pump," she explained. "In fact, I already use one, even now. I overdo even *that* — wouldn't you know it!" She finished with a self-deprecating laugh.

Mrs Sancreed felt she had offered enough objections to propitiate the gods of this good fortune. "If you're *sure*, darling?" she said.

Lorna dangled a languid wrist at her brow. "I shan't sleep a wink," she said dramatically. Then, grinning, she added, "It's all in a good cause, Mummy. Remember that!"

When Sarsfield and Drew, Solicitors at Law, opened for business at half past nine the following morning, their first customer, Miss Lorna Sancreed, was already pacing their frontage. Her interview with the younger Mr Drew was brief, for the law was uncharacteristically clear on the point that chiefly concerned her: Only natural parents had any rights in the custody of their illegitimate offspring. By custom those rights might pass to next of kin — if, for instance, both parents died — but the practice had no legal force. As for making an infant a ward of court, the judge would have to be shown some compelling cause — for instance, that the infant was in physical or moral danger — before he'd make the necessary order. "If the father were still alive," he concluded, "he might stand a chance of gaining custody. In law, the father's rights are greater than the mother's. Even there, however, the courts are becoming increasingly reluctant to separate mother and child — unless there is some flagrantly obvious reason to do so."

Lorna paid her three guineas on the spot and returned home much relieved. However, as her anxiety dwindled her bewilderment grew. "Jake Morvah's a lawyer, too," she remarked to David and Jessica, who were preparing the dining room for their meeting with Tristram Barras, the architect for the sanitarium. "He must know he has no standing in the custody of Philip. But did he really imagine he could beat me with bluff and bluster?"

David cleared his throat in a preparatory manner. Both women looked at him. "What's your opinion, then?" Lorna asked.

"I think that the custody of illegitimate children may be a topic on which old Jake Morvah might find it hard to be entirely rational. Did you know that he himself was a foundling?"

"No!" Both women stopped dead in the middle of folding the tablecloth and gaped at him.

"Yes! Literally a foundling — he was found wandering in a lane. Up Breage, I think."

"You're making it up!" Jessica accused.

"Philip never even hinted at it," Lorna added. "He always said his grandfather was Sir Stephen Morvah."

"And why d'you think the title died out with him, eh? Why didn't it pass down to Jake — if Jake was his legitimate son and heir?"

The two women exchanged glances; the incredible was beginning to seem at least possible, even if not yet probable. "How d'you know all this?" Jessica asked.

"I heard it all from Elizabeth Troy of Liston House. You know they rent that property from the Kittos — the big civil-engineering people? And Roseanne Morvah — Jake's mother — was a Kitto before her marriage to Sir Stephen. In fact, she was a Kitto when she found Jake — wandering in a lane, as I said."

"Oh yes!" Lorna said scornfully. "And the poor-law guardians allowed a young spinster to adopt a foundling? Very likely!"

David was unperturbed. "It happened just the same. If you've ever met Roseanne Kitto, you'll believe she was more than a match for any old bunch of poor-law guardians." He fixed her with a solemn gaze as he added, "There *are* women like that, you know. Ruthless ... unstoppable — especially where their children are concerned, natural or adopted. There's one or two in every generation."

"Is she still alive?" Jessica asked in some surprise.

"Very much so — the last I heard, anyway. She lives in that house out on the cliffs at Rinsey Head."

"I think I must call and see her," Lorna mused.

"I think that would be a capital notion," he replied.

"But," Jessica objected, "that doesn't go very far toward explaining why Jake should be a little unhinged on the subject of custody and illegitimate offspring — which is what you implied just now."

"Ah, well, I didn't quite tell you everything. Jake's *real* father was from quite a good family from over Falmouth way. I forget the name but he was a notorious evil-liver — to adopt the parlance of his day. He was a dope fiend and a drunkard and at the time of Jake's birth he was reduced to sleeping rough with the boy's mother. The story is that he murdered her one night when Jake was little over a year old — which is why he was wandering in a lane when Roseanne Kitto, as she then was, found him. So now d'you see?"

He put the question more particularly to Lorna. She nodded gravely and said, "It does all begin to look horribly consistent. The reason Philip fell out with his father is that he wouldn't take a commission in the navy — he preferred to serve in the ranks in the air force." She smiled at Jess. "To serve with the Chief, to be precise."

"I remember your telling me," Jessica responded.

Lorna went on: "I don't think Philip knew this story, you know. He could never understand his father's obsession with class and respectability. He just thought him a most terrible snob."

"And look at it from Jake's point of view now," Jessica put in. "His only son refuses the respectable rank of officer and gentleman in order to 'live rough,' so to speak among the mechanicals. He then lives out of wedlock with ..."

"Steady!" Lorna laughed. "That's me!"

"I know. But you see the superficial parallels, surely?"

Lorna nodded rather glumly.

"Jake must now be desperate to 'rescue' his grandson — as he sees it — and bring him back to the ultra-respectable Morvah fold."

After a longish, thoughtful pause, Lorna said, "I think I absolutely must go and have a talk with old Mrs Morvah, up Rinsey Head."

"You'd be mad not to," David agreed. "And there's one more thing you should know — more incredible than anything I've yet told you."

"What happened to the natural father?" Jessica interrupted. "The evil-liver?"

"That's what I'm coming to. He escaped after the murder. They say his family smuggled him abroad. But he came back a few years later. I don't know exactly when but it was while Jake was still a lad. And it must have been before Roseanne Kitto married Sir Stephen because she was farming up Wheal Fortune then."

"On her own?"

He nodded. "Her family always had a field or two and a few cows. Anyway, the evil-liver came back and tried to finish off the boy — and Roseanne. He threw them down a mineshaft — the country's riddled with them round there." He laughed at their expressions of disbelief and added, "I told you, didn't I!"

"But no one can possibly survive a fall down a mineshaft," Jessica objected. It was, in fact, one of the commonest ways of committing suicide in Cornwall.

"But they did," he asured them. "What the man didn't realize was that the mineshaft he'd picked was the old-fashioned kind — the kind that follows the lode down into the earth." He held his hand at a steep angle, about seventy degrees to the horizontal. "Not the modern, vertical sort. It seems they slipped down quite a way and then lodged. Then he was apprehended and they were rescued."

Lorna thought of the respectable Jake Morvah who had accosted her yesterday, so intense, so solemn. She tried to picture him as a young lad in the circumstances David had just described. It still seemed impossible — and yet it explained so much.

"And now, ladies," David said, "we have a sanitarium to build, if you please?"

*W*hen they broke for lunch the two women were ready to call off the whole idea of converting Rosemergy into a modern sanitarium and instead open it as a simple little seaside boarding house. There seemed to be difficulties every way they turned, and each solution merely opened the doors on a further set of problems.

"It's because you're not concentrating," Jessica complained to Lorna when they went out to the kitchen to cut a few sandwiches. "Not that I blame you entirely, but it's not a good omen for our cooperation in the future."

"But it's *your* house," Lorna complained back. "I don't feel I can just suggest this and suggest that all over the place."

"That's just an excuse. We've agreed on it — your investment and my property both go into the pool. And we both own the pool equally. Stop waving that knife around."

Lorna gave out a sigh of frustration. "I'd like to slip it under Tristram Barras's ribs! You know what *barras* means in Cornish? Cod! He's well named, isn't he!"

"I wish you'd stick to the point, Lorna. Even now you're going off in all directions. Is that enough bread, d'you think? I'm not desperately hungry, myself."

"Do four more. I'll bet old codface will scoff the lot. The point is, Jess, darling, that it's easy enough to agree in theory that everything is *ours*, but the fact remains that Rosemergy's your home — I mean, it's all those things you *can't* chuck into a common pool. And almost every suggestion that crosses my mind would change it so irrevocably that it could never go back to being your home again." She laughed drily. "I know — let's just buy the Riviera-Splendide and turn *that* into a large private hospital! Now there's a building I'd love to be ruthless with!"

When laughter had somewhat eased the atmosphere between them, Jessica said, "Just give me one example of the sort of change you think is too ruthless here, then?"

"All right. Take this room." Lorna ran a quick eye around the kitchen. "The heart of the house, eh?"

"Not until you came, dear — but go on."

"Isn't this the obvious place to put the lift for the patients? Extend the drive to come round here." She pointed out of the window. "So that patients can get out of cars or ambulances and move directly into the lift. Simple!"

"But they'd still have to come through the scullery."

"No — knock all that out. This would become our reception area."

"And what about the bathroom above?"

"Get rid of that, too. That's where the lift arrives — and continues on up to the new solar hydro on the roof."

"Whew!" Jessica gave out a toneless whistle, as if Lorna had winded her.

"Exactly!" Lorna said. "Now try turning *that* back into a private house! It's been our bugbear all morning, you realize? Nobody's actually said it but at the back of all our minds has been this nagging thought — *If it doesn't pan out, we'll want to turn it back into a private residence.* So we've kept on pushing all the changes to the outside edges — and, of course, it doesn't work."

By now Jessica had got over her surprise sufficiently to start considering the proposal seriously. "So we'd have to build a new kitchen … where?"

"Immediately beyond the new dining rooms, which will be the present drawing room and morning room. Anyway, it'll probably be cheaper to build a new kitchen from scratch because adapting this one to meet all those stupid Board of Trade regulations will cost the earth."

The conversation continued in this manner until they had an answer to every problem that had arisen during the morning's acrimonious and frustrating discussions. It came to a halt when they looked up to find the two men leaning, one against each door jamb, gazing up at the ceiling with expressions of angelic patience. "We've solved it all," Jessica told them, handing Barras the tray of glasses and David the jug of beer; she and Lorna followed them back to the dining room with the plates of sandwiches.

There, between mouthfuls, the two women described the carefully planned wrecking of Rosemergy and its transmutation into the finest sanitarium west of Plymouth. Barras's mouth watered far more than could be explained by even the most appetizing of Lorna's sandwiches. David turned paler with each new revelation. "But you can't possibly live in the house while all this is going on," he objected. "Where will you go? Summer lettings won't be cheap."

"It'll only be for the summer months," Lorna replied, giving Barras a meaningful "or else!" sort of glance. "I thought we might put two or three Romany caravans on the back lawn and sleep in those. I'm sure we can make an arrangement with Ben Calloway about baths and meals. Talking of which — or whom — I asked him over at around teatime to look at our preliminary suggestions. We want to keep on the right side of our neighbours, I feel?"

"Teatime *this* afternoon?" the architect asked in alarm. "But that's impossible! Out of the ..."

"Just freehand sketches," Lorna assured him. "The little drawings you did this morning were so beautiful. That's all we'll need today. There's absolutely no hurry for the detailed plans and a fully costed quantity survey. That can easily wait until tomorrow."

"Oh yes!" he exclaimed sarcastically. "Morning or afternoon?"

"Morning would be *wonderful!*" she assured him.

David patted his arm consolingly. "Treasure these moments, Barras," he advised. "I have the feeling you're going to look back on these early days as the *easiest* part of our association!"

*I*t was a point of honour with Lorna to take her first dip in the sea before Easter. It had been easy enough in 1919, when the festival had fallen toward the end of April and the nearest salt water had been along the relatively shallow and warm coastal stretch of north Somerset; last year, 1920, though still in those favoured waters, had been harder, for Easter had fallen a couple of weeks earlier. But the present year, 1921, was a real test of courage. Not only was Easter on the last Sunday in March, but the sea, though officially called the English Channel, was raw North Atlantic, deep and cold. She might therefore have decided that this was a fitting moment in her life to bow gracefully out of the habit — no matter that Jessica would surely taunt her with premature middle age; but the self-inflicted challenge coincided so neatly with the fact that old Mrs Morvah lived on the clifftop at Rinsey Head that she felt compelled to take it up for one more year at least. The only question was when? Day after day her answer was, "Tomorrow," until, as Easter week dawned, it looked as though the contest would lapse by default.

In the end it was Lorna's mother who decided it for her. She turned up on the Tuesday of that week and asked if she could "borrow" baby Philip once again; he was proving a better ambassador with his grandfather than either she or her daughter had dared hope. With Philip away that night, the emptiness of Rosemergy was all the encouragement Lorna needed to take the plunge — with both the sea and the old lady. She had heard nothing from Jake Morvah since the evening of the christening, now more than two weeks ago; but she did not let that lull her suspicions for one moment.

The following day was bright enough for a swim but rather breezy. One of the fishermen at the early-morning market assured her it would die back later and turn dead calm. However, when she returned home with her marketing, Jessica reminded her that the beach at Rinsey Cove lay to the east of the headland where Mrs Morvah's house was built. From lunchtime onward the cliffs would be shedding a lengthening shadow there, so that by mid-afternoon she'd be swimming in the chill of it, no matter how slack the breeze.

Lorna saw that the luxury of "tomorrow," which the fisherman had shrunk to "today," was at long last reduced to "now or never."

"I'll come with you, if you like," Jessica promised. "Just in case you freeze to death."

"And what'll you do *then?*" Lorna asked.

Jess shrugged. "At least I can point out to the coroner the spot where you were last seen alive."

And so, shortly after breakfast, they packed a hamper with a spirit kettle, some soup, vacuum flasks of tea, a set of fisherman's underwear, seaboot stockings, two fairisle sweaters, and a tub of embrocation. On their way through Penzance, at the foot of Market Jew Street, they made a brief halt at the railway station, where they plundered the slot machine of half a dozen penny bars of chocolate.

Lorna was at the wheel; she said it helped calm her excitement. Jessica kept a stoic silence as to what Lorna's driving — skilled though it was — did to her own nerves. As they flashed past Bill Westwood's airfield at Penzance Green, Lorna gave only the most cursory glance and wave. "He's taking someone up," she said as they sped on toward Long Rock. "His first tripper of the year, let's hope."

Jessica, who had studied the scene at greater leisure, noticed David's car parked beside the hangar. It could not be David himself for she knew he was doing town visits that morning, something he usually managed in the pony and trap. She decided to say nothing of it to Lorna — or not just yet.

Lorna said, "I asked him once what would happen if I put on a bathing costume and jumped out over the sea at a thousand feet. He said the bruises would take six months to heal."

Jessica laughed. "I'll bet you were disappointed!"

"I was — honestly. Don't you think it'd be fun to dive and dive and dive ... knowing you'd be safe, of course?"

"No! I'd rather" — Jessica tried to think of the worst chore within her grasp — "cook dinner for twenty!"

"Oh, so would I!" Lorna agreed.

"Well ... there you are — one more difference between you and me. I don't think there could be two more different people — do you?"

Lorna considered the question in silence awhile; then she said, "Do you really want to go ahead with turning Rosemergy into a sanitarium, Jess?"

"Of course I do!" she exclaimed in surprise. "What have we spent the last two weeks discussing it for, otherwise?"

"I just wondered." Lorna slowed down to take the uphill bends through Marazion.

"Do I give the impression I'm getting cold feet?" Jessica asked.

"Not in the least. I'm just asking — in an ideal world, you know — would you still do it?"

"Oh ... in an *ideal* world ..." Jessica spoke as if that were something she never considered.

"Yes. If you had enough in the funds — not filthy rich but enough to get by comfortably for the rest of your life — would you?"

"Heavens!" Jessica looked all about her for inspiration. "I've never thought about it."

"You never daydream?"

"Of course I do — but only about things that might actually happen. Why d'you want to know, anyway? Are *you* getting cold feet, perhaps?"

Lorna chuckled. "Ask me in half an hour. It'll be more than my feet, I think."

"Ha ha! But to be serious ..."

"I'm not getting cold feet, Jess — and that's quite serious." They had reached the top of the hill, beyond the straggle of houses, where Lorna slowed down for one last view of St Michael's Mount before the road turned inland. "I sometimes wish I wasn't Cornish," she said. "Imagine seeing all this for the first time! It's one of the few parts of England — of the world, maybe — where the real thing is even more beautiful and heart-stopping than the most romantic painting of it could ever be."

The words made Jessica realize, yet again, how different she and Lorna were. The romantic Cornwall so beloved of painters and summer visitors had never moved her very much; the Cornwall she treasured was more local and secret than that. The memory of some anonymous back lane, or a patch of half-regrown mine halvans, or the sight and smell of gulls wheeling over a gut-spattered quay — these could bring a lump to the throat at any time. All she said, however, was, "Yes, I do agree." She could not spend the whole morning carping on and on about their differences.

"One thing I have noticed, though," Lorna continued as they followed the road inland, where the tall stone hedges cut out the last view of the sea for several miles, "is that you were never more than lukewarm toward the other ideas. I mean, we could still make a very good go of a private hôtel, you know."

"But we've been through all that, dear. An hôtel might earn more per week, but only during the summer season. A sanitarium is all the year round."

"An hôtel could take retired people *en pension* during the off-season — like Bournemouth and Torquay. A lot of people who couldn't afford the social life in those places might come here."

Jessica slumped dramatically in her seat. "Lord! Are we going to start all that again? I thought we'd ..."

"Not at all — except that one should always think of all the possibilities. But again I notice you pour cold water on them at once."

Jessica's tone hardened. "Oh, I see! Ho ho! I see! I know your game, Miss Sancreed!"

"Really?" Lorna grinned.

"Yes! You're trying to force me to admit that if David isn't going to be involved, I want nothing to do with it! Is that it? Why not just say so? Of course I admit it. Have I ever made a secret of it?"

Lorna did not share her amusement. She stared rather fixedly at the road ahead and then said, "Suppose David became free? Of Estelle, I mean. Suppose one didn't *have* to build this sanitarium to ... er ..."

"Trap him?"

"I wasn't going to say that. I was going to say to cloak ..." She burst into laughter at last. "It was the *next* few words that made me hesitate — but you know what I mean, I'm sure."

"There is nothing going on between David and me that needs cloaking," Jessica said coldly.

"Oh-dear-oh-dear-oh-dear!" Lorna's hands tightened on the wheel. "I didn't mean to unleash this!"

"Unleash?" Jessica echoed in protest. "There you go again! What is there to unleash? How many times do I have to tell you — there is *nothing* to cloak, *nothing* to unleash."

"All right, all right! I'll buy a dictionary!"

"You won't catch *me* skulking out at Porthgwarra," Jessica added.

Lorna considered this puzzling statement awhile. "I don't follow?" she said at length.

"Oh yes you do!"

Lorna stared at her in amused surprise. "D'you think that ... Theo and I ...? Surely not!"

"Clever!" Jessica said scornfully. "But you know very well I'm not thinking about Theo."

"A girl could do worse," Lorna said playfully.

Jessica stared at the road ahead in stony silence.

They were passing through Rosudgeon, summit of the long, gentle climb up from Marazion. From here it was an equally long, gentle downhill to Praa. The gears ceased their whine and began to purr. After a while Lorna said, "If we can talk about it seriously — I mean without exploding all over the place — I take it you're referring to David, then?"

"What a brilliant deduction!"

Lorna sighed. "Not really. I've only once been to Porthgwarra Cottage with any other man than Theo, and that was with David — the day Bill took Estelle up for a spin." She laughed sardonically. "It never occurred to me that Estelle would tell *you!* I thought she'd rather die than do that."

"Oh yes! I suppose you're now going to make out it was all part of some deep-laid plot!"

"Spur-of-the-moment, actually. David and I were walking across the cliff ..."

Jessica suddenly erupted. "It's the duplicity of it, Lorna. David was to drop you off at Theo's and go on to ... wherever he usually goes when he communes with nature. Instead, the next thing I know is that Estelle comes hotfoot to Rosemergy bursting with the news that she's caught the pair of you in the act on Gwennap Head."

"And of course you believed her!" Lorna answered scornfully. "It never struck you that she herself has an axe to grind — a cupboard full of axes! I'd like to bury any one of them in her head!" Her fingers drummed the wheel. "This is the last sort of conversation I want or need this morning, you realize? We should be talking about Roseanne Morvah. What am I going to say to her? How can I get her to call off her son Jake?" She turned and gazed earnestly at Jessica. "I'm not trying to wriggle out of it, darling, but honestly — d'you think we could postpone all this about Estelle and David and you and me until the journey back?"

*T*he last time Lorna had swum at Rinsey was when she was eight. If she had remembered how narrow, stony, and rutted the lane down to Rinsey Head was, she'd have left the car at the green and walked the last half mile. But once she was committed to it there was no turning around; she was glad to arrive at the open clifftop with the springs intact. Mrs Morvah's house — built in solid granite, four-square to the elements — was still about a quarter of a mile away at the end of an unfenced cart-track that wound its way down the centre of the headland. Smoke was rising from several of its chimneys, teased rather then blown away on eddies of uncertain air. Apart from that one man-made element, the scene immediately before them was a treeless wilderness of furze, coarse grass, thrift — in fact, any sort of plant that could cower successfully against the constant battering of wind and salt spray.

"Swim first, walk down to the house later," Lorna suggested as she parked to one side among a patch of furze and mine halvans. When she switched off, the silence that followed was profound. The sea, almost three hundred feet below them, was oily calm, so the only sound was the occasional mewing of gulls and the steady, muted whoosh of six-inch wavelets, out of sight beyond the cliff edge. "We already know one thing about Roseanne Morvah," Lorna said. "She does not own a car — or surely Kitto Engineering would have done something about that lane before now!"

"Perhaps she regards a new set of springs each month as a fair price to pay to keep out unwanted trippers like us," Jessica suggested. Her tone was mild enough but, like everything else she had said since putting their quarrel on ice, it was a direct contradiction of what Lorna had said.

In fact, Lorna almost considered making a game of it — to see whether she could say anything that Jess would find impossible to gainsay. "Leave everything up here," she suggested. "I'll just take a towel down with me."

"You'll get cold," Jessica warned.

"The climb back will soon warm me up. I hate carrying empty picnic baskets, especially up a steep hill like that."

Jessica said nothing.

The path snaked steeply down, east then west then east again, to the little beach at the neck of the cove. The first stretch ran diagonally from the end of the lane to the derelict engine house of an abandoned mine, halfway down the cliff and a mere twenty paces from its edge. Built in the 1860s, it had limped along for a few decades until cheap tin from the empire had forced its closure.

The engine shaft was wide open and unfenced; the grassy edges sank inwards like the lips of a toothless old man. When they reached it Lorna rolled a large stone to its rim and sent it onward with a kick; it boomed and roared as it ricocheted from side to side in its descent, fetching down many times its own weight in loose shale, all of which plunged at last with a cavernous thunder into the water at the bottom of the shaft.

"My father once told me the story of how this place flooded," Lorna said as relative silence returned. "The stopes ran far out under the sea, you know, and apparently they arranged to hold one tribute supper way out there somewhere." She waved a hand out toward the horizon and they began the next leg of their descent, which ran westward, toward the headland, along the very edge of the cliff. "They laid all the tables that morning — white tablecloths, pewter tankards, Sheffield plate canteens ... everything. Then, about two o'clock in the afternoon, a couple of men carried down the ale, but when they arrived they saw seawater dripping through the overburden onto one of the tables. So they raced back to the winding shaft and got hauled up. And before they reached grass they heard this great roaring beneath them and the sea flooded the entire mine." She laughed. "Later I learned it wasn't this mine at all. It was the one just round the next headland at Trewarvas. But I still think of that table, all beautifully laid and abandoned down there somewhere."

Again she pointed at the sea, which was now only a hundred feet or so beneath them. Then she froze, staring intently, and a slow smile spread across her lips.

Jessica followed her eyes and saw, a couple of hundred yards out from the shore, level with the tip of the headland, a number of black specks bobbing on the water.

"Seals!" Lorna murmured. "Oh, Jess, you might as well stay up here in the sunshine. I won't be swimming down on the beach."

"Why ever not?"

She nodded toward the seals. "Those fellows. I want to go out and talk to them. I can't resist it. Sorry!" The apology was flung over her shoulder as she started on a reckless plunge down the last leg of the path, which was part-cut, part-eroded into the face of the cliff. It ended about twelve feet above the level of the sands, leaving her with a precarious scramble down over the side of a rock into which someone had once cut rudimentary footholds. She landed in a sprawling heap on the sand.

She already had her swimming costume on under her dress, so less than a minute passed before she was ready for the plunge. Behind her a freshet of water poured out of the cliff face and broke with a crackling sort of complaint on a flat sheet of rock; from there it ran out into the sand and vanished before reaching the sea. The sharpness of the sound made it seem very cold. Protesting gulls, disturbed by her sudden arrival, wheeled high above. Jessica, having taken her at her word, was back on the cliff top, gazing down at her; otherwise she was the last person left alive on earth. Even the roof of Roseanne Morvah's house was not visible from there.

The sea temperature, she knew, would be no more than the low forties — as good as freezing to a warm-blooded human. There was only one possible way to go into water at that temperature: at full gallop. With one foot she prodded her clothes into a neat pile, postponing the dread moment for another precious five seconds; the sun and the chill March air fought an equal contest on her skin, giving her reason neither to go in nor to stay out. "This will be the last year of this utter madness," she promised herself aloud.

"Coward!" The taunt floated down from the top of the cliff.

That galvanized her. She set off at a moderate lope, like a cross-country runner. The tide was out so she had a fair stretch to the water's edge; half way there she was racing; by the time she reached the sea she was sprinting as hard as she could go, and giving out the longest, loudest, prophylactic scream that had ever escaped her throat.

The slope was so gentle that for the first dozen paces she could still leap clear of the water between each footfall — that is, still hoodwink her jangled nerves into thinking this nightmare wasn't really happening. Sheets of silver rose about her at every step. She burst her way through them, unable to believe that water could be so cold without turning to ice. Then, when even her gawkiest, most ostrich-like dancing could no longer lift her feet clear of the surface, she faced that awful moment of choice between instant death and a long wade-out with the water rising inexorably to claim her, bit by bit — death by a thousand millimetres.

With a final shrill of disbelief she launched herself at the water — not just into it but under it, down to the pale, sun-mottled sand. It felt as if ten thousand icy needles were pricking her skin; she had a sudden violent headache at the back of her head. The unbelievable cold left her senses so disoriented that when she gathered her feet beneath her and leaped back into the air again, the sudden access of sunlight registered in her brain not as a visual experience but as a new, exotic smell. And when gravity bore her back into the water, the freezing embrace of it was like a blinding flash.

Memory took over — the automatic sort that lies buried in all our muscles, ready for such moments of stress — so that she swam with sturdy, even strokes, marvelling to find herself still alive. At last, when something like everyday consciousness returned to her and her pulse was back to just under a thousand, she found she was swimming well out of her depth and had already covered about a third of the distance to the headland and the welcoming (she hoped) school of seals. It was then she made the discovery that the water was not cold at all; in fact, it was tingling-hot, almost too hot to bear. She laughed and flipped onto her back to see if Jessica was still watching — admiring her courage. At first she saw no one; then she realized she was making her way toward the headland along the clifftop, keeping pace with her. Jessica waved and Lorna waved back before turning over once more and settling to a steady trudgen, keeping close to the rocky foot of the cliff in case of cramps.

The cliff face of the headland had been mined for tin and copper long before the modern Cornish industry was born — so long ago, indeed, that the two great caves which pierced it near the tip were by now as much the work of the sea as of man. Only an ancient quarry back near the beach, around which Jessica was now making a detour, was indisputably the work of human hands. Beneath it, on the seaward side, a number of low rocky shelves, mostly covered at high tide, offered Lorna the temptation of walking rather than swimming the next two dozen paces. She succumbed gratefully — but paid for it when she plunged back into the chilling sea at the outer end of the rock shelf.

Now she found herself treading water before the first of the great, square-mouthed caverns; a place of secrets and unknown treasures, it both invited and repelled her. What if it were also the home of a giant squid or some monstrous sea-serpent as yet unknown to science? Gingerly she edged toward it, telling herself she needn't explore very far — and it would at least give Jess time to catch up. Nervously she eyed the stone that spanned the entrance, some twenty feet overhead, hoping to discover a telltale crack that would enable her to trade discretion for valour. It was of no comfort to reflect upon all the storms and batterings it had withstood down the centuries; these things always give way when least expected.

In fact, by the time she reached the opening, her eyes were accustomed to the gloom and she could see that the "cave" hardly deserved the name, for it went barely more than thirty or forty feet into the rock. Perhaps it was not man-made at all, she realized, for she was still swimming in two fathoms of water, and if this was the sea level at low tide, how had they cut all that rock away below?

The moment she entered the grotto she forgot all her fears. The sea outside was slick-calm; but in here even the tiniest waves were bounced back and forth between the confining walls to create a flickering surface, so like a child's painting of the sea that she could hardly believe it was real. It was composed entirely of transient pinnacles, bobbing and falling all about her — all of identical height and all with identical concave profiles. Most eerie of all — they somehow absorbed the light reaching into the grotto from behind her and re-emitted it in a lambent, almost supernatural green. It was as if she were afloat in a sea of ghostly emerald fire.

She gave a cry of delight — and saw the green wraith of her condensed breath drift like smoke, adding to the illusion of the watery flames. The long, magical moment came to an end when she turned back toward the open sea and saw two sleek heads bobbing on the water, just outside the cave mouth, watching her keenly.

"Hallo, fellows!" she cried out gaily. "Am I keeping you out of your home?"

They slipped beneath the surface and she fought a moment of panic as she imagined them heading straight toward her, fangs bared. But no — seals weren't like that. Truly not! All the same, she swam as fast as she could, outside and seaward, making a great deal of splashing toward the next rocky shelf, which would allow her to walk a further dozen yards or so toward her ultimate goal — the school of seals near the tip of the headland.

She saw them the moment she stood up and began to walk. They, however, were not in playful mood today; those who were sunbathing on the rocks lumbered back into the water and all of them made for the open sea with a great deal of barking complaint.

"I was ready to send for the Porthleven lifeboat!" Jessica called out from above.

"Sorry! There's an amazing cave in there. You really ought to come in and see for yourself."

"No thanks!"

"And there's another one — just here. I shan't be long." Before she could get too warm in the sun she dived once more into waters, pleased to find that their chill now seemed merely invigorating.

The second cave, though outwardly similar to the first, could hardly have been more different — as she realized the moment she swam inside. For a start it ran deep into the cliff, tapering all the way. The floor rose, too, so that the inner half of it was — at low tide, anyway — exposed to the air. The sensation of swimming through green fire was less marked here because the wavelets were dissipated among the hundreds of smooth, round boulders that littered the shelving floor — polished gemstones for giants, she thought. She wriggled among them like an eel, marvelling at their smoothness, for the rocks outside had been carpeted with tiny barnacles.

Indeed, these boulders were so smooth they made it dangerous for her to stand; she picked her way forward on knees and knuckles to a small patch of sand at the very end of the cave, no bigger than a blanket. There, as her eyes grew accustomed to the even deeper gloom, she was surprised to see that the tapering sides and roof did not pinch in to a solid back wall but vanished into a narrow cleft, about her own height but no more than a foot wide. At its foot was a pool of unknown depth.

She straddled the water and, bracing her hands nervously against the sides, poked her head into the dark — expecting to find nothing but pitch black. Instead she saw a narrow strip of daylight at the farther end. This cleft was obviously the opening of a narrow tunnel that ran right though the cliff ... except that something was not quite right. She looked back toward the mouth of the cave and gauged its distance as about thirty paces; she poked her head into the tunnel again and guessed it to be no more than six paces long — plus a further three or four until it opened out again into broad daylight. So — forty paces in all, say. But the headland was surely double that, if not more?

Something didn't add up. Perhaps her sense of direction had gone awry and this tunnel pierced diagonally across the headland, coming out at the most seaward point? Anyway, it was certainly not long enough to go right across. The only way for her to find out was to work her way through the tunnel and discover precisely where it emerged into open water.

With sinking heart she surveyed the route. The pool at her feet extended all the way through the tunnel to the farther end. It was just the sort of place where giant anemones would lie in ambush, waiting for the sea to wash their unsuspecting prey into the clammy, poisonous embrace of their myriad tentacles. Or vampire cuttlefish, ready to streak out of secret tunnels and fasten all ten tentacles around her ankles ... or sea snakes ... Or (why invent phantasmogorical creatures when the sea has plenty of known examples, ready-made?) simple crabs and lobsters — not even lying in wait, just angry to be disturbed in their holes and crevices ...

She drew a deep breath and shut her mind to these terrors as best she could. The heroine who had just won her own personal Victoria Cross for taking to the sea at all this morning was not going to be put off by a few lurking crustaceans and polyps! All the same, she covered the first few paces with her feet straining desperately against the smooth walls of the tunnel, a few inches clear of the water, assisted by her hands, four or five feet higher. Thus Samson must have strained to bring down the pillars of the Temple.

She, being no Samson, could not maintain the effort. The walls were smooth and her feet kept slipping. At last, aching in every muscle of all four limbs, she allowed her feet to slide down into the stygian black of the water beneath her. It proved to be a puddle, no more than two inches deep! She laughed aloud and went splashing boisterously out into the blinding light of day.

When she could see her way about her she discovered she was in a kind of natural amphitheatre in the very heart of the headland, about fifteen paces long and five wide. The sides were almost sheer and offered no obvious way out by climbing. The floor was composed of a mass of boulders, wedged tight between the tapering walls. They were free of bird lime and so were obviously covered at high tide. In fact, she could hear the water sloshing idly about beneath her feet at that moment.

And that was a further puzzle. For if the tide flowed in here by way of the tunnel she had just negotiated, the water lying pooled among the boulders at her feet ought now to be quite still. Therefore, she reasoned, there must be another opening to the sea at the farther end of this amphitheatre and deep enough to remain connected at low water. Gingerly she picked her way over the boulders, several of which tilted and wobbled beneath her weight; and, sure enough, at the farther end she discovered the expected opening. It was no larger than a domestic bath, though it was easily a couple of fathoms deep — and it certainly connected with the open water for she could see daylight flooding in from the farther side.

She dared herself to go on — to swim through this underwater tunnel and emerge on the farther side of Rinsey Head. It couldn't be very long — probably no more than three or four strokes, to judge by the strength of the daylight pouring through it. But the snag was the hole at her feet. It was too small to dive into and its sides were too sheer to let her lower herself in gradually. The only way in was to jump — as upright and rigid as possible.

She was on the point of doing so when the tunnel darkened. There was a moving shadow on the sandy floor. She gave a cry of delight. Obviously one of the seals was coming in here for a quick look-around. She squatted at the edge, ready to give it the surprise of its life.

Only the fact that seals do not wear white rubber swimming caps prevented her from giving Roseanne Morvah the surprise of her life. Lorna did not know it was old Mrs Morvah, of course; she assumed, without time to think very hard, that it was Jessica, who, knowing of this secret way through the headland, had come dressed with her costume underneath and was now hoping to surprise her. Only the last-minute sight of the wrinkled old arm that broke the surface prevented her from crowing out the most inappropriate welcome.

The white swimming cap soon followed. There was a stertorous gasp of pent-up breath, a deal of spray, and then Lorna found herself looking down at the nut-brown face of a grinning old lady. "Ha!" the woman said. "Thought 'ee would!"

"Mrs Morvah?" Lorna asked, feeling rather stupid, for who else was it likely to be!

"Miss Sancreed." She reached up a hand, not for assistance but to be shaken. "Coming in, are 'ee, maid?" she asked. Her Cornish accent was much more marked than Lorna would have expected in a woman of her wealth. "There's soup on the hob and a pasty in the oven. You'll catch your death if you stay here."

"You know me?" she asked, slightly dazed.

"I do know *of* 'ee, maid," she said. "I just met your friend upalong, Widow Lanyon."

Widow Lanyon! It was a voice from another age. Lorna had a sudden image of Jessica, all wrapped up in a black shawl, pacing the headlands like a distraught seawife, scanning the horizon for a sail that would never fill with wind again.

"Come-us on, then!" Mrs Morvah cried. "Drop in feet-first. He's burr and wide down near the bottom. You won't hit your feet on the sides down there." And she inhaled sharply and plunged vertically to the sandy bed. Lorna watched her turn, lithe as the seal she had mistaken her for at first, and breast-stroke her way back toward the open sea.

The moment she was clear Lorna jumped in after her — before she could have second thoughts, not just about swimming but about the whole business. For old Mrs Morvah was clearly nothing like the grand old wealthy lady with whom she had conducted so many imaginary arguments these past three weeks.

*L*orna did not get the feeling back into the tips of her fingers until, some twenty minutes later, she wrapped them around a bowl of hot soup in Roseanne Morvah's kitchen. By then Jessica had returned with her clothes. "My good deed for the day," she said as she handed them over. Then, remembering the long climb down to the beach and up again, she added, "Actually, for the month."

Taking advantage of the hot kitchen range, the two swimmers changed out of their wet costumes. Mrs Morvah pushed a finger through a moth hole in the back of hers. "That shows how long 'tis since I last put this old thing up," she remarked.

"You don't swim all that often, then?" Lorna surmised.

She grinned. "Every day of the year, my lover, come rain or shine. But I don't belong to put up my old costume. The seals have no modesty, see?"

Lorna laughed as the penny dropped. "And I thought I chased them away," she said. "In fact, they were only going round to say hallo to you!"

"There's two kinds of people do come swimming at Rinsey," the old woman went on. "Those who only go so far into that cave and then turn back — I've got no time for them. And then there's the ones like you, who do go all the way through."

"You have time for them!"

"And pasties," Jessica put in.

Laughing, they carried their lunch through to the long verandah-like sitting room, which offered a breathtaking view over Mount's Bay. There they ate in silence while the two visitors marvelled at the panorama. The contrast between the two reaches of coastline to their immediate left and right could not have been greater. Westward, there stretched the mile-long sands at Praa, a favourite bathing beach of summer visitors — and the site of many a profitable wreck, too. To the east, as far as Trewarvas Head, it was all rock, some of it sheer cliff, the rest a higgledy-piggledy of outcrops, erratics, fallen boulders, and wave-washed islands. Rinsey beach itself — the only bit of sand for miles on that side — was almost directly behind the house and therefore out of sight.

Looking farther afield, Penzance, too, was hidden. It lay miles beyond the headland of Cudden Point, which beetled over Prussia Cove, the ancient haunt of John Carter, the greatest of the Cornish smugglers, who styled himself the "King of Prussia." Beyond the Point, Newlyn was just visible, together with the whole of the southern Land's End peninsula. Today it formed a blue-gray smudge that in places merged with the sky. Like Cudden Point, Trewarvas Head concealed all the coast for miles beyond. The whole of Porthleven and Loe Bar lay hidden behind it, as did all the land from Gunwalloe down to just north of Mullion. There the remainder of the Lizard peninsula came into view, but so far off as to be nothing but a darker blur between a pale sea and sky. The overall result was an almost dreamlike landscape — sharply etched beach and rock formations near by, framed by distant coasts half lost in the haze.

"We shan't have rain for a week or more," Mrs Morvah predicted confidently. "When I can count the sails out of Newlyn, I do take my umbrella, even if the sky's blue."

"There are two houses in Cornwall that I really wanted to live in as a child," Lorna said. "One is this house and the other was very like it. It used to stand on the cliffs over near Prussia Cove — or did I imagine that one?"

"John Carter's old house," Jessica said.

Mrs Morvah nodded her agreement. "It used to be a pub. They pulled 'n down back in 'oh-six." She frowned at Lorna. "I'm surprised *you* can remember it, maid."

Lorna smiled ruefully. "I was eight then. I'm getting to be quite *old*, you know!"

"We-ell!" The old woman shook her head at the general sadness of time and the passing of life. Then she grinned. "And I'll bet 'ee never thought 'ee'd come a-calling here in such a manner as today!"

"Never in my life!" Lorna agreed.

"Nor on such an errand, neither!" she went on drily.

Lorna exchanged glances with Jessica and said, "No."

"I've been expecting of 'ee," Mrs Morvah added.

Lorna licked her fingers — for they had all eaten their pasties "fitty-like" in the proper Cornish manner. She wiped them in her napkin.

"Then I take it you already know what your son is trying to do about Philip, my baby?"

"Bull at a gate," she replied scornfully. "The lawyer who represents hisself has a fool for a client, they say. He knows that so well as anyone. I've heard him say it scores of times — about other colleagues, of course. But there's no telling him now."

Lorna rose and went to the window. Her fingers drummed idly on the sill. "You see," she said, "the thing is I *want* young Philip to know his family. I'd love it if, in years to come, he could go and spend part of each summer with his grandfathers — my father and your son, I mean. And to stay here with you, too, Mrs Morvah — if you could bear it." She did not look round to see how the old woman was taking all this. "Family is so important," she went on.

"Ha!" Mrs Morvah interrupted at last. "You do understand that, then, maid!"

Lorna turned and looked at her; for a long moment their eyes audited each other. Then Lorna said, "I think I know why it is so *desperately* important to your son."

Mrs Morvah nodded gravely. "I wondered 'bout that. I was all set to explain."

"It's an extraordinary story. One can't imagine such a thing happening in these rather gray and conformist days."

The other laughed. "One couldn't 'zackly imagine it backalong then, neither, I can tell 'ee! What? Dead bodies lying in fields at nine o'clock on a Friday morn!"

Lorna, who had been thinking rather more of the time when Jake Morvah's real father returned and tried to murder him and his mother, merely nodded. When David had told them the tale she had found it impossible to imagine fifty-year-old Jake as a child, still less being pushed down a mine-shaft; yet, curiously enough, she had no difficulty in imagining this sprightly old lady as she must have been forty-five-odd years ago and in the same predicament. "Still," she said ruefully, "all the understanding in the world doesn't help resolve the case. It only helps tell us how *not* to resolve it — not to go head-on at each other in a court of law. How can I help your son to a little better understanding on his part, Mrs Morvah? How can I get him to see that his *only* way to enjoy his fair share in his grandson's life is by cooperating with me?" She smiled engagingly. "Or can I say, 'How may *we* help him to see it'?"

The old woman shrugged noncommittally. "Did 'ee come here empty-minded, Miss Sancreed? I can't hardly believe that."

The two visitors were filled with admiration for her shrewdness. They knew that she had started life as a humble field girl and had worked her way up to her present considerable fortune. Now that they had met her, neither of them doubted that luck had played only the smallest part in the process.

"I came bristling with ideas," Lorna boasted, "depending on what sort of reception you accorded me."

Mrs Morvah laughed, implying that Lorna couldn't possibly have foreseen the reception she had actually received. "No wonder you held your tongue, then!" she joked.

"I suppose there's nothing to be done in the immediate future," Lorna went on. "He had that look in his eye, you know?"

"I do know," she replied heavily.

"He'll get no joy from the courts, of course. Any lawyer will tell you that. But I expect it'll take a couple of years for him to accept the fact. Unless ..." She moved her hands about vaguely. "I don't know. If only we could cut through all that!"

"How don't 'ee just go and tell him — like you're telling me, here?"

Lorna pulled a face. "He'd think he forced me to it. It would look like a concession. It's not. It's something I've always wanted, but he'd never believe it."

Mrs Morvah shrugged. "Does that matter?"

"It does to me. I couldn't bear the thought of him laughing up his sleeve at me."

The old woman glanced at Jessica as if to ask whether she understood such nice scruples.

Jess, who was rather enjoying Lorna's discomfort, said, "What Mrs Morvah's saying, darling, is that the laugh would actually be against her son — for *believing* he'd forced you to it when in fact he hadn't."

"I know! But he'd *think* he had — and I couldn't bear that."

Mrs Morvah shook her head sadly. "One thing I'm glad I shall never be," she said, "and that's a modern husband with a modern young wife. Still" — she picked up the tray and bore it back to the kitchen — "if that's what the rules are nowadays, we shall have to think up something different."

Lorna gathered their napkins and a tumbler their hostess had overlooked. "I'd welcome any suggestions," she said as she followed her out.

Mrs Morvah unloaded the tray into the sink. "Margaret can see to them when she's back from the shops," she said. Then, to Lorna, "Doing anything Easter Monday, are 'ee, maid?"

"There's a circus in Penzance. I was going to take Mrs Lanyon's three youngsters."

"You don't have to, dear," Jessica put in. "David and I can easily take them."

"Come and spend the day here, then," Mrs Morvah suggested. "Bring the little cooze. And I shall ask Jake and missiz."

"Don't warn him, though!" Lorna said.

The other merely chuckled at that.

*L*orna was so pleased with the morning's work that Jessica hadn't the heart to remind her on the way back to Rosemergy that their discussion during the outward journey was merely suspended. At least, that was how she excused her silence to herself. The truth was she was beginning to regret she had ever mentioned Estelle's attempt at troublemaking. The whole business had become quite plain to her while she had walked along the cliff to Rinsey Head, watching Lorna prove what many had suspected during the Great War — that bravery and madness are kissing cousins. She recalled her thoughts now as they drove back to Penzance, talking of this and that and nothing in particular.

There had been a moment of panic when Lorna vanished into the first grotto; she had tarried there far longer than Jessica would have thought possible in water so close to freezing. And then, in the relief that followed her reappearance, she had been faced with all the usual "what-if" questions: What if Lorna *hadn't* come out again? What would life be like without her?

It put all the doubts Estelle had raised — and no doubt deliberately raised — in a different light. Lorna's fortuitous arrival at Rosemergy in the weeks after Ian's death had probably saved her sanity. To be able to admit that was, in itself, something of a shock. She had always thought of herself as among the calmest and most stable of people. The traditional symbol of steadfastness — the rock amid stormy seas — would have described her own emotional strength very well, she thought. Not that she was cold and unfeeling, mind. Far from it. She could experience the most violent storms; they could wash right over her — even appear to overwhelm her. But when they were past and all was calm again, there she was, strong and serene as ever, and quite unchanged, with tranquillity all around.

But now, by admitting that Lorna had helped preserve her sanity, she realized she was also, in effect, being forced to deny that flattering picture of herself. The rock that others saw above the waterline was balanced on a pebble down there on the seabed. Alone with the children, alone with her guilt that she had cheated both Ian and herself by agreeing to their marriage — to say nothing of the guilt her love for David would have heaped upon her ... who could say where it would have led?

It would certainly not have led to the situation in which she found herself today. Estelle was up and about again — and actively undermining her own marriage ties. Rosemergy was going to be transformed from a money-hole to a money-spinner. David was to be a partner in one sense — and probably more than one in the fullness of time. And all this because Lorna had turned up one Sunday afternoon last September. How foolish it would be, then, to let Estelle's poisonous words come between them.

What did it matter if, in a sudden enthusiasm of friendship, Lorna and David *had* walked hand-in-hand? Or even snatched a kiss? Or even ...

Her mind had closed in on itself at that point. She remembered how Estelle had described David's chronic infidelity, making it seem like an incurable sickness. She could discount it as long as the only person who spoke of it was Estelle — because it was perfectly obvious why the woman had blurted it all out (or pretended to blurt it out) in the first place. All Estelle was interested in was "proving" that David really loved her, Jessica. Then perhaps the pair of them would do something about it. And then Estelle would get a divorce as the injured party.

But what if Lorna also confessed that David was a philanderer? Suppose *he* had grabbed *her* hand that day on the cliffs at Porthgwarra Cottage? Suppose he had been leading her to some cosy, out-of-the-way place in order to ...

That was why she had no stomach to renew her argument with Lorna. If David was inclined a little in that direction, she didn't want to hear about it. He had always behaved like the perfect gentleman with her — without concealing his love, which only made it all the nobler — and that was the picture of him she wished to preserve and treasure. Somewhere, far off down one of the long corridors of her memory, a feeble voice was trying to tell her she had trod this path before — that these were the same desires that had blinded her to Ian's faults, too, different though they were.

"I can't help that," she said, speaking aloud to make it shut up. "That's the way I am."

"Eh?" Lorna looked at her in surprise.

They were just entering the narrowest and steepest part of Marazion, so she could not take her eyes off the road for long.

Jessica gave an embarrassed laugh. "Was I talking to myself?"

"You said, 'That's the way I am.' Do tell me! I'm still trying to work you out." Then, feeling that her prompting, which she intended as jocular, had actually sounded a little brusque, she went on to tell Theo's little fable of the frog and the scorpion. "You never know with Theo, do you," she said when she had finished. "At the time I thought he was trying to tell me not to fight against being the sort of person I am. Accept myself, warts and all, and make the best of a bad job."

"D'you think you *are* a bad job?" Jessica asked.

"The world does, I'm sure."

"I don't."

Lorna, still unable to take her eyes off the road, reached out and gave her arm a squeeze. "I'll bake your favourite cake, just for that. Actually, I was going on to say that that's what I thought at the time, when Theo first told me the fable. But on the way home I realized he could have had a more sinister purpose."

"Theo — sinister?"

"Maybe not quite sinister. Darker, anyway. He could have been trying to warn me that *I'm* the scorpion! And that in trying to cross my own particular Rubicon, unable to do it on my own, and using you, who are so much stronger and steadier than me ..."

"Oh really, Lorna!" Jessica began to protest.

"It's true. He could have been warning me not to hurt you during the transition. It was just a thought, anyway."

Jessica sighed and shook her head. Where could one even begin to contradict such an outpouring of nonsense!

"Anyway, whether he meant it that way or not — and he probably didn't, I agree — *I* can see the danger. Of hurting you, I mean. Not to take the tale so literally — I mean death and all that is a bit over-dramatic — but the danger of hurting you is real enough."

"Honestly!" Jessica began again to protest.

They were at the foot of the hill by now. Lorna suddenly pulled into the side road that ran down to the tidal causeway linking the mainland with St Michael's Mount. The tide was half up again and the carriageway was just awash.

"We'll have to find a giant frog to carry us across," Jessica joked.

Lorna grinned but immediately became serious again. "Don't run away from it, Jess," she urged. "Don't try and bury it in scorn. You could be hurt in all this toing and froing. Not because 'it's my character' — forget that bit. But just because I don't know what you really-*really* want. That's why I asked if you *really* wanted to go ahead with the sanitarium, even if David became free of Estelle."

Jessica shrugged hopelessly. The look she darted Lorna was that of a trapped animal. She opened the car door and stepped out onto the shingly patch where they were parked.

Lorna joined her a moment later.

"You're ruthless," Jessica grumbled.

"I know *why* you don't want to talk about it," Lorna replied. "Shall we walk along the beach a bit?"

"Have you got the chocolate?"

Lorna patted her pocket. "Yes."

"All right then."

They negotiated a few rocks and came to the sand, which ran without interruption for the next two miles, all the way to Penzance railway terminus.

"Why don't I want to talk about it?" Jessica asked.

"It's not easy to explain but it's something to do with the way we respond to *words*. Men and women respond in quite different ways. I've become aware of it lately, listening to Bill talking about his dream of building this racing 'plane."

"Do I detect a note of scorn there?"

"Possibly," Lorna conceded. "I shouldn't be scornful because that's exactly the difference I'm trying to explain. Oh dear — I hope I can say this right. The thing is, you see, men are more *experimental* with words than we are. I mean they use words as a way of … sort of experimenting with the world. So if I say Bill doesn't really *mean* it — about this racer of his — I don't mean he's being insincere, I just mean he's experimenting with his life. He's making a little picture, a word-picture, of one possible future for himself and he's holding it up to the world to see if the world likes it."

"And if the world doesn't?"

"Pfft! He'll throw it away and paint another. It was only a word-picture, anyway! Not a promise. It amazes me, actually — how *many* word-pictures he can paint and exhibit at the one time. But then, when you come to think of it, most men are like that, aren't they. Don't you think? *We* say they make lots of promises they have no intention of keeping. But that's because — to men — they aren't really promises.

They're just disposable word-pictures. We can't understand that because our attitude is quite different. *Our* word-pictures ... actually, why do I keep calling them that? Dreams and plans — that's what I really mean. We have the same sorts of dreams and plans as men, but we feel quite differently about exhibiting them in public. As soon as we do that, we turn them into a kind of promise. Our very honour gets bound up with them. Men taunt us for being fickle. Actually, they're ten *thousand* times more fickle than us — but that's only because nobody thinks of *their* public declarations as ..."

She stopped in her tracks and pressed her knuckles to her temples. "I'm not saying it right. I know what I mean but it sounds far-fetched. That's the whole point, you see! Words *pin things down* for us. For men they just liberate them!"

"I think I can see what you mean," Jessica offered. "Or rather, I can feel it."

"Come back to us! That's all I'm really interested in. The thing is — you have certain plans and dreams. About your children. About Rosemergy. About David perhaps?"

Jessica remained impassive.

"All right," Lorna continued. "Let it pass. And *I* have certain plans and dreams. About me and Philip. About my life. About using my capital wisely ..." She faltered.

"About Bill?" Jessica offered with a smile.

"Let that pass, too," Lorna replied heavily. "I may *understand* the fickle nature of Bill's dreams, but that isn't the same as coming to terms with it! My real point is that we're reluctant ... what's a word a hundred times stronger than 'reluctant'? *Loth!* We're loth to talk about our plans because we're afraid that will fix them for all time. As long as we keep them secret, we can change them without anybody noticing and accusing us of being fickle."

There was a long silence between them, all the more noticeable for the length of the monologue that had preceded it — indeed, inspired it. Lorna desperately wanted to prompt some response from her friend but managed to hold herself in check.

At length Jessica said, "It's true. Everything you say is true. In fact, it's even worse than you describe. Because we can even juggle quite *contradictory* dreams in different parts of our mind — all at the same time. Like wanting a new husband. Like wanting to keep my old home. Like turning it into a sanitarium. Like wanting another baby. Like wanting the children to be grown up and gone." She halted and closed her eyes. Her voice was close to breaking as she concluded:

"Like wanting to walk out of the door one morning ... and just keep walking ... never come back."

Awkwardly — for she had no idea her words would release this extraordinary confession — Lorna put her arms around her friend and hugged her hard. "Jess!" she murmured.

"It's true." Jessica yielded for a moment to the luxury of Lorna's comfort — the dependable shoulder, the bracing hug. Then she took a grip on herself and stood up straight again. "I'll speak one dream aloud — without the slightest fear it'll ever change," she joked. "The dream of chocolate!"

Lorna laughed and fished a bar from her pocket. "Slightly soft," she apologized. "But still eatable." She unwrapped another for herself.

They munched in appreciative silence and Lorna let the emotional temperature fall to normal before she said, "*All* the dreams I juggle with are contradictory! I want to be a free spirit in Paris or Vienna or somewhere. I want to be the mistress of some famous artist or ... poet ... or someone — so he won't be around me all the time. I want a husband who'll never leave my side practically. I want more babies and my own home — somewhere like Rinsey House — a million miles from the rest of the world, where it's all just a blue haze. I want to be the head chef at the one restaurant all the gourmets in the world speak about only in whispers. I want to live all by myself in a little cottage in the middle of a huge forest on a mountainside on a tiny island in the middle of a vast lake."

They laughed. Then Jessica said, "There's *the* difference between us: Your dreams make us laugh. Mine threaten us with tears."

Lorna, once bitten, put an arm round her shoulders, turned her about, and started purposefully back to the car. "If you promise to be a good little girl and give up self-pity for what's left of Lent," she said, "I'll let you have another bar of chocolate."

arcus Corvo had opened the Riviera-Splendide in time for Easter. Only one bedroom floor had been completely redecorated but the rest of the task was well advanced and he was confident of completing it before the peak of the season. Betty and the boys travelled down from London on the Wednesday, the day of Lorna's swim at Rinsey. At lunchtime the following day Lorna went over to the new dining room at the Mouse Hole, at Ben's request. He was not yet open to the public on weekdays but he was giving one of his sample free meals to the landladies of Penzance on that day and he wanted her advice — specifically, he wanted her to share the meal and be critical about it afterwards.

She was surprised to find Betty included among the "landladies" of Penzance but, as the woman pointed out, the Riviera-Splendide also offered a no-luncheon tariff. "Actually," she whispered hoarsely, "it suits me very well, pet, because I was hoping for a word in your shell-like ear." She followed this up with a confidential wink.

Lorna explained why she was there.

"That's okay," Betty said cheerfully. "I can give him the benefit of my experience, too. Free."

Lorna realized she must have looked disappointed — at least to Betty — because the woman immediately smirked and said, "Unless you'd rather I vamoosed, of course!" She nudged her heavily. "Like that, is it?"

"Stay by all means," Lorna told her. "It isn't like that at all."

It was a good spread, well up to Ben's usual standards and therefore hard to fault. Lorna had been afraid that Betty, being so pushy, would hog the post mortem; now, when the moment came to speak, she rather wished she would, for she found herself with little to say. But all Betty did was smile and offer her the centre-stage.

"Well, Ben," Lorna began — meaning to talk generalities until inspiration struck, "if you were hoping to hear me say the sprouts were too salty or there was too much browning in the gravy ... you're in for a disappointment."

"You can say that again," Betty chimed in.

"You've got a first-class cook in Martha Simmonds ..."

"No mistake!" Betty said.

"... so there can be no criticism on that score."

Ben eyed her hopefully. "But on some other score, perhaps?"

"Local girl is she?" Betty asked.

"Depends what you mean," Ben told her. "She's from up Saint Austell way."

"Cornish, anyway," Betty said.

"And that's what our summer visitors come for," Lorna went on. She had suddenly hit upon something important to tell him. "A taste of Cornwall — or what they *imagine* is Cornwall."

He frowned. "What d'you mean?"

"I mean there are a lot of genuine Cornish dishes you couldn't possibly give them. Pasties with crusts hard enough to drop down the mineshaft, for instance. Starry-gazey pie. Bread and dippy. Barley hoggan. Gerty meat. Pluck ..."

"All right!" He laughed.

"Belly timber. Fiffy duff. Burndockle. Fuggan cake. Chod! Imagine serving them chod!"

"Yes, yes!" he assured her. "Point taken. What follows?"

Betty watched this exchange with open mouth; she had never heard of one of those dishes.

"These people come down here for an imaginary Cornish cuisine — really just good country dishes and fresh-off-the-quay seafood — all the ingredients absolutely first quality and not ruined by the cook. So — our pasties have crusts a Vienna baker would be proud of. The fish pies come with the sound of the waves under the crust. Your lobsters are as red as any sunset. And as for the cream, you can stand the spoon up in it. There's no question that Martha can do all that — but can she go *on* at it, and on and on, day after day?"

Betty found her tongue at last. "That's always the problem, love. Keeping the quality once you've got it."

Lorna, seeing that Ben still only half grasped the point, added, "You see, when Doctor Whatsizname comes down here on holiday from Birmingham, where they've never had fresh fish in their lives — or not salt-water fish, anyway — and eats a mackerel like the one we've just eaten, it's an absolute revelation to him. But to Martha it's probably just the four-thousand-three-hundred-and-twenty-seventh specimen she's ever cooked."

"That's why we got old Salford," Betty chimed in. "He's so sozzled half the time he can't remember what he cooked *yesterday* unless you write it down."

"Are you saying any cook will decline after a time?" Ben asked. "Or d'you mean we should do something to prevent it?"

Lorna shook her head. "That's not really the question, Ben. You asked me to give an outsider's opinion and I'm telling you — as far as the food itself goes, you have no worries. In *my* view."

"Nor in mine," Betty agreed.

"But I'm also saying it's easy to drift. It's easy for standards to slip bit by bit — so slowly you don't notice it between one day and the next. Or even one week and the next ..."

And so the post mortem continued in this vein for the best part of half an hour, by which time Lorna had said all she could think of — and said it several times over. Then a brewery dray called with a delivery of beer and Ben had to go.

The first thing Betty Corvo said to Lorna as they walked away across the esplanade was, "You're mad to be going into this sanitarium lark, gel. Can't you tell where your heart is set?"

"With Ben?" Lorna asked scornfully.

Betty halted and stared at her in surprise. "No," she said thoughtfully. "Why did you think I meant that?" A slow smile spread across her face.

Lorna was annoyed with herself. "With cooking, you mean!" she said, trying to recover the situation. "But I've never made a secret of that, Betty. Which is why I thought you must mean something else."

"Oh yeah!" The grin did not falter.

"Yeah!" Lorna echoed. "Anyway, I can cook in a sanitarium as well as anywhere else, you know."

Betty pulled a dubious face at that. "Special diets? No salt for Mrs X. No starch for Mister Y. Only minced meat for Lady Z." She sniffed. "I'd sooner cook skilly down the Salvation Army, myself."

Lorna had no ready answer to that so she changed the subject. "You've heard we're going ahead with the sanitarium, then?"

Betty raised her hands to the skies. "Corvo can't talk of nothing else. Don't get me wrong, now. I love that man even though he's my husband. And I also respect him in lots of ways. But there's one thing I have to allow — he's the world's worst loser."

"We haven't seen much of him lately."

"Nor *heard*, either, I hope!"

Lorna chuckled. "Not since he got attacked from the air! Mind you, we haven't seen much of *anybody* lately — what with the new baby."

"Ah! I didn't know whether to ask or not."

"Good heavens!" The reply took Lorna aback. "There's no secret about it, you know. He's a little marvel. Don't start me off or I'll never stop." She smiled at Betty. "Or perhaps that's what you meant."

They had walked the full length of the Riviera-Splendide, on the seaward side of the esplanade, and had arrived at one of the stairways to the beach. "D'you want to pop down and say hallo to the sea?" Lorna suggested.

Betty looked at her flimsy patent-leather shoes and said she was afraid she'd ruin her stockings in the sand.

"I went for a swim yesterday," Lorna added nonchalantly as they continued their stroll up the seafront. "I always try and go in at least once before Easter every year."

Betty sniffed and said she hoped it wasn't catching. Then she remembered the thread of their interrupted conversation. "Corvo! I was going to say — much as I admire that man, he's not a good loser. He's never lost a battle in his life."

Lorna thought of saying he hadn't fought in all that many, either, but she managed to hold her tongue.

"But then, the thing is, you see, he's never owned a property like this before. He's always been in businesses he could drop and walk away from — make his money and go, if you follow. He never realized the difference when he took this on." She cackled. "This is bricks and mortar, see! You put things *into* it — not take them out."

"Like seven hundred rolls of wallpaper," Lorna said.

"And forty gallons of paint. And ten thousand square feet of carpet. And a couple of tons of cutlery. Oh yes — there's no end once you get started. But even worse than that: You can't pick it up and put it down somewhere else when you get tired of the view! He never thought of that, neither. The Riviera-Splendide stays put! *And* everything that goes with it. The neighbours. The town councillors. The health inspectors. The licensing justices. The bank managers. The coppers." She laughed richly once again. "You can't walk away from them, neither! It's different from London, see? In London it's off with the old and on with the new — any day of the week. But not here. In Penzance, old and new are two sides of the same penny. And he's only just woken up to it. Guess what he said to me this morning!"

"I couldn't even begin."

" 'Betty,' he says to me he says, 'guess what I've been and gone and done — only built the best-decorated chokey in Cornwall!' That's what he said."

"Chokey?" Lorna queried.

"Bridewell. Clink. And guess what I said to him? I said, 'Good! 'Cos that means you're growing up at last, my lad!' Don't you think I'm right, pet?" She nudged Lorna's arm. "Growing up is like admitting we're all in the chokey. And settling down and making the best of it. Don't you think?"

"I suppose so," Lorna replied. "Is this what you wanted to talk to me about?"

Betty laughed uproariously. "Bless you, no! I wanted to ask you about schools down here in Cornwall — boys' schools — for Augustus and Tarquin, see?"

"Are you tired of London, then?"

"No," she replied grimly. "But I'm getting a *bit* tired of what's going on down here. Know what I mean?"

Lorna took a chance and said, "Petronella?"

"Treble tops, pet! Don't get me wrong ..." She paused and looked all about her. "I don't mind the nookie. Corvo's got more than enough for both of us. I never minded that. Petronella's saved me a lot of wear and tear, I can tell you. No — it's the *other*, see?"

Lorna, who could not quite bring herself to believe she was having this conversation — and yet, on the other hand, would not give it up for worlds — cleared her throat awkwardly and said, "Not quite, to be honest with you."

"The *other*," Betty repeated as if it ought to be self-explanatory. Then, in a sing-song voice, not attempting to imitate Petronella's Cornish accent but parodying her nonetheless, she went on: "'Oh, Marcus, darling, I think you're wonderful. You can do no wrong. Everyone else is a fool.' All that caper — that's what I can't stand. I mean it leaves *me* to carry the whole burden. Being married to a man *is* a burden, you know — well, of course you know. You were *as good as*, weren't you. Next best thing, eh? You know what it's like. One man is worse than a whole flock of sheep at a crossroads."

"Ah! So you're going to move down here all the year?"

"Forty weeks out of fifty-two, anyway. I've got to put a stop to all that malarkey. I should have seen the danger at Christmas, when he thought he could frighten you off with that band. And Petronella laughing her head off and telling him he was the Three Wise Men all rolled into one. Don't get me wrong. I love that gel. She's like a sister to me. But when Corvo walks in, she's like a headless chicken. Is Truro a good school?"

Lorna nodded. "It's reckoned to be the best of the local schools. I take it you do want a local school? You don't want to pack them off to Winchester or Eton or somewhere like that?"

"No, God forbid! The good thing about Truro is they could go on the train from here. It's only a mile to walk at the other end. We could drive them *to* the station here and they could walk back. Only it's no good if the school's no good."

"What d'you want them to be when they come out at the far end, Betty? Gentlemen or scholars?"

"Gentlemen," she replied without hesitation.

"Look no further than Truro, then."

Betty was so delighted at this reassurance she flung an arm round Lorna's shoulders and hugged her to her side. "Bless you, pet!" she said. Then she laughed. "What would Ben Calloway and me do without you, eh? It's your day for putting the world to rights."

Lorna laughed with her, but not quite so heartily nor for quite as long. "Physician, heal thyself!" she murmured.

"Oh?" Betty's ears pricked up. "Anything I can do? One good turn deserves another, they say."

"I think you've helped me already, actually," Lorna told her.

"Me?" She clearly did not believe it.

"Yes — just the way you talk about your marriage with Mister Corvo. I mean, you say you love him ..."

Betty bristled at that. "And so I do!"

"Absolutely — I believe you. But it's not all starry eyed, is it — love's young dream."

Betty relaxed and laughed again. "I leave that to poor little Petronella!"

"With you it's everything — all the emotions, all rolled up in the same ... thing." She turned and stared earnestly into the older woman's eyes. "Did you have to *learn* that marriage is like that? Or did you always know it?"

Betty rocked her head uncomfortably. "I suppose I always knew it. I never had much opinion of marriage to start with, mind. So anything good about it was like a prize, you could say."

Lorna came to a halt and turned toward the railings. Gazing out to sea she said, "I was exactly the opposite. With Philip, I mean. My expectations couldn't possibly have been higher. So everything that actually happened was like ... what's the opposite to a prize — when they take things away from you?"

"Robbery?"

Lorna nodded glumly.

Betty squeezed her hand. "That's how we learn, pet."

"God, I hope so!" Lorna replied.

Shortly after morning service began on that Easter Sunday there was a brief flurry of late arrivals at the back of the church. Lorna had an astonishing premonition, which she was hard put to it to explain afterward. The skin prickled on the back of her neck and she felt every muscle tighten as she turned around to see who it might be. After such a foreboding it came as no great surprise to see her father and mother slipping into one of the rearmost pews, followed by Ricks the chauffeur and an unknown nanny, holding baby Philip. Her mother, being rather high-church ("bells and smells" as her father always complained), bobbed a curtsy in the aisle as well.

Their presence ruined the service for Lorna. She did not mind surprises — the more the merrier, in fact. But she hated being given time to consider her response to them; the brilliant riposte she could frame at leisure in her mind set a standard that not even Mary Pickford could achieve and her hard-thought-out triumphs always turned out rather limp. So she tried to forget that her baby and his grandparents were sitting somewhere there behind her.

Philip made the task easy enough for he slept soundly all through the service, as though organ music, incantation, and intonings were the commonplaces of his life. He even slept through his grandfather's singing, though it made Lorna's sought-for oblivion impossible to achieve. Colonel Sancreed could force an entire regiment to sing off-key, if only in self-defence — indeed, he had done so at every church parade he attended during the Great War. Now his cavernous and piercing baritone boomed out over the congregation and spread itself like mustard gas, an imprecise semitone higher — or sometimes lower — than all the rest.

And then, just in case she might think her parents had come to this church on impulse today, her father stepped forward to read the second lesson. The Sunday being Easter, it was taken from the Epistle to the Romans. As Lorna watched him march past her pew and on up the aisle to the lectern — eyes front all the way, as if he were at the head of a whole army of the righteous — she felt all her ancient love and hatred for this man well up inside her once more. Feelings that had been sequestered for years past — not dead but not experienced, either — caught fire and raged through her. And when she heard him speak the opening words, not reading from the page but with his eyes fixed in hers, she was ready to believe he had come all this way merely because Romans VI was the appointed text for Easter Day. He read it with such relish: "What shall we say, then? Shall we continue in sin that grace may abound! God forbid. How shall we, that are dead to sin, live any longer therein?"

She heard no more. "I'm feeling a little bilious," she murmured to Jessica as she rose to leave. "Nothing bad. You stay put."

She edged along the pew to the side aisle, murmuring an apology to the worshipers she disturbed. She avoided her mother's eye and did not turn round, even for a final glance, when she reached the porch. Few among the congregation knew her parents by sight so nobody connected her departure with their presence. Bill Westwood, who was seated with the Carnes, half rose to follow her out but was prevented by a tug at his sleeve from Estelle. Ben Calloway, who had risen at the same moment as Bill, had no one to tug him down again. So, a few moments after Lorna reached the open haven of the promenade, she heard his voice behind her saying, "Are you all right, Lorna?"

She turned with relief and held out a hand to him. He mistook her intention and shook it rather formally. She laughed and, grasping his other hand, placed it firmly in hers and held it there, swinging it gaily as she set off home again. "I am now," she replied. "Quite all right again. Bless you."

"You looked so pale," he said.

"It's hardly surprising. You obviously don't know who that was — the man reading the lesson?"

"He wasn't Caruso — I'm sure of that much."

She laughed. "Mind you — he'd be delighted to hear you say it. That — for your information — was Colonel Sancreed."

"Your father!"

"So it would seem. Though he's refused to acknowledge the fact for the past two and a half years."

He tugged at her hand, slowing her down. "Then that was little Philip they brought in with them! Shouldn't you ... I mean we ... shouldn't we go back?"

She shook her head and let go of his hand. They both came to a halt. "I can't. You go if you want. It's not right for you to miss the service." She stamped her foot. "It's my favourite Sunday of all the year, too!"

He took her hand again and resumed their homeward progress. "You needn't explain," he told her. "If you don't want to go back, that's good enough for me."

"I could accept it, you see, if they'd all piled into the car and driven over here on the spur of the moment. I could accept it, too, if they'd arranged it all in advance — as they obviously have — and then written to let me know. But *this!* It's intolerable. They could at least have telephoned."

Ben thought it over. "Do you think your father's forgotten what you're like?" he asked.

"What d'you mean?" she replied warily. "What am I like?"

"D'you think he knew that if he took you by surprise, you'd go storming out like this?"

She tried to deny it but could not. "Possibly," she answered with some reluctance.

"Then he's got you dancing to his tune, hasn't he!"

Once again she came to an abrupt halt; this time she turned and stared out over the bay. A shower had passed over during the service and she could see where further squalls darkened the water beyond Newlyn. If they didn't hurry, they'd be caught. However, she made no move. "I'm not thinking, am I. Three years apart from him and I've learned nothing! He turns up out of the blue like that and — how right you are, Ben! — I dance to his tune again."

"You know him better than I," he said. "I mean, I don't know him at all. But he must have a purpose, mustn't he? Or does he just enjoy making you twitch?"

"Oh, he has a purpose!" she said bitterly. "Never doubt that! There's a purpose to absolutely ... I mean he wouldn't even snore in his sleep without a purpose! Meddle, meddle, meddle! He can't leave anything alone. When I saw him walking down the aisle ..."

"Ow! I say!" Ben rescued his hand from her clutch and massaged it tenderly.

"Sorry! Oh, dear Ben — why can I not be calm and normal and ... God, I can't even think of *words* now! For the first fourteen years of my life that man ignored me. He wanted a son. My mother called me 'William' until I was six — in a futile attempt to placate him. Then he ordered her to stop it. Otherwise I'm sure she'd still be doing it. You may laugh!"

Now it was Ben who apologized. He crammed his fingers into his mouth — then his handkerchief. "It's just the thought of calling you 'William'! Anyone less like a boy than you ..."

"Now!" she interrupted. "You should have seen me then! Cropped hair ... riding breeches ... a toy fort and soldiers for Christmas ..."

"And what happened after the first fourteen years of your life?"

"The usual. It became rather obvious I was never going to be the son he'd always wanted. I, er ..." She grinned cheekily. "I stuck out in the wrong places."

He laughed and nodded. "I've noticed that, too."

She slipped her arm through his and encouraged him to a trot. The squall was now pouring down just beyond Newlyn harbour. "We're going to be caught," she said.

"We'll make that shelter, and it'll soon pass."

"After that" — she spoke so that each syllable coincided with the fall of her feet — "he began to interfere ... to take over ... No good!" she gasped. "Tell you when we're out of this."

Large raindrops began to fall when they were still thirty paces off. She let go of his arm and, shouting, "Last one in is a cissy!" sprinted for the glass and wrought-iron shelter.

He just beat her to it. There was a stub-partition halfway along the structure. He spun round to face her at the last second, halting with his back pressed hard against it, and crying, "One-two-three block!" as in the children's game.

Laughing she piled into him, calling out, "Not fair!" and pummelling his chest.

He encircled her with his arms to stop her and she suddenly became still. She laid her head against his shoulder and stared out to sea. *Do I really mean this?* she asked herself. She found no firm *yes* inside her — but neither was there a *no*. Wisely he did not attempt to kiss her.

The embrace was brief. She soon straightened up and gave him a rather wan smile.

"Funny your mother should have picked the name 'William'," he commented. "Bill Westwood and all that, I mean."

"Not really. My father is also a William. Actually, talking of Westwood, I think that's what this visit today is all about." She went on to give him a potted version of that day back in January when Bill had been turned down by Curnow and she had sent him to talk to her father, instead.

"You *sent him the bill!*" he commented.

She winced. "No, Ben! That's *awful!* Actually, it just seemed a delicious revenge at the time."

"But no longer?"

"I thought it was a siren song my father couldn't resist — a world speed record with the union jack all over it. *And* a substitute son called William into the bargain."

"Didn't he buy it?"

She began to pace about, demonstratively avoiding the lines between the paving flags. "I don't know. I don't care, either. And I don't want to talk about it any more. He sprang that little surprise on me this morning to see if he could still make me dance to his tune. Now he believes he can." She grinned at Ben. "So now all I've got to do is show him how wrong he is!"

*L*orna opened the door, looked at her parents, said, "I knew you'd get here first," and stood aside to let them come in. Her mother gave her a token peck on the cheek and whispered "Careful now." The nanny introduced herself as a Mrs Rose Gurnard as she handed over the swaddled baby. Philip gazed up at her and looked as if he might smile if he only knew how to. "He do need a suck now, missiz," she said — at which Lorna had to confess she had lost her milk (probably as a result of her swim, though she kept that explanation to herself). Mrs Gurnard, who was wet-nursing at that time too, carried Philip upstairs to feed him. Mrs Sancreed went with her, eager to poke around, of course.

Then came her father.

While waiting for the service to end, Lorna had prepared a dozen different greetings, ranging from the effusive to the chilly, each ready to be plucked from the air, depending on her father's opening salvo. Naturally he chose the one she had not foreseen. He strolled past her with an affable nod — as if they'd been meeting casually almost every day — looked all about him, and said, "So! This is the new centre of the universe, eh!"

The tensions that had held Lorna on the rack ever since her parents had appeared at church that morning now threatened to overwhelm her. Was ever a man more smug, more cocky, more sure of himself, more infuriating … more unique … more pathetic, more loveable? She wanted to hit him hard between those stiff, proud shoulder-blades — also to throw her arms about him and hug him half to death. She suddenly realized how long it had been since he had hugged her, or even touched her with any degree of affection.

Then the unprepared response came welling up from inside her: She hooked a hand round his shoulder, turned him to face her, wrapped her arms round him, and drew herself gently against him.

For a moment he was too surprised to respond. Then he put one hesitant arm around her, too, patted her back soothingly as if she were crying, and said, "Isn't that a grand little fellow you've given us!"

She sniffed heavily, being unaware until that moment how close she had come to tears. "And now they want to take him away from us," she said.

He gripped her fiercely by the shoulders and held her off him at arms' length, staring now into one eye, now into the other, as if he believed she might be lying. "Who?" he barked. A phantasmagoria of Church Army ladies, Health Ministry inspectors, Watch Committee bigwigs, and other licensed meddlers paraded before his mind's eye, raising his hackles; so her reply, "The Morvahs," meant nothing to him at first. He was wondering if they were some new religious sect when she added, "Actually, it's Jake Morvah. His other grandfather. I suppose the wife has no choice but to go along."

"That bastard son of a murderer?" the colonel roared. "Wants *my* grandson?" He shook his fist at the ceiling. "We'll see him off!"

Lorna suddenly noticed that Ricks, the chauffeur, was still standing in the porch — and that Bill Westwood had now joined him. "I'm so sorry!" she said, returning to the door. "Do come in." She pointed out the kitchen to Ricks and gave Bill's arm a welcoming squeeze. He responded with a nervous smile, quite lacking his usual swagger.

Her father had meanwhile overcome his shock and was now chortling to himself. "We've got them beat already," he said. "We've got the answer, eh, Bill, my boy!"

"Well, I have a few things to attend to in the kitchen," Lorna said briskly. "Bill, you know where the sherry's kept. Take my father into the drawing room and make yourselves at home."

The colonel ignored the implied command and followed her down the passage. "Kitchen?" he asked tetchily.

Lorna held her tongue. The moment she raised the lid on the soup saucepan her father's demeanour changed. "Hmph!" His compressed lips moved as if with independent life. "That smells ... ah ... ah ..."

"Good?" she suggested.

"Hmph!"

Bill appeared with three glasses of sherry expertly trapped between his fingers. "If the mountain won't come to Mahomet ..." he said, handing them round. He was still somewhat ill at ease, Lorna thought.

She tipped hers into the soup and grinned as she handed him back the empty glass. "Encore," she said. "Don't tell Jessica. She likes cooking with British brown." She pulled a face.

Ricks mumbled something about the car and went out again. When they were alone the colonel said experimentally, "He's a pretty good sort, old Bill."

"Excellent company," she agreed.

"Very important quality, that," was his mystifying response. "He'll make his mark, that fellow. He'll *be* somebody one of these days." After a pause he risked adding, "Ambition!"

Lack of ambition had been one of his many criticisms of Philip — the grandson of a baronet who hadn't the moral fibre to apply for the king's commission. So the word was loaded with barbs for Lorna. Of course, her father was well aware of the fact. He dropped the three syllables like a gauntlet to see would she pick him up on it. He was continuing the sort of preliminary skirmish his military training had taught him to pursue — probing the enemy's strengths and weaknesses before mounting the main attack.

She let the gauntlet lie where it was.

"So, Daddy dear, on the whole you're rather glad I advised him to have a word in your ear?" She sampled the soup and offered the rest of the spoonful to him.

He sipped it inelegantly and said, "Hmph!" again. "He needs a bit of settling down, though. War's a fine thing for a *young* man."

Before he could get launched she said, "It stops him from growing old as we that are left grow old."

"Yes," he said reluctantly. "I must admit it went on too long. But that was the point I was coming to. A one-year war would have been a grand thing for the empire."

Bill returned with her sherry and then went back to the drawing room again to pour one for her mother, who was coming back downstairs at that moment.

The colonel continued: "A few skirmishes, a campaign or two, then shake hands with a gallant enemy and a sporting loser, and home, tail-high, to the victory parades — that's what it should have been."

"And a lifetime spent refighting a hundred campaigns 'twixt tea and supper!" she put in.

Her father, too, knew a gauntlet when he saw one dropped. All he did was chuckle and say, "Just so. Old soldier's privilege, what — baiting the 'gentlemen in England now abed'! But four long years is too much of a good thing. It has killed off the flower of the empire's youth and it's unsettled those who came through. So now it's up to you, the women of the empire. You were spared the *direct* horrors of the conflict for a purpose, I believe."

A number of angrily flippant responses gathered in Lorna's mind, but she suppressed them all. She did not believe her father was being deliberately provocative in voicing these sentiments; he truly believed them — and considered them so self-evident that he would have been genuinely surprised and shocked at her disagreement. And so, since she wished neither to shock nor to surprise him, she merely smiled and said it was important, in the hurly-burly of life, to be reminded of the larger picture now and then — an answer that pleased him inordinately.

"You did manage to learn a thing or two during all those years of rebellion, then," he remarked.

"So it would appear, Daddy." She forced another smile. "By the way, I presume you had a word with Mrs Lanyon before you drove away from the church?"

He nodded. "Offered her a lift, of course. Ricks and I could have walked and her three brats could have sat in the dickey. They were looking forward to it, I could see. Is *she* going to marry again? Two fine boys like that shouldn't grow up in a house full of women, especially with an eldest sister. I never had a really good platoon commander who grew up with an eldest sister."

"She invited you to lunch, I'm sure?"

"Eh? Oh — Mrs Lanyon! Yes … er, good of her."

"I'd invite you, of course, but it's not really my place."

At around this point it began to dawn on Lorna what an amazing thing was happening. For almost three years this man had refused to acknowledge her very existence; yet now here they were, standing in the kitchen, doing humdrum things, engaged in their usual thin-ice conversation — as if there had never been a moment's estrangement.

She remembered a thing old Roseanne Morvah had said to her just before they parted, while she walked with them back to where the car was parked. Lorna had said something apologetic about her regret at forcing a division between the old woman and her son. And old Mrs Morvah had laughed as she replied, "Gusson, my lover. A family is a business, too — like any other." Lorna had pondered the remark many times over the past few days, realizing what a profound truth it was — and what a necessary antidote, too, to the dangerous sentimentality that increasingly surrounded the idea of "family," especially since the bloodletting of the Great War had made it seem so precious.

The colonel took the remark that "it wasn't really her place" to apply to Rosemergy, rather than to the abstract notion of "the mistress of the house." He looked about him, at the kitchen and out through the window at the garden beyond, and said, "No — fortunately."

He spoke the word so deliberately it would have been rude not to ask what he meant by it.

"As we are not yet 'twixt tea and supper," he replied, "I suppose I can risk a war story? My happiest days in the war came when the regiment was fighting for the ridge at Bapaume. Jove, how we wanted to take it! We thought of nothing else, day and night. How we lusted to plant the colours on its crest."

"And you did, too." She thought she'd help him cut to the climax and spare her the tactical steps in between.

"And I never knew another moment's peace!" he said. "A great lesson! What d'you do when you've got what you want? You turn into a snarling dog-in-the-manger — that's what! The king with his crown, the rich man with his gold, the poor man with a beautiful wife, the schoolboy with his hundred-conqueror conker — none of them will ever know a moment's peace."

"I don't see what all this has to do with ..." She waved a hand at the bricks and mortar all around them.

"You don't own it," he replied. "If you did, the whole thing would look very different." He strolled across to the window, sipping his sherry as he went. "Is that the leech's house?" he asked.

"Doctor Carne? Yes."

"Can't wait to get his hands on this place by all accounts. And the publican next door, too, I hear."

"*And* the sinner on the other side," she put in. "You're well informed, Daddy. Bill, I suppose?"

"You'll be well off out of it with him," he said.

She covered her refusal to respond by taking the roast from the oven and basting it. "I think you're going to get your crackling just the way you like it," she murmured.

The front door opened and the children came running in ahead of their mother. Lorna glanced out of the window past her father and said, "That's Doctor and Mrs Carne — taking a short cut through our garden. They must have walked home together."

"*She* has the purse-strings, I hear," he replied.

Bill *had* been talkative.

"Look!" Toby held up a flimsy cross made from a dry, plaited leaf. "It's from the River Jordan," he said excitedly. "It's where Jesus trod."

"I've got one too." Sarah held up hers and — to show how mature and fair-minded she was — added, "So has Guy. The rushes came to England in an aeroplane."

"Amazing," Lorna said.

Someone must have told Toby that the colonel had fought in the war, for he rushed upstairs and came thundering down again bearing Lorna's Christmas present to him, the trench periscope.

"By jove, eh!" The man's eyes gleamed. "Now doesn't that just take me back." Then, suddenly mock-severe, he frowned down at the lad and said, "I don't suppose anyone in this house of women has shown you how to use it properly, eh?"

Toby turned pale and shook his head.

"Come on, I'll show you. You, too!" he roared at Guy, who had just appeared with his stereoscope box under his arm.

"Lunch in thirty seconds," Lorna called after them as they fled by the scullery door.

"Yes, yes!" he growled back tetchily.

Lorna smiled at Sarah and Sarah smiled back. Jessica appeared in the doorway at that moment and said, "Oh, bless you! That smells absolutely delicious. Can I help?"

Despite her rising tone both of them took it as a dutiful rather than a genuine question. "I'll just go and ... entertain, then," she said as she returned to the drawing room.

"What's wrong with a house of women?" Sarah asked as she lifted the saucepan lid and prodded the sprouts.

Lorna shrugged. "One of these days we'll discover what it is about us that makes men so angry." She sighed. "Probably about ten minutes before the world comes to an end. That would be just our luck, wouldn't it."

*A*fter lunch the squalls died away, the wind dropped, and the sun came out. Jessica said she was going up to Mount Misery to tend Ian's grave; nobody else need come if they didn't want to. Sarah said she'd come, of course. They looked at Guy, who replied, with a sullen sort of guilt that it'd be his turn next time; Toby said, "Me too." The fact was, the colonel had promised to take them down to the beach that afternoon and teach them "scouting and recce" — which was Something Every Boy Should Know.

Bill offered to be the enemy but the colonel just glowered; he obviously had more important business in mind for the young man. Then Bill remembered some maintenance work he had to carry out on the *Star of the West,* as he now called his "crate." A famous London actor had booked him for a "spin" on Easter Monday, which, he had only just realized, was tomorrow. That pleased the colonel even less but there was nothing he could do about it.

David came over just as Jessica and Sarah were bringing out the car. He said Estelle had retired to bed with a headache and asked if they'd mind if he joined them. Of course they did not.

But the moment he had gone, Estelle herself appeared, bright as a new penny. She made a beeline for Mrs Sancreed and suggested a walk along the promenade; almost as an afterthought she added, "You too, Lorna dear, of course?"

Lorna, who could hear the barbs in the offer almost as well as if she'd added, "Just you dare!", said (which was true) that she'd missed little Philip rather badly and would sooner stay with him. In fact, she wanted to offer Rose Gurnard a more regular place as nanny here at Rosemergy. It wasn't simply that she, Lorna, had an unfashionable faith in the virtues of mother's milk, she also had a premonition that life — her life, Jessica's ... everyone's — was coming to a head and she wanted to be sure the baby was in capable hands.

Moments later she stood at her bedroom window, watching her mother and Estelle walking down the drive; like well matched mares in harness, their heads leaned inward and they kept automatic pace. She told herself she'd give anything to know what they were hatching between them — and then it struck her that, actually, she wouldn't give much more than a farthing. Once upon a time there was a Lorna who would have given a lot more, but she was now fading into memory. The new Lorna had a new baby, a new life to take care off, decisions to make, a future to plan. No — *planning* the future was still far beyond her capacities; if she could simply *face* it, that'd be a start.

The two women turned left at the gate and soon vanished behind the Riviera-Splendide. Almost simultaneously her father and the boys reappeared on the farther side of the esplanade, going in the opposite direction, toward Newlyn. The colonel had obviously decided that the sands over there had greater military potential. As they passed the Mouse Hole she was surprised to see Ben Calloway skip across the road to join them.

Collusion?

Was everybody around her involved in secret cabals?

But it was clear from the way Ben introduced himself and from the length of the conversation that followed that the two men had never met. Whatever Ben was doing, the agendum was his own. She could guess what they were saying to each other — listing off regiments, sectors, battles, rear echelons, clearing stations ... all those words she vaguely understood though each was shrouded in a mist of manly impenetrability. What *was* an echelon? In her mind it kept occasional company with words like epaulette and chevron ... something military, anyway. She could tell it had to be that sort of conversation otherwise Guy and Toby would never be so attentive. A moment later all four of them set off together, heading for the wilder part of the beach between Penzance and Newlyn.

"You want to change the li'l cooze, do 'ee, missiz?" Rose Gurnard asked.

Lorna turned from the window and saw that the woman had made everything ready — the clean nappy, the sponge and basin, the towel, the zinc salve, the powder and puff — you could have taken a photograph and used it in a nanny's training manual. Half of her was reassured — the intelligent, civilized half; but at a deeper level she felt rebuffed, excluded. A simple everyday procedure had been turned into a set-piece occasion: Mother was being granted a Chance to show her Love for Baby. Then, the little demonstration safely over, she could jolly well clear out of the nursery and leave the real work to the professional!

Lorna swallowed her primitive annoyance and told herself she couldn't have it both ways. "How charming," she said.

The nappy was filled with pale, milky excreta. It always amazed Lorna that its smell, far from being offensive, was actually ... it sounded absurd but the only proper word she could think of was appetizing!

Or *almost* appetizing. It must be Nature's way of ensuring ... something. She inhaled it surreptitiously as she worked away at cleaning his tail, relishing, too, the emergence of his soft, unbelievably fine skin as the discoloration was wiped away. "Ooh what a belly!" she cooed and, bending over him, put her lips to his navel and blew a raspberry.

Philip giggled a scream and clutched her hair; his little feet pummelled at her empty breasts.

"What a belly!" She blew another raspberry, and another, and another ... until Mrs Gurnard cleared her throat respectfully. By her lights, girls could be allowed no more than two good giggles, boys might enjoy four or five; but one mustn't overdo the orgiastic because it was only storing up trouble.

Lorna desisted, making the baby a silent promise that when life settled down again and Nanny Gurnard went (assuming she agreed to stay, that is) they'd enjoy all the tickling and raspberries and giggles they wanted.

This particular session seemed to have done no harm, however, for no sooner did she lay him to rest in his cot, with the clean nappy safely pinned in place, than he gave a shivery little sigh and fell fast asleep, thumb in mouth. Nanny Gurnard pulled it out again, saying it'd give him buck teeth; she seemed disappointed to find him so well behaved after so much dangerous excitement. She had put on an I-told-you-so face and had to take it off again.

"I suppose you have a little baby of your own, Mrs Gurnard?" Lorna asked while the woman lingered on in hope that Philip might show some late symptom of excess.

"Bless 'ee, no, my lover!" She laughed and gave up her vigil. "My youngest li'l boy, Peter, 'e's seven come Lady Day."

"Oh! I just thought ... because of still having ... milk, you know."

"Ah!" She looked down at her breasts as if they were impersonal fixtures. "Salvation, that is. I fed Peter till 'e were five, see. I only stopped 'cause the other li'l boys did tease he. Then that Mrs Tregarthen-Soames — you do know she, I speck?"

Lorna nodded. "Slightly." She was a vain, pretty woman.

"Real high-quarter doxy, she is! She didn't want no emperent babby at her breast! So ... that's how I started. And I never stopped somehow, and I don't think I shall now."

"So you've had milk for seven years!" Lorna asked in amazement.

"'Es." She looked again at her bosom, proudly this time. "They've nourished scores o' babbies, they 'ave. And people call it work! At least, they do pay for it." She glanced significantly at Lorna.

"Ah ... well, that brings me to what I wanted to say, Mrs Gurnard."

After some haggling it was agreed to give it a month's trial. Mrs Gurnard lived in Redruth, near the station, less than half an hour away by stopping train; so, if missiz would pay her fares, and bring her to and from the station, morning and evening — and give babby a bottle feed last thing at night — they could manage very well. Lorna thought the fee of twenty-five shillings a week rather steep, but then there weren't too many reliable women around with milk to spare. "I can see why you call them your salvation!" she commented at the conclusion of their bargaining.

Mrs Gurnard laughed. "My dear soul, my lover — 'tis nothing to do with that!" She gave a conspiratorial look all about them. "Don't 'ee *know?*"

"Know what?"

"While one babby's suckling, you can't 'ave another. Don't 'ee know the saying: *When the milk is in spate, the next babby must wait!* And 'tis true, I can tell 'ee. Gospel."

Lorna laughed.

"Didn't 'ee know that?" Mrs Gurnard asked again.

Making it up on the spur of the moment, Lorna replied, "Well, I heard a slightly different version: *When the milk's from the churn, 'tis the next babby's turn!* It's the same thing, though, isn't it."

It was Mrs Gurnard's turn to chuckle. "That's a good one, that is. I must remember that one."

Lorna left her to tidy everything away and went downstairs to catch up on whatever gossip Ricks might unwittingly let slip. Now that a nanny was engaged she felt more at ease than at any time since coming to Rosemergy — which was odd, considering all that was going on about her.

*L*orna took Mrs Gurnard with her to Rinsey House the following afternoon. She also took a new folding perambulator, thinking that her unconventional papoose sling might not be quite the thing to flaunt before the Morvahs. From the moment they climbed into the car Mrs Gurnard twigged that something was wrong; she didn't need to do much fishing before she got the gist of it out of Lorna. It all seemed very plain sailing to her, though. In fact, the surprises were all on Lorna's side.

In the first place, it was clear that the "shame" of being an unmarried mother meant nothing to the woman. When Lorna delicately probed this discovery she learned that in Mrs Gurnard's community of friends no man would dream of marrying a maid who wasn't "looking for a babby" by him; she thought that Methodism had stamped out all that sort of thing a century and more ago. In fact, as further discussion revealed, Methodism had made *divorce* unthinkable, even though it had been legally feasible for common folk for more than forty years. Therefore neither man nor maid would risk their only chance of progeny on a barren union, no matter how much they might love each other. Both would wait until she was "quickened for sure." If the man happened to die before the ring was on the finger, that was more of a misfortune than a shame.

Mrs Gurnard was also quite ready to believe that Lawyer Morvah would do all he could, lawful or no, to take the babby from her. That was only natural. Indeed, she came within an ace of implying it was almost right and proper. She would not have put it in so many words, but tactful steering of the discussion revealed an attitude that Lorna could not believe still survived in 1921. To Mrs Gurnard a woman's body was clearly a kind of factory where babbies were assembled and launched. The babby itself — the product, so to speak — belonged more to the man who had "fixed it inside her" (her words); the process of giving birth was really just a way of clearing the workshop to make room for the next job of assembly. Of course it wasn't quite that simple. Babbies still needed a lot of mothering after the physical cord was cut; but the older they grew, the less true that was. Therefore the less they belonged to the mother and the more they became the property — and responsibility — of the father.

And so, since Philip had no father, Lawyer Morvah was only asserting a kind of natural right to take him over. Her attitude was that Lorna should try to come to some arrangement for an orderly and amicable handover.

Or find a man to marry, of course.

Lorna's immediate impulse was to turn around and take this woman and her dangerously medieval ideas back home. Then it struck her that support from such a quarter was probably the last thing Jake Morvah would welcome — and, though it was most unlikely he would canvass the opinion of a mere wet-nurse, he'd get a sobering shock if he did. Then she realized she had no choice in the matter, anyway. *Someone* had to hold the baby during the journey, and feed him at some point during the visit.

This time she left the car at Rinsey Green rather than risk the springs on the lane to the open cliff. Fortunately the afternoon, though overcast, was dry and almost windless. In a flurry of last-minute nerves she checked everything again before they set off. Her fingers almost came to grief among the struts of the folding perambulator — which Mrs Gurnard said would be "proper job" for cutting up turnips — but eventually she got all the securing clips in place and the contraption became satisfyingly rigid. The rest was soon checked: spare nappies, powder, flannel, ointment, gripe water, rattle, her grandmother's christening gown, folding camera, new spool of film safely wrapped in silver paper ... "We forgot the gin," Lorna said. "Let's hope he can manage without for a few hours."

Mrs Gurnard laughed at that — a rare coincidence of her sense of humour with Lorna's; it was odd, she thought, that they each found the other's company so congenial (which she felt sure they did), since in every other respect their beliefs and attitudes were almost completely alien to one another.

When Philip felt the bumpy road beneath him he began to cry. But then he must have heard the effect of the jerking on his voice and his first lusty bellow turned into a laugh — or the nearest thing to a laugh that a ten-week-old baby can achieve: a kind of gurgling hiccup. Then for almost the rest of the way he lay there quite happily, giving out a long, toneless "Aaaaaaa ..." and enjoying, after his own fashion, the accidental modulations produced by the stones and ruts beneath him.

For the first minute or two Lorna found it endearing. But when it went on and on and on she began to understand how the (on the face of it) strange institution of the nanny had come about in the first place. A year of this sort of thing, she realized, and she'd be utterly incapable of sustaining any kind of adult conversation. By the time they reached the last stretch of driveway, down to the house itself, she was indulging a fantasy in which she placed a pillow firmly over Philip's face and luxuriated in the blissful silence that ensued.

It was hardly the right frame of mind in which to face someone whose main thought in life was to relieve her of this inconvenience for good. She stopped and picked him up and carried him the rest of the way, pointing out the waves, the cliffs, the old mine, the seagulls ... anything to hear her own voice rather than his. He followed her finger with his eyes and his head lolled about drunkenly, but whether he saw any actual shapes out there she doubted.

There was a cob tethered on a patch of grass beside the house and a gig with its wheels trigged beside the coalshed; so she guessed Grandfather Jake and his wife were already there. Mrs Gurnard unfolded the lace gown, which had been pinned up while Philip lay in the pram, and smoothed it out with long, gentle strokes. "My, but he's some proper 'ansum li'l babby!" she cooed at him. " 'Es 'e is! 'Es 'e is!" Then she gave an ironic laugh. "Look at 'n! Like the Grand Sultan with two women ready to do all his bidding!"

They had obviously been spied from the house for the door opened as they approached it. Old Mrs Morvah stood beaming in the doorway, arms outstretched in welcome. "My chickabiddy!" she cried. "Let me see 'n, then. Come to his great-grandmama!"

Behind her stood Jake, face black as thunder, saying, "You said nothing about this − not a word!"

And beside him his wife plucked at his sleeve, while he tried to bat her hands away, saying, "Now my dear, calm yourself! Remember what Doctor Wilson said." She was a statuesque, rather severely beautiful woman, a full six inches taller than her husband; and − in the way that English eyes can make such judgements in less than no time and on no particular evidence at all − Lorna guessed she was a cut above him socially, too.

She darted an apologetic glance at the old woman and, walking straight past her, placed Philip in the arms of his startled grandfather.

A shocked silence settled on them all − even the baby seemed to hold his breath. He stared up at Jake. Jake gazed down at him, his expression still a startled blank. Old Mrs Morvah took Lorna's elbow from behind and gave it an encouraging squeeze.

Philip smiled. The four women there recognized it as no more than a symptom of wind but Jake did not. He smiled back and then looked at his wife as if to say, "See! What d'you say to that, then?"

Her expression remained impassive.

The pain of the wind intensified the "smile" — and then brimmed it over into lusty tears.

The grandfather's expression changed to one of alarm and then, as the howls gathered pace, of panic. Again he looked at his wife. This time she took a backward pace, away from him.

He turned to his mother. She nudged Lorna forward surreptitiously. Lorna, fearing that a direct offer to take the baby back might seem too symbolically provocative, glanced toward Mrs Gurnard.

She stepped forward at once, murmuring, "Now then, li'l cooze, come to thy ol' Nanny, then!" When Jake gratefully handed the child over, she added, " 'Tis only the wind, my lover. Us'll soon fetch 'n up."

And, indeed, the moment she laid him over her shoulder he produced the most satisfying belch and fell silent almost at once.

All this while, Lorna kept her eyes fastened on Jake. It distressed her to see how much he reminded her of his son, Philip — not so much in looks, for Jake was shorter and much swarthier, but in gestures and in those fleeting changes of expression that signal strong emotion in men who are trying to appear calm. "Take him again, Mister Morvah," she said gently. "He's all right now."

Mrs Gurnard half offered the baby but the man drew back. "Later, perhaps," he mumbled.

"Certainly," Lorna pressed home the advantage. "I want a photo of you — and Mrs Morvah — holding him." She spun round. "And Great-grandmama too, of course. Something for our family album, eh — four generations all together."

Mrs Gurnard offered the baby to his great-grandmother, who took him with pleasure and carried him to the window beside the front door and stared deep into his eyes; he, meanwhile, tried to discover how far the end of her nose would move — which alone would have accounted for the tears that sprang into her eyes ... but not the simultaneous lump in her throat.

Lorna realized she had probably doubted such a day would ever come. It suddenly occurred to her that the woman must have gone to bed each night since their meeting last Wednesday praying to be allowed to live at least until this day. She herself so rarely considered death in such immediate or personal terms it came as a shock. She glanced at Jake to see how he was responding. Their eyes met and, in the way that the most complex thoughts — thoughts people would find almost impossible to put into words — can be expressed, literally "in the twinkling of an eye," the twinkle in *his* eye assured her that while his mother lived he would not dare make a battleground of her great-grandson.

Meanwhile, behind her, Roseanne Morvah and Mrs Gurnard were introducing each other. It gave Lorna her cue.

"We didn't actually shake hands last time we met, Mister Morvah," she said, stretching out her arm as she walked up to him.

He darted a nervous glance at his wife, who glanced tactfully away while he put this seal on his surrender. "Miss Sancreed," he murmured.

"I'm so glad you've met your grandson now," she said. "I hope you're proud of him? I certainly am — the one act of pride of which I refuse to be ashamed."

His wife laughed and held out her hand to Lorna. "I'm so glad we've met at last, my dear. You are everything Philip told us about you." She glanced toward her husband and corrected it to, "Or told *me* about you."

They shook hands.

Lorna was now in a quandary. She had delayed Philip's funeral for a week — for eight days, in fact — to give this woman and her stiff-necked husband a chance to repent and travel up to attend it. She had even sent them daily telegrams, none of which had they acknowledged. Should she refer to it now? What a moment to be pondering such a question! Of course, all her thoughts this past week had concentrated on protecting the baby.

But Mrs Morvah must have divined her difficulty for she said, "I'm glad, too, to have this chance to thank you for ... all you did."

Lorna nodded and, taking her heart in her hands, said, "I have brought some photographs of his grave — if you'd like to see them?"

Jake cleared his throat. "We've ... seen it."

His wife nudged him sharply.

"Yes, er, we *are* very grateful," he added stiffly. "We've put the boy down for Truro."

"Not *now*, dear!" his wife snapped.

Lorna, all tension gone, fought hard to suppress a fit of giggles. "What may I call you, by the way?" she asked — mainly to fill the silence. "D'you prefer Gran or Nan or Grannie or Grandma or what?"

The woman pulled a distasteful face at all these suggestions. "You may call me Sybil," she replied firmly.

Jake stared at her in amazement.

"Certainly!" she told him with some vigour. "You may be 'Grandad' if you like. I'm not ready to be called Grannie by a woman of fully twenty ... what are you, dear?"

"Twenty-three now," Lorna replied. "He was born a month before my birthday."

Sybil turned back to her husband. "If you want a twenty-three-year-old woman to go around calling you Grandad, Jake, then you deserve it."

"Deserve what?" he asked testily.

"Everything," she replied grandly.

"Philip and I always called you Dad," Lorna suggested tactfully. "He spoke about you often — and never with any rancour, either. I thought you might like to know that now ... Dad?"

He stared at her, speechless for one wild-eyed moment, ran his fingers through his hair until he looked like Struwelpeter — and then he turned on his heel and stalked from the hall toward the verandah. A moment later they heard, briefly, the roar of the sea as he opened and closed the outside door.

"Well done, Lorna!" Sybil said.

Lorna, who thought she'd just ruined everything, was surprised to see that Sybil meant it quite genuinely.

"Yes — truly!" the woman continued. "I was so afraid you'd go to see a lawyer yourself and turn up today spouting whole sections of the civil law."

"I told you the sort of girl she is," her mother-in-law said, offering her a turn at holding Philip.

Sybil pulled a dubious face. "I suppose he's dry?" she said, accepting him with wary distaste.

But the moment Philip discovered he had a new nose to experiment with she became quite ecstatic, pulling faces and crying out mock shouts of pain and outraged dignity. "I remember his father doing this," she said, "but not at the age of three months."

Pride prevented Lorna from correcting her. "You knew I was coming here this afternoon, then?" she said.

"I did, of course," Sybil replied. "But you wouldn't have got *Grandpa* here if he'd known."

"Has he really got a weak heart? Only you said something about Doctor Wilson?"

"Oh ... no. Stroke. He had a stroke — it was the day after he saw you, in fact."

Lorna's jaw fell. "But how *awful!* I'm so sorry ... I mean, I hope it was nothing that *I* ..." Sybil was so preoccupied with Philip — and so seemingly unconcerned about Jake's condition — that Lorna turned to the man's mother.

She shrugged petulantly. "I heard about it first time today, of course! Come-us on — shall us go through to the verandah. You too, Mrs Gurnard."

Sybil handed the baby back to the nanny and led the way. "It was nothing," she explained over her shoulder. "Or almost nothing. The paralysis was only down one side of his face and it only lasted a few hours. It was a warning, really. These clever Viennese doctors would probably say he brought it on himself as a way of going back on his vows without losing face." She laughed as she added, "Or losing only *half* his face! Anyway, it made it quite clear to him he was in no condition to go fighting battles over the custody of the child. What absurd creatures men are! They'll always reach for a blunderbuss — when a tiny drop of prussic acid will do just as well." She smiled warmly at Lorna. "Still, it brought us all together — which is what really counts, isn't it!"

Jake returned a short while later, in quite an affable mood though his manner toward Lorna was still rather clipped and uncertain. He mellowed still further as the afternoon wore on so that, by the time the sun came out, just an hour or so before setting, he was the very picture of a jovial grandfather — which was when Lorna took out her collapsible camera.

The only awkward moment came when they parted and he clearly felt an apology was called for. Lorna, even more embarrassed at the thought of it than he was, simply put her arms around him and hugged him tight, saying, "Well, Dad — starting from today, eh?"

He hugged her briefly back, cleared his throat heavily, and pushed her away to allow himself to blow his nose. "You know where we live," was all he could say without choking.

When they had gone, Roseanne Morvah took Lorna's hand and squeezed it hard. "You're some miracle-woman, you are," she said admiringly. "Isn't that a fact, Mrs Gurnard?"

Lorna, however, was beginning to feel she had struggled to the mountain top only to discover that it was the merest foothill to the *real* mountain, which had been concealed all this time beyond it. "It's easy enough," she said, "to get people to do something they've always wanted to do anyway. It's the people who don't know what on earth they want in the first place who pose the real problem."

*W*hen they drove through Penzance Green on the way home Lorna was a little surprised to see the barn door — or hangar door, as it now was — closed. Bill always left it open when he was flying, and she remembered he had been engaged to take Darcy Beaumont, the famous actor, for a flight that afternoon. More surprising still, there were no cars parked beside the building, either. Apart from the windsock, fluttering gently in the late-afternoon breeze, the place might have reverted back to an ordinary farm field. There were even cows all over the landing strip. Something must have gone wrong with the arrangements. She felt disappointed for him but made no remark to Mrs Gurnard, whom she dropped off at the station a few minutes later.

She thought no more about it, either, until they turned into the drive at Rosemergy. She had hardly got her nose in the gate before Jessica came running from the house signalling for her to stop and go back. Then she must have remembered that Philip was in the car — and the new pram and a fair pile of equipment. She abruptly changed her gestures, indicating that Lorna was to come up to the house as fast as possible.

She was so eager that she leaped across the drive before the car came to a halt and almost fell beneath the wheels.

"Sorry!" Lorna shouted jovially as she wound down the window. "D'you actually *want* me to run you over? I'll reverse if you like and try again."

"No time for all that now," Jessica said breathlessly.

"Is something wrong?"

"We don't know. Did you happen to see Bill Westwood as you passed Penzance Green?"

"No. The hangar door was shut and the whole place deserted."

"No cars? David's car wasn't there? Can you turn round now and drive me there? I must know — I've rung for a taxi, actually."

Lorna saw a movement between the side of the garage and the potting shed beyond. "Isn't that David there now?"

"Oh yes — *he's* not missing. Just his car." She looked down the drive. "Damn! There's the taxi now. Have you got half-a-crown?"

"Half-a-crown!" Lorna was scandalized.

"It *is* a Bank Holiday — and I don't want them turning their noses up at us in some future emergency."

Still reluctant, Lorna parted with the coin.

While Jessica ran down the drive to pay off the taxi, Lorna unloaded the accoutrements and left Philip in Sarah's charge; the young girl was being very solemn and reliable-in-a-crisis. Guy and Toby were quietly excited, too. She told them all to be good and went back outside. David was waiting for her in the porch.

"Jess is in an odd state," she told him, pointing to the bottom of the drive. "First she couldn't wait to pay the taxi driver and be off, now she's chatting away with him like old pals!"

"I doubt if she's 'just chatting' with the fellow," he replied as they started walking back to the car.

"What's going on, David? I didn't get much sense out of her. Has Estelle done a bolt with Bill?"

He halted and looked at her in amazement. "What do you know about it?"

"Really! Your car has vanished. Jess is running round like a headless chicken asking what I saw at Penzance Green ... It doesn't take Sherlock Holmes to add one and one and make five, does it!"

Jessica came sprinting back up the drive. "That was Mister Williams who lives at Gulval. He said his wife saw Doctor Carne's car drive across the field and shortly afterwards he himself saw the *Spirit of the West* take off with a passenger."

"When?" David asked.

"About an hour and a half ago — that's when the plane took off." She looked at Lorna. "We must go and make sure. Can you drive us? I'm in too much of a state."

"We can't just leave Sarah in charge," Lorna objected

David said he'd already sent one of the maids from Trevescan to be with her. "Lorna thinks Estelle's done a bolt with Westwood," he added as they climbed into the car.

"I didn't say she has," Lorna objected as she craned her neck to back the car down the drive again. "I said has she?"

The other two, seated side by side in the back, stared glumly at her.

She backed cautiously onto the esplanade and set off at a stately — and legal — twenty miles-per-hour. "Can't you go faster?" an agitated Jessica said.

"Faster would end up slower today," Lorna replied. "I passed two lurking constables on my way here from the station. Catching road hogs is their favourite Bank Holiday sport."

Mention of the station must have reminded them of Mrs Gurnard and thus of her visit to Rinsey that afternoon. "Aren't we awful!" David said. "We haven't asked how your meeting with the kidnapper-grandad went. He obviously failed."

Lorna laughed. "It went very well. We're all jolly old pals now — I'll tell you about it later. But what's up with you two? I can't understand why you're both so glum. If Estelle has done a bolt, isn't it what you've both been ..."

"Lorna!" Jessica interrupted sharply.

"Sorry," she replied jovially — and quite without sincerity. "None of my business, I know."

"How true!" Jessica said heavily.

"I'll just be your taxi driver, then." Lorna gave a vulgar sniff and put on a yokel's accent. "You two from up England, are 'ee — down yur on yoor 'ollydays?"

"I think Estelle may have cleared out our bank account," David said solemnly.

Lorna dropped her pantomime at once. "How d'you know? How could she, anyway? The banks have been closed for two days. Did she leave a note?"

Lorna's mind was racing now and she had to force herself not to stand on the accelerator. When was the last time she had actually *seen* Estelle? Yesterday afternoon, walking up the esplanade with her mother — after that business in the church. What had they told each other? Her mother had a very cat-that-got-the-goldfish look about her when she came back. Alone, too.

"There was no note," David replied. "That would hardly have been her style. She only ever communicated with me by actions. Usually violent. But ..."

"So why d'you think she's bolted with the petty cash?"

"I was about to say ..."

"It's none of her business!" Jessica hissed at him. Then she shouted at Lorna. "It's none of your business — any of this!"

Lorna clenched her jaws against an equally angry reply and counted down her temper. "It won't work, Jess," she replied, far more cheerfully than she felt. "I've had so much practice these past two days at turning the other cheek. I'm a reformed character."

David laughed, though not very willingly.

Jessica rounded on him. "There's absolutely *nothing* to laugh at, you idiot. You're smashed and I'm broke. Don't you understand what this means for all ..."

"Hell and damnation!" Lorna braked — then changed her mind and accelerated, pushing the klaxon handle repeatedly — *hoo-huh! ... hoo-huh! ... hoo-huh!* — as she approached a milling crowd on the harbour side.

The gathering scattered in panic. There was a flurry of alarmed faces, angry faces, raised fists, shouted oaths, and, somewhere in the middle of it all, two heads covered in blood.

"Stop!" David said as they pulled away from the mob.

"Not on your life!" Lorna told him, though she did slow down to the legal limit again.

"There were two people injured back there."

"Two tarts settling an old score. They wouldn't thank you for interfering." She glanced in the mirror. "Anyway, the police are about to arrive. Now we *can* speed safely!" She put her foot down and lurched round the corner by the station.

They were going so fast by the time they reached the bend leading down to the Green that Jessica cried out for her to slow down.

A moment later she not only slowed down but stopped. David got out and opened the gate into the airfield. He saw the cows and called out to Lorna as she drove through, "I'll have to shut it as well."

While they waited, ten yards into the field, Lorna's eyes met Jess's in the mirror. "It's all going to turn out all right, darling," she said.

Jessica gave a tight little nod. "I'm sorry I snapped just now. Of *course* it's your business, too. I shouldn't have said that. We're all in it together. Or we were. I don't see how we can do any of it now — if David's absolutely cleaned out."

"It'll be all right," Lorna repeated. "Let's just find out exactly what's happened first."

David leaped onto the running board and, clinging to the door handle, banged on the roof.

"Idiot!" Lorna muttered as they set off across the field. "I could go twice as fast if he just got inside. Little boys! You should have seen my father and Ben Calloway yesterday!"

"I know." Jessica gave a reluctant chuckle. "Guy was absolutely full of it at bathtime."

They covered the rest of the short distance in silence. As they drew up Lorna said, "Children are the glue that holds all civilization together, actually."

She halted about ten paces short of the hangar door. David leaped from the running board and raced to open it. A moment later he kicked at it angrily and rattled the padlock.

Lorna pulled out a hairpin and said, "Stand back and leave this to a professional." She had little hope of picking it but could not think of anything else to do.

To her surprise it fell open at the first touch. She realized, of course, that it had not actually been locked, merely pushed together and held by its own stiffness. But she whistled nonchalantly as she stuck the hairpin back in her curls and accepted their astonished congratulations all the same.

David opened the doors to reveal his own car and Bill's van parked side by side. And, of course, no *Spirit of the West*.

"So there we are," he said flatly.

"You didn't finish explaining how you can be so sure she's cleaned out your account," Lorna said.

"It was *her* account, anyway," he replied.

"Whose-ever it was — how can you be certain? The banks have been shut since ..."

"She left lots of pages covered with figures," Jessica interrupted.

"She didn't exactly *leave* them," David added. "We found them in the dustbin. But they made it fairly clear she'd been totting up her assets. The maid said she threw those papers away on Friday, which is when the dustmen usually collect. But, coming up to the holiday, I suppose they made different arrangements."

So, Lorna thought, if Estelle had bolted, she'd been planning it for some days. It wasn't on impulse, following something her mother had blurted out yesterday — though, of course, that might have been the last straw. Or the trigger, anyway.

David went into the hangar. "He's left all his tools," he commented.

"They'll be back," Jessica said dubiously. "They've *got* to come back, surely. Estelle's left all her clothes, all her shoes ... everything."

David and Lorna exchanged glances. Neither of them believed that was enough to make her return.

He opened the car door and said, "She even left the key in." He sat in the driver's seat.

"Stand back everyone! Take cover!" Lorna made a joke of it and raced in mock panic to the end of the building.

David didn't start the car but by now Lorna had noticed that the rain-water butts were no longer there. Her hands mimed the act of washing her face. She closed her eyes and could almost feel the suds on her cheeks.

Then Bill's lips on hers.

"Oh Bill!" she whispered. "Why?"

She leaned her forehead against the rough siding of the old barn. "Eh?"

She opened her eyes to find Jessica standing not three feet away, staring at her with a mixture of amusement and concern. "Did these ears of mine hear right?"

Lorna grinned. "Just trying to provoke myself — don't worry. Just trying to see if there was any feeling left, that's all."

"And is there?"

Lorna shrugged. "A bit of sadness, perhaps — sentimental. He kissed me here once."

"When?"

"Oh ... about twenty years ago! A couple of days after we met. He didn't believe in wasting time, old Bill!"

"Nor did Estelle, it seems. Why did she do it?"

Lorna drew breath to answer, thought better of it, and then shrugged.

"I say!" David called to them from the door. "I think I'll drive the old jalopy back home. We shouldn't stay away too long. I'm sure Estelle will phone the moment they land, wherever that is — if only to stop me from going to the police. Are you coming? There's nothing to hang about here for."

"We'll follow you," Jessica promised.

"And pick up the bits," Lorna added under her breath.

"Can you get the padlock locked again?" he asked.

"Fear not! All will be as it was when we arrived," she promised. "Outwardly, anyway."

He started the car, crashed the gears a couple of times, and lurched out across the field, narrowly missing Jessica's car in passing.

Lorna started back toward the door but Jessica put a hand against the wall to bar her way. "Tell me — what were you going to say just now?" she asked.

"When?"

"When I asked what made Estelle do such a thing — throw away her reputation. I only half-meant it as a question but you ..."

"I only half-meant to answer it!" Lorna capped her.

"Yes."

Lorna sighed and looked around for aid. "Oh dear!"

"Please?" Jess begged.

"Isn't it better to draw a line under everything now — all those blotted-copybook pages? Pretend they're what Estelle threw in the dustbin. Start fresh from this very moment?"

"Please?" Jess repeated.

Lorna nodded once, twice — a gesture of defeat. "I suppose it's only right, really." She linked her arm in Jessica's and, turning their backs to the hangar, started to stroll aimlessly across the field. "In the end, I think, the only reputation Estelle cared about was the one in her own mind — her self-esteem. All those months lying alone in bed, trying so hard to be ill ... and failing. Alone with her own thoughts — her own guilt."

"Guilt?"

Lorna nodded. "Are you sure you want to hear about it, darling? You see, her guilt was directed toward you."

"Me! But she hated me! Not so much lately. In fact, she's been very strange lately. But since ..." She hesitated.

"Yes?" Lorna encouraged. "Since when?"

"All those years."

"Since when?"

Jessica looked at her in surprise. "Well — since she took to her bed, of course."

"And when was that?"

"God knows! I'd have to look in my diary."

"No you wouldn't, Jess. Not if you really understood. Think!"

Jessica shook her head, still uncomprehending. "Around the end of the war, anyway."

"*Just* before it? A *month*, for instance? A month and *three days?*"

Jessica frowned. "But that was when ..."

Lorna nodded slowly.

Jessica became exasperated. "I was rather preoccupied with ... other things at that time — as you know very well!"

Lorna said nothing.

Jessica suddenly became aware that the cows had formed a loose semicircle behind them. She flapped her arms at them and shouted, "Shoo!"

They scampered a few paces away and then began to creep back once more.

Lorna took her arm again, firmly, and continued their stroll. "They won't come close. They're just curious — like me, really. Waiting to see how long it'll take for the penny to drop."

After a silence, Jessica said, "Are you implying that Estelle's ... illness, or whatever it was, had something to do with ... Ian's accident?"

"I haven't the slightest doubt that it had," Lorna replied. "D'you still want to go on?"

"Yes! More than ever now. What possible connection could there be between ..." Her voice trailed off.

"*Connection* is a very good word for it, Jess. A bit cold and legalistic, perhaps ... but precise."

"Estelle and Ian ..." She murmured, looking about them as if she no longer knew where this field was.

"Or Ian and Estelle. His last forty-eight before the accident. When he thought he'd surprise you."

"And I was away in Scotland!" She turned to Lorna suddenly. "Did Estelle tell you all this?"

Lorna shook her head. "Not in so many words — but only because she realized she didn't need to."

"You could be wrong about that! You could have jumped to the wrong conclusion? She could have thought you understood something entirely different?"

She shook her head again but this time said nothing.

Jessica turned half away from her and stared blankly at the cows. "All because of *that?*" she murmured.

Now it was Lorna's turn to utter a surprised, "Eh?"

Jessica looked at her and gave a baffled laugh. "Now I hear you say it — Estelle and Ian ... Ian and Estelle — it doesn't really surprise me. It's almost as if it's been waiting for someone to say it." She sculpted imaginary ideas floating in the air around her head. "As if I've half thought it for a long time."

"Shall we go home now? It's turning a bit chilly, don't you think?"

They scattered the cows again as they made their way back to the car. Several times before they arrived, Jessica repeated the two names: "Estelle and Ian!"

"Names from the past, eh!" Lorna said when they finally reached the car.

*J*essica was still looking rather dazed. Lorna got out to shut the gate behind them. When she returned she was surprised to see a smile beginning to twitch at her friend's lips. "You're a bit of an oddity, Jess," she said. "When you think it's a simple case of bolting with the money, you're like a bear with a sore head. When you hear the bolter herself committed adultery with your husband, you start to smile!"

Jess laughed. "I wish Theo were here. He'd say something that would make all this seem so ... *petty!*" She stared at Lorna. "Don't you think it's petty? Why *do* we make such a fuss?"

"About adultery?" Lorna was tempted to confess her own venture in that direction with David; somehow she didn't think Jessica would be quite so tolerant of *that!* The temptation did not last long. "If you'd known about Ian and Estelle," she said, "would it have made any difference with you and David?"

She prepared for an explosion, remembering how Jess had responded to such probings in the past. But the woman thought it over quite calmly and then said, "No."

"It's marriage or nothing for you, then? No matter what others may do?"

"No." This time Jessica grinned.

"What then? It doesn't make sense."

"I know. It's pointless trying to make sense out of it. You only end up ..." She hesitated.

"Lying in bed pretending to be ill?" Lorna suggested.

"Probably!" Jessica laughed. "Yes — certainly. I'll tell you something. You remember the day David and I met Theo?"

"The same day I took Ben to Hell's Mouth." Suddenly she wanted to see Ben very much, to tell him everything that had happened, to bring him into the circle.

Jessica said, "Mmm," as if she hadn't really listened. "We took the brats to Porthgwarra Cove, remember? They decided that the transatlantic cable needed burying, so David and I left them to it and walked back up the lane. We were going to the car to fetch something, I don't know what. And on the way we stopped and I kissed him."

"Or he kissed you? It doesn't sound like David to let the woman ..." She caught Jessica's baleful eye and said, "Sorry! You kissed him. And ...?"

"And I'd have gone on to ... do anything." She became agitated. "If Theo hadn't come walking down the lane! Anything, you know! I'd have ... I was ready ..." She swallowed hard.

"Yes-yes, darling! All right. I do vaguely understand these things by now."

Jessica breathed heavily several times, as if she had just been running. Then, in quite a different tone, she asked, "Why did you say that just now — about 'it doesn't sound like David to let the woman take the lead'? That's what you were going to say, wasn't it!"

"I was going to say it wasn't like him to be backward in coming forward. Same thing, I suppose."

"Has he ever ... you know? Suggested anything to you?"

Lorna chuckled and made her eyes flash in parody of a vamp. "The very sight of him suggests *all sorts* of things to me, Jess! What had you in mind?"

"No! Be serious. Has he ever made an improper suggestion?"

Lorna pretended to think it over.

"Good heavens!" Jessica exploded. "Surely you know without having to think!"

"He kissed me under the mistletoe at Christmas," Lorna allowed.

"All right. But apart from that?"

Lorna let go of the steering wheel and patted her arm. "I had even less luck than you, Jess."

She bridled. "What may that mean?"

"It means I tried — and was spurned."

"When?" It was like a gunshot.

"Good lord! D'you want a forensic report? The very first evening, if you want to know. When he drove me back to Morrab Road to collect my bags? I tried to kiss him. I was like that in those days."

"And?"

She patted her arm once again. "*Calme toi, chérie!* He froze me out."

"And when you went to Land's Ends with him that time?"

"We were like brother and sister."

"Hah!" Jessica laughed and clapped her hands delightedly. "I knew it! I knew it was just Estelle's poison. She tried to poison me against David. And you. You thought she was your friend, didn't you! You should have heard some of the things she said to me about you! Oh!" She let out a long sigh of relief and settled back in the leather of her seat.

Lorna blessed the instinct that had led her to tell such a thorough-going lie. Now it was time to direct Jessica's attention forward again.

avid bought half a ton of fish and chips on his way home. They all sat down in the kitchen and ate them at once, straight out of the newspaper in which they were wrapped. "Good heavens!" Lorna exclaimed when she moved the fish and a headline caught her eye. "Did you know — the French have marched into Düsseldorf!"

"That was two weeks ago!" Jessica said scornfully. "I'm much more up to date. Britain has acquired Ruanda!"

They both looked at David to see if he could cap that. He pretended to stare at his paper before saying, "Huzza! Mafeking's relieved! They've got the Mahdi!"

Their good humour persisted throughout the meal. As they were wiping their fingers and congratulating themselves on having nothing but their tumblers to wash up the maid came running over from Trevescan. "Please, Doctor Carne, sir, it's the missiz on the phone."

"Now?" He was already half out of the door. "Or am I to ring back?" He started running across the grass.

The maid turned to the two women. "She rung off. She said not to ring back. She never left no number."

Lorna went to the back door and called him back.

"Where was she ringing from?" Jessica asked meanwhile.

The girl fished out a scrap of paper. "She made I write 'n down," she said as she handed it over.

"Cherbourg!" Jessica exclaimed. She passed the slip to David, who returned at that moment. "They've gone to France!"

He stared at the paper. "Is that all she said? She didn't say they'd crashed — or been forced down or anything? Just Cherbourg?"

"That's all, sir. Just to tell 'ee that she was all right and not to worry and then I was to write down that. France, is it? No wonder I couldn't hardly hear!"

"I wonder if the exchange could trace the call?" Jessica mused.

"Probably just an hôtel," David replied. "Estelle doesn't know anyone there. Of course, Westwood might. Two-oh-four was stationed near there, wasn't it?"

They looked at each other — each knowing that none of them was going to follow it up. The stable door was bolted. What did it matter where the runaways had called from — Cherbourg or Timbuctoo!

Shortly after that David went home to attend to an emergency caller, a lad with a sprained wrist. Jessica went up to bath the two boys — or to stop them from splashing half the bathwater over the floor — and Lorna, helped by Sarah, fed and attended to Philip before Sarah took her bath and put herself to bed.

David and Jessica finished before Lorna. They were already pouring themselves coffee in the drawing room as she came back downstairs to join them — and just in the nick of time, too, for as she took the last few steps she heard Jessica saying, "Lorna has confessed to me about what happened between you that time."

She could almost see David's face blanch as he echoed the word: "Confessed?" She took the last three steps in a single bound.

"Yes," Jessica went on. "In the car — when you went to collect her bags that first night."

"Oh — *that* time!" He laughed with relief.

"Yes. I'm proud of you, David!"

By then Lorna was standing in the doorway, winking for all she was worth. She just managed to stop before Jess turned and saw her.

Behind Jessica's back he raised his eyes to the ceiling and let out a long, silent whistle.

"You don't mind, darling?" Jess asked nervously. "It's all water under the bridge now, eh?"

"It was a great temptation," David admitted, lifting his arm for Lorna to creep underneath it.

Taking her cue she snuggled against him and said huskily, "What d'you mean — *was?*"

One look at the horror on Jessica's face, however, and she sprang away from him and then fell upon the sofa, laughing hysterically. "Jess!" she called out when she got some breath back. "*Do* something about it, for heaven's sake."

"Like what?" she asked, half bemused by this buffoonery, but also half affronted.

"Whatever you like." Lorna became serious again. "Anything's better than nothing. I wouldn't let the sun go down on another wasted day." She looked out of the window and saw that it had, in fact, gone down already. "Or rise," she added.

Jessica sat down.

Lorna poured herself a coffee and went on, "Can we have a moment of seriousness? We may all be a little shell-shocked by ... what's happened, but we can't blink the fact that it has changed ... well, absolutely everything."

"She wants to back out," Jessica said to David.

"I didn't say that," Lorna told her.

"No, but that was behind your questions to me the other day — did I *really* want to ..." She broke off and stared at Lorna with something like horror in her eyes.

"What now?" Lorna asked, alarmed.

"You didn't just say that! You said *if David were free of Estelle!* My God! Were you *expecting* this to happen?"

"I thought it was quite on the cards," Lorna replied stoutly. "Didn't you? I never dreamed it would happen so swiftly."

"Anyway," David cut in impatiently. "What about it? If I were free of Estelle ... how did the question go on?"

"I asked her if you were free, would she still want to go on with the sanitarium — that was all. And there's no *if* about it now, is there!" She turned to Jess. "So — do you?"

Jessica turned to David. "You see — she *does* want to back out."

Lorna closed her eyes and clenched her fists. "Oh, for one small drop of prussic acid! Just answer the question, Jess! I know it's tantamount to asking are you and David going to get married as soon as you possibly can — but since that's the thought which is uppermost in all our minds at this moment, or so I imagine, it ought to be quite an easy one to answer."

"What is the alternative?" David asked, trying to soothe the atmosphere.

Lorna rose and paced angrily to the window. She did not, in fact, feel in the least bit angry but instinct told her that calm, reasoned discussion, would lead them nowhere. "God, I have to do everything around here!" she exclaimed, thumping the window sill with her clenched fist. "All right!" She spun round, eyes blazing. "If you want it straight from the shoulder, chaps. I *do* want to back out — and for the best of all reasons. The idea that the three of us might try to run a sanitarium between us was always folly. There'd have been at least one murder before a year was out."

"Excuses!" Jessica sneered.

"Just hear me out! I would far rather be a neighbour — a friendly neighbour — to Doctor Carne and the new Mrs Carne."

"And what are we supposed to live on — David and I — for the three years before the divorce is ..." David put a hand to her arm and she fell silent.

"Go on," he said to Lorna. "Finish it."

"Finish *us!*" Jessica murmured.

"I would like to buy either Rosemergy or Trevescan. I don't really mind which. Both are fine houses and either is suitable to my purpose."

"Which is?" Jessica challenged.

Lorna gave a cajoling sort of laugh. *"Think,* Jess! What's the *one* thing I'm suited to?"

The woman's eyes brightened and she looked as if she could suggest half a dozen — if it weren't for mixed company.

"Cuisine," David said.

"Cooking!" Lorna insisted.

"Which you couldn't possibly do in a sanitarium, of course!" Jessica sneered.

Lorna looked at her scornfully. "Diets based on quackery and ignorance? Carbohydrate? Protein? Fat?" She spoke each word as if it had excretory associations — which, for her, it had. "How can anyone make good food out of muck like that? Good food is cream and eggs and butter and rich red meat marbled with fat and herbs and spices and ... and ... and *love!* How can you love a *vitamine!"*

Jessica looked at her blankly, then at David. "What's that?"

"I don't know," Lorna replied. "Nor does he, so don't look at him! No one's ever *found* one but they'll all swear that food is absolutely crawling with the stuff. Well not *my* food, I'll tell you that!"

Her earlier words had just begun to sink through Jessica's pessimism, her determination to see their future in the darkest light. "Buy Rosemergy?" she said.

"Or Trevescan. Either will do for a cookery school. I don't mind. You decide between you." Lorna saw the two of them exchange disbelieving glances. "I'm not saying decide this very minute, for heaven's sake!" she said. She laughed and added, "I'll give you *five* minutes, if you like."

Jessica, who was just beginning to glimpse all sorts of impossible, wonderful things, was forced to laugh at last. Then, before euphoria swamped her, she said, "But suppose for argument's sake I decide to sell Rosemergy to you. I mean ... what do *I* do then?"

Lorna crossed the room to her and, taking her by the elbow, led her back to the window. "You stay here, Jess," she said quietly. "You stay with me just as I stayed with you. The same easy terms! Only now you'll have ten thousand pounds to do what you like with." She lowered her voice still further. "You go on living here. That man goes on living there. Darkness falls every night. And dear Estelle has even provided a gate between you!"

Jessica swallowed heavily. "D'you think we could?" she whispered.

Lorna grinned. "D'you think we could *stop* him? You know the reputation this man has!"

Jessica punched her. Tears were brimming in her eyes now. "It's never worth ten thousand," she said.

"You saved my life, darling." Lorna leaned forward and kissed her lightly on the brow. "Let me decide what that's worth, eh?"

The tears began to flow. Soon they were both clinging to each other, unable to explain it, unable to stop.

Even David had to turn his back on them and blow his nose rather heavily — and never mind his reputation.

Envoi

*L*orna put a finger to her lips — not that Philip understood the gesture yet but he watched her with interest — and she slipped quietly round the back of Porthgwarra Cottage. There she caught Theo fast asleep under a fruit-laden apple tree in the middle of the back lawn. She was about to tiptoe away again and join Ben down on the beach when one of the apples fell, striking Theo on the arm. "Not content!" he shouted as he woke up. He looked about him, blinking and rubbing his eyes, and was just about to settle to sleep again when he saw her standing there. And Philip on her arm.

"Mrs Calloway!" He rose affably, stifling a yawn and ambled toward them. "I'd forgotten. Forgive me — it's Sunday, of course."

"The twenty-first after Pentecost." She kissed him and passed over Philip for him to hug and hold.

"And how's Master Calloway?" He squinted at Philip, who giggled and hid his head in Theo's wattles. "No *Mister* Calloway today?"

Lorna pulled a face and settled in one of the empty deck chairs. "Kaiser misbehaved disgustingly in the car on the way here. Ben's taken him down to the beach to try to shake the rest of it out of him. He'll be back soon."

Theo held Philip up into the branches of the apple tree; little baby hands stroked ripe fruit with anxious curiosity, amazed at its colour and coolness.

"Apples," Theo told him. "Ap-ples."

Philip's lips framed the first syllable. "Gagaga?" he said.

"Perfect!" Theo told him. "We'll start on Greek after tea. Talking of which ..." He looked guiltily at Lorna.

She laughed. "Never buy food to entertain *us*," she said. "I've told you. The one thing we're never short of is food."

"You've had a good summer."

"We've had a marvellous summer. We're still having it, too."

"And you're still in favour of matrimony — obviously."

"I'd better be!" she said heavily, laying a hand on her tummy.

He broke into a broad smile. "Really? Wonderful!" Then he looked at Philip on his arm and frowned. "A bit quick, though, isn't it?"

She nodded and pulled a guilty face. "I didn't think it was possible, see? Got a bit careless. I've only just found out."

"Ben knows, of course?"

"Oh yes. I told him this morning." The guilty face turned naughty. "I thought we might as well enjoy *one* more Saturday night. He'll get over the shock, of course."

Theo frowned. "You mean he's not happy about it?"

"Oh, ecstatic! I can't get his feet back on the ground. Unfortunately he thinks I should creep into a chrysalis — I can hear him coming up the lane, by the way — creep into a chrysalis and not come out for the next six months." She sighed. "But, as I say, he'll get over it. I'll be rolling beer kegs by Christmas."

"Six months!" he exclaimed. "That's next February." He looked again at Philip.

"It'll be fourteen months between them — aren't I the scandal of Penzance!" She raised her voice and shouted, "Ben? Round the back!"

The gate clicked open and shut. There was a brown streak among the straggling grass that bordered the drive and a lively dachshund leaped out at them. Philip reached a hand toward it and laughed.

"Kaiser!" Lorna called severely.

The creature hung his head and yawed unwillingly toward her. She put a finger an inch from his nose. "No more smells!"

He licked her finger.

"Theo!" Ben came round the corner, hand outstretched.

Theo, hampered by the baby, grasped it upside down and shook it. "You're looking well. You're both looking well."

Ben grinned at Lorna. "Have you told him?"

She nodded. "Just."

He turned back to the old man. "Isn't it grand? I can't wait to tell David and Jess." He sat down in the other spare deck chair.

"Have you heard from them?" Lorna asked Theo.

"I had a card from them this morning." He hit his forehead. "No. Yesterday morning."

"Postmarked?"

"Wednesday — Cherbourg. They're still there. Or were until Wednesday. The card is very uninformative, of course. Deliberately so, I suspect. If they wrote a letter they'd have to be more specific."

"They said nothing?"

"Just that it was all going very amicably. Estelle radiant. Bill harassed ... working all the hours God sends ... but doing well. I suppose it's all we're entitled to know."

"When you think how it *might* have turned out!" Lorna said. "I was afraid Estelle would overwhelm him." She leaned back and closed her eyes, lifting her face to the afternoon sun. "What a year it's been!"

"It's not over yet," Ben said.

She opened her eyes again and stared at him. "It is, you know."

He was nonplussed.

"The date," she said. "What happened a year ago today?"

He closed his eyes, trying to think. Then he frowned and raised his hand to his brow. "My God — Ian's funeral!" He opened his eyes again and stared at her.

"Yes." She rose and slid into Theo's still unoccupied chair so that she could hold his hand.

"I'll go and put the kettle on," Theo said. "Are you coming with me, young man?"

"Gagaga," Philip replied.

"Oh no!" Theo said as he wandered away. "I'm afraid you're much too young for apples!"

"I never realized!" Ben said apologetically. "What a crass ... unfeeling ..."

She slapped his hand playfully. "Stop it!"

"I should have remembered, though."

"All right, if it makes you happy — you should have remembered." She leaned back again and stared up into the apple boughs. "The only thing I can remember is how miserable *I* was."

"Naturally."

"No, not at Philip's death — or not so *much* at his death as at the way I'd wasted my life. And spoiled his."

"I'm sure *he* didn't see it like that!"

"So am I. But *his* delusion doesn't create a truth."

Ben gazed wistfully after Theo. The old philosopher would surely have a ready answer to a statement like that.

Lorna saw his dilemma and smiled fondly. "You mustn't think my life with Philip was anything like *our* life together, darling. It wasn't even a preparation for it." She squeezed his hand hard.

He smiled gratefully at her. "I still can't believe it," he said.

"Nor can I. I thought I'd never be able to love anyone. I thought I'd have to settle for something close. Now ... sometimes ... I love you so much I feel I'm going to burst with it."

"Me too." He swallowed heavily. "God — I hope it lasts this time! It *must* last."

"It will. To the end."

"To the end of what?" he asked, as if to accept her simple assurance would be like challenging the Fates to destroy them.

"To the end," she repeated simply.